250

The U.S. Army's AH-64 attack helicopter (also represented on the front cover) is shown here in an anti-tank scenario. The target is designated by lasers from a scout helicopter (with assistance from a ground unit). The attack helicopter launches missiles that home in on laser-marked tank.

ON THE FRONT LINES OF
THE WORLD'S LAST WAR:

ARMY SPECIAL FORCES CAPT. FRANCISCO MARTINEZ: Multilingual, slim, fast, and lethal—he was a fighting soldier in a world that pretended to be at peace. Now as war flares, they need him and his combat-ready forces—in three places at once!

MORRIS REISMAN: A combat veteran of Vietnam, now a journalist, he's still attracted to the world's hot spots—like a moth to flame.

1ST LT. ESTEBAN ALVAREZ and M. SGT. ARTURO CHAVEZ: They're Martinez's battle-tough right and left hands, trained in the arts of lighting-swift and silent war.

CAPT. GEORGI KURLOV: Behind his chiseled features lies a computer-swift military mind. With his Soviet Spetsnaz combat team at his back, he'll face any military force on the planet. Assignment: Estonia.

AIR FORCE CAPT. MARIE FRANKOWSKI: Along with her husband, John, she's one of the USAF's elite jet jocks. But on a routine flight to Saudi Arabia, she lands in the middle of a firefight—and a revolution.

CAPT. FIRST RANK MIKHAIL INBER: Carrying explosive sealed orders and a crack team of Soviet marines, he's ordered to pilot his nuclear-armed submarine into Cuban coastal waters.

STEVE MacKENZIE: A young fanatic, whose infiltration of Red China with counter-propaganda material could cause the world's largest and most repressed population to explode in a whirlwind of unpredictable rage.

PREMIER TAN TRI VAN: The North Vietnamese leader trying to keep his people from being used as a pawn in the great struggle between the Chinese Red Army and brutal Soviet Forces.

MAJOR RICHARD BRIZZOLA: The assistant operations officer at Florida's Eglin Air Force Base, who may have to handle the first military conflict on or anywhere *near* U.S. soil in the past fifty years.

Other Bantam Falcon titles that may be of interest:

GLOBAL WAR

Book

I

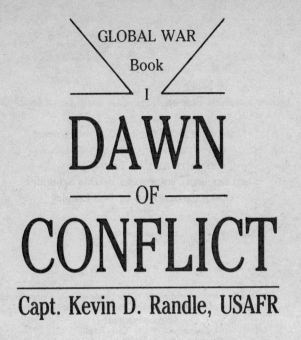

DAWN

— OF —

CONFLICT

Capt. Kevin D. Randle, USAFR

FALCON™

BANTAM BOOKS
NEW YORK · TORONTO · LONDON · SYDNEY · AUCKLAND

DAWN OF CONFLICT
A Bantam Falcon Book / December 1991

ISBN 0-553-29436-9

Published simultaneously in the United States and Canada

Bantam Books are published by Bantam Books, a division of Bantam Doubleday
Dell Publishing Group, Inc. Its trademark, consisting of the words "Bantam
Books" and the portrayal of a rooster, is Registered in U.S. Patent and Trademark
Office and in other countries. Marca Registrada. Bantam Books, 666 Fifth Ave-
nue, New York, New York 10103.

PRINTED IN THE UNITED STATES OF AMERICA
RAD 0 9 8 7 6 5 4 3 2 1

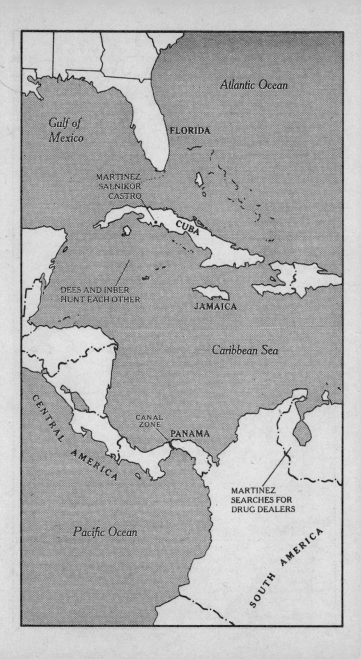

THE HOLIDAY INN
HONG KONG

Sitting at the elegant wooden desk that faced a large window, Morris Reisman couldn't believe all that he was being told. He stared at the interpreter, a Chinese woman who sat to the side and spoke in a low voice, and wondered again if she was telling him the truth.

Reisman considered himself a young man. He'd just turned forty-five and had ignored the birthday because he didn't feel older than he had when he returned from Vietnam more than twenty years earlier. Then he'd felt like an old man, having seen friends die in hideous ways and having killed men and women in hideous ways as they charged across rice paddies or out of the Vietnamese jungle. Then he'd felt old.

But now, as a member of the working press, having seen the horror of the world in all its full-color, multipart glory, he again believed himself to be young. This was the job he'd be doing for another twenty or thirty or maybe forty years, if he could live that long and still move without the benefit of mechanical assistance.

Reisman was a thin man, believing that health came through proper diet and that overeating was as dangerous as cigarettes or warfare. He was tall, standing three inches over six feet. He had dark, curly hair that held no trace of gray, making him appear younger than he was. There were those in the office who accused him of using Grecian Formula so that the managing editor would continue to hand him the rough assignments.

His blue eyes sometimes turned slate gray and other times became sea green, depending on his mood and the clothes he wore. They were the dominant feature on his face, and many people said the eyes had been wasted on him because the rest of his face was rather plain. A sharp nose and a pointed chin made it look as if he hadn't had a good meal in a couple of weeks.

Now he sat very straight in the high-backed chair, his elbows propped on the polished mahogany of the desk, and listened to the young Chinese woman tell of the horror she'd witnessed only a few weeks earlier. Reisman stared into her eyes and realized they were the eyes he'd seen a hundred times, a thousand times, as he'd interviewed the survivors of the world's tragedies. Old eyes that had seen too much in too short a time.

"The soldiers didn't care who they killed," the interpreter said, repeating what she was being told. "They shot those who ran and bayoneted those who stayed."

Reisman made a note and glanced out the window behind the woman. Everything in the room—the large double bed, the combination dresser, chest, and TV stand, and the two wingback chairs—faded into the background. Outside, across the bay filled with sailboats, junks, and ferries, he could see Kowloon with its high-rise hotels and tourist buildings. Beyond that, invisible because of the buildings and the hills of the New Territories, was Communist China.

The two women were talking in low tones, the interpreter's voice stronger than that of the other, who was crying, the tears streaking her face.

"The soldiers lost control. They didn't care who they

killed. They just wanted to kill. Everyone who stood there, many with their hands in the air, were gunned down. Children, with their parents, were shot.''

Reisman turned his attention to the witness, watching as she spoke, rattling in Chinese so fast that the words seemed to grow together.

"They used machine guns, firing into the crowd. In the panic, people were trampled. Bodies piled on bodies as the soldiers forced us back, into corners and next to walls, so that there was no escape.''

"Then how did she escape?'' Reisman asked.

The interpreter asked the question and then waited. The woman looked at Reisman and began to answer slowly.

Translating almost simultaneously, the interpreter said, "My brother fell toward me and I caught him. There was blood on his face and chest. I tried to hold him up, but couldn't. I staggered back and fell, my brother on top of me. He tried to speak, but the blood came from his mouth, splattering my face and neck. He shuddered once and then collapsed, pinning me to the ground, his blood staining my clothes.''

The woman looked at Reisman, continuing to speak, tears dripping to the soft cotton of her blouse. She didn't try to hide her tears.

"The soldiers were chasing us. Now I couldn't get up, and they were coming closer. I closed my eyes and pretended to be dead. I prayed that the soldiers would not shoot me or bayonet me to make sure I was dead. I prayed that my brother's life had not been wasted.''

Reisman wrote down what she was saying, ignoring the tape recorder that was running nearby. With hours of tape, he needed a way to cut through it quickly. His notes would help him find the right parts of the tapes.

"They shot him again as they ran by. I could feel the bullets striking his body. He jerked as they hit him and I wondered if he might have been alive. I prayed they wouldn't see me.

"Then the noise was past me. I could hear more shooting and screams of pain, but that was far away. Around me there were moans from the wounded and the dying. I opened my eyes to see bodies lying everywhere. Dozens had been killed. The odor of the dead filled the square, hanging over it, oppressing us all."

Reisman sat back and stared at the woman. The story struck him as too pat. It sounded too good. A dead brother who had protected her from the soldiers.

But then the emotions seemed genuine enough. Her face took on a chalky appearance. She lifted a hand and wiped her eyes, but stared straight at him, as if defying him not to believe her story.

In the last two weeks he'd heard a dozen reports of the massacre that sounded like those that had come from Tiananmen Square in 1989. Soldiers from outside districts moving through a crowd of demonstrators, using their weapons because everything else had failed.

Reisman picked up his camera, took a single shot of the woman as she rattled off her story. As she ran down and the interpreter stopped talking Reisman set his camera on the desk. He slipped his chair to the rear and stood up. He walked around them to the windows so that he could look down on Hong Kong. During his few months there, he had detected a frantic undercurrent to the city. In a couple of years the colony would be handed back to the Chinese on the mainland and all the blazing nightlife, the decadence, the free enterprise would be buried under the Communist bureaucracy.

He turned and looked at the woman. Her head was bowed and she cried softly. He stared for a moment and then returned to his seat. He was going to shut off the tape recorder and then decided against it.

"How did she get here?" Reisman asked. "The Chinese authorities have been trying to round up everyone who witnessed the massacre."

The interpreter translated the remark and then waited.

The woman looked up and shrugged. She hesitated and then started talking, quietly.

"The soldiers were not worried about the dead. They ran past where I fell and were killing the others. It was hard for them to see everything in the dark. When I was sure that no soldiers were close, I worked my way from under my brother."

Her voice broke then and she began crying again. The room was quiet, except for the sound of her crying. She looked up at Reisman and began again.

"I ran to the edge of the square," the interpreter translated. "I ran as fast as I could, running away from the lights and the shooting and my brother. I saw some soldiers and they yelled at me, but I ignored them, running for my life. I could still hear the shooting from the square. I could hear people screaming."

"No," said Reisman. "I want to know how she got out of China. The authorities have been watching the borders. They've been working very hard to keep the people in."

The question was translated and then answered. "We moved at night, staying off the roads. We had to hide from the army, which was looking for us. People gave us food and shelter. They hid us from the army. Everyone was afraid of the army. The army was shooting anyone who resisted them."

"Then why were the people hiding you?" Reisman asked.

"They were under the thumb, too. They helped me because they hoped that if they needed help, there would be someone to help them."

"Sure," said Reisman.

"They helped me to get to the border. The army was there waiting. Hundreds of them, but there were thousands of us. They couldn't line up on the border shoulder to shoulder. They couldn't catch all of us."

Reisman wasn't sure about that. Had the Chinese wanted to stop the people badly enough, they would have.

"We waited for the dark of the moon. The night was overcast. A guide, not Chinese, but someone who knew the area, was there. He led us to the shore and we slipped into the water so that we could swim to Hong Kong."

Reisman knew that people had been escaping from China by that route for years. Everyone knew about it. Hundreds had been killed, drowned, having misjudged the distance or lacking the endurance to make it all the way.

"You swam?"

"At night. I don't know how many left with us. A few

of them drowned and some were spotted and arrested by the authorities. Some were shot by men in boats.''

The story was typical. He'd heard dozens of them, read dozens of them, and written a few of them himself. There were ways to get out of China. Reisman sometimes wondered if the Chinese didn't let people escape to Hong Kong because they thought they could arrest them when Hong Kong became Chinese again. Or maybe they were using the escape routes to get the dissidents out of the country.

"Did you know the guide?"

"No. He just asked for money before taking us to the shore. When he had collected it, we followed him down. He told us to stay close and then began to swim."

"But he wasn't Chinese? Was he Asian?"

"Not Chinese, but he was big. Not like the Vietnamese or the Thais. Maybe Japanese."

Reisman couldn't think of anything else he wanted to ask. He didn't care about it anymore. People would read only so many accounts of a massacre before they became numb. They had already read too many horror stories of kids being gunned down by the Chinese government. They had reached the saturation point.

"I think that's all I need," he said.

The interpreter asked, "Are you going to need me again today?"

Reisman finally shut off the tape recorder. "No. That'll be it."

"What's going to happen to her?"

Reisman shrugged. "I'll take her down to the refugee center and then it'll be their problem."

The interpreter gathered up her notebook, pen, and purse. "She answered your questions and helped you."

"No. She answered the questions, but that doesn't help me."

"You wouldn't have a story without her."

"Hell, I don't think I've got one now. People don't want to read about this. Kill a hundred, or a thousand, and people don't react. Kill one and the world is outraged."

"Her brother," said the interpreter.

"Was one of hundreds. A faceless name used to fill

newspaper space. No one cares about him. Kill a little kid sitting on the railroad track while the city burns and the Japanese invade, and you have outrage. Kill a thousand people, run over them with tanks, and people are numb.''

"So you're going to cast her aside.''

Reisman laughed. "You're free to take her with you. Find her work and give her money.''

"I haven't exploited her.''

"Neither have I,'' said Reisman. "I'm just a story-teller. Nothing more than that.''

The interpreter headed toward the door. She didn't wait for the other woman. "Wait,'' said Reisman.

"I have my own life.'' The interpreter was out the door a second later.

Reisman turned and looked at the girl who had been left with him. Slender, with a round face, jet-black hair chopped off short, and almond-shaped, brown eyes. An attractive woman.

"You may go now,'' Reisman said, speaking slowly. And then he laughed again. Americans believed that if they talked slowly enough, all foreigners would under-stand what they were saying. That was the secret to inter-national communication. Talk slowly and loudly.

He gestured at her, but she didn't understand that either. She sat quietly, waiting for Reisman to do some-thing. If they had been at the bureau office, he'd have brought in one of the Chinese reporters or secretaries to translate, but Reisman had insisted on privacy. He hadn't wanted anyone else stealing his story, if he'd found one.

He picked up the phone, got the front-desk clerk. "I need someone who can speak Chinese to come to my room.''

"Dialect?''

Reisman shook his head. "I don't care. I've got a ref-ugee woman up here that I need to get to the center.''

"One moment, please.''

"Sure.''

An instant later another voice came on the line. "May I ask what you are doing with a refugee woman in your room, sir?''

"No," said Reisman. "I just want someone to take her to the center."

"One moment, please."

Reisman ran a hand through his hair and then turned. The woman was sitting quietly, watching him with dead eyes. She had accepted her fate, whatever it was, and was now waiting for it to fall on her. Reisman tried a smile but the woman didn't respond.

"The police are on the way."

"No!" Reisman shouted. "I didn't want the police. Just someone to translate."

"The police will be there in five minutes."

Reisman looked at the phone. He said things into it and the person at the other end refused to listen. The police were on the way. The problem was solved.

"Thanks," he said finally. He hung up and looked at the young woman. She had listened to the exchange but didn't seem to understand it. She sat there passively, letting the events whirl around her as if she had no influence on them.

Reisman sat down. "It would be so much easier if you could speak English."

She didn't say a word.

Reisman picked up the phone again. He glanced at the paper pasted to it and then touched the buttons. When room service answered, he asked them to bring up some tea, some biscuits, and some jam.

After he hung up, he rewound the tape. When it hit the end, he touched the play button and listened to the beginning, making sure that he had recorded the interview.

Finished with that, he didn't know what to do. The woman watched him, waiting for him to do something. He hadn't thought to ask her what it had been like in the refugee center, or if she had friends or relatives living in Hong Kong. He'd concentrated on the massacre and her escape, searching for holes in that story.

There was a knock at the door, and Reisman walked over to open it, thinking that room service had been pretty fast. Instead, he was facing an Englishman wearing a gray suit, white shirt, and striped tie. He looked to be forty, maybe as old as forty-five, and had dark, greased hair. Beside him was a Chinese man, also in plain clothes.

"Who the hell are you?"

One of the men pulled a badge from his pocket and said, "Police business."

"No reason for you to be here."

"We'll see that the woman gets to the refugee center unharmed."

The second man moved toward the woman. He spoke to her in Chinese. She stared up at him and then climbed to her feet, her head bowed, waiting for orders.

Reisman watched the woman head for the door. She didn't look back or protest. Reisman wanted to do something, say something, but was at a loss. He couldn't even tell the woman he was sorry, because she wouldn't understand.

As the two police officers and the Chinese woman walked out the door, room service arrived. The waiter, a young Chinese, wore black pants, a white jacket, and a red tie. He held the tray in one hand with a white towel over the other. He jumped back, out of the way, as the police and the women hurried from the hotel room.

The waiter looked in at Reisman. "Room service."

"Perfect," said Reisman. "Just perfect."

RUSSIAN ARMY HEADQUARTERS
MOSCOW

General Andrei Stepanov sat in the high-backed leather chair in the ornate conference room and faced the movie screen at the far end. To his left was a polished conference table surrounded by a dozen other officers. Sitting in the center of the table was a silver samovar, filled not with tea but with vodka. In front of each of the officers was a leather pad and a silver pen in case someone wanted to make notes.

Stepanov had passed his sixtieth birthday a couple of years earlier. He was a short, squat man with broad shoulders, a massive chest, and a high waist. He moved with the grace of a younger man, and even his dark hair, just beginning to turn white, fooled many. They'd never guess he was as old as he was.

The lights in the conference room had been dimmed, but Stepanov could still see the red banner of the Soviet Union in one corner and the painting of Lenin holding a flag and looking as if he was leading an assault on the rest of the world.

A junior lieutenant stood near the screen, partially hidden by a lecturn with a tiny light on it. His head was bowed as he tried to read the notes that he'd placed there a few minutes earlier. He turned to the screen and watched as the color film began to play.

"These pictures," he said without preamble, "were taken late yesterday afternoon in Tartu, Estonian Socialist Republic." He moved closer to the screen and pointed at the crowd surging down the street, thousands of people carrying banners and signs demanding reform and freedom and a voice in the government.

The scene shifted as the mob reached a government building. A few soldiers, and fewer police, stood in front of the doors. The soldiers were armed with AKs and the police held shotguns or pistols. Now the crowd rushed forward, screaming. One of the soldiers lowered his rifle and fired. Just a single shot, but it was a good one. A woman holding one side of a banner was hit in the stomach. She dropped the banner, wrapped her arms around her middle, and collapsed.

"The mob wasn't intimidated by the soldiers. In fact, the shooting had the opposite effect," said the lieutenant, without looking at the screen.

Stepanov and the others watched as the crowd overran the soldiers. There was some firing, but there are too many angry people and too few soldiers.

"They forced their way into the offices." As the lieutenant spoke they saw a chair crash through a window and fall to the street. Fire broke out and smoke burst from the upper windows.

The lieutenant waved at the screen and returned to his place at the lecturn. "The rest of the film shows more of the same. Fourteen soldiers were killed and twelve injured. The police lost eight killed and twenty-two injured. There are forty-seven weapons unaccounted for and assumed to be in the hands of the terrorists."

The screen darkened. The last scene was of the government building engulfed in flames, with the mob holding the fire fighters at bay.

"Status this morning?" asked Stepanov.

"Our soldiers reestablished control of most key installations about midnight, but it's shaky. There are many indications that all the citizens will be back in the streets today."

"What indications?" asked Stepanov.

"Workers not arriving at the factories, students staying home from school, and people already gathering at various points around the city."

"Have them dispersed," said one of the other officers. "Do not give them the chance to assemble."

The lieutenant looked troubled and fumbled with his notes. "The few attempts to disperse the people have turned into confrontations. Shots have been fired and people have been killed."

"I don't understand this," yelled a colonel. "I simply do not understand this. An armed man should be able to turn a mob. A dozen armed men should be able to end a riot. If a crowd refuses to obey the orders of the soldiers or the police, why are they not arrested?"

"Colonel Shishmarev," said Stepanov, "you forget the world press. After Lithuania in 1991, the world watches our every move. They are watching us very closely now."

"The world press is of little interest to me."

"That is why you will probably remain a colonel for the remainder of your career, Shishmarev. World opinion has become important. Western politicians listen to their people, and if those people see our soldiers shooting helpless citizens in the streets of Tartu, then they will change their policy accordingly."

"Force the press to leave," said Shishmarev.

"You refuse to understand. We no longer live in a vacuum. There are too many ways for information to get out. It is not Hungary in 1956 or even Czechoslovakia in 1968. The world situation was different then. The Americans had either just come out of a war or were involved in a war, and what we did in our satellites did not interest them."

"The Americans are weak."

"Colonel," said Stepanov, "your opinions are worse than useless. They are dangerous. You refuse to grow with the times." He turned to face the officer and then grinned.

"Even if the Americans are weak, there are problems in Europe. One Germany is a danger to us all."

"But NATO is as dead as the Warsaw Pact."

Stepanov shook his head and asked the lieutenant, "What is being done now?"

"Extra troops have been dispatched, but their orders are to guard the government buildings and protect the officials. They are to avoid confrontation with the people."

"Western journalists?" Stepanov asked.

"They are trying to get to Tartu now. We are slowing the process, but there isn't much that can be done without raising suspicions."

Stepanov nodded. "All right, Lieutenant, thank you. You may go now."

"Certainly, Comrade General." The young officer picked up his notes, turned off the reading light, and headed for the door.

"Subtlety," said Stepanov. "That is what is needed now. Not the iron hand of Moscow smashing another city hoping for freedom. We must be subtle."

General Stepanov stood at the edge of the tarmac and looked at the short line of soldiers in front of him. They were supposedly members of a Russian boxing team that was going to tour bases in the West, pitting their abilities against those of the best American, British, and German soldiers. But the trip wasn't scheduled for another month and the team sparring matches had been canceled.

Stepanov looked at the young captain standing in front of the team. He was dressed in black fatigues that included black buttons and black zippers and black insignia that disappeared into the black background, making it nearly impossible to discern his rank.

Stepanov stepped closer and then stopped. The captain popped off a salute and said, "Boxing team ready for inspection, General."

"Thank you, Captain Kurlov. If you will be so kind as to accompany me."

"Certainly, Comrade General."

Captain Georgi Kurlov was six-two, with blond hair and blue eyes. His tight black uniform showed broad shoulders and a narrow waist. He moved with the grace of an athlete and with the bearing of a military officer. Kurlov had big hands, and the Tokarev pistol he carried was nearly invisible when he drew it.

Stepanov walked along the line of soldiers, all dressed in the black uniforms. They were an elite, chosen from among the best, and in spite of obvious physical differences, they had one thing in common. All were in superb shape. The Spetsnaz team was ready. For anything.

"Very good," said Stepanov. "They look very good. What is the schedule?"

"We take off in an hour. Equipment has already been loaded onto the aircraft. We should hit the target area about two hours after that, and we'll have three hours on the ground until the first light."

"You may dismiss the men now."

Kurlov said, "Sergeant Yerikalin, have the men fall out and take them into the operations building. Wait there until it is time to board the aircraft."

"Yes, sir. I'd like a chance to check our gear before takeoff."

"Check with the operations sergeant. Leave Corporal Chuykov in charge."

"Yes, sir."

"Come with me, Captain," said Stepanov. He walked across a small patch of grass and reached a metal door covered with flaking gray paint. A soldier standing close to it opened it and Stepanov entered, followed by Kurlov.

The interior was air-conditioned. To the left was a concrete staircase with metal strips on the edges of the risers. They climbed the stairs, reached another metal door, and entered a hallway. Stepanov led Kurlov into a small office that held only a desk, two chairs, and a tiny bookcase loaded with military manuals.

The general sat down behind the desk. He closed his eyes and pinched the bridge of his nose. Opening his eyes, he asked, "Do you understand your instructions?"

Kurlov stood at attention in front of the desk, his eyes locked on a point a half foot above Stepanov's head. He said, "Yes, sir."

Stepanov gestured at the other chair. "You may relax and sit down, Captain."

"Thank you, Comrade General."

"I wanted an opportunity to speak to you in private," said Stepanov. "Secrecy in this mission is imperative. Secrecy will not be compromised. If the mission cannot be accomplished in total secrecy, then it is to be sacrificed."

"I understand, General."

Stepanov reached into a pocket and extracted a map. He laid it on the desk, flattening it with the edge of his hand. "You've had your final briefing?"

"Two hours ago, General. We based our plan on that assessment of the situation."

"Tell me," said Stepanov.

Kurlov stood and moved to the map. "The dissidents have occupied the government complex here and the building here."

"Those your only targets?"

"Yes, General. We're not concerned with the people on the streets. They're supporting the people occupying the buildings, but they have no organized leadership."

"You're sure?"

Kurlov shrugged. "That is what intelligence has reported to us."

"And you accept that."

Kurlov grinned. "No, General. However, the information is not critical to the first part of the mission. We must clear the buildings first. Then we can worry about the leadership of the mobs."

"You must accomplish that under the eyes of the Western press without letting them know that you're doing it. We have been forced to allow a contingent of them into Tartu. So just how do you plan to do it?"

"We have loaded four canisters of a harmless gas. It is odorless, colorless, and will put anyone who catches a whiff of it to sleep within thirty seconds. The gas is less dense than air and will slowly rise, so that within six hours all traces of it should be gone."

"You have identified the leadership in the buildings?" Stepanov asked.

"A few of them. We'll see what we see when we get

in there. We've had to leave the second phase of the mission open because of the fluid nature of the situation."

"I'll want to be kept informed," said Stepanov.

"Of course, Comrade General."

"I'll be airborne over the scene from thirty minutes before your insertion. Radio contact using the RM scrambler system will be employed. Your radio operator should be prepared to both transmit and receive using the scrambler."

"I shall make sure that he is prepared."

Stepanov opened one of the desk drawers and took out a bottle of vodka. He smiled as he set it, and then a couple of glasses, on the desk. "It is no accident that this office was available for our use."

"Yes, General."

Stepanov filled both glasses and pushed one at Kurlov. The captain hesitated. "A single toast will not impair your ability to function, Captain."

Kurlov picked up a glass. "Needs a little pepper."

"I am not uncivilized," said Stepanov. He reached into the drawer and took out a pepper grinder. He used it on his own glass and on Kurlov's, then lifted his glass. "To a successful mission, Captain."

"To the mission." Kurlov lifted the glass and drank. When he finished, he said, "Will that be all, General?"

"Yes. Remember, a successful mission will mean promotions for everyone. Failure can mean death."

"I understand."

"Good." Stepanov lifted his glass in a final salute. "You may join your men."

Kurlov set his glass on the desk and saluted. "Thank you for the opportunity to serve, Comrade General."

Stepanov returned the salute and watched the young officer leave. He shook his head and wondered if he'd ever been that young and that enthusiastic. If he had, it had been a long time ago. Long before he had seen the political influence on the military and before he'd seen men promoted not because they were good soldiers, but because their fathers were influential.

Under his breath, he said, "Good luck, Captain. If you fail, you will be shot."

• • •

Kurlov walked down the stairs and entered a hangar area. The concrete floor had been waxed a hundred times, so that it was a shiny, slick surface, easy to clean. Painted yellow lines marked the walkways and parking areas of the aircraft. There was a marshaling bay at one end, separated from the rest of the hangar only by the yellow lines on the floor. Overhead were banks of lights, most of them off.

Kurlov's men were sitting on the floor near the hangar door. One man was sharpening a combat knife; another sat reading a manual by the light of a flashlight. The others were sitting quietly, waiting to board the aircraft.

As he walked up Kurlov said, "Sergeant Yerikalin?"

"In the aircraft, checking the equipment."

"Corporal Chuykov?"

"Over there, checking the chutes a final time."

In the dim-lit hangar Kurlov could just make out a shape. There was a flash of light. Chuykov was inspecting the thunderbows, which resembled a stubby, wide wing more than a conventional parachute.

Kurlov waited until Chuykov returned, then checked his watch and nodded. "We've got about thirty minutes. Get the men moving."

"Yes, sir." Yuri Chuykov was a small, stocky man, with black hair, dark eyes, and thick features. His nose had been broken more than once. He turned to face the troops. "Let's move it."

The men stood. The one with the knife slipped it into the scabbard that was taped upside down to his web gear. The man with the manuals gathered them up and tucked them under his arm. Together, the men walked across the hangar floor.

Chuykov stood in front of the thunderbows like a supply sergeant in front of his equipment. He watched as each man picked up a sail and moved off.

Kurlov grabbed one and began to slip into the harness. He adjusted it, twisted it, and reached back to grab one of the straps. He hooked it into the capewell in the center of his chest. He bent, grabbed two more straps, and pulled them up between his legs, trying to avoid crushing his balls. Again, he snapped the ends of the straps into the plate. With the thunderbow set on his back, he began to tighten the straps so that the sail wouldn't shift as it deployed.

The door at the far end of the hangar opened and Yerikalin appeared. When he was close to Kurlov, he said, "Looks like everything we asked for has been loaded on the aircraft."

Kurlov checked the time, pulling the black sleeve of his jumpsuit up. The watch was digital, purchased in the West, and his prize possession. Almost no one had one like it. Nearly everyone in the Soviet military preferred the classic watch made by the Swiss.

"Get into your sail. We're running short of time."

"Yes, sir."

Kurlov moved to the locked rack that stood to his left. That was where the weapons had been stored. Now it was time to distribute them. Each man had selected the weapon he preferred, zeroed it, and cleaned and oiled it. Kurlov took a key from his pocket and unlocked the rack.

His weapon, an AK-74, was at the end of the rack. He slipped the thick chain through the trigger guard and let it fall away. He picked up the weapon, worked the bolt, and tried to look down the barrel, but there wasn't enough light in the hangar. He'd have to use a flashlight.

The men lined up and began removing their weapons. There was no ammo for any of them. That had been stored on the plane, and the aircraft commander would have to unlock the storage containers once they were airborne.

"We about ready?" Kurlov asked.

"Yes, sir," said Yerikalin.

"Get the men over to the door. I don't suppose anyone thought to arrange transport to the aircraft."

"I saw no sign of it out there, sir," said Yerikalin.

"Great." Kurlov opened the door and stepped out. The evening was muggy, and a light mist hung in the air, creating halos around the airfield lights. A yellow tug was sitting on the ramp near the nosewheel of the aircraft. An auxiliary power unit was hooked into the side of the plane, and parked near it was a staff car.

Kurlov ducked back inside and said, "We're going to have to look sharp. I think there's some brass out there."

"General Stepanov?"

"No. The general has probably left to get on the communications plane. I don't know who it is."

Yerikalin nodded and turned to face the rest of the men. "Let's try to look like soldiers for the next few minutes."

"That mean we're going to march out to the plane?" asked one of them.

"No," said Kurlov. "But let's not look like a mob, either. Just board the plane, find a place to sit, and buckle in. When the brass leave, you can fall back into your normal, slovenly manner."

"Yes, sir," snapped one of the men.

Kurlov slung his weapon, barrel down, and put on his cap, pulling it low so that his eyes were barely visible. He pushed the door open and stepped out. Using the sidewalk, he headed in the general direction of the aircraft. Now he could hear the low rumbling of the APU and the whine of a smaller engine.

The men followed, forming a line behind him. At the edge of the tarmac Kurlov hesitated, almost like a kid looking both ways before crossing the street. Then he stepped off, angling toward the rear of the aircraft where the ramp had been lowered.

The plane was painted flat black with little in the way of markings on it. That was to inhibit radar returns and prevent IR from locking onto hot spots on the fuselage during the day. It was a four-engine aircraft designed to deliver troops and equipment into hostile environments, either by dropping them by parachute or landing them on short unimproved airfields on even pieces of highway.

As he reached the rear ramp Kurlov glanced at the engine pods. In the past they had been designed simply as exhaust pipes for hot gases. Now they dispersed those gases, cooling them as they fed them into the air. This, too, was meant to defeat infrared. It made the rear of the engines look as if they had exploded.

He climbed the ramp. The interior of the aircraft looked as if it had been stripped. There were no real seats, just a dull gray webbing that provided little comfort for the soldiers. In the center was the equipment they would need. It would be broken into small loads as they approached the destination. Everything they needed would be carried down by the men. Nothing would be thrown out to be collected later.

Standing at the far end of the aircraft were two men. In the dim, red lights of the interior, Kurlov could tell almost nothing about them. He was sure that they were high-ranking officers.

As Kurlov approached, one of them said, "Captain, I am Colonel Vladimir Kerenko."

"Colonel?"

"I wanted to wish you well on your mission."

"Thank you, sir."

"I hope that you have found our limited facilities here to be adequate."

"They have been fine." Kurlov glanced at the second man, who was wearing an officer's uniform with no insignia on it. He neither spoke nor looked at Kurlov, just stood there like he was part of the aircraft's airframe.

"Well," said Kerenko. "I know you have things that need to be done, so I'll leave you to them." He turned and with the other man, moved through the hatch on the left side of the airplane.

Yerikalin said, "What in the hell was that all about?"

"I haven't the faintest idea, but I'll bet that one of them was KGB. Maybe both."

"KGB interested in this operation?"

"I would think so. They haven't had much luck stopping the insurrection. Maybe they wanted to get a look at the competition. Besides, if we succeed, they can now claim they consulted with us before we were deployed."

"Not much of a consultation."

"But enough," said Kurlov. "And it wouldn't be wise to deny their assistance, if they make such a claim."

"No," said Yerikalin, "I don't suppose it would be."

"Let's get everything set for takeoff."

"Yes, sir."

SCHOOL OF THE AMERICAS
PANAMA

Army Special Forces Captain Francisco Martinez sat in the air-conditioned, cinder-block briefing room and waited. His beret was on the table in front of him, where his files and notebooks would have been had he had any files or notebooks. It wasn't normal to jerk a man out of the jungle, rush him back to the base, and then tell him to report to a conference room without time for a shower and change of uniform.

Martinez was five-nine, with a slender build, but he was deceptively strong. His short-cropped black hair, brown eyes, and sun-darkened olive skin made him look like a native, but though he spoke fluent Spanish, those in the know could tell it was Texas Spanish, heavily accented with the inflections of that region.

He rubbed a hand through his hair and then wiped the sweat on the front of his fatigues, almost as if defying military regulations. The general would notice the ragged stain, but then, his uniform was already mud-splattered and torn.

"How long?" asked First Lieutenant Esteban Alvarez. Like Martinez, he was Hispanic, born in California but raised in New Mexico. He could speak Spanish like a native of Mexico or of Spain, depending on the assignment, Italian like a resident of Rome, and Chinese like a man from Hong Kong. Alvarez had an uncanny ability to mimic native accents perfectly.

Martinez took a deep breath and shrugged. "I haven't the faintest. What do you know, Master Sergeant?"

Arturo Chavez glanced to the right. Hispanic, too, he was bigger than both officers, taller, stockier, and more heavily muscled. He sported a pistolero mustache that the brass on the various camps and bases hated. Military grooming regulations demanded that the edges of the mustache not extend beyond the corner of the mouth. Chavez always agreed to shave in conformity with regulations but always forgot to do it.

"I'm in the dark, too, sir."

"I thought all you sergeants always stayed in touch," said Alvarez.

"We do, but this is something different. The general hasn't been revealing everything to his clerks." Chavez grinned. "The intelligence system only works when the officers need to have paperwork typed."

The door opposite Martinez .opened and a major in starched fatigues stepped through. He moved to the right, out of the way, and announced, "The commanding general."

The three Special Forces troopers climbed to their feet as the general entered. He glanced at them and then walked to the head of the conference table. He hesitated and then sat down, glancing at his aide. The major closed the door and hurried forward, setting a file in front of him.

The general adjusted the folder, took a gold pen from his pocket, set it on the table, and then looked pointedly at Martinez. "Your uniform is filthy."

"Yes, sir," said Martinez. When the general didn't say anything, Martinez continued, "We were involved in a jungle warfare training exercise this morning."

"And you didn't take time to clean up?"

"No, sir. We were told to report here immediately, which we did."

"Ah." The general picked up the gold pen and made a note. "You have no idea why you're here."

"General," said Martinez, "I"—he waved a hand— "we, were in the field this morning. A chopper landed and told us that we were required to be here, immediately, so here we are."

The general looked at the major, who spoke for the first time. "Gentlemen, everything said in this room from this point is classified secret."

The general opened the file and pushed the papers at Martinez. "As you may know, the president has again directed the army to take a more active role in the interdiction of drug trafficking."

Martinez looked down at the conference table and felt his stomach flip. The regular army had been used to interdict the drug trade in the past and it had resulted in a bloodbath. Attempting to play by society's rules, the army had tried to arrest members of the various drug cartels when they found them. But the drug runners hadn't been hampered by rules. They shot and killed, ran ambushs, and even attacked army camps much like the VC had done during the Vietnam War. In the end, the army had withdrawn, explaining that law enforcement was not part of the army's role. Hire additional men and women for the DEA and the FBI if that was what they wanted, but leave the army out of it completely.

The general studied Martinez. "You have a problem with that, Captain?"

"General, are we free to speak?"

"Certainly."

"Unless the rules have been changed radically, I don't think this is a good idea."

The general rocked in his chair and dropped his gold pen onto the notebook. "You don't think it's a good idea? What's not a good idea?"

Martinez wiped a hand over his face and decided there was nothing to lose. "We are hampered by rules, but the other side is not. I don't understand why we always feel we have to play by a different set of rules than the enemy."

"Not enemy, Captain. Drug dealers."

"Sir, if you're planning to send my men in to interdict, then they're the enemy. Hell, these people, the drug runners, have been trained by Cubans in the various arts of warfare—"

"We don't know that," said the general. "There is no proof that the Cubans have ever been involved."

Martinez shrugged and conceded the point. "They've still been trained by someone in basic military tactics. They demonstrated that against the regular army units sent against them a couple of years ago."

"That policy has been reevaluated," said the general.

"I don't want to use my men if our hands are going to be tied."

"Captain, I don't believe I asked for opinions. You were brought here to listen, not hand out advice."

"Yes, sir."

The general picked up his pen and twirled it in his fingers. He studied it carefully before issuing the orders. "Your team will infiltrate into the jungles of Colombia, study the terrain, locate but not engage the drug runners and the drug-processing areas. Once the information has been secured, you will quietly withdraw."

"For what purpose?" Martinez asked.

"They'll be targeted by both American and Colombian drug enforcement authorities. They will be attacked and destroyed, the men operating them arrested and tried. Any fields growing the crops will be burned and the farmers arrested and jailed. The supply is going to be choked at the source once and for all." The general's voice had risen slightly as he worked himself into a fervor.

Martinez looked at Alvarez and then Chavez. Chavez shrugged slightly but kept his eyes on the general.

"I don't pretend to understand the inner workings of your Special Forces units, Captain," said the general. "But this is going to be a full-blown tactical mission. You will operate just as if you were about to parachute into enemy territory or behind enemy lines. Questions?"

"How many people will know about this?" asked Alvarez.

"Well, Lieutenant, we're going to keep it as limited as possible. I'll know, of course, as will Major Jamison here. Your B team will know about it, too."

Martinez rubbed his chin. "I think Lieutenant Alvarez is wondering how many people outside the army will know what we're doing."

"Ah. Well, there is a DEA liaison officer who will be kept advised."

"But he won't know the details of the mission?" Martinez asked hopefully.

"What are you suggesting?"

"During the Vietnam War," said Martinez, "Special Forces missions had the tightest security. When the regular army and then the Vietnamese were brought in, there were leaks."

"Are you saying that the DEA can't keep a secret?" asked the general.

Martinez knew that he was on shaky ground now. He looked into the general's eyes and then glanced at the ribbons above his left breast pocket. For those who understood the code, a man's career could be read by the ribbons. The general had a few combat awards, including a Silver Star. He wore ribbons denoting service in Vietnam, in Panama, and in the Persian Gulf. He had a combat infantryman's badge and jump wings. The general had been around enough to understand what Martinez meant. He wasn't an officer who had taken the easy way up the ladder.

"I'm suggesting, General, that the fewer people who know our business, the better off we'll be."

"I understand that. But DEA has requested our assistance and the president has decided to give it."

"Yes, sir, I understand. But is there any reason we have to tell them, tell anyone outside, when we'll be in the field or where we'll be?"

"Jamison?" said the general.

The aide shrugged and took out a small notebook. "I'll check around."

"But discreetly," said Martinez. "Very discreetly."

"I know my job, Captain," said Jamison.

The general looked expectantly at Martinez, who asked, "What are the rules of engagement?"

The general smiled slyly. "Thought we'd get to that. You're to initiate no action, but you can return fire for fire received. I don't want a massacre, but then I don't want your men jeopardizing themselves." He put down the gold pen again. "The American press—hell, the world press—will support anything we do against the drug cartel members. As long as there is no doubt the action was directed against the drug cartels and was not a full-scale invasion of Colombia, we'll be in good shape."

"Do we hit the field as American soldiers?" Chavez asked.

"The planning and execution of the mission is entirely in your hands. You'll be given the latest in available intelligence, maps, and equipment. How you put it to use is up to you. There is no reason to disguise yourselves."

Martinez looked at the two men with him, and when neither asked anything else, he said, "I guess that covers it."

"Fine," said the general. "I'll expect a full report in the next week." He closed his folder, picked up the pen, stuck it into his shirt pocket without unbuttoning the flap, and stood up.

Martinez climbed to his feet and watched as the general and his aide left the conference room.

"Well," said Alvarez, "now what?"

"Looks like we get the team assembled. Have Gibson check with Intel and see what's available. We'll want him to put together a report on the environment, likely locations of enemy camps, and the attitudes of the locals."

"Yes, sir," said Alvarez.

Martinez looked at Chavez. "You've got a problem, Art?"

"Hell, Captain, I don't like jumping into territory that we haven't fully reconned, let alone having civilians aware of our plans. I don't want to say anything derogatory about the DEA, but those guys are exposed to a hell of a lot of money."

"Meaning?" said Martinez.

If I handled a million dollars a day from drug runners and suddenly someone offered me a big piece of it to leak the plans of a bunch of army pukes I didn't know . . ."

Martinez shrugged and stood up, ready to leave. "Let's not worry about that problem now."

"Yes, sir."

Master Sergeant Arturo Chavez stood on the concrete steps outside a barracks twenty minutes later and watched a canvas-covered truck drive into the tarmac parking lot. It pulled around the half-dozen cars parked there and then backed up close to the steps. The brakes squeaked as it stopped, the diesel engine rumbled, and a cloud of black smoke belched from the rear.

As soon as the truck stopped, the canvas flap was flipped up out of the way, and the sweat-drenched face of Staff Sergeant Raoul Munyo appeared. He hesitated and then asked, "What the hell is going on?"

"Just climb on down," said Chavez.

Munyo dropped to the pavement and turned, waiting for someone to hand him his weapon. The sleeve of Munyo's dirty and sweat-stained fatigues was ripped badly and there was an angry red welt on his arm.

As he received his weapon he turned and looked up at the two-story tan building. Red tile covered the roof and the deep greens of the jungle-like vegetation reached down from the hill behind it, almost to the southern side of the structure. The colors were so bright and sharp that it looked more like a color photograph than a real jungle.

Grinning, Munyo said, "You're not going to get me complaining about this."

Sergeant First Class Leroy Jones didn't say a word as he dropped to the concrete. He stood with his hands on his hips and then grinned broadly. Jones was the only black member of the team, selected because his diminutive stature and his ability to speak Spanish made him look like a Panamanian. The senior medical specialist, he was also an expert with explosives and light weapons. If there were no patients to treat, he wasn't above creating a few.

Sergeant First Class Juan Ortega stopped in the rear of the truck. "Yeah," he said. "I could get used to this."

"It's only temporary," said Chavez. "Until we can get into isolation."

Ortega took a deep breath. "How long?"

"Not before noon tomorrow, depending on what the captain can arrange."

"That's plenty of time."

A final man climbed out of the truck and opened the tailgate. Reaching in, he snagged the last of the equipment and dragged it toward him. As he dropped the gear to the tarmac he slapped the rear of the truck. "That's got it, Mac. You can take off."

The starter ground, caught, and the truck coughed out another cloud of diesel smoke. Grinding gears, the driver dropped into low and lurched forward.

"Rest of the team is coming in later," said Jones. "They got on a different truck."

"Where'd they go?" asked Chavez.

"Made a PX run just in case things didn't work out well here," said Jones. He shrugged. "You know how the army sometimes organizes things."

"Yeah," Chavez agreed. He turned and pointed at the tan building. "We've got two-man rooms on the second floor. We'll be quartered here until further notice."

"Beer?" Munyo asked.

"More importantly," said Jones, "babes."

Chavez said, "You're all adults here. Remember that we've got meetings tomorrow morning and you're required to be present. Captain didn't leave instructions for anything this afternoon."

"Then it's showers, clean clothes, and into the heart of Panama City," said Munyo.

"Just as long as you're here tomorrow morning, ready for the briefings."

"Yes, Drill Sergeant," said Munyo, mimicking the response of men in basic training.

The men shouldered their gear and climbed the steps to the building. Chavez watched them go and then shook his head. Some things stayed the same no matter how much the army changed. Men coming out of the field always showered and then headed into the nearest town to look for good food and willing women. And the thing was, both could always be found regardless of the circumstances. People would sell the good food and the women would sell themselves. The politics of the situation never mattered.

Chavez watched as the last of the men entered the building and then pulled at the sleeve of his jungle fatigues so that he could see the time.

SOVIET TRANSPORT
NEARING TARTU, ESTONIA SSR

Kurlov stood next to the bulkhead and watched his men distribute the equipment. They were eerie-looking shapes, hard to see in the dim red glow of the aircraft. Yerikalin grabbed something from one of the equipment pods and handed it to Kurlov.

They were goggles with an assortment of lenses, like tiny telescopes, attached to the front. The night-vision goggles, which magnified the ambient light so one could see in the dark, made the interior red lights seem ridiculously unnecessary.

Yerikalin, wearing his chutes and equipment and carrying his weapon, now fully loaded, said, "We are ready to jump, Captain."

Kurlov looked at his watch. If they were holding to the schedule—and no one had suggested they were late—they were within ten minutes of jumping.

"You've made the equipment check?"

"Yes, sir. All is in readiness."

"Let's get the men lined up and in the door."

"Yes, sir."

An aircrewmen moved down the aisle to one of the side doors. He turned back, looking at Kurlov.

"The ramp," said Kurlov. "We'll go out the ramp." That way they could jump in formation, almost all of them stepping into space at once.

The crewman moved to his left and stood next to a button mounted on the fuselage.

The soldiers slipped forward and stood at the edge of the ramp. Now they were less than five minutes out. When a red light set near the button began to glow, the crewman pushed the button and the ramp began to lower slowly. Cold air surged into the rear of the aircraft.

Kurlov stepped forward and looked out. The sky was a charcoal and the ground was black. Few lights burned. A road wound its way to the north and there was a single car on it, the headlights bouncing.

"Two minutes," yelled the crewman.

Kurlov put his foot up on the ramp. He kept his eyes on the burning red light and prayed that the aircraft commander and his navigator would be able to find the right targets in the dark. He thought he could see the outskirts of the city.

"One minute."

Now Kurlov walked closer to the trailing edge of the ramp. His men were clustered around him, ready to leap as soon as they got the word. Nervously, Kurlov glanced to the right, where Yerikalin stood. They had talked about combat jumps before. Both had made similar jumps in the past, but Kurlov was always nervous. Especially at night. Especially when jumping into an urban area.

"Thirty seconds."

Kurlov suddenly thought of a dozen things that needed to be done. Things he'd accomplished as they had ridden to the target but that he suddenly couldn't remember doing. As always, he wanted to shout, "Wait!" and as always, he kept his mouth shut.

The light changed suddenly to green and the crewman slashed a hand through the air, signaling Kurlov that it was time. The captain felt a bump to his rear and knew that it was the man behind him pushing forward.

Without thinking about it, Kurlov took two quick steps and fell into space. The sudden blast of air was like a cold, dry slap in the face. He stretched out, aiming toward the top of the center building, trying to remember the aerial photos he'd studied, trying to identify the target as he fell toward it in the darkness. He felt the air whip by him as he plummeted toward the ground. Finally, he yanked at the ripcord and heard the thunderbow spill from the pack with the sound of spilling ripstop nylon. A sudden, sharp yank sent splinters of fire through his body, and his descent was noticeably slowed.

Spread out below him was a series of tall buildings and wide streets. Soviet engineering had cleared away old sections of Tartu and replaced them with the beginnings of a modern city. There was movement on the streets, a few vehicles and a few people, violators of the curfew ordered by the police.

The target building loomed just below him; he was finally positive he knew which one it was. He yanked at the toggles, spilled air from his canopy, and changed directions as he corkscrewed in. Against the black of the building's roof, he could see the duct work, a slant-roofed shed, and tiny caps for the elevator shafts. A couple of smokestacks and a small field of antennas with a network of guy wires created the obstacles he'd have to avoid on landing.

The building rushed up at him. Glancing at the charcoal horizon and then back at the building, Kurlov jerked right and then left and saw that he would land in the center of the roof, away from the obstacles.

He hit feetfirst, ran three steps, and stopped, the chute collapsing behind him. He whirled, jerking at the toggles, and then fumbled with the capewell, dropping the harness so that he wasn't yanked over the side of the building by an unexpected gust of wind. Around him, the rest of his team landed as silently. One man hit and stumbled into the antenna array, crushing one and bending another. Kurlov grinned and tried not to laugh.

Kurlov pulled a small radio from his side pocket and

touched the transmit button. The small UHF radio didn't have much power, but then it didn't need much. The huge antenna system on the Soviet-built Il-76 Mainstay would be able to read his signal and relay his message to General Stepanov. Whispering, he said, "Igor has landed."

Yerikalin appeared and whispered, "We're all down. No sign of the enemy."

"The enemy would be the police," said Kurlov.

"Yes, sir. No sign that anyone is aware that we're on the roof."

"Let's get going." They'd have to pick up the chutes later, but at the moment it didn't matter. Kurlov unslung his weapon and touched the safety to make sure that it was on. He reached out and touched Yerikalin lightly on the right shoulder. "Go."

The sergeant whirled, snapped his fingers at two of the men, and ran toward the top of the stairwell. One man diverted right and the other left. Yerikalin crouched to the left of the door and reached across to grab the knob. He turned it and pulled. The door was locked.

While Yerikalin pressed thermite around the knob, Kurlov moved the rest of the men into position. They fanned out, forming a half-moon around the door, ready to fire into it if anyone happened to be standing there, barring the way.

There was a quiet spurting, a flare of flame, and the doorknob fell away. Yerikalin reached in and yanked the door open. The stairway was dark.

Kurlov nodded and three of the men ran to the edge of the building. They fastened ropes to the fixtures close to the edge and threw them over.

Chuykov looked back at Kurlov, who nodded. The corporal fastened the rope onto the rings hanging from his belt and then stepped over the short wall. He disappeared, rappelling down toward the street. The other two followed him. They were going to break into the basement of the building and use the gas.

Kurlov moved back to the door and pulled the night-vision goggles down so that he could see, but there was nothing of interest in the stairwell.

"Have the men put on their masks," he said as he

pulled his own free from its case. He removed the goggles.

"Yes, sir."

Kurlov didn't like the masks. They made it difficult to breathe, they were hot, and in hot weather, the eyepieces tended to fog with no way to clear them. Only officers and senior NCOs were supposed to have masks with voice emitter boxes, but Kurlov had circumvented that rule. He wanted all his men to be able to communicate with him.

The radio chirped once and a quiet voice said, "We're down and moving."

Kurlov didn't respond. He pointed into the stairwell. Yerikalin entered and descended. The rest of the team followed, with Kurlov bringing up the rear.

They reached another door, this one not locked. Yerikalin opened it slowly. He stepped back into the dark as two of the team ran through, one facing right and the other left.

"Clear," said Yerikalin quietly.

The team filtered out into the hallway. The top floor of the building seemed to be deserted. Kurlov was surprised by that. Although he hadn't expected to find protesters on the roof—aerial photos had shown that the roofs were clear—he figured they would have occupied all floors of the building.

Yerikalin leaned close and whispered, "They must be lower."

"Right."

The radio crackled once. "Gas released."

Kurlov looked at his watch. It'd take thirty minutes to disperse through the whole building. Removing his mask, he donned the goggles and then slipped on his mask. He could now seen better, though his vision was slightly distorted and he had no depth perception.

With his team, he moved along the hallway, looking at the closed doors. He twisted the knob on one and pushed it open. The interior was dark, but with the goggles he could easily see the furniture, the desk, and the bookcases along one wall. There was no indication that anyone had been there. Certainly no protesters, angered over years of repression. The office was immaculate.

The team worked its way along the hallway, checking all the offices. They cleared the floor and found no evidence of the protesters.

Kurlov checked the time. Fifteen minutes had passed since they'd landed here. Another fifteen minutes and everyone in the building should be asleep.

They reached the stairwell and again found a locked door. That might explain the absence of protesters, who had no way to force the doors. Instead of battering themselves against them, they had retreated.

Yerikalin forced the door again, burning it off the hinges. Kurlov didn't like this because it left evidence of their presence, but there was no alternative.

"Go," he said.

Yerikalin sent one group down to the next floor. Then he, Kurlov, and the remaining men descended two flights, emerging into a dark hallway.

Through the night-vision goggles he could see the floor littered with trash, broken and overturned furniture, and three bodies. Kurlov moved forward slowly, his weapon pointed at the unconscious forms. He knelt near the first and stared down at the face. A young man with a bruise on the side of his face and dried blood on his shirt. Apparently the police had succeeded in stopping him.

He moved to the second form, a young woman with long blond hair pinned up so that she had a boyish look. Kurlov examined her face and recognized it immediately. She was one of the student leaders of the protests. She had been seen on news reports in Moscow and he had examined photos of her before beginning the mission.

Without much thought, Kurlov pulled a pistol from inside his jumpsuit, a small, black automatic that had been designed to be concealed and to kill. It wasn't the type of weapon a soldier would carry into combat because it was inaccurate at five meters, it jammed easily, and its caliber was not compatible with military weapons.

From a pocket, Kurlov took a silencer. He snapped it over the barrel of the small automatic, making sure that the slide would work properly when he fired it. Satisfied, he put the end of it against the girl's ear and pulled the trigger once. The weapon coughed, the sound of the shot so muffled that Yerikalin standing next to him didn't hear it.

The girl's body spasmed as the bullet slammed into her head and punched into her brain. She moaned once, almost inaudibly, as blood began to stain the floor under her head.

Yerikalin moved on, looking at the last of the people in the hallway. He knelt next to an older man with graying hair. Kurlov looked at the face that Yerikalin had turned toward him and shook his head. The old man wasn't important.

The men worked their way along the whole corridor but found no one else on that floor. The offices had been trashed. Equipment and furniture had been destroyed, files and books ripped apart and set on fire, and walls and windows broken.

They reached the stairwell at the far end and leap-frogged down, avoiding the next floor, where the second part of the team would be working.

On the next floor they found more of the protesters. Dozens of them were scattered in the halls, all asleep, thanks to the gas that Chuykov had released.

Kurlov reached up to wipe the sweat from his face, forgetting about the mask. He was miserable in it. Sweat was dripping into his eyes, stinging them. His breathing was ragged and he felt like he was suffocating.

The men swept forward slowly, looking into the faces of the sleeping people. One of the men recognized a protest leader and killed him with a shot to the head, then moved on quickly, checking the next body.

Kurlov grinned behind his mask. That was the advantage of working with professionals. They did their job, no matter what it was, and moved on.

Kurlov started down his side of the hallway, looking at the prone forms. Men and women were everywhere. He opened a door and spotted two naked bodies. For a moment he couldn't figure out the tangle of arms and legs and then realized that the couple had fallen asleep in the middle of making love because of the gas. Kurlov had never seen two people doing it, never blundered in on his mother and father or seen his sister as she tried to earn enough money to escape her family.

He moved forward and studied the scene. The woman was slender, almost skinny, with black hair fanning out around her head. The man was heavier, thicker, and hid most of her. Kurlov wondered what their reaction was going to be when they woke up in a couple of hours. Back in the hallway, he saw that his men had reached the far end of the corridor and were waiting there for him.

They worked their way down through the building, checking each floor, looking for the leaders who had been identified through news photographs and GRU sources. Kurlov found two more suspected leaders and killed them both.

They reached the bottom floor thirty minutes later. Kurlov spotted Chuykov standing near the entrance, a double glass door. Beyond it was movement. Nothing rapid and nothing with purpose. Chuykov approached and said, "We had to eliminate two people down in the basement. They caught us putting the gas into the system."

"No problem." Kurlov looked at his men and then crouched. Using a penlight, he examined his map of downtown Tartu. When Yerikalin looked over his shoulder, Kurlov pointed to another building. "We need to check this one."

"Yes, sir. It's about three hours to sunrise."

Kurlov didn't move. He checked the time and reached up to rub his face but the gas mask was in the way. "Let's get out of here."

"Stick close to the walls and stay in the shadows," said Yerikalin.

"Right," said Kurlov. "Everyone outside."

The men filtered through the door. As soon as they were outside, Kurlov stripped off the mask. He took a deep breath of the muggy but fresh-tasting air. He could feel the sweat drying on his face and wiped it with the sleeve of his black jumpsuit.

"Sir," said Yerikalin.

"I know." Kurlov took another deep breath and then pointed at a building across the street.

Before his men could move, a figure came at them.

Kurlov turned as a police officer, pistol at hand, moved closer, demanding, "Who are you?"

Kurlov half raised his hands and moved toward the police officer. "Soldiers."

"What are you doing here?"

"We have orders." Kurlov could see one of his men edging to the side, away from the confrontation. Kurlov reached inside his jumpsuit. "I have my orders right here."

The police officer raised his pistol and pointed it at Kurlov's face. "Show me your hand. Slowly."

Kurlov grinned. "Certainly."

As he drew his hand out slowly, his fingers stiff, the soldier struck. He hit the police officer on the side of the neck as he grabbed for the pistol, jerking it to the side. In the quiet of the early morning, the sound of the finger breaking seemed loud. As the police officer fell the soldier hit him again in the side and then kicked him in the kidney. The police officer hit the ground without a sound.

Kurlov moved toward the prone man and touched his throat. He drew his knife and then struck the officer in the head a dozen times. The skull splintered, cracking under the force of the assault.

Looking up at his men, he said, "Drag the body inside the door there."

Two of the men grabbed the dead man. They pulled him back into the building and shoved him to one side, near the door.

"Less than three hours, Captain," said Yerikalin.

Now there was more noise around them. A few cars were on the street, their headlights flashing on the glass of the nearby buildings.

"No more time," said Kurlov. "Back inside."

They reentered the building, but Kurlov didn't order them to use the masks; the gas had dissipated. Kneeling near the body of the dead policeman, Kurlov took the pistol he'd used to kill the woman on the top floor and the two men on lower floors and put it in the corpse's hand. Without too much trouble, the police would be able to prove that the dead officer had killed the people. Persuasive KGB officers would help them reach that conclusion.

"Chuykov, get the men up the stairs, to the roof."

"Certainly." Chuykov pushed the door open and began waving the unit through. "Move it. Move it."

Kurlov and Yerikalin watched as a police vehicle moved along the street with a searchlight swinging from side to side. Three men were standing in the rear, one manning the machine gun and the other two searching for the protesters.

"We got in here pretty easily," said Yerikalin.

"Meaning?"

"Shouldn't this building have been surrounded by the police?"

"Probably have the whole area cordoned off," said Kurlov. But even as he said it he knew that wasn't right. If they'd cordoned the area, there wouldn't have been a single man on patrol. He'd have been traveling with four or five others. "We'd better get moving."

Yerikalin looked at the body of the dead officer. "Too bad," he said.

They headed to the door and began to climb the stairs, Yerikalin leading the way. Kurlov stopped at the first landing and looked back the way they had come. There was no one in the stairway. He turned and hurried on up.

When they reached the roof, Kurlov saw that his men had spread out and were gathering up their chutes. One man was using a penlight, searching for anything they might have dropped. Kurlov took out his radio and extended the antenna. He listened to the carrier wave for a moment and then said, "Igor is prepared for pickup."

There was a moment's hesitation and then, "Helicopters are inbound, Igor."

"Roger. We are four bingo."

"Understood."

Kurlov collapsed the antenna and turned. The men had collected the chutes and thrown them into a pile. Chuykov was checking the perimeter of the roof to make sure that there were no wires or antennas that could foul a chopper's rotors.

"Strobe light," said Kurlov.

"Right here."

"Chopper should be approaching from the west," he said, pointing.

"Yes, sir."

Kurlov watched his men spread out across the roof of the building. They didn't have to defend it from the enemy, the protesters, or the police. No one knew they were there. No one knew that they were escaping. He turned and walked back toward the stairwell and stared at the burned door handle. No proof that Soviet troops had burned through the door. Nothing except a hole so that someone could defeat the lock, and that someone could easily have been one of the dissidents occupying the building.

In the distance he heard the beat of helicopter rotors. He turned and looked up toward the dark star-sprinkled sky. There was a black shape in the distance but that was a cloud.

"There," said one of the men, pointing to the northwest. "Right there."

Yerikalin pointed his strobe at the chopper and touched the button on the side. Kurlov had heard pilots tell others that the strobe looked like muzzle flashes when seen from the air. But the pilot of the inbound chopper would know it wasn't a muzzle flash. No one in Tartu would be shooting at him.

"We have everything?" Kurlov asked.

Yerikalin nodded. "Yes, sir. Everything."

The drone of the chopper increased in volume and Kurlov could now make out its shape against the dark sky. The first faint traces of daylight were beginning to push their way up. Kurlov would be gone long before it was light enough for anyone to see.

"Let's mark the touchdown point."

"Yes, sir." Yerikalin snapped his fingers and one of the men ran forward with a strobe light. He turned it on and set it on the roof, away from the tangle of wires and antennas and vents and smokestacks.

As the man retreated the helicopter crossed the edge of the building. Kurlov was caught by the rotor wash blowing at him with nearly the force of hurricane winds. He stumbled back and slipped to one knee, leaning forward.

The helicopter hovered for a moment, the roar of its engines overwhelming all other sound, then settled to the rooftop. As the wheels touched the surface the wind suddenly died away and the roar of the turbines diminished. A door on the side slipped open.

The men stood up, some of them ducking their heads, as if afraid of the rotors, although the blades were fifteen feet over them. They leaned forward, anticipating the hurricanelike winds, their eyes closed against the blowing dust and flying debris.

"Hurry," Yerikalin ordered.

As the men scrambled into the helicopter Kurlov used his radio for the last time. "Igor is vacating."

"Roger, Igor."

Kurlov collapsed the antenna and then ran to the side of the chopper. Hands reached out, grabbed him, and hauled him aboard. It seemed that as his feet left the roof, the helicopter leaped into the air. They were on their way out.

SCHOOL OF THE AMERICAS
PANAMA

Martinez and Alvarez stepped out of the conference room into the humidity and heat of the early afternoon. The sunlight seemed to be hotter and brighter than it was farther to the north. The cloudless sky was so blue that it nearly hurt the eyes to look up into it.

"I'll get the jeep."

Martinez just nodded and watched Alvarez walk into the parking lot and climb behind the wheel of a standard military jeep that had been declared obsolete but was still used. The lieutenant slipped behind the wheel, using his shoulders and feet to keep his butt off the sun-hot seat. Slowly he sat down and then drove to the waiting Martinez.

"Need a ride, soldier?"

Martinez touched the seat and shook his head. "We should have thought of that." He finally climbed in, trying to ignore the heat.

"Where to?"

"Intelligence offices over on Howard."

"Yes, sir. Will we have time to eat at the club there?"

"If you feel it necessary," said Martinez.

"Great." Alvarez dropped the jeep into gear and popped the clutch.

They drove along the canal and then turned, slowing at the gate of Howard Air Force Base, but the guard there recognized them and waved them through. Following the main road for a short distance, they climbed a slight hill. Both sides of the road were covered with thick vegetation. Martinez often wondered why the vegetation hadn't been cut back. If the Panamanians ever decided to overrun the base, the bushes, trees, and grasses would provide them with a good cover. When they reached the top of the hill, they could look down on the large, white buildings marking the various command functions of the air force at Howard.

"We need to head that way." Martinez pointed. "Main intel office is there."

Alvarez turned on a side street and then pulled into a large parking lot opposite the headquarters building. Surprisingly, the lot was filled with American-made cars. A few of them looked to be classics from the late sixties and early seventies, but many were only a year or two old. Alvarez parked in a spot marked for offical vehicles. He leaped out and then tilted the seat forward so the sun wouldn't hit it.

Martinez got out the other side and followed suit. Together they walked across the street to the building. Every time Martinez entered a building, he was surprised to find that it was air-conditioned. The army and the air force spent a great deal of money to make sure that their soldiers and airmen and women wouldn't be uncomfortable in the tropical environment. For a moment Martinez was cold.

They walked down the wide, carpeted corridors, glancing at the pictures of aircraft in flight. There was a display case holding dusty models of aircraft that had flown during World War II, Korea, and the Vietnam War. Near them were pictures of the chain of command starting with the president of the United States and working down to the officer in command of the building.

At the far end of the hall was a closed door. It looked to be made of wood, but Martinez knew it was reinforced with steel. An enemy force attacking would not be able to breach the offices beyond the door easily. It was designed to give the staff time to burn secret documents.

Martinez stopped at the door and touched the button set beside it. With the quiet hum of the air-conditioning and the thickness of the door and walls, he wasn't sure if the buzzer had sounded.

A moment later a small window opened and a clerk looked out. "ID," she said.

Martinez pulled his wallet from his pocket and showed the woman his military form two, the ID card. She studied it, then his picture, and finally disappeared for a moment. The door opened then and she pointed at a clipboard sitting on a table. "Sign in."

Martinez did as instructed and then handed the pen to Alvarez. The woman asked, "Now, what can I do for you?"

"We need to get a briefing on the current status of the various armed forces in Colombia, including the drug cartels," said Martinez.

The woman shook her head. "I'm not sure what we've got on hand here."

"Isn't the intelligence all filtered through your communications facilities?" Martinez asked.

"We pass it along, but if we're not an addressee, we don't bother with making a hard copy for ourselves. Our function, regardless of congressional thinking, is still defense."

She turned and headed across the room. It was cavernous, filled with battleship-gray metal desks and a few five-foot dividers. Men and women were working at the desks. At the far side were offices and in the center of the wall was another door that led deeper into the building, toward the vault where the classified material was stored.

She opened a door into a small conference room and reached in to turn on a light, letting the two men enter and sit down. "Please wait here."

A moment later another women entered. She glanced at both Martinez and then Alvarez before moving toward them. She held out a hand and said, "I'm Victoria Ord."

"Frank Martinez and Steve Alvarez," said Martinez. He got up and pulled out a chair.

Ord smoothed the back of her skirt and sat. She leaned forward, elbows on the table. "Now, what can I do for you?"

"I need a good briefing on the military operations in Colombia to include paramilitary forces, outlaw organizations and firepower capabilities."

Ord shook her head.

"What?" Martinez asked.

"You have no need to know."

Martinez looked at her carefully. A tall, slender, blond woman with bright brown eyes and sharp features. She looked to be no more than thirty and could have been twenty-two or twenty-three. To Martinez, she looked like a clerk. Someone sent to get information for the colonels and generals and GS-15s.

"I don't think you understand," he said. "Not to mention that you're not in a position to make that determination."

Ord shook her head. "You want a generalized briefing on the various terrorist organizations of South America, that's no problem."

"We need to target Colombia," said Martinez.

Ord rocked back in her chair and grinned. "Why just Colombia?"

Martinez glanced at Alvarez. "Need to know?" he said.

"That's not going to cut it," said Ord. "I'd like to help, but you can understand."

Martinez rubbed his face. Security was rearing its head everywhere. She wouldn't provide the information without Martinez giving her information. And he wouldn't give her information that she didn't need to have. He wouldn't do it because it could compromise his mission. The fewer people who knew what he was doing, the safer he was going to be.

"Generally," he said, "what can you tell me?"

"Most of it is classified secret," she said.

"We're both cleared for top secret," said Martinez. "Your access roster should have shown that."

"Yes." Ord stood. "If you'll give me a couple of minutes, I'll see what I can pull." She left the room, closing the door behind her.

"Good-looking woman," said Alvarez.

"But mean," said Martinez. "Won't cut us any slack."

"So we'll get Gibson over here and he can get a good briefing."

"No," said Martinez. "I don't want a bunch of outsiders knowing what we're doing. We'll have to get someone else to get the intel for us. We'll put a request through B team and then we won't have half the military knowing our business."

"Then what the hell are we doing here?"

Martinez shrugged. "Getting a feel for current events."

Ord returned with a file folder and set it on the table in front of her. There was a pink cover sheet on it that announced the contents of the folder were secret.

"Best I can do for you is to share the current intel traffic and provide a short report on the military forces in Colombia."

"We're familiar with those aligned with the government. We're more concerned with the paramilitary and the men training them."

Ord nodded. "I'll give you what we have. Please, do not take notes."

"Of course," said Martinez.

"Militarily," said Ord, "Colombia has a relatively small force, just over seventy thousand, the majority of which is army. Their navy is little more than gunboats and coastal vessels and the air force is nearly nonexistent."

"How is the army organized?" Martinez asked.

Ord shook her head. "I don't have that information available. I would guess into infantry battalions with little in the way of artillery support. Small, automatic weapons, some larger, squad weapons, and little else."

"Terrorist organizations?" asked Alvarez.

"Several have been reported to be operating in Colombia but they are directly related to the drug industry. The majority of Colombia's land is forested, with only about a quarter of it available for agriculture. That limits the areas where the drug cartels can secure their product."

Martinez pointed at the file. "Anything in there on the numbers of drug dealers or terrorists. What kind of strength they have?"

Ord shrugged again. "One man with a machine gun can cause a lot of damage and the seventy-thousand-man army can't do much to prevent that sort of thing."

"Which doesn't answer the question," said Martinez.

"I don't think anyone ever looked at them as a military force before."

Martinez said, "I read that in Vietnam every military-age male was considered to be a potential enemy soldier, so that there were various studies giving numbers that could be fielded."

"We are not at war with Colombia," said Ord.

"Then you don't have any figures on the number of military-age males," said Martinez.

"I could get those. I do remember, off the top of my head, that the population distribution is forty-nine decimal five-percent male and fifty decimal five-percent female."

"But no breakdown according to age?" Alvarez asked.

"Nope. I could find it," she said, "but I really don't see the point in it."

"I thought your job," said Martinez, "was to provide intelligence information for those who desired it. I wasn't aware that your job was to also evaluate the necessity for that information."

"My job is to do what I decide to do and not what you believe it might be," she snapped.

Alvarez said, "Anything else that you can tell us?"

She glanced at him and then said, "Terrorist activity seems to be drug related rather than politically motivated. It's directed toward the judicial system and police officials rather than the legislative or executive branches of the government. Except in rare exceptions. During the presidential elections of 1990, they assassinated a number of candidates."

"That doesn't tell us anything," said Martinez. "Hell, they could attack us as a protest against American intervention in the drug trade."

"I never said you'd be safe," said Ord angrily. "Just that the targeting is driven by monetary rather than political motives."

"Shit," said Martinez. He stood up. "Thanks for nothing."

"Come back with the proper documents," said Ord, "and I'll be more than happy to cooperate."

"Sure," said Martinez. He spun and grabbed the doorknob.

"Don't forget to sign out," said Ord levelly. "I'd hate to dispatch the MPs."

Without a word, Martinez opened the door and exited. He headed across the floor without waiting for Alvarez to catch him.

Alvarez caught him near the desk as he reached for a pen. "No need to antagonize her."

"No?" said Martinez. "Why not? All she has to do is sit in this air-conditioned office and provide us with a little information now and then. But instead she's got fourteen different reasons why she shouldn't have to do it. God, I hate these fucking civilians." He finished signing out and threw down the pen.

Alvarez signed out and then opened the door so they could leave the intelligence section. "Now what?"

"Hell, I don't know. Back to the barracks and see if Chavez has everyone rounded up."

"And then?"

"See what develops there."

The isolation area was set off from the rest of the fort, surrounded by a high, chain-link fence that was topped with huge loops of razor wire. A guard shack squatted on the road that led into the area that was not yet occupied. Set back, out of sight of the guard shack and the fence, was a series of white one-story buildings. These were the living quarters for the team, the supply depots, the briefing and messing facilities, and the equipment storage area.

Martinez and Alvarez arrived early the next morning,

after a quick dinner, a little gambling, and then a short night's sleep. Alvarez drove the hummer, the army's replacement for the old, reliable jeep. When they stopped at the gate, Martinez got out, opened it, and waited until Alvarez had driven through. Then he stepped up to the guard shack and looked in. No evidence that anyone had occupied it for several weeks.

As he returned to the hummer and climbed in, Alvarez let out the clutch. "No guard?"

"No guard, but then we haven't started yet."

They drove up to the closest of the buildings and stopped outside of it. As Alvarez turned off the engine the front door opened. Chavez appeared there, dressed in starched jungle fatigues.

"Good morning, Captain. Lieutenant."

Martinez climbed out of the hummer. "You have the whole team here?"

"Yes, sir."

Martinez took a deep breath. "Everything we need here?"

"Haven't had a chance to inventory yet, but it looks very good."

"Let's go on inside," said Martinez. He let Chavez open the door and was surprised to find the interior was air-conditioned. "I don't remember this."

"Lot's of changes," said Chavez. "Even have cable TV hooked up. We can watch the news from around the world."

"I was about to say I couldn't think of a good reason for cable TV, but that seems to be one," said Alvarez.

"Not to mention the good movies on HBO," said Chavez. "Last night they were showing *The Green Berets*. Gave me lots of good ideas."

"Really?" Alvarez asked.

Chavez rolled his eyes. "Where did you find him anyway?"

Martinez ignored this. "You get anything from headquarters on this yet?"

"Nothing new," said Chavez. "I put the men to work cleaning rifles and the like. I had each man select an

M-16 and an AK. Figured we'd go either direction and that would give us a jump on this.''

"No brand-new individual assault weapons?''

"There're a couple of the Heckler and Kock's G-11s and some of the Colt ACRs but I just don't like them. I prefer the old standard.''

"Same arguments have been going on as each generation of assault rifle was developed. The old-line soldiers reject them out of hand.''

"Hell, Captain, when I hit a combat situation, I don't want to have to worry about the reliability of the weapon I carry. I know what the AK and the M-16 will do. I just don't know about these new beasts.''

They had entered the building and were walking down one of the hallways. The interior was cinder block and green tile, a cold, sterile environment with no sign of dust anywhere. The doors on either side of the hall were made of metal and were all closed. No signs identified any of them.

"Got the boys in one of the larger conference rooms,'' said Chavez.

"Let's head there first,'' said Martinez. "Then we can decide what we're going to do.''

Chavez stopped and opened a door. As Martinez stepped in he could see the floor was carpeted. The round table had been shoved into one corner and the half-dozen high-backed chairs that went with it were stacked out of the way. The members of the team sat on the floor, their weapons near them, broken down as the men worked to clean them.

"I'll want a chance to zero these,'' said Davis. He hadn't even bothered to look up to see who had entered. He just kept working, a dirty rag in his hand.

Martinez stepped over the stripped down parts of an AK and pulled one of the chairs around so that he could sit down. Chavez closed the door.

"We'll worry about zeroing the weapons later,'' said Martinez. "Gibson?''

"Yes, sir?''

"You'll have to get over to S-2 for a briefing on the current trends in Colombia focusing on the drug trade. I want everything you can get without revealing anything about the mission.''

Martinez laughed. ''I sometimes wonder what I'm good for.''

''Hell, Captain,'' said Chavez. ''We need you to take the blame when things go wrong.''

''I guess that's true.'' He looked at the men around him. All were professionals who had volunteered for the army, volunteered for jump training and then volunteered for the Special Forces. They had spent their time in the Q Courses, at the John F. Kennedy Special Warfare School, and in various environments learning survival. They were the best-trained, most highly motivated soldiers in the world.

''You ready to give us a quick briefing on what you learned?'' Martinez asked.

''Without knowing the specific target or the mission, I'm not sure how relevant the information is going to be,'' said Gibson.

''Drug interdiction,'' said Martinez.

''Oh, shit,'' said Gibson. ''I was afraid of something like that.''

''Just tell us what you've got without the commentary,'' said Martinez.

''Location of the mission?'' Gibson asked.

''That'll be driven by the intelligence.''

''Yes, sir.'' Gibson stood up and wiped his hands on one of the rags that had littered the floor.

THE KREMLIN
MOSCOW

General Stepanov sat in a high-backed leather chair behind the massive desk in his huge office and stared at the report in front of him. To his right were four tall, thin windows that looked out on a nearly deserted square. To his left were floor-to-ceiling bookcases that held forbidden volumes from the West. When he rocked back, the leather creaked under his weight. He reached for a gold pen in a gold holder at the front of his desk, just beyond the red blotter. Other than a pool of light on the center of his desk, the office was in shadow.

Stepanov initialed the report and then dropped it to the blotter. He closed his eyes for a moment and thought about sitting in the rear of the Il-76 Mainstay, listening to the radio broadcasts from all the sources in Tartu, listening for the quiet messages from his Spetsnaz team as it moved through the building. It had been a cold time, with the air-conditioning inside the aircraft on high to keep all the electronics cool enough to function properly.

It had been frustrating sitting in the darkened aircraft, unable to do anything except listen and hope that the various orders, issued by Moscow, the KGB, the GRU, and the local military district were properly obeyed by the subordinates.

That was the problem of command and reaching general officer rank. Generals weren't allowed into the field. That was the province of younger men. They obeyed orders, they executed the plans designed by the generals, and they were the ones who lived or died. But Stepanov itched for the action of the field, even though his reflexes had slowed and his senses had dulled.

He opened his eyes and reached over toward the intercom set on the corner of his desk. "Please have Captain Kurlov come in now," he said.

The door opened and Stepanov stood. Kurlov walked across the expanse of carpet, stopped short, and saluted. "Captain Kurlov reporting as ordered, General."

"So formal?" Stepanov asked quietly.

Kurlov couldn't contain his smile. "With generals, one never knows. It is best to be on the side of safety."

Stepanov nodded, returned the salute, and then gestured at one of the two chairs in front of his desk. "Please relax and be seated."

"Thank you, Comrade General."

"I trust our facilities have been adequate?"

"Certainly, General. The new uniform fits well."

"The rest of your gear will be forwarded here. You can arrange to pick it up in the morning."

"Yes, sir."

Stepanov sat down and picked up the report. He flipped through it quickly and then looked up. "Tell me about the raid."

"It's all in the report," said Kurlov.

"No. Tell me about the things you left out of the report. The feelings. The textures. The underlying conditions."

For a moment Kurlov was silent, as if he didn't understand the question. Then he spoke. "Navigation by the pilots was flawless. Put us over the target area just as they were supposed to. Intelligence was flawless. Almost everyone on our list was found inside the building.''

"What was it like?"

Kurlov knew what the general wanted to know. He was asking what it felt like to kill a helpless, sleeping human. Kurlov shrugged, afraid to put the feelings into words because the words weren't the ones people wanted to hear. Everyone had the idea that shooting helpless people was horrible and only the lowest of human life could do it without feeling something.

But the truth was, Kurlov had felt nothing. The people were the enemies of the state. They had made clear decisions that put them into that building. They had known that failure could mean a short life in Siberia, at the best. They understood the rules before they had occupied the building, and if they didn't understand the rules, it was too bad.

"Captain?" said Stepanov, prompting him.

"I feel nothing," he said. "They made their own decisions."

"You killed a young woman," said Stepanov. "Certainly you felt something then."

"Is this relevant, Comrade General?"

"No. Not relevant. It is a question that I can ask now. It is something that I have to know."

"She was the enemy. Just as the men were the enemy. They were violating the law and they had killed soldiers during the day. They shouldn't believe that they can do as they please and that there will be no consequences."

"She was another human being," said Stepanov.

"She was the enemy," Kurlov repeated. "We are trained to kill the enemy. In war, you do not give them the opportunity to surrender. You kill them."

"It was not war."

Kurlov shrugged. "I am not a police officer. Our mission was to help crush the lawless rebellion."

Stepanov nodded. "That you did. With the leaders dead, the rest filtered out, slipped home, and then reported to work."

Kurlov grinned. "Because they saw what happened to the leaders. Assassination."

"That might have been part of it."

"General," said Kurlov. "If I might be so bold as to ask you a question?"

"You've earned a few favors," said Stepanov.

"Why the interest in my feelings over the completion of the mission?"

"Ah." Stepanov rocked back in his chair and steepled his fingers under his chin. "I was a youngster during the Great Patriotic War."

He fell silent for a moment. Suddenly he was a youngster again, freezing cold, near the camp of Nazis. The ground was littered with the bodies of the men killed in the battle, and the center of the village was filled with the dead women and children, shot in retribution. The Nazis took no prisoners. They wanted no witnesses.

It was dusk and his hands were stiff, his fingers numb. The Nazi sat near a bare tree, sheltering himself from the icy winds blowing across the open snowfields. He was huddled in his great coat, and his head was bowed. Stepanov slipped up on him slowly, thinking only of the treasures the soldier would yield. Food, weapons, ammunition, and warmth.

As he got close he could hear the man singing quietly to himself. Stepanov didn't recognize the song. He didn't care what it was. He just kept inching closer until he was less than a meter from the enemy. He stood then, the knife held in his hand, and leaped. The Nazi grunted in surprise and whirled, reaching for his rifle. Stepanov plunged the knife into the man's chest, feeling it rip through the coat, grate against a bone, and then sink into the soft flesh. Stepanov yanked the knife free and struck again and again. The air was filled with the odor of hot copper and loosened bowels as the Nazi died.

As the enemy slumped to the side Stepanov ripped the great coat open and slit the belly of the soldier. The steaming guts spilled out and he shoved his hands into them, letting the blood of his enemy warm him.

The thing about it was that he'd never felt revulsion. He'd never felt guilt. And he'd felt nothing as he'd shot other Nazis. He'd been glad to see them die and wished for more opportunities to kill them.

"I learned," said Stepanov suddenly, "during the Great Patriotic War, the enemy deserves to die. That a soldier does not regret the taking of an enemy's life. I wondered if you felt the same thing."

Kurlov shrugged but didn't speak.

Stepanov stared at the young officer for a moment and then closed the folder. "As you know, your mission was a success. Western journalists are blaming a police officer who went berserk and was killed by the protesters. With the leadership gone, the protests have evaporated. Now the advocacy for social change is in the chambers of government."

"Where nothing will happen," said Kurlov.

"Where change will be slower, but there will be change. A few deaths to prevent many deaths. A good change."

"I'm glad that you approve of the results," said Kurlov.

"Your plans now?" Stepanov asked.

"I'm going to take a few days off," said Kurlov. "Return home to visit with my wife. I have been away for a long time."

Stepanov nodded. He touched the report, flipped through the pages, but didn't bother with it again. Instead, he said, "When you come back, there may be another assignment for you. Like this last one. Discreet but important."

"Of course. I'll be ready," said Kurlov. Then, grinning, he added, "Though the boxing team is due to tour the various Western bases in a few weeks."

"Your new assignment wouldn't take that much time," said Stepanov. "Of course, if necessary, we can postpone the trip."

"Valuable intelligence will be lost."

"No, Captain, such intelligence is no longer valuable and will not be lost."

"Certainly, General." Kurlov hesitated, realized that the interview was over. He stood to salute.

"A car will be waiting downstairs to take you home," said Stepanov. "A small luxury but a well-earned one."

"Thank you, Comrade General."

Kurlov was surprised by the driver standing at the rear of the black Lincoln Town Car. The vehicle, imported under a trade agreement with the Ford Motor Company, was one of many used by the highest-ranking officials at the Kremlin. The driver opened the rear door, let Kurlov enter, and then rushed around to climb behind the wheel. He started the engine, touched the button for the stereo, and drove for the main gate.

"Home," said Kurlov.

The driver glanced into the mirror and nodded. He'd been well briefed.

As they entered the traffic Kurlov looked at the scene around him. The streets were full of cars, many of them of American or Japanese manufacture. Under the reforms started five years earlier, the productive power of the West and the Far East had been brought to Moscow. Waiting lists filled with years-old orders melted away. Consumer goods filled the stores and the people rushed to buy them. Neon lights, once considered signs of Western decadence, now decorated the main streets, advertising McDonald's, Pizza Hut, and Kentucky Fried Chicken.

Kurlov knew exactly how far the changes went. In the past no one published maps of Moscow, the belief being that good maps would aid invaders. Now, with tourists flocking behind what had been the Iron Curtain, good maps were essential.

They left the main part of the city and drove into the rings of apartments that had been constructed during the late sixties and early seventies. Concrete structures that all looked the same and that all had the same faults. Gaps around the windows, doors that wouldn't close, roofs that leaked, and floors that were buckled. Beyond them were newer apartments, built by Western contractors. These were smaller, more expensive, but in better shape. Kurlov had been lucky to get one of the first built.

The car pulled up outside the door of a massive building that would have been considered ugly in the West. It stood fourteen stories and stretched for two blocks in either direction. It was a massive, utilitarian-looking complex. Kurlov didn't care that it was not aesthetically pleasing.

As he opened the rear door the driver asked, "Will that be all?"

Kurlov shrugged. "Yes. I won't be needing you again."

"Thank you, Captain. And welcome home."

Kurlov looked at the glass door and then up the front of the building at the lighted windows. Behind one of them, his wife waited, not knowing that he was about to pop in on her. All she knew was that he had been in the field for two weeks and would be home sometime in the next. She was used to this unpredictability.

Slowly he walked up the sidewalk, avoiding the grass planted around it. Grass to absorb the summer heat and the carbon dioxide of the thousands of new cars. He reached the door and entered the foyer. There was a rental office to the right, rarely occupied because there were still waiting lists for apartments. To the left were the elevators, which worked well.

Kurlov went to hit the button and was suddenly afraid. He had thought of the fun it would be to surprise his wife. Now he had second thoughts. What if she was fooling around because he was gone so often? What if she was in their apartment now with a male friend?

He hesitated with his hand over the number, and then decided it would be better to know. And it would be better to trust her. She had never complained and she had never given him reason to suspect her of cheating. He pushed the button, heard the servos kick in, and felt the elevator begin to rise. He tried to remember exactly how she had looked when he'd left on his last assignment, down to what she had worn, how her hair was fixed, and how she had stood as he walked out the door.

The elevator stopped and the door slipped open. He stepped out and looked down the long, straight hallway. Doors lined both sides, and ceiling lights created pools of brightness. Starting down the hall, he was sure that he wouldn't like the scene that would greet him. Try as he might, he couldn't force the picture from his mind.

At the door he hesitated. He was tempted to put his ear to it and listen. Instead, he reached down and turned the knob. It was unlocked. He'd told her a dozen times to lock it if she was home alone, but she never did.

He threw the door open and saw a single light burning in the alcove they jokingly called the kitchen. She stood in front of the refrigerator, a huge thing with a double door manufactured by Amana. She was stripped to the waist and pulling at something in the freezer section.

She turned at the sound, stared at him for a moment, and then said, "What?"

"I'm home."

She stood flat-footed, water staining the blue jeans she wore. Her blond hair was tied in a ponytail. She had rubber gloves on her hands but his eyes fixed on her nipples. The cold had stiffened them.

"Home?" she repeated, and then threw herself at him.

He caught her and held her as she wrapped her legs around him, pressed herself against him, and kissed him. She held him tightly, as if afraid he would escape.

"I'm glad you're home," she said. "Very glad."

Suddenly Kurlov was, too.

CIA STATION
HONG KONG

Reisman had heard several things that bothered him during his interview with the Chinese woman. Her story of escape sounded good and fit the pattern of those told by others. But she had a few new wrinkles, and that had set him to thinking. Rather than stay in the city room making phone calls, he decided it was time to get out among the real people. Work on the phone could only accomplish so much and Reisman liked to be in the room with those he interviewed. There was so much that facial expressions and body language revealed.

Out on the crowded, noisy Hong Kong street, Reisman breathed the humid air that trapped the gases expelled by the thousands of cars, the jets at the airport, and the manufacturing areas. It was a gray, soggy day that depressed him as he fought the crowds on the street.

He was going toward the heart of the city, to a little-known area filled with government buildings and offices.

The CIA had a satellite facility that was registered as an annex of the American embassy, a ruse that fooled no one.

As he walked up the steps he tried to come up with an approach to use. Sara Keller, a young woman who had been posted to Hong Kong only three months before, was smart enough to know that she shouldn't talk to the press. But she also knew that Reisman could become an enemy if she wasn't careful. Reisman needed her as a source and she needed the assistance he could provide. They both walked a thin line between dishonor and exploitation.

Reisman opened the door on a dim, dirty hallway, its tile gray from accumulated grime. An unoccupied receptionist's desk at the back of the hall was flanked by doors and a wooden stairway to the second floor. He took a step toward the closest door, hesitated, then yanked it open as if he expected to catch someone in flagrante delicto.

The lone woman in the room asked, "May I help you?"

"Sara Keller. My name is Reisman."

"One moment please." She lifted a phone and spoke into it, then pointed at another door. "You may go right in."

Reisman moved to the door, tapped on it, and then opened it. He spotted Keller sitting behind a large desk, a bank of windows right behind her. If the sun had been out, it might have been difficult for him to see her. He wondered if she ever worried about a rifleman.

"Come on in." She stood up, her hand out. Keller was a short, slender, brown-haired woman who liked to dress in short skirts and tight-fitting blouses because it made the men stare and gave her the upper hand in the conversation. If they were watching her body, hoping to see something they weren't supposed to see, they wouldn't be concentrating on the topic at hand. She had a narrow face with a pointed chin and wide-set blue eyes. Her hair was cut in bangs that brushed her eyebrows. Periodically she would use her fingertips to brush her hair to the side.

Reisman entered and looked at the leather visitor's chair. It did not look clean.

"Have a seat," she said. "And tell me what you need from me."

"Maybe it's a social call," said Reisman.

"Nope. You would have phoned and met me at one of the bars or restaurants."

Reisman shrugged, sat back and crossed his legs, putting an ankle on his knee. He watched her sit down behind the desk and pick up a pencil. "I do have a question for you."

"Personal or professional."

"Professional," said Reisman. He grinned as he said it, thinking of the other directions the conversation could have taken.

"Go ahead and I'll do my best."

"Are the Japanese operating in China?"

She sat still for a moment, blinked twice, and said, "Sure. They've had trade agreements with the Chinese for the last four or five years. Major exports to China include—"

"No." Reisman rubbed his forehead, stared at the ceiling, and tried to rephrase the question. "I mean an unofficial presence."

"I don't know what you mean."

Reisman shrugged and decided that he had nothing to lose. "I mean, I've heard a report that Japanese were helping the Chinese get out of China."

"You sure it was the Japanese?"

"I've talked to one witness who said it was a Japanese who helped her escape."

"We," said Keller, waving a hand to indicate the others in the building, "have nothing on Japanese infiltration of China. Are you suggesting there is some kind of, ah, intelligence function being mounted by the Japanese?"

"I don't know."

Keller scratched her head in thought. "One of the conditions of the Japanese surrender at the end of the Second World War was that they would not enter the arena of world affairs, either with a standing army or navy, or in the intelligence field. They have taken a larger role for their internal defense, but I don't know of any attempts to set up an intelligence community. I would think that the various world powers—us, the Soviets, the Chinese, and the Europeans—would not allow it."

"Wouldn't an intelligence function, by its very nature, be secret?"

Now Keller smiled. "It would be. But you've got to remember that we, meaning the United States, have had a hand in their internal politics since the end of the war."

"That was fifty years ago. Things have changed radically. We haven't had much luck with them as a trading partner. High tariffs on our goods going in, and government supports on theirs to keep the prices down."

"What are you saying?"

"That the Japanese, fifty years after the war, might be attempting to expand their power. Hell, I don't know."

"This is based on a single report from a frightened Chinese?"

"Only would have taken one person to blow the whole deal on Pearl Harbor," said Reisman.

Keller took a deep breath. "Right now we have nothing to suggest that the Japanese are interested in spying on the Chinese or anyone else. I think they're pleased at not having to waste a large portion of their gross national product on defense. They can divert those monies into programs that are more beneficial."

"But if you had anything," said Reisman, "it would be classified and you couldn't talk about it."

"Off the record?" Keller asked.

"Off the record."

"If I had anything suggesting it, I would try to guide you in the right directions. There has been nothing to suggest an official presence."

"Unofficial?"

"No," said Keller. "I think you might have someone operating there on his own. Helping his fellow humans, but nothing sanctioned by the government."

"You've been a bundle of noninformation," said Reisman. "You can report to your bosses that you've done your job well."

"No reason to get nasty. It's not my fault that your information hasn't worked out."

"Sorry." Reisman stood up. "I've taken enough of your time."

Staring him in the eyes, she said. "Come back sometime when it's not all business."

"I'll do that." Reisman retreated then, before she brought in the reinforcements. He knew what she was doing and wondered why. Women normally did not throw themselves at him. He needed to work at it. Take them to dinner, take them out dancing or to the theater.

At the door he stopped and turned. "Thanks for your help."

"Sorry there wasn't more that I could do for you," she said, smiling coyly.

As he left the office the double meaning of her words was not lost on him.

Reisman reached the office and then walked up to the second floor. In the old days the newsroom would have been a dark, cluttered place where reporters built makeshift warrens to hide from the editors. The remodeling, done a couple of years earlier on the theory that the Chinese would not throw the press out of Hong Kong, had changed the dark interior into a spacious, brightly lit cavern where the editors at one end could easily see the reporters at their desks. Bright colors were splashed on the walls and the carpets. Burnt orange was the dominant color. Amber or green glowed on the screens of computers.

Reisman walked across the room, nodding at his fellows, than collapsed into his chair and stirred around in the stack of papers on his desk.

"Hey!" he shouted. "Who the hell's been sitting at my desk."

A woman turned around and said, "Me. What's your problem?"

"I had a phone number on a piece of paper. I can't find it."

"I didn't take anything. Besides, that's what a Rolodex is for. Phone numbers."

"If you can't keep your hands to yourself, stay the fuck away from my desk."

Another reporter yelled, "Hold it down. Some of us are trying to think."

Reisman leaned back and listened to the noise around him—the clacking of the keyboards, the roaring of the big fans that circulated the air because the massive air conditioners weren't up to the job of cooling the city room, and the buzzing of the phones with the dozens of one-sided conversations—and felt the anger boil in him. Too much noise and too many distractions. He didn't know how anyone could get anything done in the city room.

But then, his story wasn't there. It was outside. In Japan, regardless of what Keller had told him. The lead was weak, there was no denying that. But he'd started major stories with less. The trick was convincing the editor that it was necessary to go to Japan.

He stood and then glanced at the glassed-in offices of the editors. Slowly, trying to ignore the noise from all the other people, Reisman walked toward them. He stopped outside of one and watched as the man inside wrote on a sheet of paper and then tossed it into a basket.

Reisman stuck his head in and asked, "You got a minute?"

Ralph Carmichael, an older, heavyset man, leaned back in his chair and waved. "Sure. Shoot."

"Got a story from a refugee who has made some interesting claims." Reisman smiled weakly, knowing the story didn't have much zip.

"And?"

Reisman rubbed his cheek slowly. "That's the problem. I'm not sure that there's much in the way of an and. I'd like to follow it up and see where it takes me."

"How much time you want to spend on this?"

"Couple of days. Maybe a week."

Carmichael leaned forward, elbows on his desk and his chin propped in his hand. "That's a pretty flimsy story. I don't know about this."

"It's just a couple of days to follow the lead. If it plays out, we'll have something. If it doesn't . . ." Reisman shrugged.

Carmichael took a deep breath and blew it out audibly. He opened a drawer, took out a file. "Right now, I don't see anything coming up that will affect you. Okay. Three days, but if you find nothing, that's it."

"Thanks." Reisman turned to leave but then stopped. "I can get the voucher this afternoon?"

"Voucher?"

"For the plane fare to Japan."

"Now, wait a minute. You didn't say anything about going to Japan for this."

"Where else would I go?" Reisman asked. "That's where the story will be found."

"Leads in Japan?"

Reisman shrugged. "I've got a source with the CIA that will provide me with an introduction in Japan. I never suggested that it would be easy."

"And you couldn't do this from here?" Carmichael gestured at the newsroom.

"Could, but I wouldn't be able to get at the good stuff. It's easier to lie on the phone. They can hang up on you. But if you're standing there, watching them, it's another ballgame."

Carmichael sat back in his chair and closed his eyes. After a moment he shook his head and looked at Reisman.

"Airfare to Japan isn't that much," said Reisman. "Hotels are—"

"Damned expensive. And you can't get a hamburger for under twenty-five dollars."

"Thank God for expense accounts." Reisman grinned.

Carmichael held up a hand. "You sure that this story is worth it?"

"I think we should pursue it."

Finally Carmichael said, "Okay. Take five days."

Reisman nodded. "Thanks." He stood and left the office.

ISOLATION AREA
PANAMA

Martinez was sitting in a small office, his feet up on the battleship-gray desk, his fingers laced behind his head, studying the ceiling. His mind was blank. He was waiting for something to happen so that he could get started.

There was a tap on the door and Chavez opened it slightly to look in. "Sir, they've arrived."

Martinez dropped his feet to the tiled floor and stood up. "They're late."

"Not much," said Chavez.

"Where are they set up?"

"In the conference room."

They walked down the tiled hallway, past the pictures of the Pacific chain of command. Chavez opened the door to the conference room and Martinez entered.

The in-processing staff had pulled a couple of the tables together and were sitting behind them. They had boxes of records, typewriters, stacks of forms, a laminating machine, and two walkie-talkies in case something important happened somewhere in the world and they were suddenly called away for an emergency in-processing.

Part of the team was already in the processing line. Martinez joined the end of it and worked his way through, checking his insurance forms, his will, and then being asked if he wanted to sign a power of attorney. They checked his financial records and allotments, his dog tags and his ID card, making sure that all the information was current and accurate. He read forms, signed forms, and when asked about his religious preference, said, "Druid."

The clerk searched his list of "authorized" religious affiliations and then shook her head. "I don't find Druid on here, sir."

Martinez shrugged. "Put down Catholic, then."

"Yes, sir."

Finished, Martinez moved away from the tables and turned around. When Chavez joined him there, he said, "Napoleon said that an army moves on its stomach. Ours moves on its triplicate forms and paperwork."

"But think of all the trees we're destroying by creating this paper."

"What I want to know is where they store it all. They never throw out anything. You can still find after-action reports from the Civil War if you want to read them."

The last of the team finished with the in-processing and the officer in charge of the clerks walked up to Martinez. "I think we're through here, sir."

"Thank you for your effort, Lieutenant," said Martinez.

"Yes, sir."

The lieutenant returned to his clerks. Martinez leaned closer to Chavez and asked, "Are they getting younger?"

"Just seems that way."

Changing the subject, he asked, "The updated briefing packages arrive yet?"

"Still waiting on them," said Chavez.

"Why not have Gibson head out and see if he can scare up anything? I'd have thought the packages would be here this morning."

"Yes, sir." Chavez walked toward Gibson.

Martinez watched the two men talk and then left the conference room. He headed back to the tiny office, worried about the mission already. Too much had been happening out of channels. First the general briefed them without telling them much and now the sequencing of events was slightly askew. He didn't like it much.

As he reached the door Alvarez approached him. "Got the briefing packages."

"How?"

"Courier just brought them in. I had to sign for them."

Martinez nodded. "At least that suggests they're paying some attention to security." He glanced at the thick manila envelopes in Alvarez's hand. "You got mine there?"

"Yes, sir." He pulled it out and handed it over.

"Okay, why don't you get those distributed and then come back here?"

"Yes, sir."

As Alvarez disappeared down the hallway Martinez opened the door to the office. He tossed the envelope on the desk and then stared at it. He didn't want to open it because he knew that it was going to be bad news. Walking around the desk, he pulled the chair out and sat down. He reached out for the envelope, opened the flap, and reached in for the thick bundle of papers that included aerial photographs, pictures of the target area, maps, and detailed information about the target. Everything that he would need to plan the mission was there, assembled by intelligence officers from around the world and then reviewed by the SF headquarters, the SFOB, directing the operations of his team.

Martinez arranged the material in front of him, first looking at all the photographs just because it was easier. Some of them were satellite images, stamped "secret" top and bottom, but not because of the subject. The Soviets would love to know just how good the cameras on the new spy satellites were.

The pictures themselves, except for the few showing people or ground facilities, told him nothing. He pulled a bright red file folder that had a DEA logo on it from the stack. Statistics on drug abuse in the United States, including the infiltration routes for various drugs, their short- and long-term effects on the human body, the number of deaths attributed to each drug, and theories about drug abuse. It also contained a breakdown of murder statistics, concentrating on those that were drug-related or drug-induced. It was a propaganda package designed to enrage the reader and provoke him into action. Too many lives were being wasted by "the plague of drugs on the land."

Martinez laughed at that statement. The plague of drugs. It could be stopped, immediately, if the right pressures were applied. Make selling drugs a capital offense, eliminate the lengthy stays of execution. Let the drug dealers know that dealing drugs was a death sentence pure and simple and the glamour would be gone.

The problem, Martinez knew, was that society wouldn't allow that to happen. Not when people who used drugs "recreationally" and gave them to their friends were seen as "respectable" outlaws. "He wasn't selling drugs. Why should he go to jail with the real criminals?"

But none of that was Martinez's problem. His job was not to worry about drug dealers in the States, or about the penalties they faced. The propaganda package from the DEA was useless to him. They didn't have to convince him that the mission was a good idea.

Martinez pushed that part of the material to one side and picked up the intel package put together by the military. It contained an outline of the military presence in Colombia, but ignored the Colombian military. It detailed the suspected presence of Cuban, Israeli, and Nicaraguan advisers. It detailed the locations of the camps used by those military forces, lines of communication from those camps to the coast, and the weaponry of the various forces as well as the mission of the advisers.

Martinez used a yellow legal pad to make notes on the military forces, including the closest town to each of the camps. He'd plot those on a map later.

Finished with that, he pulled the last thick packet from the envelope. It contained the mission scenario. It was to be a "strac recon." He and the team were to avoid contact. They were to sneak in, lay low, and watch. They would patrol, but stray no more than twenty or thirty klicks from their operating base. The mission briefing also included a set of coordinates. Martinez plotted them on one of the maps of Colombia. They were to land in the jungle south of Cartagena. They would be able to watch the city and search the surrounding hills for signs of drug production and manufacture. Aerial reconnaissance had discovered a number of breaks in the jungle canopy. There were hints of rough airfields.

The mission was simple. Slip into the area, watch, learn, and pinpoint the drug centers, headquarters, and fields. Plot them on the maps, and then exfiltrate. The information would be turned over to the DEA and the Colombian authorities for interdiction later.

Martinez finished the reports, glanced at his watch, and realized it was lunchtime. He gathered the material together, stuffed it back into the envelope, and left the office. At the conference room he found that all the clerks were gone, taking their records with them. He walked down the hall and found the dayroom, which held a small kitchen. The men were in there.

"Just about to come and find you, Captain," said Chavez. "Davis is heating up some of the old C rations. Anything you want?"

"The pound cake."

"Oh no, sir. Since I found them, I get the pound cake."

"Fine. What's he preparing?"

"Sort of a military goulash. Dumped a lot of the stuff into a pot, added some spices, and is heating it."

Martinez shook his head. "I think we could get something better brought in. Good, hot food and not just heated C rats."

"Yes, sir," said Chavez. "Why don't you take a seat?"

Martinez nodded and sat at one of the card tables. Three other chairs surrounded it. There was another table with chairs, a couch pushed against one wall, a refrigerator on another, a TV set, radio, and a rack holding paperback novels and magazines. There was a bank of windows that allowed them to look out into the compound. He could see the top of the fence and beyond that the vegetation-covered slopes.

Davis moved toward him and said, "Where's your plate, sir?"

Martinez pushed his chair back but Chavez said, "I've got one here, sir."

Martinez took the paper plate and waited. Davis scooped a spoonful of the meal and dropped it on the plate. Martinez studied it for a moment. "What is this?"

"Combination of spaghetti, beans and franks, boned chicken, and ketchup."

"Good God!"

"No, sir, it's very good, really. Just think of it as barbecue."

Martinez used the plastic fork Chavez had supplied to stir the steaming mass. He had to admit that it smelled good. He lifted a bit to his mouth and tried it. Davis stood there watching and waiting.

"Okay," said Martinez. "It's good."

"It's a question of knowing what to do with the stuff and how much of each ingredient to put in. Can't just slop it into the pot wholesale. You have to be careful."

"You're an artist," said Martinez.

He ate quickly. Chavez passed out Cokes pulled from the refrigerator. As he set a can in front of Martinez he said, "We're going to need a PX run, Captain."

"We're supposed to be in isolation."

"Yes, sir. But there are some items we need in here, including a couple cases of Cokes."

"And we've got to zero the weapons," said Davis as he slopped more of the goulash on a plate.

Martinez put his fork down and closed his eyes. "Two men to the PX this afternoon. In civilian clothes. With lists of what we'll want there. I don't want to have to do this again."

"Yes, sir," said Chavez. "I'll draw up a duty roster."

Martinez looked over at Davis. "We'll get the weapons zeroed in the next couple of days." He turned his attention to Espinoza. "You been briefed on the radio gear?"

"Yes, sir." Staff Sergeant José Espinoza was the youngest man on the team, selected because of his talent with radio gear. He could cobble together a working radio from spare parts, bits of wire, and a two-year-old Eveready battery. He'd been fascinated with radios from the moment he learned that messages could be intercepted from the air around him. A short, stocky man with black hair and brown eyes, Espinoza looked as if he had escaped from high school only a few days before. When he was out of uniform, no one suspected that he was Special Forces.

Martinez turned his attention to Jones. "Medical briefing to include the hazards of the environment this afternoon?"

"Sixteen hundred, sir?"

"That'll be fine."

Martinez finished his food and pushed the plate away. To Davis he said, "I'll admit that it wasn't bad, but I think I'd prefer a thick steak."

"You get one, sir, and I'll broil it."

Martinez sat quietly for a moment, watching the members of the team. When nearly everyone had finished eating, he asked, "Everyone have a chance to review the material in the mission packages?"

There were mumbled answers and a few men nodded. Martinez continued, "We need to get a planning session going on this. Lieutenant Alvarez and Master Sergeant Chavez, will you join me in my office?"

"Yes, sir," said Alvarez.

"The rest of you," said Martinez, "take a look at your specific mission requirements and let me know what you'll need this afternoon. I want a detailed plan established by nineteen hundred."

Martinez sat off to one side of the conference room while Espinoza briefed the men on the communications equipment he would be carrying into the field. He had two of the radios out on top of the table and was explaining, in detail, the techniques of preparing the tapes for a burst transmission. This would allow them to send twenty to thirty minutes of material in less than two seconds. The short duration of the transmission made triangulation by enemy forces almost impossible.

When Espinoza finished, he asked, "Any questions?"

"Which units are you going to take with you?"

"Depends," said Espinoza, "if we'll be sending information back or if we'll just be contacting net control for check-in and then extraction."

"There going to be any problems with the commo?" asked Alvarez.

"No, sir," said Espinoza. "Not with the satellite links available to us. We don't need line of sight."

Martinez turned to Davis to check on the backup. Each man had two jobs on the team. "What frequencies are we going to be operating on and what are the normal check-in times with net control?"

Davis answered without hesitation. Martinez nodded. He looked at his watch and said, "Jones, you ready for the medical briefing."

"Ready, sir."

"Then have at it."

Jones grinned. "The first problem I want to talk about is poisonous snakes. There are coral snakes and rattlesnakes in Colombia. They are related to those we have in the United States. Coral snakes have to chew through the skin, so boots and heavy clothing defeat them. Besides, they're timid and flee when they have the chance."

Jones fell silent, glanced at his audience, and then grinned again. "But there are other snakes that are very deadly. The bushmaster can grow to eleven feet and lives at low altitudes. It likes the forests and often hides in animal burrows. Sometimes it conceals itself along trails, but will remain motionless unless touched, and then it probably will try to flee. Bites from the bushmaster are rare and usually not fatal.

"My personal favorite is the fer-de-lance, but only because of their bright colors—greens, reds, or yellows. One source claims that the fer-de-lance is only found on Martinique, but I saw a bright yellow one near Panama City a couple of years ago. Their venom attacks the blood and nerves, and the indications are that the mortality rate is high."

"Antivenin?"

"There are antivenins available, but not all antivenins

are effective against all the snakes. I mean, you need one antivenin for the rattlers and another for the coral snakes. Some of the antivenins don't travel well and there is discussion whether the so-called antivenins work on the neurotoxin."

"Terrific," said Martinez.

"The British, however," said Jones, "have come up with something that might work if we can get our hands on it. It's a small black box that puts a current, four hundred volts, into the snakebite area. Apparently the current breaks down the structure of the poison, so that it is no longer toxic. It also keeps the skin around the wound from putrefying. It's the latest in snakebite treatment."

He stopped and waited, looking at Martinez. The captain merely nodded. Jones continued, "There are ants, wasps, and spiders in the area. The bites of most are not fatal unless you happen to be allergic to them."

Martinez asked, "Anyone have a problem there?"

"We're all good," said Chavez. It was a ritual they went through every time.

Jones then began to describe the edible plants in the jungle environment. He told them what to avoid. The list was long and took twenty minutes to work through. Finished with the exotic, the cattail, the wild mulberry, and the coconut, Jones told them that twenty-six percent of the land was farmed. They could eat the grains and vegetables grown there. Domestic animals were widely distributed, and they could always shoot a cow for meat.

"There's the steaks you wanted, Captain," said Chavez.

Ignoring him, Martinez asked, "Diseases?"

"The things that you would expect. Malaria, dengue fever, yellow fever, and encephalitis are real problems and are all carried by mosquitoes. We'll have to watch out for dysentery, sand flea fever, and typhus. Any cut could become infected. There are leeches and flatworms that can cause sickness."

Martinez interrupted him. "Ortega, take over."

Ortega stood up and asked, "You want me to continue with the diseases?"

"No. Give me the preventative measures."

"Yes, sir." He hesitated and then said, "To prevent malaria each man should be taking the pill." He laughed. "Even if it gives you the shits. If shots are up-to-date, there should be no problems with yellow fever, typhus, and dysentery. In the field we need to camp on the high ground away from swamps, use mosquito netting or smear mud on the face, and keep all clothing fastened down so mosquitoes can't get in to bite. That'll help prevent most of the diseases."

Chavez interrupted this time. "Captain, we're getting close to suppertime."

Martinez looked at his watch and nodded. "Okay, Ortega, you're off the hook now. Let's break for food."

With dinner out of the way, Martinez moved the men back into the conference room. He pulled out a chair at the head of the table, put his foot into the seat, and leaned forward, elbow on knee. To Alvarez he said, "Let's have a look at the mission profile."

Alvarez stood up and flipped the cover off the map sitting on the easel. He pulled a pointer from his pocket and opened it.

"The target zone has been determined for us." He snapped the pointer against the map. "In the designated area, there are four good drop zones."

"Infiltration by air?" Martinez asked.

"Only way to do it," said Alvarez. "We're too far from the coast to use it. We'd spend two, three weeks walking in and then have to be resupplied by air if we were going to remain on station very long."

"Go ahead," said Martinez.

"Drop just before dawn so that we have the cover of darkness for the drop but then a whole day to get off the DZ and into the jungle."

"No problems there," said Martinez.

Alvarez then described the construction of their base, the use of the terrain to conceal their presence, and the patrolling by the men. Always six men at the camp with two- or three-man teams operating in the jungle. They would stay out two or three days, depending on the circumstances.

"Exfiltration," said Martinez.

"That's the major problem. There are a dozen areas that could take helicopters. There are farmers' fields where they could land as well."

Martinez nodded and Alvarez grinned. He pulled an aerial photograph and set it on the easel. "There's an airfield here where a C-130 could land if we wanted it to."

"What's the air force say about that?"

"They say they could make it. The problem is the DEA and the Colombians. Obviously this is a drug dealer's strip. Indications are that it hasn't been used in six months. The real problem is being intercepted by Colombian fighters once we come up off it."

Chavez chimed in. "Colombia doesn't have any fighters to launch against us. By the time we cross the coast and American fighters pick us up, the IFF will tell them who we are. That's a nonissue."

"You still haven't addressed the question of exfiltration. How are you going to do it?"

"I think the C-130 is the best bet," said Alvarez. "Puts us back into Panama in an hour or two. We have diplomatic overflight clearances. If the plane sinks below radar coverage for five or six minutes, no one's going to scream too loud."

Martinez stood and walked to the map. He studied it and then picked up the aerial recon photo. "Strip doesn't look too good here."

"No, sir, but that's why it's good. If the drug runners were still using it, it would be in good shape. Since it's abandoned, it'll be good for us."

"We'll need to check this out more closely," said Martinez. "I see a couple of shadows on the runway. Those could be potholes."

"Yes, sir."

Martinez returned to his chair, pulled a couple of documents, and read them quickly. "I think that's got it."

"Sir?" said Chavez.

"I'll want to look at refinements for the plan and I'll want detailed plans for the FOB and the patrolling activities, but in general, I think we've got it."

"Yes, sir," said Alvarez. "Does that mean I pass out the beer?"

"It means that we'll call it an evening. Davis, I want a schedule for zeroing the weapons." He stopped to think. "Anything I'm overlooking?"

"No, sir," said Chavez.

For two days they worked on refining the basic plan, on studying the environment they would encounter, on learning the idiosyncrasies of the radios and other equipment. They worked carefully, each man learning the roles of the others. If disaster struck, they would all have the knowledge needed to extract them from the problem. In Special Forces there was no special knowledge limited to one man. Each could take the role of anyone else if it became necessary.

On Friday morning at ten, it was time for the briefback. Martinez had the conference room set up to accommodate the four men from the SFOB headquarters, who were coming in to listen to the plan the team had devised. If they thought the plan would work, if they believed that all options had been covered, they would give the go-ahead. If it was a no-go, Martinez and his men would be given the opportunity to reconstruct the plan, or they would be taken out of isolation. Another team would then take the mission.

Martinez had tried reading in his office but failed. He had tried pacing, but the office was too small. He had tried to forget that the briefback was coming, but it was always in his mind ready to leap up at him. Finally he gave up and walked out into the hallway.

Chavez appeared. "Not long now, sir."

"Not long." He looked at the master sergeant. "It is a good plan, isn't it?"

"It's a fine plan, Captain. Hell, there's not much we can do for this since the mission is to gather information. No bridges to attack, no military targets to eliminate. We just sneak in, keep low, and sneak out."

"This is the worst part," said Martinez. "A test in school, except to fail here is as bad as it gets."

"No, sir. To fail in the field is as bad as it gets."

"You know what I mean," said Martinez. "Very few teams have ever received a no-go."

"How many other teams are in isolation on this?" asked Chavez.

"I don't know. I suspect they've got a dozen teams set to go into a dozen different locations, each operating independently."

Ortega appeared and said, "Guards report that the cars have cleared the gate."

Martinez took a deep breath. "Here we go."

When Martinez saw the delegation coming down the hallway, he wanted to scream. Along with the general, his aide, and two Special Forces officers, was Victoria Ord.

The general moved toward Martinez. "You ready, Captain?"

"Yes, sir." He hesitated and then asked, "Should the civilian be here?"

"The civilian is authorized to see everything that goes on in here."

Martinez wanted to challenge that but knew from the tone of the general's voice that no more discussion would be tolerated. Ord was going to sit in on the briefback whether he liked it or not.

"We're set up in the conference room, General," said Chavez. "If you'd like coffee?"

The general looked at Ord pointedly. "Victoria, would you care for coffee?"

"Yes, General, I believe I would."

"Sergeant, two cups of coffee."

"Yes, sir."

They reached the conference room and Martinez opened the door. "Gentlemen, General Keaton."

The men got to their feet as the general and his staff entered. Keaton moved toward the front and pulled a chair to the side. "Victoria?"

She sat down and crossed her legs slowly. "Thank you, General."

Martinez moved to the front of the room where a blackboard had been set up. Next to it was an easel holding a series of maps and charts. Off to one side, on one of the card tables brought from the dayroom, were the radios, some of the rifles, and a display of other equipment.

Keaton waited for the others and then sat down. He pointed at Martinez and said, "You may begin, Captain."

"Yes, General." He turned and looked directly at Ord.

Smiling at him, she nodded. "I have the proper clearances, Captain."

"Yes, ma'am," he said.

"Let's get on with it," said Keaton.

"General, pardon me for being obtuse, but this should be confined to a need-to-know basis."

"You may proceed, Captain."

Martinez focused his attention on Ord. She grinned broadly at him but made no move to leave. She folded her arms across her chest.

"Captain," said Keaton. "Begin."

Now Martinez looked at the two Special Forces officers who were sitting in the front row with Keaton and Ord. They had to understand his feelings, but neither said a word. They just sat there waiting.

Martinez rubbed his face. He was suddenly hot and felt the sweat bead on his face and begin to drip down his sides. He felt trapped, unable to speak, unable to move. The situation was one that he didn't understand and one that he didn't like.

"Captain," said the general, "is there some problem?"

Martinez shot another glance at Ord. She was a good-looking woman, and he would have liked to know her better if the situation had been different. But she seemed to be as ruthless as any of the men he knew, and because he didn't know her well, he didn't trust her. Not when his life and the lives of his men hung in the balance.

Martinez turned his back and looked at the charts on the easel. He focused his attention for a moment, thinking only of the mission. It was like jumping into enemy territory. It wasn't a combat jump, though it was the next thing to it. Even if the woman compromised them, they should be able to get clear.

And then he laughed once. It was a single, short bark.

He knew he was rationalizing the situation. The woman was as dangerous as an enemy spy. She was not military and she had not been trained by the Special Forces.

"Captain," Keaton snapped.

Turning, Martinez said, "Insertion will be just before dawn on the twenty-second of the month because of the full moon."

"Finally," said Keaton.

Martinez then ran through the mission scenario, leaving out details because he didn't think the woman needed to know them. He glanced toward the Special Forces officers, who sat there stone-faced, staring at the maps. Martinez knew that they had protested Ord's attendance and had been overridden. That told Martinez something about the mission. It was not something he cared to know.

ISOLATION AREA, PANAMA

The team sat in the stifling rear of a covered deuce-and-a-half, waiting for the truck to begin the journey to the airfield. They had slipped out of the isolation area under the cover of darkness, loaded their gear into the truck, and then climbed in after it. Chavez had pulled the flap down so that no one would be able to see them.

Martinez sat on the end of the wooden bench, his weapon in his hands, muzzle pointing up. His head was bowed and his eyes were closed as he concentrated on the last few hours.

As soon as the briefback ended, General Keaton had stood up and moved toward Martinez. "Congratulations. You're a go."

He hadn't accepted that. Keaton wasn't in his chain of command. Instead, he looked at the two Special Forces officers, but neither of them had said a word.

Ord had pushed her way forward and held out a hand. "I hope you didn't mind my sitting in that way."

Martinez shook her hand and said, "It was fine."

"You don't sound as if you mean that."

"Normally we don't have civilians attending the briefback. Once we're in isolation, contact with outsiders is supposed to be limited."

"I'm not an outsider," she said.

Martinez shrugged. "Whatever."

"I'm sorry you're annoyed, but there's a good reason for me to be here."

Before he could answer, one of the Special Forces officers stepped between them and said, "If you'll excuse us."

Martinez and the officer moved to the side. The officer lowered his voice. "That wasn't a complete briefing."

"No, sir."

"It wasn't a complete briefback either. You never mentioned alternative extraction plans."

"There are four LZs near our FOB, all of which could take two CH-53 Sea Stallions. Escape and evasion to the coast would take no more than a week and extraction could be accomplished there."

The officer grinned. "Then you have worked out all the details."

"Yes, sir. I just didn't want to open everything up with the civilian sitting there."

"I can give you a no-go if you want. I can make it stick, even if I have to work all the way up to the Pentagon."

Martinez looked past the officer's shoulder. He watched Ord move close to the general, listening to everything he was saying. The mission had been compromised already; they should go back into isolation to come up with another plan or scrub it altogether.

Instead, he heard himself say, "I think we'll be all right."

"You sure?"

Martinez nodded. "Yes, sir."

"Then you're a go."

Martinez felt a thrill pulse through him. Those were

the words he had wanted to hear, and not from Keaton. He wanted them from his own officers. It meant they approved of his work, that he and his team had a good plan.

"Thank you, sir."

The Special Forces officer walked off as Alvarez and Chavez approached. "Well?" asked the lieutenant.

"We go."

"Yeah!" Alvarez shouted.

Martinez turned. "Let's get ready to move." He saw Ord moving toward him again.

"You're going?" she asked.

Martinez let both Chavez and Alvarez walk away. "Need to know?"

She grinned at him, and suddenly he thought she looked good. Maybe it was because he had gotten back at her. The old security chestnut was a good one.

"Well, good luck anyway," she said.

"Thank you."

Now he sat in the back of the truck and listened to the rumbling of the engine and smelled the stench of the diesel smoke. Maybe he should have taken the easy way out and declared the mission compromised when he had the chance.

The truck lurched once, stopped suddenly, and jerked forward again. Davis slipped from the bench. "Shit!" Those around him laughed. Chavez said, "Steady there."

"Here we go," said Alvarez.

Martinez didn't say a word. They were about to fly into the face of an armed enemy, one that was different, unknown. An enemy they'd never faced or experienced; no army had.

He thought about that. The drug dealers, drug runners, the drug pushers were no better than the Vandals that had sacked Rome, or the Huns that had spread across Europe. They hadn't been real soldiers, though they had sometimes acted like soldiers. They had forts or camps and attacked villages. The drug cartel did the same thing, though not on such a grand scale.

No, they were about to go into combat against an armed enemy. He would have to keep that in mind as they jumped into the jungle. Treat the enemy like a foreign army. Treat them like an armed enemy because that was what they were.

Martinez leaned close to Chavez. "I want each man briefed on the enemy again. I want it reinforced that the enemy is as dangerous as any that we've ever faced."

"Yes, sir."

"I don't want anyone killed or wounded because he's thinking in terms of due process or police action. This is a wartime environment."

"They understand, sir."

Martinez nodded and the truck rolled to a stop. From the distance came the whine of jet engines. Martinez pushed aside the canvas cover and peaked out. They were sitting on a ramp, a floodlit building visible at the edge of the tarmac. A single hummer was parked there.

The truck reversed. Martinez dropped the flap and waited. The truck stopped again and the engine raced. The back of the truck lifted and they inched up a ramp. It leveled out and stopped.

Again, Martinez looked out, but this time all he could see was the interior of an aircraft. He then tossed the flap up, out of the way.

"Let's go," he said. He stepped up on the tailgate and dropped to the deck of the aircraft. He worked the chains and opened the tailgate. Chavez jumped out and turned as two of the men in the truck began to shove the equipment pods forward. Martinez and Chavez grabbed them, tossing them to the side.

Jones appeared and said, "That's got it." He sat down and then slipped out of the truck.

The rest of the team dropped down, and once they were clear, the truck drove out. As it disappeared an airman standing near the ramp reached out to push a button. There was a whine from a small servo and the ramp began to close.

A loadmaster moved from the bulkhead near the cockpit. He began to stack the equipment pods in the center of the aircraft. With belts attached to rings in the deck, he tied it down.

Martinez moved out of the way. Red troop seats with webbing behind them were attached to the fuselage. He sat down and stretched out slightly, watching his men help the loadmaster stack the gear.

Alvarez stepped over a pod and sat down next to Martinez. "We're on our way."

Martinez glanced at his watch and shook his head. "Not quite yet. We're going to be on the ground for a while longer." He reached up and wiped the sweat from his face.

The team slowly spread out. The loadmaster made sure that everything was locked down, tied in place, and stored out of the way. He moved closer to Martinez and leaned over. "We'll get some cool air in here. Be a while before takeoff."

"I understand."

"We'll get airborne soon and then orbit the field, if you've got everybody with you."

Martinez said, "We're ready."

"Anyone going to need earplugs?" the air-force man asked.

"No." Martinez fingered the plastic container chained to his pocket flap.

"I'll make a final walk-through before we lift off."

"Thank you." Martinez turned to Alvarez. "Let's get everyone strapped in."

"Yes, sir." Alvarez stood up and moved along the troop seat, telling the men to buckle up, then returned to Martinez.

Cool air began to filter into the aircraft. Martinez glanced to the side and saw that the door on the left forward side at the base of the cockpit was opened. A man in a gray flight suit stood there, looking out. A moment later he closed the door and climbed into the cockpit.

One by one, the engines started. With the first, there was a little noise inside the aircraft, but the men could still hear one another talk. With each engine start, the noise level increased. Martinez used his earplugs. He saw that Alvarez was trying to say something. He leaned in close.

"Here we go."

Martinez grinned and nodded but didn't say anything. There was always one man who had to say that. Usually it was the youngest man on the team. The new guy who hadn't been out on a real mission. But someone always had to say it.

The cool air that had been filtering in turned warm and moist and smelled of jet fuel. There was a whining near Martinez's head from the servos. The aircraft vibrated and then began to move. Martinez glanced across the fuselage at Sergeant Chavez. The master sergeant nodded and held a thumb up.

Martinez knew what was happening now. It was the adrenaline rush at the beginning of the mission. An excitement in the pit of the stomach that made him want to stand up and run, to scream. They were on their way, first to jump out of the airplane at night, and then live in the jungle for two, three weeks, surrounded by the enemy. An enemy who might not be real soldiers but who would kill them just as dead.

This was the most difficult part of the mission because there was nothing that he could do. He had the energy burning through him. Suddenly he could hear better and see better and his sense of smell improved dramatically. The odor of JP-4 filled his nostrils. He could smell the man next to him. He could smell the garbage that hadn't been cleaned out of the rear of the aircraft since its last mission. Everything was pressing in on him and he was bathed in sweat, his body radiating the heat. He wiped his eyes, took a deep breath, but that didn't help.

The aircraft rumbled on, stopped, and the engines quieted for an instant. The cabin lights flashed once, and then, suddenly, they were racing down the runway. Martinez was shoved to the rear, leaning to his right against Alvarez, as the aircraft picked up speed. The fuselage vibrated as the aircraft suddenly broke free of the ground.

They seemed to leap into the air. There was a whine and a thud as the landing gear was retracted. The air temperature cooled slightly. More servos whined as the pilots trimmed out and continued the climb.

Alvarez shouted, "I make it three hours to the drop."

Martinez checked the time and nodded. He looked at the rest of the team. Two of the men were sitting back, their eyes closed, trying to appear calm. The rest were sitting forward; Davis, his elbows on his knees, looked like he was going to be sick.

The loadmaster came forward, tethered to the intercom system by a long cord. He held a tiny black box in his left hand, his thumb on the button. By depressing it, he could talk to the pilots, the navigator, or the flight engineer.

Kneeling by Davis, he shouted something, and Davis looked up. His face was chalky and the collar of his uniform was sweat-soaked. The loadmaster held out a barf bag. Davis shook his head.

Standing, the loadmaster walked over to Martinez. He crouched and shouted over the roar of the four engines, "You can move around now, if you want."

"How's Davis?" Martinez pointed across the fuselage.

The loadmaster glanced over his shoulder. "He claims he'll be all right. I told him he'd clean up any mess he made."

"He always looks sick," Martinez yelled, "but I've never seen him do it."

The man nodded and stood up, moving away.

Alvarez said, "Are we going to review the mission now?"

"No," said Martinez. "Let's settle down first. Give the men a chance to relax a little. Then we'll get to it."

"We going to use the same DZ that you briefed back?"

"Of course. Thought I had made that clear." Martinez was quiet for a moment and then grinned. "But I'm moving our forward operating base. Only SF knows where it's going to be."

Alvarez laughed. "I thought you had gone soft. Didn't want to irritate Ms. Ord."

"Screw her," said Martinez. "It's not her butt in the field. We'll protect ourselves."

"Yes, sir."

Martinez unbuckled his seat belt and moved to the center of the aircraft, near the equipment pods. He crouched and waited as the men slowly joined him.

"One last time. Let's run through it all one last time." He looked at Banse. "Start."

Staff Sergeant Timothy Banse crouched near Martinez.

He was growing a mustache. He ran through a ritual of growing one for a few months, shaving it, and then growing it again. He looked at the captain and said, "Yes, sir. Drop will be just before daylight in an LZ selected by the team."

Banse ran through most of the mission before Martinez stopped him and told Cline to take over. Sergeant First Class Robert Cline, a huge man with small hands, light hair, and features that looked shoved together in the center of his face, moved toward the center of the group and continued the briefing, including the survival information that Jones had given them.

"Weapons," said Martinez, and pointed at Munyo.

"We're carrying the AK-47 which fires the seven-point-six-two round but not the NATO standard. The round is shorter and can't be used in NATO weapons."

"Continue, Ortega," said Martinez.

Ortega took over, explaining the cyclic rate of fire and the operating procedures of the weapon. He continued on with the field stripping techniques.

When he ran down, Chavez glanced at Martinez and said, "Think that's got it, Captain."

"I agree, Sergeant. Let's check each other's gear one more time and then look into the equipment pods to make sure everything is stored properly."

They ran through that, one man checking the gear of his partner. They made sure straps were pulled tight, all clips were fastened, and that nothing was hanging loose that could be torn free as they stepped out of the aircraft.

Chavez stepped over the equipment pods and yelled at Martinez, "That's got it, sir."

"Let's relax for a few minutes," said Martinez. "We're still about thirty minutes out."

The loadmaster had moved to the rear of the aircraft and opened the troop door. The noise level increased suddenly. The rush of the wind of the slipstream combined with the roar of the engines. The internal temperature dropped as cold air filled the aircraft.

"Five minutes," the loadmaster yelled.

Chavez moved to the door and raised a hand, telling

the men to stand. They hooked the static lines to the cable strung about head high. Slowly, they shuffled forward, each with an equipment pod in front of him. The equipment would be shoved out in front of the jumpers.

The loadmaster, still hooked into the aircraft's intercom, listened and then yelled, "Two minutes."

The tiny light on the side of the door was glowing red. The rushing of the wind made conversation impossible. Chavez was using hand signals to direct the men. The loadmaster was holding up his hand, fingers extended, telling them how much time was left until they reached the DZ.

Martinez stood first in line, looking out into the night. The ground under him was dark, no sign of light anywhere. No electric lights and no firelight. Just a black mass that spread toward the horizon. Charcoal breaks marked some of the clearings.

The sky was filled with stars, and there was no sign of any aircraft around them. A definitive line marked the horizon. Jumping into the night would not be a real problem.

"One minute," yelled Chavez.

Martinez turned his attention to the red light on the door and began counting slowly to himself. When he reached forty-five, the light snapped to green and Chavez yelled, "Go!"

The loadmaster pushed the first of the equipment pods out the door. Martinez shoved out another and then centered himself there. He stepped out into the darkness and fell away from the aircraft. He was facing to the rear as he heard the drag chute pull free. The main chute spilled from his pack with a rustling of canvas and silk. Not silk, he knew, but ripstop nylon. Parachutes hadn't been silk for decades. He tensed and felt the sudden tug on his harness as the chute filled with air.

Looking back, he could see the others jumping as the aircraft, a black shape against the brightness of the night sky, continued to fly on. Blue flames shot from the engines, but the nav lights had been turned out. Overhead, the canopy was nearly invisible against the night sky. It was a black shape that blotted out the brightness of the Milky Way.

He turned his attention to the ground, watching it come up toward him. Tugging at the toggles, he steered toward the center of the clearing, and flexed his knees slightly. He touched down, ran a step or two, and then whirled, looking back as the canopy collapsed. Hitting the quick release on his chest, he let the harness fall free.

He whipped his weapon around and dropped to one knee, surveying the ground, searching the edge of the jungle, listening for signs that someone was hidden in there watching.

Chavez loomed out of the darkness. Leaning close, he said, "We're all down without injury."

"Equipment?"

"Getting it gathered now."

Martinez pulled out his pocket compass and checked the luminous dial. "Get someone in the trees there." He pointed off to the southeast.

"Yes, sir." Chavez was up and moving.

Martinez got to his feet and walked slowly toward the towering trees of the jungle but stopped ten or twelve yards short. He crouched and watched. All he heard was a muted cry from a bird and the scrambling of small feet. Satisfied that the men couldn't be seen from the jungle, he moved back toward the center of the DZ. Alvarez was crouching next to an equipment pod, removing the gear.

"Top popped," he said quietly. "Can't tell if there's any damage."

"We've got ten or fifteen minutes to get moving."

"Yes, sir. We're about ready now. I've got Munyo and Espinoza out as point. They're in the trees now."

"Leave Davis and Cline behind to clean the DZ."

"Shouldn't be necessary," said Alvarez. "It's not like we're in a combat situation."

"I want the DZ cleaned," said Martinez. "Those two can follow after ten minutes."

"Yes, sir."

Chavez appeared again. "Looks like we're set. Equipment is distributed. Everything is accounted for."

"Then take the point."

"Yes, sir."

Quickly, the team formed. Chavez glanced back at them and then took a compass reading. He moved off, to the southeast, stepping carefully. The team spread out behind him, letting the darkness dictate the extent of separation.

They slipped into the jungle and closed up. As Martinez walked passed Davis and Cline he saw them stretch out behind the thick trunk of a giant tree so they could watch the DZ.

But even as they entered the jungle the darkness began to brighten. The eastern horizon turned pink as the sun began to force its way higher. The team became dark shapes moving among other shapes.

Birds were beginning to call to one another. Monkeys were chattering in the trees. The leaves rustled as the monkeys scampered through the canopy.

After only ten minutes Chavez called a halt. They were no more than a hundred yards in the jungle, but they could have been miles from the DZ. Martinez moved up and slipped to a knee next to Chavez, who had out a map and a compass. It was still too dark to see anything on the map, but the compass needle was bright.

"I think we're walking downhill," said Chavez. "If I remember the map correctly, we'll end up in a valley about a mile across and maybe fifty long. No roads to it, though there was a railroad someone built at the turn of the century that passes within three miles."

Martinez reached up and wiped the sweat from his face. He rubbed his hand on his fatigues. The air was hot and damp with no hint of a breeze. The leaves in the canopy rattled, sounding as if a breeze was blowing, but there was no hint of it at ground level.

The jungle began to brighten slowly until it was possible to see the trees and bushes and ferns as something more than dark shapes. Chavez stood finally and began to work his way away from the DZ. A moment later Cline and Davis joined the team. Davis moved toward Martinez and in a normal tone of voice said, "Nothing left on the DZ."

"That was quick."

Davis shrugged. "Nothing obvious, anyway."

Martinez nodded. "Take up the rear and keep your eyes open. Some of the drug runners will open fire without waiting to identify the targets."

"Understood, sir."

They moved down the slight slope of the hill. Chavez found a trail and began to follow it, winding back and forth like a highway climbing a mountain. They crossed a shallow stream with water so clear that the stone bottom was easy to see. A few fish were swimming in the water.

They continued, stopping for a break every fifty minutes. Martinez, knowing that drug dealers were in the area, insisted that security be posted. He also realized that Colombia was one of the few places in the world where emeralds could be found. There was a chance, a slight chance, they might run into men protecting the precious stones.

It was noon when they reached the center of the valley floor, and Martinez ordered them to stop to eat. They ate the new MREs in shifts and then buried the remains of the meals. They started out just after one o'clock, and by three, they found what they were looking for.

Chavez had halted them near an outcropping of rock. There was a slight rise behind it that gave them a view of most of the valley. A source of water was close, and if they ran into trouble, they could defend the outcropping almost as if it was a castle built on a hillside in England. Espinoza told Martinez that he could run an antenna up one side of the hillside and they would be able to communicate easily with net control.

"Then let's get the base set up," said Martinez.

He watched as Chavez climbed to the top of the outcropping. The rest of the team spread out, slowly surveying the site. They found no evidence that anyone had been there in a long time. It was the perfect place for them. To get to the suspected areas of drug production, they had to climb one side of the valley or the other. The camp was protected by the hills.

"Tomorrow," said Martinez, "we begin patrolling."

Chavez led the first patrol. It was to be a short one. Up over the hill, down the other side, and then a search of the jungle. Aerial recon had put some kind of a camp there, no more than ten miles from them. There had been no way to identify it from the air without revealing an interest in it. Chavez and the patrol would do that from the ground.

They left at dawn, when it was light enough to see. Chavez ordered them to operate as if they were now behind enemy lines. Even if the drug runners weren't soldiers, the practice would be good for them; it would teach them to slip through the jungle undetected.

They reached the top of the hill easily and began the descent into the next valley. They listened to the noises of the jungle, learning the sound of it so that a change would be obvious to them. They stepped slowly, carefully, watching the ground for snakes. They searched for signs of the jungle cats and heard the shrieking cries of the monkeys, stopping often, drinking water to cool themselves. The jungle held the humidity like a steambath. Sweat didn't dry, but soaked the uniform, threatening to rot it from the body in a matter of days. Dehydration was a concern. Chavez had them cool themselves in the streams that flowed across their paths.

They listened and they searched, moving along the valley floor, and when it seemed that they would never find the enemy's—the drug runners'—camp, they heard the distant, insectile buzz of a small aircraft.

"Where's it going?" asked Ortega.

Chavez didn't answer. He turned his face up and stared at the deep green of the jungle canopy. The sound of the engine changed and the plane came back toward them. Chavez didn't move, but Ortega hid himself in the deep shadows of one of the trees.

"They're not searching for us," said Chavez.

Again the sound changed and the airplane slipped closer to the ground. Through a break in the canopy, Chavez caught a glimpse of a small helicopter that flew without the popping of rotors that gave choppers their distinctive sound. The engine was gasoline-powered, not a turbine.

"They're searching," said Ortega.

"But not for us," said Chavez.

Gunfire burst to the west. Chavez dived for cover and then scrambled around. For a moment his heart hammered in his chest and sweat beaded and dripped, and then he realized that no one was shooting at him. The firing was a mile away and aimed at someone else.

"What's going on?" Brown asked, in a whisper.

Chavez shrugged. He didn't have any idea except that someone was shooting. The firing died suddenly. Chavez lay there, listening to the jungle. And then the firing erupted again, this time shorter-lived. At the end it was punctuated by grenade detonations. Five or six of them.

"Ambush?" Ortega asked.

"No," said Chavez. "The grenades would have gone off first. Then a high volume of fire followed by single shots as the survivors are eliminated."

"Then what?"

Chavez grinned. "Sounds like firing on a range."

"What?"

"Sounds like the firing on a rifle range with a little grenade practice thrown in."

Now Ortega smiled. "You're kidding, right?"

"No." Chavez got to his feet, ignoring the temptation to brush the dirt off his chest. "Whoever it was, I think they've pointed the way to their camp. Let's get going. And let's remember they've got automatic weapons."

They moved out slowly, listening to the sounds around them. Chavez realized that the noise of the helicopter was gone now. Maybe it had landed, or maybe it had been chased away by the gunfire on the ground.

As they approached the area where the camp had to be Chavez began to find signs that someone was around. Some of the bush had been cut back, making it easier to walk through the jungle. He found the broken blade of a machete and tin cans that had held food. Cans that had once been part of old C-ration meals.

Now another sound joined those of the jungle. It was a continual low hum. Chavez knew exactly what it was. He crouched and waved his men closer. Pointing to the north, he whispered, "Generator."

"We found their camp?"

"We've found something." Chavez pointed right and then left, letting the other two men slide into position. He then moved forward, using the shadows as he worked his way closer to the sound of the generator. But now he was crouched low, moving cautiously, sticking to the shadows and the cover.

He came to the edge of the jungle. It looked as if someone had scraped the ground and cut down all the small trees so that only the tallest were still standing like pillars holding up a ballroom ceiling. Overhead, the canopy was still thick and interwoven, making it impossible to see the camp from the air. The only break was on the northern edge, where it looked as if a helipad had been constructed.

The camp was nothing more or less than a military outpost. It was surrounded by a high barbed-wire fence that included watchtowers at each corner. A road led up to the gate, but Chavez couldn't tell where it went. It had to deteriorate a few hundred yards east of the gate.

Behind the wire was a series of low, long buildings looking like the barracks seen on any military base. They were built in neat rows. A single, two-story building with a flagpole stood near the gate. Sitting in front of that structure were three jeeps and one car.

As Chavez watched, two men exited the building and walked to the backdoor of the car. The driver, in uniform, got out and opened the rear door for one of the two men. The two men spoke quietly and then shook hands.

When the one man had entered the car and the driver had slipped behind the wheel, Chavez studied the rest of the camp. There weren't many men moving around it, but he could see that it wasn't the camp of drug runners or pushers or manufacturers. It was a military base. Men in uniform armed with military weapons. Not the Uzis and the MAC-10s favored by drug merchants, but assault rifles complete with bayonets. Military weapons designed for soldiers.

Chavez watched them for a moment, trying to get a good look at the uniforms they wore. He didn't think that the Colombian military would construct a hidden base, though it might be some kind of training facility. What he was reminded of was stories he'd heard from the Vietnam veterans; the camp looked like some of the bases built by the Viet Cong in the central highlands of South Vietnam.

He slipped to the rear and found both Brown and Ortega. Ortega asked immediately, "What'd you find?"

"I don't know. I want to move in closer for a better look. You two stay with me. There's an armed force in that camp and we don't want them to see us."

Chavez moved to the base of the slope and then turned back to the north. He could hear the constant, muted hum of the gasoline-powered generator and once there a bark of laughter. Due west of the camp, he halted, crouching between the two of them.

"I'm going to move in closer for a recon. You wait here and cover my ass."

"You got it," said Brown.

Chavez wiped a hand over his face and then rubbed the sweat on the front of his uniform. For a moment he wondered if he should pull back to change into civilian clothes. The last thing anyone wanted was a confrontation between soldiers of Colombia, or whoever, and the United States. Still, it was only a recon. No one should even see him, and if they did, civilian clothes wouldn't do him much good.

He pushed off again, moving through the light scrub to the edge of the jungle. It looked like the manicured parks in the United States. Short grass leading up to the barbed-wire fence. Now he could see a single soldier walking on the inside of the fence, looking like a man on guard duty.

From the new angle he could see a number of low buildings; a couple of them seemed to be poured concrete. Off to the north was a rifle range. There was a tower and a berm designed to stop the rounds. It looked as if there were a half dozen, maybe a dozen firing points.

He took out his binoculars and studied the soldier. He carried an AK-74, but that proved nothing. Chavez had an AK, too. He wore a dark green uniform that could have been manufactured in a dozen different places. The insignia looked Cuban, but it might have been Nicaraguan or even Vietnamese. To identify it exactly, he'd have to get closer and that he couldn't do.

He studied the camp, saw the obvious hole in the defense that they could exploit if they decided to take it out, but that was a decision to be left to Martinez. His immediate job was recon, and it was now time to get out. The longer they spent in the area, the greater the chance of getting caught.

Chavez started to move and then heard a rustling in the jungle. He froze. The quickest way to be spotted in the jungle was to move suddenly. Slowly he turned his head in the direction of the sound. He let his eyes play across the patchwork of shadows and leaves, searching for anything that didn't belong. He felt his ears twitch as he listened.

Suddenly the jungle was alive with sounds. Birds and lizards and animals. Insects seemed to fill the air and the monkeys were screaming overhead. Chavez slipped to a knee, sliding to the right so that he could put the thick trunk of a tree next to his shoulder. From the camp came the sound of a voice yelling Spanish parade-ground commands. The enemy wouldn't be shouting commands if they knew they were being watched.

He reached up and touched his combat knife. He'd spent days honing the blade until it was razor sharp. It would slice through thick leather, canvas, and human flesh with ease.

And then he spotted the enemy soldier. He might have been a guard thrown outside the perimeter as a listening post or a picket. There was no telling. It could be some kind of punishment tour. Chavez didn't care. Now that he knew where the man was, he could slide off into the jungle and the man would never know that he had been there.

Before Chavez could move, the man tossed away his cigarette. Chavez was surprised that he hadn't smelled the smoke, but the light breeze was blowing in the wrong direction. The man shouldered his rifle and stepped toward him.

There was no sign that Chavez had been seen. The guard was just walking toward him. Just walking in the wrong direction. There was nothing Chavez could do. It was obvious that the man was going to trip over him. Any move would reveal his presence to the man.

When the soldier was two feet in front of him, Chavez stood up. Before the enemy could react, Chavez's left hand shot out, grabbing the man by the throat, choking him so that he couldn't scream. Then he struck with the knife, driving it into the man's chest just under the breastbone. He felt a slight resistance and then saw a splash of hot blood. The man sagged as the knife cut into his heart. Chavez held him upright and twisted the blade before pulling it out.

Carefully, he lowered the man to the ground, keeping his hand on the man's throat. The enemy bucked once, tried to kick, but there was no energy behind it. Chavez stared into his eyes and watched them glaze. There was the odor of bowels and he knew the man had died.

He wiped the knife on the dead man's uniform. He was going to cut the insignia from it, for the intelligence value, but knew when the men in the camp found the body, they would know they'd been discovered. Instead, he stole the man's wallet and watch, hoping that the enemy would believe it was a robbery. The idea was thin, but it was all he had at the moment.

Searching around, he found a shallow depression with a huge, flowering bush hiding most of it. Chavez rolled the body down and tried to conceal it. That might give him a couple of hours, maybe a couple of days. Maybe they would think the man had run off.

He slipped to the rear, back to the other team members. "It's time that we go." He didn't see any need to tell them about the dead man here. Getting away was the priority.

"We're ready." Then Brown noticed the blood. "You okay?"

"Had to take out one of theirs and then hide the body. Brown, you've got the point. Back to the south for a klick or so."

"We running away?" Brown asked.

"No," Chavez whispered, "we're returning to camp for reinforcements."

Now Brown smiled. "That's all I wanted to know."

SAN ANTONIO, TEXAS
AT A FACULTY PARTY

The small knot of men stood with drinks in their hands and watched the big-screen television that in normal times would have been tuned to a football or baseball game. Now it was tuned to CNN, where the good-looking, blow-dried anchors were attempting to analyze the latest information coming from Western Europe, the Middle East, and the northern reaches of the Soviet Union. They were trying to tie all the events together into a neat, comprehensive package that could be explained in the two minutes before the important commercial break.

Sandi Paulding, a martini in her delicate hand, hovered around the edge of the group, glancing occasionally at the screen. The information being given by the news team was two days old. Paulding, as a reserve intelligence officer, had already read the classified traffic message that had been issued by the CIA, army intelligence, and DIA. She'd often said that the only difference between CNN and the intelligence community was that the intelligence people obtained the information faster. The news media was able to disseminate it faster.

She sipped the martini and realized again that she didn't want it. The host had insisted that everyone have a drink, even in the enlightened university environment, where millions had been spent investigating the harmful effects of alcohol on the human body and human society.

"Getting scary out there," said a voice.

Paulding turned and looked at Larry Jennings. A tall, slender man with salt-and-pepper hair, he bent his head and lifted his glass, sipping. Unlike some of the other teachers, he was well dressed, his dark suit looking as if it had just been pressed, his shoes highly polished, and his striped tie perfectly knotted. His black rimmed glasses had slipped partly down his nose. It was the only thing out of place about him.

Paulding nodded, wishing that Jennings would leave her alone. Ever since her divorce had come through, he had taken every opportunity to talk to her. He wasn't pushy, wasn't even annoying, he just seemed to always be there as if waiting to pounce on her.

She had never thought of herself as particularly good-looking, though her military training and her teaching schedule kept her in good shape. Her blond hair, which normally hung to her shoulders, had been pinned up for the party in much the same way she pinned it when she was working with her army reserve unit.

Jennings gestured at the TV set. "What do you make of that?"

Paulding watched as the female anchor talked about the police officer in Tartu, Estonia, who'd gone berserk and shot a number of dissidents who had occupied a government building. He'd then been beaten to death by the survivors, but the event had ended, at least temporarily, the riots in the Soviet republics.

"I find it an amazing coincidence," said Paulding. "Soviets want the protests ended and a berserk policeman manages to do it for them."

"Seems like the entire world has suddenly gone nuts. I thought with the crumbling of the Warsaw Pact and the realignment in Eastern Europe, world tensions would lessen because of the peace dividend that the media is so fond of talking about.''

"The news media tend to reduce everything to its lowest common denominator." She grinned. "I heard something just the other day. A television reporter, being unusually candid, suggested that they didn't know that much about anything. They scrambled to learn what they could about a story and then moved on to the next."

"Meaning what?"

"Simply that a politician talks about a peace dividend. That has a nice ring to it and the reporter can see the weakening of Soviet influence throughout the world. Suddenly that reporter can't see any reason for spending billions on defense and he or she begins to suggest that in the news."

Jennings took a sip of his drink, glanced at the TV, and then said, "Then you don't think there is any such thing as a peace dividend."

Paulding shook her head. She was now getting into the same discussion she'd had with her students in the last few months. Too many people watching the television news and not enough of them asking any hard questions.

"I think that the threat of the Soviet Union is as real as it was five years ago. They're still spending most of their gross national product to arm soldiers. Their desire for world domination hasn't lessened in the last few years. The focus might have changed, but the desire is still there."

Another man appeared and broke into the conversation. He put a hand on Paulding's bare back and grinned. "No private seminars, you two."

"Sure, Grant," said Jennings, smiling. "We were just discussing the sudden collapse of the protests in Estonia. An amazing thing."

"Sandi," said Grant Hackett, "I know you've got a few inside sources. How about that?"

Paulding finished her martini, ate the olive, and then shrugged. "It's an amazing coincidence, Grant."

"Yeah." Hackett laughed. It was a cross between a snort and a laugh. "Back in the old days, when I was a graduate assistant, our campus used to erupt into protests about the Vietnam War each spring. Students in the streets throwing rocks and overturning cars. I never could figure out how burning some poor schmuck's car was going to end the war in Vietnam . . . but every spring the students were all out there, burning cars and taking over buildings."

"The point, Grant," said Paulding.

"Simply that no police officer ever went crazy and shot just the student leaders of the demonstrations. Kids were killed at Kent State, but that was a different thing. It wasn't targeted just at the leaders. The National Guard fired into the crowd and a few innocent bystanders were hurt. Not like in Tartu, where only the leaders were killed."

"Has the nuclear clock now progressed closer to midnight?" Jennings asked.

"Oh, for God's sake," Paulding snapped. "It seems that some people like to live on the edge of nuclear destruction. The Soviets have moved to stop a destructive riot in their own country. It does not suggest that they are about to launch a world campaign to eliminate capitalism."

"A rather ruthless solution," said Jennings.

Paulding shook her head slowly and wondered if Jennings had ever studied any political science. He seemed to know nothing about the world situation.

"The Soviets crushed an uprising in Hungary in 1956. They have sent troops and tanks into other Eastern European countries in the past. It was only recently that they have allowed their iron curtain to rust away."

"But . . ."

"If the Soviets did engineer that, they did it quietly, with the world press watching, and I haven't heard one reporter suggest that the Soviets unleashed a wholesale slaughter. They took advantage of the situation as it developed," said Paulding. "I'd hope we'd be smart enough to do the same thing."

The news analysis ended and Larry King appeared on the screen. One of the men reached over and turned off the program. He didn't like the way King interviewed people. In the first thirty seconds anyone could tell whether or not King liked and respected the guest.

The group of men headed toward the open bar or the table loaded with cold cuts, vegetables, dips and chips, and a dozen different cakes and pies. One of them said, "Goddamned Russians still know how to handle criminals."

Hackett's wife, a very young woman, came out of the kitchen, looking more like a student than the wife of a department head. "Are you Major Paulding?" she asked Sandi. She acted as if she believed the answer would be in the negative.

"Yes."

"There's a call for you." She blinked, still not believing it.

Paulding handed the empty glass to the woman and walked into the kitchen. She glanced at the students brought in as servers for the party and then picked up the phone on the counter. Quietly, she said, "Major Paulding."

"Sorry to bother you at the party, Major. We need you to come out to the post."

"Tonight?"

"Yes, ma'am. As soon as you can."

A hundred questions flashed in her mind, but she knew that she'd get no answers over an unsecured phone line. "Is this a drill?"

"No, ma'am. This is not a drill. When should I tell the general you'll be arriving?"

Paulding grinned at that and glanced up at the wall clock. "Probably be an hour."

"No, ma'am. The general would like you to get here ASAP."

"Then twenty minutes if I hit the lights right and I don't go home to change."

"I'll tell him twenty minutes."

"Thanks." Paulding hung up and left the kitchen. She found Hackett still talking to Jennings. "I'm sorry, Grant, but I've got to leave."

"What?"

"This have anything to do with the Soviet Union?" Jennings asked.

She hesitated and then realized that Hackett knew she'd received a call from the post. If she went out without a word, the speculation would run wild.

"No. They've scheduled one of those idiot recall exercises. Every year they drop one on us to see how fast the staff can respond."

"Sounds silly," said Jennings.

"Well, they do send a nice check every month. Helps pay the rent."

"I'm sorry you have to leave. Will you be able to get back this evening?" Hackett asked.

"I'm afraid not. Once we're there, we've got to inventory the equipment on the deployment pallets to make sure we've everything the TO and E requires."

"TO and E?" said Jennings. "You still speaking English?"

"Table of organization and equipment. I'm sorry, I've got to go."

"I'm sorry, too," said Hackett.

"It was a nice party." She moved to the door and Hackett opened it for her. She stepped into the cool evening and looked up at the clear, star-studded sky.

Her car was parked half a block away. After she climbed behind the wheel, she sat quietly for a moment and considered possibilities. The general often called his top staff people in for discussions about the world situation, the running of the armored division, or exercises. He liked to think of himself as an active-duty general even though he held a reserve commission and was assigned to a reserve unit.

Paulding knew that she could resign, but she liked the classified intelligence summaries her job supplied. Although she could not quote sources to her students, she could dazzle them with her inside knowledge. It gave her a leg up on the others in the political science department. It actually made her teaching job easier because she didn't have to sift through all the information contained in the news magazines or the newspapers. The government paid clerks to do that, refine it, and then put out summaries,

some classified and some not, that told her what she
needed to know.

She put the key in the ignition and started the engine.
Music filled the car. She touched a button and found the
all-news-all-the-time station. Unfortunately they were
caught in the middle of a sports report.

Fifteen minutes later she was at the base gate. Although she had a sticker on the bumper of her car, the
guards still stopped her. The security was tight tonight.

"Need to see your ID card, ma'am."

She opened her purse and held her card up. The MP
used a flashlight to examine it and her carefully. "Thank
you, ma'am." He saluted.

Paulding dropped the card on the seat beside her and
drove toward the headquarters building. As she pulled in
she saw that the parking lot was already filling. It looked
like the primary staff along with their deputies, assistants,
and top NCOs had been called. Now she felt strange in
her party dress. It was shorter than she would have liked
and cut lower than she would have liked, considering where
she was. But she'd had no choice.

An MP in camouflaged BDUs opened the HQ door for
her. He was armed with the new standard assault rifle and
a holstered pistol. The general was pulling all the stops
on this one.

"They're in the main conference room, ma'am."

"Thank you."

Paulding hurried down the dimly lit, carpeted, and air-
conditioned hallway. The bricks of the wall were a dull
red, the doors were wooden with windows in them, each
with the name of the office etched in the glass. There were
a couple of bulletin boards hung on the walls, displaying
a variety of memos, orders, and charts telling the soldiers,
both male and female, what they needed to know.

She pushed her way through a double door and turned
into another corridor. At the far end was a single door
where another guard stood.

"Major Paulding, they're waiting," the guard said as
she approached. He opened the door.

Almost everyone was in civilian clothes, some of them
looking as if they had been working around the house,

others, like Paulding, looking as if they had been out. A few were in uniforms, Class A or fatigues or BDUs.

One of the men pointed at a vacant chair. "We saved your place."

"Thanks." She pulled the chair out and sat down. The general's staff sat around a conference table, with a vu-graph projector sitting on the end of it. The screen had been pulled down, and a single vu-graph shone on it, telling everyone there that they belonged to the Twelfth Armor Division, U.S. Army Reserve. Around the walls the lower-ranking officers and a few NCOs were sitting in chairs, conversing.

The door opened again and the general's aide looked in. "Ladies and gentlemen, our commanding officer, General Norman Beal."

The men and women stood up, one or two of them looking toward the general. He walked to the head of the table and pulled out his chair. "Let's be seated."

All eyes were on the general, a short man with gray hair cut so close to his head that in the right light he appeared completely bald. He wore a khaki uniform that held only his combat decorations, a combat infantryman's badge and jump wings. The two stars of a major general gleamed on his right collar and the armor insignia on the other. Most generals wore the stars on both sides.

He waited until the conference room was completely quiet, with the exception of the fan in the vu-graph projector, then opened the leather folder in front of him and glanced at his watch, ignoring the clock hanging on the wall.

"Thirty-seven minutes from the beginning of the alert until we're ready to go. Not bad, but I'd hoped for thirty minutes flat."

"We had trouble tracking down a few of the people," said the deputy commander, a brigadier general in battle-dress uniform, a BDU. "Major Paulding was at some kind of party."

The general looked at her. "Sorry to interrupt your party." He didn't look sorry. In fact, he seemed annoyed that any of his officers had a life outside the post. It was as if he wished they were stacked in boxes, waiting until the urge to play soldier hit him. Then he could shake them out.

"Yes, General," she said.

"Now," he said. "This is not a drill. This is a paid formation and I'm not sure when we'll be released."

A buzz of conversation broke out around the table. The general looked up and everyone fell silent. "The world situation," said the general, "is in a state of flux and we might be caught in it."

"Shit," said a lieutenant colonel at the far end of the table, a fat man who'd avoided the Vietnam War by conspiring with his professors at college to keep him in school and with a draft board that handed out deferments to anyone who had enough intelligence to write a letter to them asking for one. He had no active duty except for the two weeks of annual training every year and a few weeks in basic training nearly twenty years earlier.

"Resignations," said the general, looking at the colonel, "will gladly be accepted in the morning. I'm sure there are majors in the division who would like the opportunity to be lieutenant colonels."

"No, General. Sorry."

"All right, Jim," said Beal. "You want to start the briefing?"

"Yes, sir." Jim Wheeler, the general's aide, moved to the side and dimmed the lights. One of the NCOs moved to the vu-graph and changed it.

"The fluid nature of the world situation," said Wheeler, "is throwing critical planning into a cocked hat." At the sound of a discreet cough, he looked at the general. "Oh. This briefing is classified secret and will not be discussed outside this room."

Paulding wondered why the general's aide was giving an intelligence briefing. That was her job. Had the general called her, she would have been able to put something together for the meeting. If he'd asked. She wondered if she was about to be phased out.

That was the thing about the military. They ran in cycles. First they would be attempting to integrate women into all phases of military life with little regard to the congressional ban against women in combat roles. Then someone would wonder what would happen if the units were called to fight. Some critical slots would be opened because women filled those slots. The division needed an intelligence officer who wouldn't be left behind if the division was suddenly called to active duty and deployed to combat zone. Suddenly Paulding wondered if a realignment was coming.

"There are two current areas of acute concern," Wheeler was saying. The vu-graph had switched to one showing both the Middle East and Asia.

Again the vu-graph changed and the Middle East was featured. "There are rumblings again from Iran and Iraq. They have traded a few surface-to-surface missiles but little damage has been reported by either country. Casualties were termed light by both governments."

Paulding could contain herself no longer. "That is nothing significant," she said. "They've been taking pot-shots at each other for years."

Wheeler looked at her and nodded. "Yes, ma'am. I bring it up only because the last two missile launches took place in the last twenty-four hours, and there are indications that there will be more of them. This after their much-touted peace initiative, it's a little surprising."

"No, sir," said Paulding. "The surprise is that the peace lasted as long as it did."

"But the important fact," said Wheeler, "is the turmoil in Saudi Arabia."

Paulding had to break in again. "There has been internal tension there for some time. It's a family power struggle, but there is no indication of a destabilizing effect."

"Major Paulding," said General Beal, "please let Captain Wheeler continue."

"Yes, General. Sorry."

"Our concern," said Wheeler, reading from the notes he held in his left hand, "is that the internal struggle of the ruling family in Saudi Arabia will create a power vacuum which will induce the Iraqis to try something there."

Again Paulding wanted to speak but held her tongue. She'd already been told she had been late and that her opinions didn't matter. It could only mean that she was being eased out of her position and that wasn't fair.

"In the past," said Wheeler, "whenever the various countries and factions in the Middle East warred, we could count on the Saudis to remain quiet, especially after our deployment there in 1990 and 1991 for Desert Storm. Even our pullout in late 1991 reinforced the status of the Saudis. But the recent death in the ruling family has created the vacuum at the top, and there are half a dozen men trying to fill it."

Paulding shook her head and remembered that a vacuum had not been created when King Faisal was assassinated by his nephew. But then, one man was attempting to take control of the government. With the unexpected death of the king, the line of succession, which wasn't hereditary, was open to question. She turned her attention back to Wheeler.

"Saudi Arabia's economy is dominated by oil. The wealth of Saudi Arabia is oil. Its known reserves rank it first and it is among the leaders in the production of oil. With that oil, you might say the Saudis hold the rest of the world over a barrel." Wheeler waited for the laughs, but they didn't come.

Shrugging, Wheeler continued. "The major concern at the moment is the Soviet Union. Now, I know that there has been a considerable lessening of tension between us and the Soviets during the last few years. But the Soviets still have a couple of items on their wish list. They have always wanted a warm-water port that does not involve narrow straits that lead into the world's major oceans. And they would like to become oil independent. Saudi Arabia meets both those needs."

"Excuse me, Captain," said Major Victor McGregor, "but the Straits of Hormuz block the entrance into the world's oceans."

"Yes, sir," said Wheeler. "But those straits are much wider than the Straits of Gibraltar at the end of the Mediterranean Sea. I think the Soviets are looking at that. And the oil reserves make Saudi Arabia an attractive target."

Now the general interrupted. "You're not suggesting

that the Soviets are going to attempt something in Saudi Arabia, are you?''

Wheeler glanced at the vu-graph and then at his notes. He hadn't prepared the briefing himself, so he didn't have an answer to the question.

He hesitated for a moment, looked unhappily at Paulding, and then said, ''With the vacuum at the top, there is the possibility that the Soviets will try to expand their influence.''

''Do you have anything else, Captain?'' the general asked.

''Yes, sir. I have a brief history of Saudi Arabia since the late thirties and a discussion of the internal politics.''

''Thank you,'' said the general. ''I think that'll be enough for us.''

''Yes, sir.''

As the lights came up Beal glanced at the men and women around the table. ''I'll want a full review of Oplan 24–17 with whatever modifications and recommendations are dictated by the current situation. And we'll want to review Oplan 91–52 in case we're deployed into Central America.''

''Is there a deployment coming?'' asked a major at the end of the table.

The general looked at his folder. ''I am only aware of changes in the world scene that suggest a heightening of various tensions, but I've seen nothing suggesting that our life of luxury and ease here is about to change. There was a period of warning before the deployment of U.S. forces in 1990. I just want to be prepared for any contingency. Questions?''

''Is this a paid drill?''

The general laughed. ''You would want to know that, McKinnon. And if you were paying attention, you would already have that answer. But, yes, it's paid. If there is nothing else, review those plans.''

Wheeler said, ''Ladies and gentlemen.''

Beal stood, as did everyone else in the conference room, and looked at Paulding. ''I'd like to see you in my office at your convenience.''

''Yes, General.''

As Beal walked out of the conference room Paulding thought, Here it comes. I'm fired.

She followed him across the hall to his main office. The reception area was nearly as large as the conference room, with two desks, one for Beal's secretary and one for his aide, as well as couches, chairs, and a coffee table that held magazines and newspapers. All the lights in the office were on, and Paulding blinked in the brightness as she walked in.

The secretary smiled and said, "You may go right in."

Paulding stopped at the door, wishing that she was more suitably attired, then knocked, and the general invited her in.

Like all offices belonging to general officers, this was a big one, with a massive desk in one corner, a bank of windows that allowed him to look out on the post, a couch, two high-backed leather chairs. Off to the side a floor-to-ceiling bookcase contained books on military history.

The general looked at her and Paulding grinned. "I don't know if I'm supposed to report officially when in civilian clothes."

"Have a seat, Sandi," he said, gesturing toward one of the leather chairs.

Paulding sat down and crossed her legs. She felt like a little girl caught wearing her older sister's clothes.

"First, let me say that you have nothing to worry about."

"Sir?"

"That was a canned briefing distributed through army headquarters with orders to brief as soon as the staff could be assembled to listen to it."

"Sir?" she said again, not quite sure what was happening.

The general picked up a letter opener that resembled a miniature M-1 bayonet and tested the point with his index finger. "Your job is not on the line. I wanted Wheeler to get some experience briefing line troops. He didn't do too well, but then, it wasn't his briefing either."

"Yes, sir."

"Anyway, I wanted to know if there was anything

you'd like to add to what was said tonight. Something for my consumption alone."

"I'm not really prepared. . . ."

"I understand that."

Paulding leaned back in the chair and closed her eyes. "The Soviets do want a warm-water port, but not in another country like Saudi Arabia. They want a port whose cross-country access they control."

"Then you think the assessment is wrong?"

"No, General. I'm merely saying that the motivation for it is different. It probably revolves around the oil. The Soviets would much rather have Iran because that gives them the port facilities they want." She grinned. "If they controlled both countries, then they'd be in the power seat. They could cut our oil supplies drastically."

"You think that will happen in this world of glasnost and perestroika?"

"Hell, General, if we were suddenly handed a club, or at least given the opportunity to pick up a club with which to hammer our enemies, do you think we'd refuse it? We might not use it, but we'd take the club just in case the situation changed suddenly."

"Then the situation in Saudi Arabia bears watching?"

"Yes, sir. Definitely. But I wouldn't read anything into this power-vacuum theory that Wheeler was talking about. Right now, there is a clear-cut order of precedence for selecting the sucessor to the king."

"Thank you, Major. I'd like something a little more formal for the normal staff meeting on Friday."

"Yes, sir. No problem."

Beal grinned. "And I'd like to say that you look exceptionally lovely tonight, but then the feminists of the world would call me a dirty old man."

"Thanks for the thought anyway." Paulding grinned broadly.

"Friday."

"Yes, General." She stood up to leave.

ALONG THE CHINESE COAST

Captain Chin Lee Wang crouched behind a boulder, looking down on a long stretch of white beach. The breakers were small, making it easier for the boat to navigate toward the sheltered cove. Forest covered one finger of land, providing concealment for a force of marines armed with small arms and machine guns.

Through his binoculars Wang watched two small boats that had been launched from a Japanese fishing vessel work their way closer to the beach. Four men in each of them used the oars to pull themselves to the coast of China.

"I see no arms, Captain," said one of the sergeants.

"They'll be armed," said Wang. "Spies, saboteurs, and invaders are always armed."

"Yes, sir."

Wang lowered the binoculars and glanced to either side. Forty marines, all armed with Type 81 rifles, crouched near him. A few had grenade launchers, and two manned a heavy machine gun that would fire at the fishing boat, though it was at an extreme range. The 12.7mm machine gun was effective to just over three klicks.

"Let them reach the beach," said Wang. "That way there can be no doubt about their mission."

One of the sergeants moved along the line, warning the marines to hold their fire until the commander's orders. He touched each man on his back, waited to receive a response, and then moved on.

The lieutenant, who also had binoculars, asked, "What are they doing?"

"It doesn't matter," said Wang. "They invade our coast. The penalty is death."

Wang raised his binoculars again. Now he could see the boxes stacked in the bottom of the boats. Cardboard boxes that were taped shut.

"Give me a grenade launcher." One of the enlisted soldiers moved closer and slapped the weapon into Wang's hand. Lowering his binoculars, he said, "Thank you."

Slipping down, his back against the sun-hot boulder, he broke open the weapon and checked the load, a high-explosive round designed to throw out shrapnel, killing the unprotected within a twenty-five-meter radius.

For a moment Wang shut his eyes, visualizing the scene: his round exploding as the boats reached the beach; then, the ambush from within the woods, forcing the enemy up the beach to seek protection in the rocks. Finally, the men with him firing down at them, killing them. Two minutes. That was all it should take. He opened his eyes, snapped the weapon shut, and peeked over the rocks. The boats were in the shallow water now. A man from each had leaped out into the thigh-high water and was straining to drag the boats up to the sand.

Wang moved the sight, setting it for a hundred meters, and aimed. He pulled the trigger, felt the impact against his shoulder, and heard the metallic whump as the weapon detonated. An instant later there was a flash on the beach, near the tide line, and sand, mud, and water fountained up.

One of the men was spinning, blood staining his shirt.

He emitted a high-pitched wail as he fell, his head under-water, his feet on dry land.

Shooting erupted from the forest. A dozen Type 81s firing on full auto. Bullets slammed into the boats, splintering the wood. Others hit the ocean, splashing. Two men toppled from the boats. One floated facedown, obviously dead. The other struggled toward the beach, was hit again, and collapsed.

Others leaped from the boats, grabbing their weapons. They used the bobbing boats for cover, firing at the men in the trees. Heavy firing erupted, the sounds combining into a single, drawn-out detonation.

Wang turned to the men on the ridge with him and waved his arm. "Open fire. Open fire."

There was a rattling of weapons as the men began firing. Rounds poured down at the trapped men, ripping at their boats. The outboard engine in the rear of one was hit. Gas poured from it and then burst into flame. Black smoke erupted over the tiny battle.

Two of the enemy turned and began firing up at the ridge line. Wang heard a round snap by his head. He dropped down flat, scraping his cheek on the stone, moved to the right, and glanced down again. Half the enemy were sprawled on the sand or were floating in the water, crimson spreading around them.

Wang snapped his fingers and received another grenade for his launcher. He leaped up, aimed, fired, and dropped again. He then tossed the weapon away and grabbed his binoculars. The fishing boat had yet to move.

"Hit the boat," he yelled.

The heavy weapon began to chug. Green-glowing tracers danced out, floating across the water, splashing up near the side of the boat. Black smoke suddenly billowed from the stacks and the boat began to move.

But it wasn't quite fast enough. The machine gunners had gotten the range; the tracers smashed into the side of the vessel. Pieces of it flew upward. Tiny fires broke out on the deck as the boat turned its stern toward the shore.

Wang turned his attention back to the firefight on the beach. One man was firing at the forest and then up at the ridge. Suddenly the man realized he was alone. He dropped his weapon into the water, raised his hands, stood up, and slowly walked to the beach. Once he glanced at the body of one of his fellows, the sand under the man a bright red.

Wang didn't want any prisoners. Not this time. "Kill him," he ordered.

Someone stood, aimed, and fired. The man on the beach dropped, dead as he hit the sand.

Now the only weapon firing was the heavy 12.7mm machine gun. The fishing boat was pulling out of range and was barely visible, only the black smoke from its stack and the fires burning on its decks marking its position.

And then it was gone.

"Cease fire!" ordered Wang. "Cease fire."

The sudden silence was deafening. Wang used his binoculars to survey the scene below him. One of the boats, and part of its cargo, was burning and sinking. Two dead men floated in the surf, and the others were scattered around the boats.

A patrol exited from the finger of forest, moving up the beach along the high-tide line. Wang watched them spread out, moving directly toward the dead men and checking the bodies. They dragged one of the men up, out of the water, and were crouched around him.

Close to Wang, the radio crackled. "Sir, we have one who is still alive here. Badly wounded."

"Kill him." Wang gave the handset back to his radio operator and then stood up, his binoculars hitting him in the chest. He touched his holster as if to make sure that his pistol was still there and then ordered, "Everyone remain here. Lieutenant Chung, you will be in charge here."

"Yes, sir."

Wang climbed up over the boulder, noticing a couple of bright streaks where bullets had struck it. He began working his way down a narrow path, used the exposed root of a twisted tree to pull himself around another boulder, and then slipped down to the thick, coarse sand of the beach.

As he marched forward, watching his men check the bodies, move the cartons from the boat that wasn't burning, and try to put out the fire, the officer in charge spotted him and ran toward him. "All invaders are dead, Comrade."

"Good."

"There's one thing that you should see." The officer walked back toward the bodies and grabbed one of the dead men by the hair, lifting the head. "Westerner. Probably American."

"The others?" Wang asked.

"Japanese."

"Documents?"

The officer snapped his fingers and a man rushed over. He held a couple of sheets of paper and a wallet stuffed with money.

"That's it," said the officer. "Nothing of any value."

"Those papers?"

"Maps of the coastline. No names on them and no locations pinpointed."

Wang stood up looked at the ridge line where the rest of his soldiers waited. "They were going to be met by someone."

"Unless they heard the shooting and ran away."

"What's in the boxes?"

The officer moved toward one of them. Using his combat knife, he slit the top, peeled back the cardboard, and pulled out a black book, which he handed to Wang.

"A Bible?" said Wang. He thumbed through it, seeing the English words and the few full-color pictures depicting Christ. He shook his head. "Why would the Japanese be smuggling English Bibles into China?"

"Maybe," said the officer, "they were paid for it. They don't care what it is, as long as they're paid for it."

Wang tossed the Bible back at the box. "I want all this garbage burned."

"Bodies, too?"

"No. Leave the bodies on the beach to rot. Let those who come after them see what the fate of smugglers and counterrevolutionists is."

"Yes, sir."

Wang headed back across the beach toward the rocks. Without looking back, he began to climb to the ridge.

COLOMBIA

Chavez crouched near Martinez and repeated the same thing that he'd said several times. "I'm sure there were Cubans there. I didn't see any signs of Colombian soldiers."

And Martinez repeated the question he'd asked each time Chavez said this. "You're sure they were Cuban?"

"Yes, sir." Chavez pointed at the map. "There. About half a day's march, maybe a little more."

Martinez nodded slowly, studying the map and the aerial photos they had brought with them. There were no indications of a camp, Cuban or otherwise, on the map or in the photos.

"Seems that we need to get some documented proof," said Chavez. "Pictures of that camp would help."

"There are those who still won't believe it. They'll insist that we faked the pictures."

"Yes, sir, but who cares about that? We get a few shots

of the camp and the Cubans and we're going to have the right people interested."

Martinez nodded and studied the map, then said, "Our mission is to locate the sites of drug factories and production facilities, not prove a Cuban presence in Colombia. Even a secret Cuban presence."

"Except there are those who think that the Cubans are training the drug runners." Chavez grinned suddenly. "Besides, is any intelligence ever wasted?"

Martinez held up a hand. "It really doesn't matter. We've got to prove this. I think a full patrol. Six men with a camera or two. We'll photograph and map the site and then withdraw. Unless the situation dictates otherwise. Other six holding back as reinforcements or an ambush to stop pursuit."

"Yes, sir."

"Half the team, including me, you, Espinoza, Ortega, Cline, and Banse. I'll leave Alvarez in command of the other team and the blocking force. Throw him out to the east of here."

"We leave in the morning?"

Martinez checked the time. "In an hour. We'll have three or four hours of daylight and it'll put us into the enemy camp early tomorrow morning. Or we can lay low through the heat of the day and then slip up on them in the evening. Gives us light to reconnoiter."

"I'll alert the others." Chavez started to stand and then stopped. "What are the rules of engagement?"

Martinez was silent for a moment and then grinned. "We're not supposed to be here and I'll bet my jump pay that the Cubans aren't supposed to be here. We'll have normal rules. Return fire for fire received, but we do not initiate the fight."

"Yes, sir. I understand that we're cleared to fire if we're fired on first."

"I don't like giving the enemy the first shot, but there's no other way to handle it. Of course, what the general says goes. We do not allow ourselves to get killed because we were slow on the trigger."

"Yes, sir."

•   •   •

Crouched amid the jungle foliage, Martinez surveyed the enemy camp. He studied the watchtowers until he was sure that no one was in them. A single guard walked around the perimeter, his weapon slung. A cigarette dangled from his mouth.

Leaning close to Chavez, he whispered, "Not much in the way of a guard."

"Had pickets out yesterday," said Chavez. "In the little time I watched, I didn't see any signs of a real guard."

Martinez touched his lips. Suddenly, with the enemy no more than a hundred yards in front of him, he was thirsty. He knew it was psychological. If he concentrated on it, it would become maddening in a few short minutes.

"Guard towers," he said.

"I believe they'll put someone up there at dusk," said Chavez. "They'll feel safe during the day."

"They've enough space for two, three hundred men. I don't see any emplacements for heavy weapons. I would imagine 12.7s in the guard towers." Martinez turned his attention to the main buildings. "Two-story headquarters." He spotted a cinder-block structure behind the headquarters. From the antennas on the top and the wires running from it, he believed it was the radio and generator shack.

Martinez pointed it out and handed his binoculars to Chavez. "First target?"

"Let Banse and Cline take it out."

Martinez nodded. "We've got to take out the guards in the towers."

"If there's anyone in them."

"And the pickets you mentioned."

"Yes, sir."

Martinez slipped back, letting the branches of a bush close behind him, screening off the camp. He shut his eyes for a moment, thinking about the layout.

"The information we want will be in the headquarters. You and I'll search it, with Espinoza and Ortega providing us with security. Alvarez and the rest will form a blocking force here."

"What time we going to hit them?" Chavez asked.

"Just like the VC used to do. At the worst possible moment. Just about two-thirty or three o'clock."

"Until then?"

"We study the camp, take pictures of everything, and afterward lay low."

Chavez killed the guard. They'd watched him walk out the gate about dusk and work his way into the jungle. He stopped near a large tree, leaned against the trunk, and lit a cigarette. He was the only man who came out. Martinez figured he had been sent out as punishment. They waited to see if he would move off, or if he would be joined by others. But once he was out the gate, it was closed, and as the hours slipped by it was obvious that no one would be relieving him.

As the time for the attack neared Chavez began working toward him, stopping to listen and to feel his way closer. He could smell the man, even over the stench coming from the jungle floor, and he could hear everything—the animals in the canopy overhead, and those on the ground. He ignored them, concentrating on the target.

The man, who was smoking another cigarette, turned his back on Chavez. When he did, Chavez struck, leaping the last few feet to his target. He clapped a hand over the mouth and nose of his victim and lifted. As soon as the throat was exposed he cut it. The razor-sharp knife sliced with a whisper like the ripping of silk. The dead man sagged back as his blood splashed the front of his uniform.

Chavez lowered the body, but this time didn't worry about hiding it. Before the enemy would find it, he would be gone. He knelt, picked up the man's rifle, and cut the chest pouch holding the spare magazines. He ignored the already sticky blood on it. Rejoining Martinez, he held up the chest pouch like an Indian holding a scalp. Martinez nodded and then pointed at the camp.

Taking the lead, Chavez began working his way toward the wire fence. They could see the guards, who'd climbed into the towers after dark. Periodically a face would appear, stare off into the jungle, and then vanish again.

At the edge of the jungle, no more than fifteen feet from the wire, Chavez halted. He glanced right and then left, up at the guard towers. Satisfied that no one was watching, he began to crawl forward.

As he did Martinez said, "Espinoza, once we're inside, you're going to have to kill the guards."

"Yes, sir."

Chavez reached the wire and halted again, listening to the sounds from inside the camp. In the dark he could see nothing moving. The few lights that had been burning earlier had been extinguished.

Reaching up, he touched the wire and then rolled to his left, pulling out his wire cutters. Carefully, he cut the bottom strand, holding both ends so that it wouldn't snap back, but it was slack and didn't recoil. He cut again and then rolled to his back, pushing himself under the wire. A moment later he was inside. As he moved to the right, rolling to his belly and watching the camp, Martinez followed him in and then waited for Banse, Cline, Espinoza, and Ortega.

When they were together, Martinez climbed to his feet. He pointed at the closest of the guard towers and Espinoza. Espinoza nodded and began moving toward the tower.

Banse and Cline didn't wait. Crouching low, they ran toward the stone building that housed the radios. They disappeared into the dark an instant later.

Now Martinez and Chavez began working their way toward the headquarters. Neither of them spoke. They concentrated on moving, placing their feet carefully, their heads swirling back and forth as they looked for the enemy and for obstacles. When they reached the front of the building, Chavez climbed the steps and flattened himself against the stone. He turned, glanced at the window, but could see nothing inside. He reached for the door, twisted the knob, and pushed. It swung open silently. That was the thing about military installations. No one locked doors because everyone was stopped at the front gate.

Martinez stepped through the door. He slipped to the side, his back against the wall, and then dropped to one knee. Chavez followed him and then closed the door; the floor creaked under his weight. He froze, waited for a light to come on, and when it didn't, moved toward the stairs at the back of the room.

"Where?" he asked, his voice quiet.

"Main offices upstairs," said Martinez. "Admin down here. We should be able to find what we want in the admin files. You check the ones on the right."

Without a word Chavez moved off. He reached out, feeling for the wall, and then followed it to the first door. There was no sign on it. He tried the knob, found it locked, and grinned. Using his knife, he slipped the lock in under ten seconds.

He'd found an office. A bank of file cabinets stood against one wall. Two desks were pushed together in the center of the room, and a large gray square marked the only window.

He walked to the desks and leaned close. There were files and papers spread across them, but nothing of importance should have been left on them. He sat down and heard the chair squeak. It was louder than an artillery simulator.

He pulled out his flashlight and made sure the red lens was covering the bulb. Holding it down, close to the floor and under the kneehole in the desk, he switched it on. Then he began to rifle the drawers.

There was nothing of interest there. Orders written in Spanish, but all listing Colombia as the home station. The names were Spanish, and given a computer, enough intelligence, and six months, they might be able to link some of the names to the Cubans. Maybe.

Finished there, he turned off the light and moved to the second desk. Deciding there would be nothing interesting in it, he stepped to the file cabinets and began searching for anything that would link the camp to Cuba. He pulled a number of folders that looked promising, but didn't take the time to read them. He gathered data that looked good. He'd let the intelligence officers sort it out.

Martinez appeared at the door. "You through?"

"Yeah."

There was a single shot then. Both Martinez and Chavez dropped to the floor.

"Where?"

Chavez glanced to his right. "Near the guard tower."
"Shit."

There was a burst of fire. An AK on full auto, all thirty rounds burned off.

"That wasn't one of our guys," said Martinez. "Let's get going."

Chavez grabbed the files and stuffed them into his fatigue jacket. He touched the safety on his AK, snapped it off, setting it for single shot.

Together, they reached the door as the northern side of the camp erupted. Outside, the night was filled with muzzle flashes and tracers. The glowing green balls flashed, drawing lines in the dark. Some of them pointed up, at the guard tower. Others lanced across the ground, hit, and then tumbled.

"Espinoza," yelled Martinez.

In Spanish, Espinoza shouted back. "Pinned down. We're okay."

"Banse and Cline," said Chavez.

"They're on their own for the moment."

Banse had reached the solid stone of the radio shack and then the solid metal door. From the inside he could hear the hum of the generator. That had to make it difficult on the radio operators. He felt the door and then tried the knob. It didn't turn. He glanced over at Cline and whispered, "If it was easy, it wouldn't be any fun."

He moved along the building and found an open window. He pushed it to the side and then looked inside. The generator was chugging away, filling the room with diesel fumes. Banse ducked back and took a deep breath of fresh air.

He glanced at Cline and pointed back toward the door. Cline nodded and retreated. Banse lifted himself, twisted around, and stepped through the window. The vent pipe for the generator was leaking fumes into the room. Given the rest of the night, it might fill the radio shack, killing those inside.

Banse moved to the door and then hesitated. When he opened it, the noise from the generator would fill the building. That might alert anyone who was inside.

He leaned against the door, his ear pressed against the wood, but could hear nothing other than the noise of the generator.

He slung his AK and pulled his pistol from inside his fatigue jacket. Army regulations prohibited the carrying of concealed weapons. Army regulations prohibited a dozen things that soldiers in combat ignored. He fastened the silencer, also against regulations, to the barrel of the .22-caliber automatic. It fired ammunition that didn't crack the sound barrier. When it was fired, the loudest noise was the working of the slide as it ejected the spent round and loaded a new one.

Taking a deep breath, Banse pushed open the door and stepped through. He slipped to one knee, watching the other door, but there was no movement of the knob. Standing, he inched to the right and opened the main door, letting Cline in.

The two of them returned to the other door and took up positions on either side of it.

Cline reached down to open it. As he did Banse leaped into the tiny room. It was occupied by a single radio operator wearing headphones. He was sitting with his feet up on a console, a high-intensity light focused on codebooks. There were half a dozen radios, alive with glowing lights and dancing meters, but the radioman held no microphones and was not working a keypad. He was listening to traffic, not sending.

Banse lifted the silenced .22, aimed at a point just behind the ear, and fired. The man spasmed, jerked rigid, and then fell from his chair. The headphones were yanked off his ears.

Banse jumped forward and felt for a pulse. There was none. He sat down in the chair and checked the radio equipment. The traffic sounded routine. There was a loose-leaf notebook listing codes, radio frequencies, and alert rosters. Each page was stamped, indicating the document was classified.

Next to it were operating instructions for the camp and for the radio room. Banse picked both those up.

"What'd you find?"

"Good stuff." He stood and began pumping rounds into the fronts of the radios.

"What about the generator?" asked Cline.

"Wire it," said Banse, "and then we'll get out of here."

Cline disappeared. Banse took a block of plastic explosive, pressed it against the front of one of the radios, and pushed a detonator into it. He worked his way around the room, wiring it. The explosion should hide the evidence that they were ever in there.

Then, from outside came a shot. Banse snapped his head around and held his breath. Firing erupted, all of it AKs, which meant nothing.

Cline stuck his head into the room. "I'm ready. Set the timer for ten minutes."

Banse nodded, set the clock, and left the room. At the main door he hesitated, looking out. For the moment he could see nothing. He could just hear the firefight that was developing.

Espinoza stood under the ladder that led up into the closest of the guard towers. He looked up at the trapdoor in the floor and wished that he could just blow it up. It'd be so much easier that way. Glancing to the left, he saw that Ortega had taken up his position, crouching in the darkness, using the shadows. Espinoza nodded and put a foot up on the bottom rung of the ladder. He'd slung his weapon and was carrying a .22 pistol.

He climbed the ladder and put a hand onto the trapdoor. The next step was tricky. He had to open the door, get up far enough to see into the guardhouse, spot the occupants, and shoot them all before they could warn anyone.

For a moment he hesitated. Surprise was on his side. The enemy didn't know the perimeter had been breached. They figured they were safe and weren't paying attention. They'd never been attacked and didn't know that American soldiers were close.

Finally, he just shoved the trapdoor and scrambled up the ladder. As he emerged he spotted the guard facing him, a look of surprise on his face. The man was un-armed. He'd set his rifle down in a corner.

Espinoza didn't hesitate: he raised his pistol and fired. The bullet struck the man just below the breastbone. He grunted, sounding as if he'd been punched. He dropped to his hands and knees. Espinoza fired again and the man collapsed without a sound. Espinoza climbed the rest of the way into the guardhouse. He crouched there, checked the body to make sure the man was dead, and then inspected the interior. Nothing of importance.

He returned to the ladder and climbed down. On the ground he hesitated again, searching the area around him. The guard tower in the other corner was too far away from them to see anything easily. Besides, they'd be watching the jungle, if they were watching at all.

Ortega moved forward. Quietly, he asked, "How'd it go?"

"Piece of cake. I'm trying to figure if we should take out the other one."

Ortega shook his head. "Too far away. We're in good shape here. Let's get the wire open and then wait for the others."

Espinoza slipped his pistol inside his fatigue jacket and took out his wire cutters. He attacked the perimeter, quietly cutting the fence.

"Shit," said Ortega. "Someone's coming."

Espinoza stopped working and crouched. He turned and slipped his weapon off his shoulder, waiting. The man walked straight for them, never hesitating.

It had to be the sergeant of the guard making his rounds. Espinoza drew his silenced pistol, but before he could fire, the enemy stopped.

"Hey!" he called. Then suddenly he dived to the right. He began to raise his weapon and Ortega fired once. The bullet slammed into the man, killing him.

"That's torn it," said Espinoza. He leaped up and tore at the wire, finishing the opening.

"Here they come," said Ortega.

Espinoza thought he meant the rest of the team, but when he turned, he saw a dozen men running toward them. Even in the half-light of the camp, he could see they had responded quickly. They were without shirts and boots. Half of them carried weapons and one man had a flashlight.

One of the men stopped, threw himself to the ground, and opened fire, holding down the trigger. The muzzle of his weapon strobed, lighting the ground and those around him. Tracers flashed, snapped overhead, and vanished into the night.

Ortega fired back in short bursts. Three of the enemy went down. He dodged to the right, next to one of the fence posts, and fired again. The rounds hit the ground near one of the enemy soldiers.

Now all of them were shooting. The guard in the far tower opened up, the muzzle flash pinpointing him. Espinoza aimed into the center of the flash and fired a quick burst. Firing from the guard tower stopped suddenly.

"We've got to get out," said Ortega.

"We've got to cover the others."

Martinez watched the firefight for a moment, making sure he knew who was where. The first rule in combat was to identify the target. He slipped along the porch of the headquarters and stopped next to the wooden railing. In the strobing of the muzzle flashes, he could see the dark shapes of the enemy. Their movements were slow and jerky.

"Grenades?" asked Chavez.

"Right." Martinez set his weapon on the wood porch, operating lever up. He pulled a grenade and yanked the pin free. Then, like a baseball player, he threw the grenade at the enemy soldiers.

Chavez followed suit. A moment later there were two detonations and the firing tapered.

"Let's go," Martinez yelled. He scooped up his rifle and vaulted from the porch. As he hit the ground he spotted more enemy coming at them. He whirled, dropped to a knee, and opened fire with a short burst and then a longer one. The enemy soldiers vanished, running for cover.

Chavez jumped down, glanced at the fleeing soldiers, and started toward Espinoza and Ortega. When he was halfway there, he stopped, threw himself to the ground, and waited.

Martinez was moving then, running for the hole in the fence. He leaped over a body and ran to the guardhouse. He spotted one of his men next to a fence post, ran through the hole in the fence, and then took cover, facing back.

"Banse and Cline?" Espinoza asked.

"They'll have to get themselves out of there."

For the first few minutes Banse couldn't see anything. The fighting was hidden behind the headquarters building. He turned, looking back at the barracks.

"We could do something there," he said.

"Everyone's awake. They'll be pouring out."

"Couple of big charges thrown back there. Impressive explosions. That'd slow everyone down."

"Let's do it," said Cline.

They ran around the side of the radio shack and looked at the barracks. No lights had been turned on, and if it hadn't been for the shooting, it would have seemed that the enemy was still asleep.

"Somebody's trained them well. Not running out into the night."

Cline nodded. He stopped at the edge of the shack and crouched. He worked the plastic explosive, added a detonator and a fuse. "Two minutes?"

"Thirty seconds," said Banse.

"Right."

Cline finished and then stepped out of the shadows. He tossed the plastic, saw it bounce and then roll under the building.

"Now let's get the hell out of here," said Banse. He turned, ran along the side of the radio shack, stopped at the edge, and then sprinted to the side of the headquarters.

From there he could look along the porch. Near the fence he could see shapes moving, men firing, and watched as the tracers hit the ground to bounce up into the sky.

A moment later there was a crashing explosion as the plastic detonated. The roar overwhelmed the firing. The flash of fire lit the camp like the noontime sun. For an instant everything was laid out bare. And then the bright-

ness faded and the debris began to rain down. There were
shouts, screams, and fires began to burn. Cline stood to
run, but Banse stopped him.

"Let the radio shack go up."

Cline nodded and turned to watch their backs. He saw
something and fired at it. It fell, rolled, and was still.

Now there was movement everywhere on the camp.
Men were screaming at each other. The heavy machine
gun in one of the guard towers began to fire into the jungle. The tracers floated out and then disappeared.

Three men ran from one of the barracks, stopped at
the door to the radio shack, and then burst inside. An
instant later there was an explosion from inside. Fire and
flame burst through the doors and windows and the few
lights that had been on suddenly went out.

"Now," said Banse.

He leaped around the end of the porch, spotted the
gaping hole in the wire, and ran right for it. As he got
close he said, "Coming at you," in English.

Espinoza yelled, "Hurry the fuck up."

Banse dashed through the wire, turned, and dropped,
rolling to his belly. He swung his rifle around and for the
first time saw the damage in the camp. The one barracks
they'd attacked was a wreck, fires burning its entire length.
Other, smaller fires burned in some of the other buildings. Part of the headquarters was on fire.

There were two dozen bodies scattered over the field.
Firing was coming from a dozen points, the rounds poorly
aimed. They hit the fence posts high overhead. They
slammed into the jungle behind them.

"You okay?" Martinez asked.

"Yeah," said Banse. "Radios are destroyed. Got the
codebooks."

"Good," said Martinez. He raised his voice. "Espinoza. Ortega. Let's drop back now. We'll cover."

"Right."

Martinez rolled to the right, took out his radio, and
whispered into it. "Five. We're getting out now."

"Roger. Ready."

Espinoza and Ortega ran through the wire and stopped.

Martinez called out. "Chavez, let's start moving to the rear."

"Yes, sir."

Firing from the camp had slowed as the men inside tried to figure out what had happened. But then men began swarming toward the hole in the wire. Martinez yelled, "Stop them."

Everyone opened fire at once. The weapons hammered and the tracers flashed. The area strobed with sudden intensity. And the enemy assault broke in a moment, the soldiers diving for cover or fleeing in fear.

"That's got it," said Martinez. "Let's get the hell out of here."

COLOMBIA

The two teams rejoined for a moment. The enemy in the camp was busy trying to figure out what happened and there was no sign of a pursuit. Martinez, crouched near Alvarez, said, "I want to split the team. You take half the men and parallel our course about a klick away. No ambush would get us both."

"Can't split up the intelligence, Captain," said Chavez.

"Why not? Half of it with Alvarez. One of the cameras. That way some of it will get back if we're stopped."

Chavez nodded. "I mean we couldn't duplicate it."

Martinez wiped a hand over his face, surprised by the sweat there. He hadn't realized how hot it was. The humidity had remained high, even with the sun gone.

"Alvarez, you wait here for an hour and then begin your escape and evasion. We'll take off now."

"No problem, Captain."

Martinez nodded. He looked up at the young officer but couldn't see much in the dark. A hint of his shape and that was it. "Good luck to you."

"Sure thing, Captain. You've done the hard work. Now it's time to get the hell out of here." Martinez hurried up the slope with the others strung out behind him. They moved slowly, carefully, listening for signs that the enemy was around them. Martinez had ordered a standard combat patrol. He was assuming that the Cubans would shoot first and ask questions later. Crouching low, Chavez moved off, toward his half of the team. Whispering, he ordered Banse to turn the notebooks and manuals he'd found over to one of Alvarez's men. Then he slipped to the moist earth and waited for his instructions.

At dawn, Martinez halted, giving them a chance to eat a quick, cold breakfast of MREs. Ten minutes later they buried the evidence of the meal and prepared to get moving again. Chavez, watching the jungle, slipped close to Martinez and in a quiet voice said, "Something's changed."

"What?"

"Don't know, Captain, but the jungle doesn't feel right this morning."

Martinez closed his eyes and let the impressions wash over him. It was cooler, though the air was still heavy with humidity. Everything was coated with a light film of moisture that had settled during the night.

"I don't feel anything."

"Yes, sir," said Chavez. "Just thought I'd let you know that I don't feel right about this."

"You still going to take the point?"

"Yes, sir."

"Lead on," said Martinez.

Chavez checked his weapon, opening and closing the bolt to make sure that the round was seated properly. He put the weapon on safe, but kept his thumb on the safety so that he could snap it off if he needed to. He took a step, stopped, and looked back over his shoulder. The rest of the patrol was spread out behind him, facing in different directions. Each man held his weapon in his hands, at the ready, though no one expected anyone to be shooting at them yet.

Chavez moved forward between two trees. The brush, ferns, and vines grabbed at him, but he ignored them. He avoided the easiest route and what looked like an old trail, preferring to stay in the trees.

The ambush was sprung by accident. There was a faint click and then a shot. Chavez dived for cover, rolling up against a rotting log. Martinez jumped to the right and fell next to the thick trunk of a tree.

"Where'd that come from?" he shouted.

A volley crashed then, the rounds striking the tree, shaking it. Martinez rolled right and scrambled around so that he was sitting with his back to the tree, the trunk between him and the enemy.

Firing erupted to the right and left, but it was all AKs. He couldn't tell if it was his own men or the ambushers. He hadn't seen one of them yet.

"Anyone hit?" he asked. There was no answer.

Firing slowed for a moment and there was movement to the east. Martinez stood up, his back to the tree, and peeked around the trunk. He saw a flash as someone dived to the right. There were two shots and then silence.

It wasn't like the firefights he'd seen on TV or in the movies, where the two sides fired at one another on full automatic with lots of yelling and screaming. Martinez lifted a hand and wiped at his mouth. He glanced down at his weapon. He'd yet to fire it.

He turned so that it looked as if he wanted to hug the tree. He heard someone running and a shout in Spanish. Martinez had to grin to himself. The ambushers had assumed that he couldn't speak the language.

"Chavez?" he yelled.

"Here, sir."

"Coming up on the right."

"I've got them."

There was a single burst of fire. Five or six rounds and a scream that sounded like tires on dry concrete. That was answered by a second, longer burst.

Martinez used that as cover and jumped to the left. He landed behind a large log. Now he caught a flash of movement in front of him and fired without aiming. The man fell, tossing his rifle into the air.

Suddenly firing erupted from both sides of the line. Rounds whipped overhead, slashing through the jungle vegetation. Bits of leaf, bark, and twigs rained down.

Martinez spotted one of the muzzle flashes and fired into it. He held the trigger down, burning through the whole magazine before diving back for cover.

"They've got the flank," yelled Banse. "Coming on in."

"Hold right there," Martinez ordered. He crawled along the log and then got up on his knees. There was movement in front of him. He fired at it. "Take them out."

Firing opened on his right—four or five short bursts. Someone screamed in sudden pain, the cry rising like a siren and then dropping off suddenly.

"We're going to have to fall back," shouted Chavez.

"Two at a time," said Martinez.

"Ortega, you're on me," said Chavez.

"I've got Banse," said Martinez. "Everyone ready. Espinoza? Cline?"

"Set."

"Go," Martinez yelled. Then he was up, firing as fast as he could. The rounds burned through the weapon, heating the barrel. He could smell the oil cooking off, and the odor of cordite filled the air.

Something loomed out of the shadows, coming at him. It was screaming and firing, its head down. Martinez turned to meet the new threat. He fired once, twice, but the man kept attacking. Martinez fired again and saw dust fly from the man's uniform. A wet stain began to spread, dripping down, toward his crotch. The enemy staggered forward two steps, dropped his weapon, and collapsed.

Martinez ripped the spent magazine from his weapon, dug out a new one, and slammed it home. He hadn't expected a sustained firefight.

"Pull it back," Chavez yelled.

Martinez saw Banse rise up and turn, running back the way they came. As Banse disappeared into the jungle two men appeared suddenly, running after him. Martinez got a good look at them and there was no doubt they were Cubans. He aimed and fired. Both went down like rag dolls, dead before they hit the ground.

Now Martinez turned to run. He leaped over a fern and dodged around a tree. He heard someone crashing through the jungle behind him but didn't turn to look. To do that would cost time. In the jungle he had to watch where he put his feet.

"Drop, sir!" yelled one of his men.

Martinez didn't even think about it. He fell to the ground. He clawed at it, trying to disappear into it. He was aware of the odor of rotting vegetation.

His men opened fire, all five of them on full auto. He heard the rounds snapping through the air overhead. There were sudden screams and someone crashed into the brush.

"Let's go," Chavez yelled.

Martinez was up and moving. He caught a glimpse of Banse as he disappeared into the jungle. He dodged to the right and saw Chavez.

Chavez stopped and turned. He looked right at Martinez. "Hurry it up, sir."

Martinez caught him and whirled. Looking back, he saw no signs of the Cubans in pursuit. There was noise, he could hear someone shouting orders, but couldn't make out the words.

"We better find a place to regroup," said Chavez.

"Don't want to get caught in a running gun battle. They've got the numbers."

Chavez pulled the magazine from his weapon and looked down into it. He slammed it home and turned. "Let's get going. Up the hill."

"Go," said Martinez. "I'll cover. Wait at the summit for me."

"Yes, sir."

Chavez started up the hill, moving rapidly. Martinez watched the jungle behind them and then turned to follow the others. The Cubans were still out there, but they didn't seem to be pressing the advantage. That bothered him. The camp could have held two or three hundred men. It meant that someone might have filled in behind them. If they ran into a blocking force, they could be wiped out in a matter of seconds.

Martinez scrambled up the hill. He reached the crest just behind Cline. The sergeant was kneeling next to a tree, facing the way they'd come.

"No, sir. Looks clear."

Chavez moved toward them. "If we move to the north, we'll fool them. We can double back later."

Martinez looked at his watch, but didn't see the time. It was just something to do. "Let's get moving. You've got the point."

"Terrific, sir."

Martinez said suddenly, "Wait. Head back toward the enemy camp."

Chavez was about to say something and then grinned. "Yes, sir. I get it."

"Cline, you've got the slack. I'll take the rear. Let's get moving."

Chavez moved into the jungle. Banse, Espinoza, and Ortega filled in, slowly moving out behind Chavez. Martinez hesitated, watching the slope. There didn't seem to be any sign of the Cubans.

Chavez slipped from the crest of the hill to a point about ten feet down. He was weaving a path through the trees and bushes and ferns.

They moved rapidly for ten or fifteen minutes and then slowed. Now Chavez was trying to slip through the jungle without leaving any signs of his passing or making any noise. He didn't want to alert the enemy.

Martinez stopped once and turned, slipping to one knee. He couldn't see more than five or six yards behind them because the vegetation was so thick. And he could hear nothing. No sign of a pursuit, but then if the enemy was good in the jungle, Martinez might not hear them.

Satisfied they had slipped the Cuban ambush, he hurried after the rest of the patrol. Through a gap in the vegetation, he saw the back of one of his men. He caught up to them again and fell into line.

Chavez kept them moving for another four or five minutes and then stopped. He turned, looked at Martinez, and waved him forward.

When the captain was close, Chavez whispered, "There's someone in front of us."

"You know who?"

"Nope. But they're out there."

Martinez crouched and stared at the ground. He wiped the sweat from his face and then turned, looking to the rear. He turned his attention back to Chavez.

"There might have been two hundred people at that camp," said Chavez.

"You think they've got other patrols out."

"Makes sense now, Captain. After what we did to them last night, they'd be out hunting for us."

Martinez pulled his map from his pocket. The surrounding territory didn't give him much in the way of landmarks. There was the ridge line they had climbed and the valleys they had seen. From his point there, surrounded by the thick jungle growth, he couldn't see anything else.

"Maybe we'd better just slide down the hill and get the hell out of here."

"And warn the others?" Chavez asked.

Martinez nodded and moved to the rear. He found Banse kneeling next to a tree, his weapon pointed toward the jungle. "Need to make radio contact with the others and let them know what happened. Tell them that they're patrols out looking for us."

"They should have heard the shooting."

"Should have isn't quite good enough. I want to make sure that they know." He hesitated for a moment and then said, "I think it's time to call for extraction."

"Yes, sir." Banse was grinning broadly.

They waited for only a few minutes, listening to the sounds of the men working their way through the jungle fifty or a hundred yards in front of them. The enemy climbed the slope, grabbing at the vegetation, slipping and sliding around, and then crossed the crest, moving down the other side.

When they were gone, Chavez returned to Martinez and leaned close to him. "We go?"

Martinez showed the master sergeant the map. "Let's

hit the PZ. That's where the rest of the team's going to be.''

Chavez studied the map. "Down the slope to the valley floor and then to the south."

"You've got the point."

"Why am I always so lucky?" asked Chavez.

"I think it's your personal charm."

"Thanks."

Martinez stood up and moved back along the line, checking on each of his soldiers. Satisfied that everyone was ready, he turned and signaled Chavez.

They moved down the hill carefully. They knew the enemy was out there searching. It was a tedious way to move, but it gave them the opportunity to listen to the jungle. If the Cubans were moving toward them, they would hear them.

After fifteen minutes they halted for five. Chavez took off again, walking for twelve minutes and then stopping for three. The random movement was designed to trip up anyone who might be following them, but Chavez could detect nothing.

At noon they halted, ate a quick meal of MREs, drank the lukewarm water in their canteens, and then started off again. But the Cubans had now turned and Chavez could hear them in the distance.

He stopped the patrol and told Martinez, "I think they've picked up our trail."

"I don't want to lead them to the PZ," said Martinez. "How many are there?"

"No more than a dozen."

"Let's take them."

"Yes, sir." Chavez grinned evilly. "They're coming in this direction."

"Take the anchor end of the ambush. I'll take the other end. Rest of the team between us."

Chavez disappeared behind a tree, while Martinez moved along the line, setting up the ambush. Ortega was placed behind it to watch for the enemy from that direction. Martinez then settled in. He took one grenade and set it in front of him. He checked his weapon and then made sure that he could get to his spare magazines easily.

Now he could hear the enemy soldiers. There was the rustling of a bush against cotton. A twig snapped and two birds leaped into the air, squawking. He squeezed his eyes shut for a moment and listened to the jungle, to the insects and birds and animals. He opened his eyes and stared into the shadows, watching for signs of the men following them.

There was a flash of movement. Martinez reached down and picked up the grenade, pulling the pin. He waited for a moment and saw the first of the Cubans appear. He was a short, dark man with a helmet pulled low. Behind him were two more soldiers, each armed with an AK-47.

Martinez cocked his arm and waited until he could see another three of the Cubans, then threw the grenade, aiming at the last man in the line. An instant later it detonated with a flat bang that tossed dirt and debris up into the air. A second and third explosion followed as the other members of the team threw grenades. Firing erupted as the men tried to cut down the Cubans.

One of them dived for cover and then popped up four or five feet closer. Martinez fired, missed, and shot again. The Cuban whirled and fired, the rounds snapping past Martinez's ear. He dived to the right, rolled, and came up, firing on full auto. The rounds stitched the Cuban from shoulder to hip. Blood spurted as the man flipped to the rear and didn't move as his heart gave out.

The firing died out as quickly as it started. The Cubans were all down and none of them was moving. Martinez stood slowly, his weapon pointed at the ambush site. He stepped forward, his eyes on the one man he could see.

The patrol slowly filtered out of the trees, watching the men lying dead in the jungle. Martinez kicked an AK away from an outstretched hand. He crouched and reached out to the corpse's blood-soaked pockets. The odor of hot copper filled the air. Martinez took the man's wallet and a pack of papers that was stuffed in next to it. He wanted to take the weapon to deny it to the enemy, but a state of war didn't exist. His taking a single AK or half a dozen wouldn't make any difference.

Chavez and Banse moved among the dead, searching

their pockets, taking anything they could find. That was standard operating procedure. Take anything that might be of intelligence value. In the field they didn't know what would be important, so they stole it all.

Martinez stood up. "Let's get the hell out of here."

"You want me to take the point?" Chavez asked.

"No," said Martinez. "Banse. Take the point. Chavez, you've got the rear."

They moved out, forming up, filtering through the jungle. Now they moved faster, trying to get away from the ambush point before the Cubans could respond. They ran, or tried to, but the jungle was too thick. The thorn-covered bushes and the sticker-ladened vines grabbed at them; other plants tugged at them, holding them back.

They broke out of the jungle suddenly and into a long, narrow clearing with thick, waist-high grass. Banse hesitated at the edge, glancing up at the sun. He looked back at Martinez and then sprinted into the center. A moment later he reached the other side. He stopped there.

The rest of the team followed him and, once on the other side, took a short break. They fanned out in a ragged circle, each man covering the man on his right and left.

Chavez slipped up on Martinez. "We're still four or five miles from the PZ."

"I know."

"We're going to have to get out of the jungle. Too many Cubans around now."

Martinez hesitated. "Any reason we can't use this clearing for the pickup?"

"It's big enough," said Chavez.

"You have a clue as to pickup times?"

"No, sir. I just told Banse to get it arranged."

Martinez got out his map and worked his way around. "We're going to secure this clearing, Banse. I want pick up arranged here."

"Yes, sir. I'll do what I can."

Martinez returned to Chavez. "Make a quiet sweep around here. I don't want the Cubans sneaking up on us."

"I haven't heard anything in the last thirty minutes or so," said Chavez.

"We'll just make sure."

"Yes, sir."

Martinez moved to the edge of the jungle and looked out over the sun-drenched clearing. The helicopter pilots wouldn't like the deep grass because obstructions—tree stumps, logs, rocks—could be hidden in it. They'd be afraid of impaling their choppers.

But they couldn't survey the clearing because he didn't want anyone in it until the choppers were inbound. Now, looking back, he could see the paths they had taken as they ran through it. The grass hadn't recovered. The trails were obvious, but there was nothing he could do about it.

Banse appeared at his elbow and whispered, "Everything's set. We'll have to throw smoke."

"ETA?"

"About thirty minutes."

"Thirty minutes?"

"Yes, sir. They were standing by, and when the first call arrived, they got airborne. One chopper will divert to us and the other two will pick up Alvarez and his team."

"Thirty minutes." Martinez couldn't believe it. If only the pilots would be smart enough to bring the cold beer, it would be perfect.

Chavez came back. "There's someone out there," he said, his voice a hoarse whisper.

"How far?"

"Half a klick, maybe more. They're not coming directly at us, but they're coming in this direction in a very roundabout fashion."

"We've got maybe twenty, twenty-five minutes to the pickup," said Martinez.

"It's going to be close."

Martinez slipped to the rear and found Banse. "You better get on the horn and see if you can stir things up. We've got some company coming."

"Yes, sir."

Then he found Cline. "I want you to get the men organized here. Coordinate with Banse and throw the smoke when the lead pilot calls for it. We need to get the choppers in and out as quickly as possible."

"Where will you be?"

"Sergeant Chavez and I will be out there watching for the Cubans. We'll be on the chopper before lift-off."

"Yes, sir."

Martinez and Chavez slipped deeper into the jungle, moving toward the Cuban soldiers that Chavez had spotted. They left the rest of the patrol a hundred yards behind them and found a point where they could see fifty yards through light scrub and hanging vegetation.

"This is perfect," said Chavez.

Martinez dropped to one knee and then didn't move. For a few moments he could hear only the natural sounds of the jungle: lizards and monkeys and birds. Some of them ran through the canopy overhead, rustling the branches and chattering at one another. Then, from the distance came another sound. Martinez turned slightly and recognized the quiet pop of rotor blades. He glanced at Chavez. "Let's go."

But now there was noise in front of them, too. The Cubans had turned and seemed to be heading directly toward the PZ. Martinez pointed in that direction. Chavez nodded. Neither of them moved.

The chopper was coming closer. They could hear the whine of the turbine. Martinez stood up and glanced to the rear. He still hadn't seen the Cubans. They didn't seem to be moving any faster.

Chavez slipped to the right. "I think we'd better get out of here now."

"I'm right behind you," said Martinez. As he moved he could see purple smoke billowing up through the trees. The helicopter was was almost there.

Chavez caught him. "Cubans coming up. They're running at us now."

"Go," said Martinez.

Chavez pushed his way thorugh the jungle, heading toward the rest of the patrol. Martinez followed for a moment but then stopped and whirled. Now he could see the Cubans. They had closed the gap.

The helicopter was hovering near the ground, the noise from the engine and rotors filling the jungle and overpowering the other sounds. The rotor wash was tearing at the vegetation, forcing it down, and swirling it around like the winds of a cyclone.

A single shot rang out and then a short burst. Martinez dodged right and then left. He whirled, saw one man, and opened fire. A short burst and then a longer one. He saw the enemy diving for cover. Now Martinez spun and started to run again. He only had to stop the Cubans for a few seconds. Then he'd be on the aircraft, flying out.

He caught Chavez at the edge of the jungle. He stopped there and watched the helicopter come in. It hovered ten feet above the ground, the rotor wash flattening the grass. The purple smoke from the grenade was sucked up by the rotor, twisted around, and blown off.

Cline and the rest of the patrol were now running at the chopper. It dropped slowly as the pilots searched the ground under them, making sure they weren't going to crash into something.

Martinez burst out of the trees, right behind Chavez. "Go," he yelled. "Go."

Cline reached the chopper as it settled into the grass. The door on the cargo compartment was open and a man was standing in it, watching. He looked bewildered by the dash made by the men in the jungle.

Firing erupted from the jungle. Martinez ran straight for the side of the helicopter. Through the windshield he could see both the pilots, one of them sitting with her eyes wide open. Tracers were flashing overhead.

At the nose of the chopper Martinez turned. There was movement inside the jungle. The muzzle flashes sparkled in the shadows of the trees.

Cline was now peeking out of the cargo compartment. "Come on, sir."

Martinez squeezed off a sustained burst, holding the trigger down until the magazine was empty. He whirled and ran toward the cargo compartment. The whole patrol was inside now. Cline and Chavez were leaning out, hanging on, reaching for Martinez. He grabbed Chavez's hand and felt himself lifted from his feet. He was jerked toward the interior of the chopper and fell, sprawling on his face.

The chopper seemed to jump into the air. It spun quickly and the nose dipped as the pilot took off. Martinez turned and glanced out of the cargo compartment. The ground was racing by under him as they climbed rapidly into the sky. He watched the Cubans spill into the PZ, their weapons pointed up at the chopper, but not shooting.

"Did it," Chavez yelled. "We fucking did it. Got the hell out."

Martinez grinned and asked, "Anyone bring the beer?"

TOKYO, JAPAN

Had Sara Keller refused to provide the information, Reisman would never have found the tiny warehouse. And if Keller hadn't called ahead, warning those in the warehouse that Reisman would be coming, he would never have gotten inside the door. They would either have refused to answer the buzzer or refused him entrance. As it was, they let him inside to look around.

A man dressed in shabby and shapeless jeans and a ripped old work shirt, with a cloth strip around his head, met him at the door. Reisman looked at the Japanese and shook his head. "I might be in the wrong place."

"Your name?"

"Reisman."

"You have ID?"

Reisman pulled out his wallet and showed the man his New Mexico driver's license.

"Anyone can get driver's license."

Reisman showed his press card and a couple of credit cards. The man took the wallet, looked at the money, selected several bills, and handed the wallet back.

"You follow me."

Reisman stuffed the wallet into his hip pocket. "I'm right behind you."

They walked down a narrow hall, past a couple of doors that looked like bank vaults and a couple of doors that looked as if they were about to fall in. At the end of the corridor, a single bright light hung down, illuminating the floor. Reisman stopped in the center of the light. The man reached out and touched the button on the frame.

A small eyehole opened, closed, and then the vault door began to swing in. The man there said, "I'll take over now."

The first man nodded, turned, and began to walk away. The new man said, "Come on in."

"Thanks."

As the man closed the vault door Reisman looked around. The room wasn't big, not much more than twelve by fifteen feet. The walls were smooth metal, and if someone dropped an atomic bomb on Tokyo, the room would probably survive. If the bomb wasn't too big and hit a mile away.

Cardboard boxes were stacked along one wall. Metal shelves were against another, and each shelf held hundreds of bibles. All kinds of bibles, from the King James Version right up to the latest edition from Reader's Digest that held full-color illustrations and black-and-red text.

More boxes against the back wall contained various items—toothbrushes, soap, razors, toilet paper, a few canned goods, and boxes of crackers or cereal. All sorts of things that couldn't be found, bought, or stolen in China.

"What the hell is going on here?" Reisman asked.

One of the men, who had been sitting on the floor, stood up. "You are?"

Reisman moved toward him, his hand out to be shaken. "Morris Reisman. I'm a reporter with the—"

"Christ! That's all we need. A reporter."

Reisman studied the man. He was tall and young,

looking as if he'd been out of college for a year or two, with light-colored hair, blue eyes, and narrow features. He looked out of place with the Oriental people in the room.

"Sit down, Steve," said one of the women. She was a small women with long, black hair.

"Steve?" said Reisman.

"MacKenzie. And don't get your hopes up. I'm not going to introduce the others. You don't need to know their names."

"Okay," said Reisman. He'd been in hostile environments before. The moment he identified himself as a reporter, the subjects clammed up, figuring him for the enemy. But if he stayed quiet, asked an occasional, non-threatening question, they would open up for him. "What's going on? Smuggling Bibles to the Chinese?"

MacKenzie sat down in front of a large carton. He picked up a Bible and flipped it open, showing Reisman that the interior had been cut out and a videotape hidden inside.

Reisman knelt beside him. "What the hell?"

"We figure that—this is all off the record?"

"Of course."

"Okay. We figure that the Chinese will figure we're smuggling the Bibles, hidden among the consumer goods, into China. They won't look further than that. But what we're really doing is smuggling in the tapes."

"Why?"

"Tapes show what it's like out in the real world. This month it's a walk down Rodeo Drive. It shows to all what our glorious capitalism can do for you. Opulence as far as the eye can see. Dozens, nay, thousands of well-dressed, decadently rich Americans of all persuasions—black, white, yellow—walking among the shops that are filled with consumer goods."

"I'd think it would look staged."

"Hell," said MacKenzie, "I would think they all look staged, but then, when the tapes of New York City, with the burned-out buildings and rubble-strewn street lots are used, there are always cars on the streets and pedestrians carrying boom boxes. It sends conflicting messages and starts the Chinese citizens thinking.''

''I don't get it,'' said Reisman.

MacKenzie put down the Bible he held. ''The theory is that the Chinese see our problems, but they also see the people on the street with boom boxes and cars. They see all the conflicts, but the visual evidence is that everyone is rich in America. Or more importantly, that there are lots of consumer goods available to everyone.''

''My point,'' said Reisman, ''is that the Chinese are going to see the trouble in our country.''

''But the Chinese government tells them that America is decaying and on the verge of collapse.'' He grinned and picked up one of the cassettes. ''Our own tapes suggest that.''

''Exactly.''

''But then the Chinese people look at the tapes carefully. Who owns all those cars? Why does the black man carry a huge tape recorder and radio around? Why do all those people have bright clothes? Conflicting messages.''

Now Reisman nodded. ''So that the citizens realize that their government is filling them with propaganda. Our tapes say, sure, we have troubles, but not like the ones you face.''

''The only thing I worry about,'' said MacKenzie, ''is whether there are enough video recorders in China to play the tapes. The smuggling doesn't do much good if the person at the other end can't watch it.''

''You remember back—what, five, six years ago—when the students were attempting to win reforms. There was that big democracy demonstration in Beijing?'' said the woman.

''Yeah?'' said MacKenzie.

''Well, the students at American universities were faxing information to the students in Beijing. Who would have thought that any Chinese student would have had access to a fax machine?''

''Good point,'' said Reisman.

''Information,'' said MacKenzie. ''That's the way we're going to destroy the Communist world. In the old days, when information about the rest of the world could be restricted, you could tell your people anything and they would believe it. Today, with satellite communications, telephone lines into everywhere, and videotapes, you can't stop the flow of information. People can see with their own eyes everything going on.''

"Is it working?" Reisman asked.

"Hell." MacKenzie grinned. "We don't know. We're just sending the tapes in. But it's a lot cheaper than funding a new weapons system. The B-2 costs what now? A billion dollars a plane or something equally ridiculous.''

"Have you smuggled anything into China yet?"

MacKenzie looked at the others, who bent to their work without saying anything. For a moment he stared at the Bible he held in his hand.

"We've made several trips into China. We leave from Kagoshima and hit the Chinese mainland near Shanghai.''

"Successful?"

"The stuff reached China. Our feeling is it doesn't really matter if it's intercepted by the officials or not. As long as the material arrives intact.''

Reisman had caught the glimpses from the others. He knew that something was going on that he wasn't being told. He waited, letting the silence descend in the room. After a couple of minutes, when no one spoke, he asked, "Would it be possible for me to go on one of the trips?"

"What for?"

"See the whole operation.''

"We're going to an enemy coastline, kind of like drug smugglers approaching Florida. Where our Coast Guard would arrest the drug smugglers, the Chinese open fire.''

Reisman let that sink in for a moment. He looked at MacKenzie and realized that he was speaking from experience. He wasn't suggesting that the Chinese might open fire. He knew they would.

"When'd it happen?"

MacKenzie didn't answer the question. Instead, he said, "The last thing we need is to have a reporter killed.''

"I want to see the operation.''

"Maybe. I don't know.''

*   *   *

It had taken two hours, but all the cartons had been packed. The tapes inside the Bibles, only three or four in each of the boxes, were hidden in among the toothbrushes and toilet paper and soap. They had figured that any tapes that got through would be traded among those who found them. One tape could be seen by several hundred people. It didn't take many of them.

Reisman, allowed to stay because he helped load the cartons, watched as two of the men carried them from the warehouse, loading them in the back of a covered truck. It was an old Mercedes with an engine that sounded as if it was on the verge of stalling.

Leaning against the doorjamb, he counted the cartons as they were carried out. All were labeled with Chinese characters. MacKenzie came out of the warehouse, looked into the rear of the truck, counted, and punched something into his handheld minicomputer.

MacKenzie watched the two men bring the last of the crates out, push them into the rear of the truck, and close the tailgate. The men walked around and climbed into the cab, but they didn't leave. MacKenzie hesitated and then walked up to the cab. He spoke to the driver and stepped back. Gears ground and the truck lurched down the alley and disappeared around a corner.

As he returned to the building MacKenzie said, "This is the easy part. The Japanese don't care if we're driving Bibles, videotapes, or bathroom articles through the city. Even if they're stopped and the truck searched, we've done nothing illegal."

"Now what?" Reisman asked.

"They drive to the docks and the cartons are loaded onto the boat that will take the stuff to China."

"Then that's where I want to go."

MacKenzie looked at Reisman. "That's funny. You don't look particularly stupid."

"You can call your counterpart in Hong Kong. She'll tell you that I'll play fair."

MacKenzie laughed. "This is a very low-level, unimportant operation. It gets compromised and we find another way of doing it. There's not much that you can do to harm it."

"So why can't I see the docks. The other end of the pipeline, so to speak."

"Fine," said MacKenzie. "How did you plan to get down there?"

"Thought maybe I'd ride with you."

"My function has been completed. Now everything is in the hands of the others." MacKenzie pushed past Reisman, entering the warehouse.

"Then tell me the destination of the truck and I'll get myself down there."

"Oh no," said MacKenzie. "I'm not going to have you poking around down there by yourself."

"I can make a few phone calls. . . ."

"Don't bother," said MacKenzie. "I'll take you down there. I'm just not thrilled with making the drive, that's all. Roads are crowded and you'll be surprised what a gallon of gas costs now."

"It's not coming out of your pocket, is it?"

MacKenzie shrugged. "Either mine or the taxpayers' back in the States. It's almost the same thing."

"Then I'll buy the gas. Let the news service pay for it."

"And you'll buy the dinner?"

Reisman had to laugh. "Sure. I'll buy the dinner."

"Then we'd better get going. We can have something to eat along the way. Truck's not due to the docks until two in the morning."

MacKenzie hadn't timed it quite as well as he thought. When they reached the dock, the truck was already there. Half a dozen men were moving the cartons to the edge of the dock, where a fishing boat was tied up.

Reisman asked, "You using fishing boats?"

"Yeah. They make a poor radar target, they're so abundant in the area that no one thinks twice about them, and they can get close to the Chinese coast easily."

"Can we go on board?"

"I hope you're not planning on taking a trip."

"I just want to see the operation."

They started across the dock, but a man loomed up out of the dark. He said something in Japanese. Reisman started to reply in English, but MacKenzie answered in Japanese. That explained what MacKenzie was doing in Japan.

The man didn't seem happy, but then MacKenzie opened his wallet, handed him a couple of bills. That ended the discussion. The man stepped aside.

"What was that all about?" Reisman asked.

"Guard. He knew me but I gave him a couple of bucks—yen, actually—to make him happy."

They walked across the dock, the odor of fish and salt air heavy. The fishing boat bobbed slightly, the thick ropes creaking against the pilings of the pier. A couple of men stood at the head of the gangplank, but neither seemed inclined to come ashore.

"You let me talk to them," said MacKenzie. "It's their boat, and if they don't want us on it, then we're not going to get on it."

"Sure," said Reisman.

MacKenzie moved to the edge of the gangplank and spoke to the men on board. For a couple of minutes, the men shouted answers at one another. No one was trying to hide his presence. There was no secrecy involved.

Finally MacKenzie turned and waved. "Come on."

As he approached, Reisman said, "You were pretty loud about it."

"Keep telling you. We're doing nothing illegal here. The Japanese government doesn't care if we load the boat with Bibles and tapes. Nothing wrong with it."

Reisman walked up the gangplank and felt the urge to salute the flag, the men on deck, anything. That was what happened in all the war movies. Instead he stepped down and turned.

"Nothing interesting here," said MacKenzie.

Reisman shrugged. He walked to the stern and looked down into the black water. He turned and then saw that recent repairs had been made to the boat. He stepped closer and wished he had a flashlight. The little light coming from the dock area didn't help much.

"What'd you find?" asked MacKenzie.

Reisman pointed at one small area. "Looks like a bullet hole," he said.

"The Chinese oppose the operation. The Japanese do not. They encourage it."

"Anybody been killed?" Reisman asked.

"That's not our worry."

"These guys here, the ones I've seen. They don't look like your average fishermen."

"What's that mean?"

"It means that there's more going on here than meets the eye."

"Nope," said MacKenzie. "All that's going on here is that we're smuggling Bibles and tapes into China. There is no hidden agenda, nothing hidden beneath the surface here. What you see is all there is."

"Fine," said Reisman. "I want to go to China."

"That," said MacKenzie, "is an incredibly bad idea."

"Why?"

"Because you could get killed."

CARSWELL AIR FORCE BASE, TEXAS

John Frankowski sat at the dinner table with a bottle of wine in his hand and leaned forward to fill Marie's glass. She shook her head and put her hand over it. "I'm flying in the morning."

John looked at the clock and asked, "What time is your takeoff?"

"Nine. Yes, I know that the regulations read eight hours before the flight, but I've had enough already."

John leaned back. "You're sure?"

"Yeah, I'm sure." She patted her lips with her napkin and dropped it on the table next to her plate. Marie Frankowski was one of the growing number of female pilots in the air force. She was a tall woman, slender, with short brown hair and big brown eyes. Early in her career she had fought for her long hair, pinning it up daily as regulations demanded. But she'd grown tired of that and one day had it chopped almost as short as her husband's. It made it simpler to care for and made life easier.

Her husband, John, was also an air-force pilot. He outranked his wife, but just barely. He had been promoted to major two months earlier and she was on the list to be promoted in a couple of months. They had joked about it, but she had known that if she had gotten promoted below the zone, he would have had trouble dealing with it and would also have taken a quite ribbing from his friends. He would have said nothing about it to her.

John Frankowski was an inch taller than his wife, had darker hair, and blue eyes. He was slim, bordering on skinny, a result of playing racquetball and handball, jogging, and playing center field on the base softball team. He wasn't scheduled to fly. In fact, he was scheduled down for the next week. He'd accumulated too many flight hours in the last thirty days. He didn't have to worry about regulations and the consumption of alcohol.

"Wine's almost gone," he said. "Little more won't hurt you." He held up the bottle.

"I'd expect that from someone else, but you're a flier yourself."

John shrugged and dumped the wine into his glass. "Just wanted to make sure you didn't want it."

"Since I have to fly tomorrow, are you going to do the dishes tonight?"

"Nope. But I'll put them in the dishwasher."

"That's all I wanted." Marie stood up. "While you do that I think I'll go watch a little TV."

"I didn't say that I'd do it right this very minute."

"You let them sit and the stuff crusts over. Makes it harder to rinse them off."

"I don't understand this. We have a dishwasher, but we have to clean them before we put them in there."

"The dishwasher kills the germs," she said. "But you have to get the food off them or it'll clog up the drains."

"Okay, okay," said John. "I'll do it your way. What are you going to be doing?"

"I said I was going to watch some TV, but I think I'll take a shower first."

John nodded and picked up his plate. "And I'll just stay in here and do the dishes."

Without another word Marie left the tiny dining room. The house had been cheap because it was small. It had a formal dining room that was little more than ten by ten, only two bedrooms, and one bath. It was designed for a young couple without kids, starting out in life. But it had been the only thing available when they had been transferred to the base and it was more than adequate for their needs. They'd turned the second bedroom into an office they shared and they rarely used the formal dining room, so that the table became a second desk.

The master bedroom, however, was the house's single concession to luxury. It was huge, with walk-in closets, one for each of them. A fireplace was built into the corner. Their king-size waterbed, a dresser, and a chest fit easily. Marie had brought in a chair and there was a cedar chest at the end of the bed.

She slipped out of her clothes, dropping them on the bed. She walked to the closet, grabbed her robe, and then thought better of it. As she walked naked to the bathroom she considered taking a bubble bath but decided against it. That would be too relaxing, and the last thing she wanted to do was relax completely.

She turned on the water, tested it with her wrist, and then stepped into the tub, closing the shower doors. She pushed the little button and stepped back, waiting for the spray to come. When it did, she moved forward carefully, letting the flow bathe her ankles, shins, thighs, and then belly. She moved closer and turned, letting the fine streams of water vibrate against her back. The warm water hitting her just below the shoulder blades was almost hypnotic in its relaxing pulse.

She finally picked up the soap. She bent slightly, soaping her thighs slowly, feeling the soft skin there. Grinning to herself, she realized that the shower had done its work quickly. She was more than ready as long as John had finished with the dishes.

Now she rinsed, turning slowly, letting the water spray against her back and breasts. The tiny streams of water sent shivers of red-hot ice through her. When she had turned off the water, climbed out, and was reaching for the towel, she caught a glimpse of herself in the foggy full-length mirror on the back of the bathroom door. She leaned forward and used the soggy towel to wipe away the mist.

Hers was a good body, she decided. Still firm and trim, even after seven years of marriage. She turned and looked over her shoulder, putting her hands on her hips to mimic the famous picture of Betty Grable. Sometimes she wished she had a picture of herself, nude, just like that. Other times, she was glad that she didn't.

She wrapped a towel around her body to hide her breasts and glanced down. It barely covered her. She opened the door and walked out of the bathroom, but instead of heading for the bedroom she turned toward the kitchen. At the door she stopped and waited for John to turn around.

"You done?" he said without turning. He leaned over, stuck a dish into the bottom of the dishwasher, and then glanced back at her.

As he did she unhooked the towel, held it in place momentarily, and then let it fall to the floor. She grinned at him but didn't move and didn't speak.

"This was planned," he said, staring at her. There was a hint of a tan. Small white marks where the bikini had covered her. Just a touch of color on her legs, belly, chest, and back.

"I'll be gone for three or four days," she said.

"Do I have time to take a shower?"

Marie shrugged. "If you feel it necessary. I can wait. But not long."

Unbuttoning his shirt, John left the dishes in the sink, the dishwasher opened, and a dish towel on the floor. "I'll hurry," he announced as he left the room.

Laughing, Marie walked to the sink to assess the damage he'd done. Actually, he'd nearly finished. Most of the dishes had been cleaned and all the silverware had been loaded into the basket. Marie finished, closed the dishwasher, and then wiped down the counter. There was something slightly obscene about doing the dishes naked. It added to her excitement.

The task completed, she walked into the living room and then jumped back. Someone had forgotten to close the drapes on the picture window that looked out on the front yard. Picture window was right. She turned off the kitchen light, slipped along the wall, and used the cord. With the drapes closed, she sat down and used the remote control to turn on the television.

She wasn't interested in anything until she came across CNN. The news reader was talking about turmoil in the Saudi Arabian capital. The line of succession for the throne was not clear and there was a minor power struggle as three factions pushed their candidate to the front.

John appeared suddenly, a towel around his waist. He stood there and then let the towel drop away. It was clear that he was as ready as she was.

"No courting?" she asked innocently.

"You'd like flowers?"

"Of course. Or a kind word."

"I like your outfit," he said. "It suits you well. You should wear it more often."

"CNN is talking about some trouble in Saudi Arabia. I wonder if that'll affect our flight."

"You know," said John, "with you sitting there like that, the last thing on my mind is a flight in the morning. I don't care what CNN has to say."

"I can see you're ready."

"You going to sit there all night?"

Marie stood up and realized she was slightly weak in the knees. She moved toward him and then stopped. He wrapped his arms around her and pulled her closer.

"Should we go to the bedroom?" he asked huskily.

"Eventually," she said. "But not now."

It had taken them two hours to get into the bedroom, but by then they were too tired to do anything but sleep. Marie set the alarm for 5:30 and climbed under the sheets. Neither of them had bothered to find any clothes.

When the alarm went off, Marie climbed out of bed to shut it off. John had rolled over but seemed to have gone back to sleep. She went in the bathroom, closed the door, and started getting ready to fly. Finished in there, she slipped into the bedroom, opened a drawer, and found underwear. She carried it into her closet, closed that door, and turned on the light.

She put on her panties and then bra. She pulled a flight suit from a hanger, climbed into it, and zipped it up. Like most pilots, she'd had it tapered slightly for a better fit.

Leaving the closet, Marie glanced down at John. He opened his eyes and asked, "You have to go now?"

"Couple of minutes. Got to find my boots."

John rolled over and propped himself up on an elbow. "What time do you take off?"

"In theory, about nine o'clock. But you know how that works with the piles of paperwork."

"Why so early then?"

"I want to check in with intelligence again. See what they have on the situation in Saudi Arabia."

"You going to eat breakfast?"

"Go back to sleep," she said. "I'll have something on base, if I decide to eat anything." She moved toward him and leaned over, brushing his lips with a kiss. "See you in a couple of days."

John laughed. "I might be out on a flight when you get back."

"Sometimes the schedules just don't work out." She touched him on the shoulder. "See you later."

She walked toward the front of the house and opened the front door. The morning newspaper was sitting on the porch. Marie picked it up, stripped the rubber band from it, and tossed it into the bushes. She wondered if the newspaper carrier ever searched the bushes near the front doors of the houses. There were probably hundreds of rubber bands in them.

She turned and stepped back in, using the hall light to review the headlines. At one time newspapers had carried national news on the front pages, but in the days of CNN and satellite dishes, newspapers ran local features and local news on the front page. She flipped through it, looking for something about Saudi Arabia, but found nothing there. The death of an obscure king in a Middle Eastern country didn't rate a single paragraph, even if that king controlled the majority of the world's known oil reserves and his country had been the focal point of a massive military buildup a few years earlier.

Finished, she dropped the paper on the table by the door. She opened the closet there, retrieved her overnight case and flight bag. She looked back to the rear of the house and then opened the front door again. After she set the lock, she pulled the door closed.

The heat had broken during the night. Dew was on the grass, and when she grabbed the handle to lift the garage door, it was wet. Her car was a sleek, low, black thing that resembled a fighter aircraft. She'd fallen in love with it the moment she'd seen it but resisted the temptation to buy one for three years.

Climbing behind the wheel, she put the key into the ignition. The engine caught immediately and settled into a low rumble. She turned on the radio, listened to the rock and roll, and then switched to the all-news station. Unfortunately she found the local news, weather, and sports. It'd be twenty minutes before they returned to the national scene and she could learn if there was anything new from Saudi Arabia.

It was a short drive to the base, one that took her through a couple of residential areas. She turned on the main drag that led into the front gate. She slowed, let the security guard see the sticker on the bumper just under the headlights, and then sped up as the guard saluted.

She drove toward flight operations and then turned, putting her car into the lot reserved for those on overnight flights. The security police watched it more closely than the other lots on the base because everyone knew the owners were gone for an extended time.

Leaving her gear in the car, she got out and headed toward the hangar, walking up the stairs to the offices on the second floor. Offices for maintenance and squadron operations and plans and intelligence. Everyone wanted intelligence close so that the officers would be handy for last-minute briefings.

Marie walked along, glancing into offices that were dark. The maintenance area was alive with activity. Aircraft were scheduled in and out all day and all night, so maintenance was an around-the-clock function.

The door to the outer office of the intelligence shop was open. The backdoor was closed and locked. The office was empty, but someone had left a cup of hot coffee. Marie sat down behind the desk and looked at the news magazine sitting there.

She had to laugh about that. She'd once heard a lieutenant colonel chewing out one of the intelligence captains for reading a magazine. The man sat quietly, listening, and when the colonel finished, the captain said, "This is my job. I evaluate all sorts of sources in an attempt to stay current." The colonel had then slipped away.

"Can I help you?"

Marie looked up and saw a young lieutenant standing in the doorway. He looked as if he had completed college sometime the week before. His uniform didn't seem to fit him quite right.

"I wondered if there was anything new on the Saudi situation?"

The lieutenant entered the office. He held a pack of papers in his hand, the top sheet a pink cover for classified information. Sitting down in the visitors' chair, he started flipping through the documents. "Let's see what we've got from the message center." He scanned the papers and then pulled a sheet from the stack. "Got a CIA assessment of the current situation."

Marie took it and noticed that it was classified secret. She flipped through the preliminaries, which addressed the procedure for selecting the new king, and read the material on the situation in Saudi Arabia. When she finished, she glanced up at the young lieutenant.

"The CIA doesn't seem to be very concerned. I heard on the news that the situation is volatile."

The lieutenant leaned back in his chair. "You know how the news media is. Everything is a crisis. Everything is a disaster. But according to my definition, a crisis is a decisive point or a climax. It can't be drawn out over six months or a year."

"I'm not interested in semantics, Lieutenant."

"Sorry. I think, given the message traffic, that it is

business as usual in Saudi Arabia. They had—what?—a caretaker force in place until they get their new king elected or appointed or whatever. I guess it's kind of like the period between the election and the inauguration of a new president here.''

Marie nodded and looked at the cover of the news magazine. ''I understand there have been some demonstrations.''

''I'm not sure how much importance to put on those public displays. You know, when the Iranians took our embassy staff hostage, there were Arabs in the street chanting, 'Down with the IRS.' Some reporter put them up to it.''

Marie laughed. ''It's too early in the day to hear things like that.''

The lieutenant scanned the papers again. ''I haven't seen anything to suggest that Americans will be in danger in Saudi Arabia. It should be a quiet, normal transition.''

''That your official opinion?''

''Yes, ma'am. It's based on everything I've seen in the last few weeks, since their king took ill and then died. Stability is the watchword in Saudi Arabia.''

''Then I don't have to worry about landing my airplane there later today.''

''No, ma'am, I wouldn't think so. As I say, I've been watching that situation, along with what is going on in the whole of the Middle East. As long as you stay away from Iran and Iraq, you shouldn't have any problems.''

Marie couldn't contain her curiosity. ''What's happening there?''

''Nothing new from that area,'' said the lieutenant.''Standard hate-the-Americans syndrome. We think there's some Soviet agitation behind it, but very low key.''

''Has the Soviet presence in there increased significantly over the last few months?''

''Nope. They've shipped in some equipment and technicians, as they always do, but it hasn't been significant. Besides, we've seen no combat troops going in, though I suspect some of the advisers could function in a combat role. That's they way they do it.''

Marie nodded again. "Then I can assume that Saudi Arabia, even with the death of the king, will be safe."

"Sure," said the lieutenant. "No reason to suspect anything else."

Marie stood up. "Well, then, I guess I'll walk down to operations and see what's happening there."

"Yes, ma'am." The lieutenant stood and tried to think of something witty to say. He'd already spotted the wedding ring on her finger, but wasn't that concerned about it. He knew that some of the officers wore wedding rings to keep the men away from them.

But Marie Frankowski walked out the door without the lieutenant ever thinking of anything to say. She disappeared around the corner and kept on going until she reached the flight planning room where the navigators hung out. There was a Coke machine, a refrigerator, and shelves holding maps and charts of the entire world. Everything the navigator needed to do his job.

"Morning, Marie," said one of the two people working in there.

"Morning, Liz. You the nav on this one?"

"Looks like. Davidson is sick, so I'll be filling in for him. How come you're here so early?"

"I wanted a chance to check the intelligence reports before takeoff."

"Anything interesting?"

"Nope. Looks like everything is going to be smooth as silk," she said.

PANAMA

The helicopter had landed in Cartagena first. It had seemed like a long flight over jungle, open fields, and finally over a small corner of the Caribbean as they made the approach into the airfield. They had gotten clear of the PZ, stayed low, using the trees for cover, and once they were a couple of miles away, had climbed to five thousand feet.

Martinez pushed himself up off the deck and looked at Chavez. "Everyone out?"

"With us, yes. I haven't heard about the second half of the team."

"Find out."

"Yes, sir."

Martinez sat up and pulled the magazine from his weapon. He looked down into it and pushed it into his pouch. He thought about reloading, but they were airborne, heading out of the jungle; no reason to load his weapon now. He ejected the live round from the chamber, watched it bounce across the deck and then out the open cargo compartment door.

Chavez crouched next to him and yelled over the sound of the engine and rotors. "Pickup has been made. Everyone's out and heading to Cartagena."

For the first time since they had jumped out of the C-130, Martinez relaxed. They were clear of the jungle, the enemy was left behind, and if the pilots didn't screw up, they'd be back in time for a big steak dinner. Nothing to worry about.

And then he thought about the Cubans. He thought about them searching for his team just as if they were in enemy territory. They hadn't been just wandering around: the Cubans were looking for them with an eye to kill them, just as the Viet Cong had searched for American soldiers in Vietnam. That would be for the intelligence officers to worry about. Once the debriefing was over, his concern with the mission would be over.

He leaned back against the gray soundproofing and closed his eyes. Slowly he realized that his whole body ached. A result of the long run through the jungle with an armed enemy in pursuit. Although he had been in good shape prior to the jump into Colombia, Martinez realized that he had pushed himself to the limit of his abilities.

Chavez leaned close. "That was a mile closer than I care for it to get."

Martinez didn't open his eyes. He grinned. "But it's always good when you win."

"We cut and run," said Chavez.

"And rightly so," said Martinez. "We were outnumbered, outgunned, and out of ideas."

Now Chavez laughed. "There are those who would believe that we need to die in the middle of an unwinnable fight to prove our bravery."

"Would those be the paper pushers in Washington whose greatest accomplishment is getting to work each morning? Would they be the men and women who have never tasted real combat or real bone-crushing fear, whose solution is to send in combat troops?"

"The very same."

"Then fuck 'em."

"Yes, sir."

Martinez fell silent, letting his mind roam. Now he didn't have to concentrate. His life was in the hands of a pilot who was as good at his job as Martinez was at his. The pilot would get them safely to Cartagena and that was all that Martinez cared about.

They had landed at Cartagena and had been hustled across the sun-hot tarmac into the operations building. They had wanted to shower, shave, and find clean clothes, but that had been impossible. Rumor had it that a C-130 was coming for them from Howard and the ETA was any moment.

A sergeant brought them Cokes, bought from a collection taken up by the people working in operations because none of Martinez's men had money. No one jumped into a combat environment carrying money.

They had been kept waiting, with the promise that the airplane would be there any minute. They'd sat around the operations building, a clerk watching them, afraid they'd damage the cheap furniture. They drank their Cokes and then demanded something to eat. Banse and Ortega stretched out on the floor and tried to sleep.

Food was brought from the mess hall. It wasn't very good, but it was hot and kept them happy for a few minutes. When they finished eating, Martinez demanded to know when the plane would be arriving. He was told that it would be any minute. They would have to stay close.

The delay became longer, with the messages to them coming faster. Martinez knew what was happening. The pilots didn't want to have to wait around once they were on the ground. They had ordered Martinez and his men to remain close so there would be no delay on the ground. No one cared that they had just come out of the jungle. It'd be too bad if the air-force people were inconvenienced.

But the aircraft finally arrived and they were rushed out. They had climbed into the rear, strapped themselves into the uncomfortable troop seats and waited while the aircraft turned, taxied, and then prepared for takeoff.

Martinez was only mildly irritated. He'd been given a mission to fight drug runners. He'd attacked a Cuban camp, been ambushed and then chased through the jungle. They had killed people, nearly been killed themselves, and then had to sit around waiting for the aircraft to take them to Panama so that someone else wouldn't be inconvenienced. No one seemed to give a fuck about them. S.O.P.

They took off moments later, and almost as soon as they became airborne he fell asleep, waking only when the loadmaster was shaking him, telling him they'd be landing shortly.

And then they had been on the ground at Howard Air Force Base, right back into the heat and humidity of the tropics. It was quite a contrast to the air-conditioning of the operations building and the comfort of the C-130 at altitude. Sunlight that seemed brighter than normal reflected from everything, making it hard to see. Holding a hand over his eyes, Martinez dropped to the concrete. A blue crew van left the operations building, heading toward them.

"Looks like we're going to get a ride."

Chavez shrugged. "I don't think I like that. Every time we get some kind of little courtesy, someone has a rotten deal coming up for us."

"You're just naturally pessimistic."

"No, sir. Realistic. I've been in this here US of A Army for a long time and they just don't go out of their way to take care of the troops unless they're about to fuck with them."

The van pulled close and the driver leaned out the window. "Either of you Captain Martinez?"

"I'm Martinez."

"Yes, sir. I'm to take you to headquarters. If you'll hop in, sir."

"What about the rest of the team?"

"They'll be taken care of."

"Sure. Sergeant Chavez, find Lieutenant Alvarez and have him keep the team together. I'm sure someone will appear for the debriefing. Can't believe they'll let that go. I'll get there as quickly as I can."

"Yes, sir. Shall I hold dinner for you?"

"Nope. I'll get there when I can, but if you get a break to go eat, take it. Leave word for me."

"Yes, sir."

Martinez shouldered his gear and started around the front of the van and then stopped. He returned to Chavez and handed him his rifle. "You take care of my gear?" He reached up, touched his side where his pistol was tucked away, and decided to keep it right where it was.

"Yes, sir. Happy to."

For a moment Martinez stared at the sergeant. Quietly, he said, "And see that the documents get into the proper hands just as quickly as you can."

"Yes, sir. No problem."

Martinez then moved to the passenger's side of the van and climbed in. "Lead on, James."

The driver nodded and drove back toward the operations building and then around the side of it. They hit one of the main streets, waited for a break in the afternoon traffic, and then entered it.

Martinez knew not to ask the driver what was going on. He wouldn't have any idea. All he'd know was that he was supposed to pick up an officer and drive him to the headquarters. Martinez would just have to wait.

A few moments later they pulled up next to one of the entrances to the headquarters. Martinez glanced at the driver. "Do you wait?"

"No, sir. I'm heading back to operations now."

"Well, thanks for the lift."

"Yes, sir."

Martinez, suddenly aware that he was in a dirty, ragged uniform, walked up the steps to the headquarters. He entered and found a man in a starched uniform waiting for him.

"You Martinez?"

"Yeah."

"Come with me." The man turned and started down the hallway. As they approached a solid, wooden door the soldier said, "You should have cleaned up."

"Right," said Martinez. "I'm in the jungle and then met at the airfield as the aircraft lands. I'm brought directly here. Now, when should I have cleaned up?"

"General isn't going to like this."

"Then fuck him. I haven't had the chance. Now, you want me to go take a shower and find a clean uniform, I'll be back in thirty, forty minutes."

"No, the general is waiting." The man grabbed the doorknob.

They entered a new section of the headquarters, one with carpeting on the floor and six-panel doors. The walls looked to have been recently painted and were hung with color photos of the men and women in the chain of command, each with a small brass plaque under it. The air-conditioning, noticeable as Martinez entered the building, had been turned to full blast. It was like walking into a freezer.

"It's cold enough," said Martinez.

"You get used to it."

"Used to it," Martinez repeated. He remembered a dozen conservation messages that said to set your air-conditioning no more than ten degrees below the outside temperature. That conserved fuel and resources and prevented illness. Of course, if the general wanted to live in a refrigerator, that was his business.

They came to a large, wooden, double door. The man opened it and let Martinez enter first. The general's aide sat behind one huge desk and his secretary sat behind the other. The secretary was a young woman who wore a sweater to keep warm. Martinez decided that he wouldn't be surprised to find a small space heater under her desk for her feet. Waste all over the place.

"This is Captain Martinez," said the man.

The aide stood up and examined Martinez. "The general is not going to be happy. You should have cleaned up."

"Major," said Martinez, "I was in the jungle a few hours ago. I was on an airplane flying here twenty minutes ago. I came directly here. You want me to go change, I'll be more than happy to do so."

"No, the general is waiting."

"Right," said Martinez. "I'm just getting a little tired of everyone commenting on the condition of my clothing. No one seems to give a shit about my health."

"You wait," said the major, ignoring the comments. "Don't sit down anywhere."

"Oh no," said Martinez. "I certainly wouldn't want to get anything dirty."

The major ignored the sarcasm and knocked on the general's door. There was a quiet reply and the major opened the door. "You may go in."

Martinez entered the office, a huge room with a huge desk, a library, and what looked like a conference area. The general sat behind his desk wearing an immaculate uniform complete with all his awards and decorations. It was quite a stack and included a few for combat heroism.

Martinez stepped briskly to the desk and then was lost. Military customs and courtesies dictated that he report to the general in a proper, military fashion. But line units often ignored what they considered training command procedures. The Special Forces rarely followed such customs and courtesies, but then, the Special Forces rarely approached flag officers who were not Special Forces qualified themselves.

Deciding that a little grease never hurt the wheels of the military machine, Martinez saluted and said, "General, Captain Francisco Martinez, U.S. Army Special Forces, reporting as ordered."

The general dropped the pen he was holding and returned the salute. He grinned and said, "It's nice to see that you Special Forces troopers can act like soldiers. Too bad you can't dress like them."

"I'm fresh from the field, General," said Martinez, feeling like a broken record. "I was ordered here immediately with no chance to even shower."

"Oh hell, man, don't worry about it. We soldiers know that sometimes the book is thrown out. Have a seat and tell me how things went in Colombia."

Martinez stepped to the rear and sat down in one of the high-backed leather chairs. He felt the comforting press of his concealed weapon against his flesh. He nodded at the general and said, "Until I'm fully debriefed, I'm afraid that I can't answer that question."

"Then let me hand a little bit of information to you,

just so you can decide if it's important. We've gotten un-confirmed reports that Fidel Castro is in deep trouble with his Communist brothers in Moscow. Intelligence has it that a coup of some kind is planned.''

''What?''

''We don't know much more. Only that it appears that Castro is on the way out. There'll probably be a scramble to fill the vacuum created by that.''

''Jesus H. Christ in a go cart.''

''Oh, that little tidbit is classified.'' The general laughed. ''I know what you're thinking. Our classifying that news isn't going to do much because it'll eventually come out. Right now we're protecting our sources, not to mention trying to get confirmation of it.''

''Yes, sir.''

''Now here's the bad news. You and your team are required to prepare to deploy.''

''Am I to assume a connection?''

The general picked up his pencil and examined it. ''I would say that making assumptions about military opera-tions is often a mistake, but given what we know, I would say yes, there is a connection.''

''How soon?''

''Transport is sitting on the ramp waiting for you and your team.''

''Jesus.'' Martinez rubbed a hand over his face and felt the accumulation of dirt and the growth of his beard. ''I'd like time to clean up and to get some decent food. They're probably going to have us back in the field in only a few hours if they have an aircraft waiting for us.''

''How much time?'' asked the general.

''Three hours,'' said Martinez. ''We'd need that for equipment checks.''

''You can draw fresh equipment here.''

''And then we'd have to zero the weapons. We'd have to check out the radios, probably change the crystals in them. Fresh equipment isn't the answer.''

''How long to get everything ready?''

''A good eight hours, if we don't stop to eat, piss, or shit,'' said Martinez.

"I can live with that."

"Why us?" Martinez asked.

The general looked at him. "The majority of your team is Hispanic and everyone on it speaks fluent Spanish. You can blend into the background easily. Hell, man, that's what you've trained for. I think you can figure that out for yourself."

"The eight hours?"

"I can't see where that's going to be a problem. Get yourself cleaned up, buy a steak, and drink a beer. I'll schedule the flight for nineteen hundred."

Martinez stood. "Thank you, General. Oh, I'm going to need transport."

"Tell my aide."

Martinez saluted. "Yes, sir." He turned and walked out of the office, closing the door behind him. To the major, he said, "You're supposed to find me some transport so that I can re-join my team."

"You'll have to wait," said the major.

"I think the general meant for me to have the transport right away."

The major stared at Martinez for a moment and, when the Special Forces officer didn't back down, said, "I'll have a hummer and a driver out there for you in ten minutes or less."

"Thanks." Martinez spun and walked out the door. No one escorted him out. No one seemed to care that he was roaming the halls. He headed for the front door and stood there, watching the traffic on the street. When a hummer dived out of the traffic, Martinez hurried out and climbed in the passenger's seat.

"Where to?" asked the driver, an army corporal.

Martinez wiped a hand over his face. He told the driver where he wanted to go and then sat back. Suddenly the luxury that he'd felt, the sudden lack of pressure, evaporated. He felt like he did when he was first entering isolation to plan a mission. He found himself tensing up. He had to think about relaxing.

But found that he couldn't. He knew what the planners in the Pentagon were thinking. If Castro was in trouble with the big boys in Moscow, now might be the time to get rid of him. His team would be dropped in there with the idea they could shoot Castro and no one outside of Cuba would care. That had to be it.

The thought of it filled him with excitement. No, not excitement. Dread. No one had been able to get close to Castro in forty years. People had tried and people had died. Castro was too well guarded. But that didn't stop the men at the top from trying to get it done.

He forced the speculation from his mind. At the moment he didn't need to think about it. He needed to stay calm and relax. After the time in the field, he needed the decompression.

The hummer pulled up near a compound surrounded by chain-link. Martinez pushed open the door and said, "Thanks for the lift."

"Yes, sir."

Martinez climbed out, approached the guard at the gate, flashed his ID, and waited as the man checked the access roster. Satisfied, he let him in.

"I believe your men are in Building T-234. To the right."

"Thanks." He entered the compound and headed toward the building. Since he was inside a guarded compound with a restricted access, there were no more checkpoints. He entered the building, saw a man sitting behind a table, looking more like a receptionist than a guard.

Before he could say a word, the man pointed and said, "You want to go to conference room six. Down that hall."

Martinez walked down the corridor. It was markedly different than the one in the headquarters. The air conditioner wasn't working as well, the floor was tiled, and the cinder-block walls needed a new coat of paint.

He found the conference room and hesitated outside. The information he had wasn't something he wanted to share with the men. They weren't going to like it. Finally, he opened the door. The room was dominated by a large, oval-shaped table. His men sat around it, along with the debriefers, an intelligence officer, and one man to record everything said.

"Captain Martinez," said one of the debriefers. "Glad you could make it."

"I hope you've covered the high points," said Martinez, "because the session is over."

"No, sir. We have plenty of work to do here. The session must continue. Especially once we get the translations of the documents your men brought."

"You don't seem to understand. It is over now. Sergeant Chavez, get the men out of here. We'll get back to our quarters, get cleaned up, and then we're going to dinner."

"Yes, sir."

"Captain, you don't seem to understand. We have a job to do," said the debriefer. "An important job."

"I understand that, but the situation has suddenly changed." He stopped and thought for a moment. "You can continue this, on the aircraft, after nineteen hundred hours."

"I'll have to check."

"That's your problem." Martinez watched as the men pushed back their chairs and got to their feet. They collected their gear and left the conference room. When they were all outside, Martinez turned to go.

"Full combat gear?" asked Chavez.

"Yes, though we should have a chance to restock our supplies before we hit the field."

"Yes, sir. Don't they have another team?"

That stumped Martinez for a moment. It was the thought that had been bouncing around in the back of his mind. "Maybe the rest of the teams with our attributes are in the field. We're the only ones available."

"Funny how that works," said Chavez.

"Just a minute, Captain," said the debriefer. "What in the hell happened here?"

"Damned if I know," said Martinez. "All I can say is that we're going to be on an airplane at nineteen hundred, flying off to the north." He didn't mention what he'd heard from the general, though it was in the back of his mind, circling there like a vulture waiting for something to die.

"I'll be there, too."

"Sure," said Martinez. He left the conference room without another word.

EAST CHINA SEA

For the first few hours Reisman had thought he was going to be sick. The small boat rocked constantly, the deck falling away as they dropped into the troughs. Then, just as suddenly, the deck leaped up, threatening to buckle his knees as he stood at the rail, looking down into the swirling depths of the ocean. He waited to throw up but couldn't.

MacKenzie had stayed with him for a few moments and then decided that he didn't want to stand out in the chill morning air. He walked up to the wheelhouse, entered it, and stood back out of the way.

After a while Reisman decided that he wasn't going to be sick. He was used to the constant motion of the boat. The sweat that had beaded on his forehead and dripped down his sides evaporated, and he felt better. He moved around the crowded deck, looking at the boxes that were stored there. He sat down among them, letting them protect him from the breeze blowing across the deck. He braced his elbows on his knees and let his head droop.

MacKenzie approached him a few minutes later. He stood leaning against a couple of the boxes, a cigarette in his hand. "You look horrible.".

"Thanks. Never been on a tiny boat out in the middle of the ocean before."

"It was your idea. You didn't have to come along."

"I wanted to see the whole operation."

"There won't be much to see," said MacKenzie. "You'll have to wait here, on the boat, as the boxes are moved to the beach."

Reisman was about to protest and then realized that he wasn't up to riding in a rowboat as it crashed through the surf. He wished they would turn around and head back to Japan.

MacKenzie was paying no attention to him. He was smoking, his eyes fixed to the mast behind the wheelhouse. He spoke almost as if he was lecturing a college class. "You'll be able to watch everything from the deck here. We'll be standing a klick or two from the shore."

Reisman nodded dumbly. He could smell the cigarette smoke and it was adding to the turmoil in his stomach. He wanted to tell MacKenzie to get rid of it but was sure that MacKenzie would just move closer and blow smoke in his face.

"Everything will be visible."

"How long?"

MacKenzie shrugged. "Hours yet. It's not just a hop across the ocean and this isn't a jet."

"Great." Reisman dropped his head as his stomach turned over and the sweat popped out on his forehead again.

MacKenzie turned and flipped his cigarette over the railing. He blew out the smoke and straightened. "Breakfast is in a few minutes."

"If I'm not there, start without me."

"Sure."

By noon, Reisman was feeling much better. He was walking around the deck, watching the men go through the motions of fishing, casting out the nets, dragging them, and then hauling them back onto the boat. As the nets came out of the water they raced ahead, toward the coast of China.

The sky was a cloudless, deep blue. Sunlight reflecting from the water made it next to impossible to see. Reisman was looking back over the stern, watching the boiling of the water in their wake, when MacKenzie suddenly appeared, his face looking white. He swiped at the sweat and yelled, "You've got to get out of the open."

"What?"

He pointed northeast. "We've got something spotted on radar."

"Radar," said Reisman, surprised that the old fishing boat would be equipped with radar. Looking up at the mast, he saw the small antenna rotating rapidly.

"Something's coming at us. We've got to get out of the open."

"What's the problem?" said Reisman. "We're still in international waters."

"Don't be stupid," said MacKenzie. "We're out here all alone. You think the Chinese are going to worry about us in international waters. Especially with what we've got stacked on the deck."

Reisman understood then. The Chinese would sink the fishing boat, and that would be the end of it. The Japanese, who were fully aware of the cargo, would pretend that no distress signals had been sent. And the Chinese, aware of the ramifications of destroying an unarmed fishing boat, would pretend it had never entered the East China Sea.

"What are we going to do?" Reisman asked.

"We're going to try to get the hell out of here."

It was then that Reisman noticed the Japanese crew swarming over the vessel. They were hauling in the last of the lines. They cut one net free, letting it sink. As soon as that was done the boat began a quick turn to the starboard.

Two of the Japanese grabbed one of the cardboard boxes and tossed it over the side. It hit with a small splash and floated for a moment.

"Hey!" MacKenzie yelled as they seized another box. "Hold it."

The men looked at him but didn't stop. They threw the box into the sea. MacKenzie moved closer and reached out to stop them. In Japanese, he told them that it wasn't necessary to throw the boxes over yet. That they could get rid of them if the patrol boat got closer.

Reisman watched this exchange and walked around to the other side of the boat. He scanned the horizon, searching for the oncoming vessel. He couldn't see a thing.

MacKenzie joined him and pointed. "It should be over there. Probably just below the horizon."

"How do you know that it's Chinese? Might be another fishing vessel."

"It's coming at us," said MacKenzie. "That means it's hostile."

A moment later one of the men called out, pointing. Reisman moved to his right and saw the prow of a ship burst over the horizon.

"Looks like a gunboat," said MacKenzie. "Coming right at us."

"Closing," said Reisman.

The Japanese sailors moved back to the boxes and lifted one of them up. MacKenzie held up a hand to stop them. "Wait a moment."

"You wait and it won't do any good to throw them over," said Reisman. "The Chinese will be able to retrieve them."

MacKenzie kept his eyes on the gunboat, trying to identify it. There was still no evidence that it was Chinese or that it was hostile, other than the fact it was running straight at them.

"Could be North Korean," said MacKenzie.

"Too far south," said Reisman. He didn't know that. He just believed it.

MacKenzie stood on the deck, his hands gripping the rail. He glanced up, toward the wheelhouse, but there was nothing to see in there. And there was no indication that they were slowing. The boat's captain was making a run for it.

Then, suddenly, a fountain of water erupted fifty yards

to the starboard. A moment later the boom of a cannon drifted to them.

"They're firing at us," said Reisman.

"No big thing," said MacKenzie. "They want us to stop."

But their speed didn't slacken. The engines roared as the captain tried to get the last few knots from them. The boat smashed into the waves, the bow knifing down and then popping up, throwing seawater everywhere.

Now the Japanese began throwing the boxes overboard again. Four of them were working at it. Two lifting and handing the cartons to the men near the railing, who tossed them over. A fifth man stood with a shark rifle, pumping rounds into the boxes, trying to sink them.

The gunboat was getting closer. Reisman could see it easily. It seemed to dominate the sea around it. The cannon on the bow fired again. Reisman saw the smoke roll from the barrel. Water splashed again and the boom finally reached them.

"We're going to have to stop," said Reisman.

"You want to spend a couple of years in a Chinese prison?" MacKenzie asked.

"They can't take us prisoner," said Reisman, knowing that the side with the guns could do whatever it wanted. North Koreans had boarded an American naval vessel in 1968 and held the sailors for eleven months. International law meant nothing to the terrorists.

The water on the starboard side of the boat erupted into a dozen fountains. The splashes walked toward it, hit the wood, and splintered it.

"Machine gun," said MacKenzie, diving to the side.

Reisman crouched, one hand on the rail. But he wanted to see what was happening. "They can't kill us," he said, more to himself than to anyone else.

The Japanese had finished dumping the cargo over the side. Half of the cartons bobbed in the water. Several of them were taking on water, the cardboard discolored. They were sinking faster than Reisman would have expected.

"Another fifteen minutes and we'll be able to stop," said MacKenzie.

From the north came the roar of jet engines. A fighter

flashed overhead, began a steep climb, and then turned back.

"Japanese?" asked Reisman.

"No. It was Soviet-made."

Reisman felt the disappointment overwhelm him. He thought that the jet was coming to their rescue. Now it looked as if it was just a Chinese MiG.

But the plane wheeled around and dived at the gunboat, roaring over it at fifty feet. As it passed by it began another steep climb.

"Markings are Chinese?" Reisman asked.

"Didn't look like it." MacKenzie was now on his feet, watching.

The jet whirled again and dived again. This time the water near the gunboat erupted. The splashes seemed to run toward it, jumped out of the water, and flashed over the deck, tearing it up. The machine guns on the boat opened fire, their tracers lancing upward at the fighter.

"What the hell?" said Reisman. He was standing upright, a hand shading his eyes. "Who the hell is that?"

The gunboat turned suddenly, heading back toward China. But the fighter wasn't content to let it go. It dived again, the machine guns firing down, the water around the boat boiling.

"That an Su-27?" Reisman asked.

"Hell, I don't know," said MacKenzie.

"He Russian?"

"Yeah. I think so."

The rear of the Chinese boat burst into flames, but the fire was short-lived. A rocket lifted off, aimed at the jet. The aircraft pulled up suddenly and then turned into the missile, as if the pilot wanted to ram it. The missile tried to follow the abrupt maneuver, but failed. The IR lock was broken and the missile turned toward the hottest, brightest thing it could find. The sun.

"Missed!" MacKenzie shouted. "They fucking missed."

The jet retaliated. Two missiles flashed from under the wings. Fire pushed them down and an instant later they exploded, both short of the boat. Now all the machine guns of the vessel were turned upward, filling the sky with tracers. The pilot didn't seem to care. He continued to dive, firing back at the boat. His rounds were tearing at the deck, wheelhouse, and the engine compartment. Fire broke out, the black smoke climbing upward.

Then, in an instant, the aircraft was gone. There was a shattering explosion in a violent cloud of flame and smoke. Parts rained down, slamming into the water.

"Jesus," MacKenzie yelled. "Jesus."

For a moment it was quiet on the sea. The Chinese had stopped firing. The engines of the gunboat were too far off to be heard.

A second plane appeared a moment later. It came in low, only a few feet above the water. This one was armed with a Gatling gun and sounded like a slow buzz saw just warming up. But soon that roar overpowered everything else as thousands of rounds poured from the weapon and whipped the water around the gunboat into a seething froth. It looked as if the sea had been put into a blender turned on high. Water exploded upward, hiding the enemy boat. A fine mist, with sunlight reflecting through it, masked the end of the Chinese vessel. Then there was a loud, flat detonation. A bright orange-yellow fireball, tinged in black, boiled upward. Debris filled the air.

"Oh yeah!" MacKenzie screamed.

The Japanese sailors were cheering, dancing, clapping each other on the back.

The jet circled the smoking ruin of the Chinese gunboat for a moment and then turned. It flew toward the Japanese boat, circled, wiggled its wings, and then took off, back toward the north.

Reisman moved to the stern and watched the jet disappear. As MacKenzie approached he said, "I think it was Russian."

"So," said MacKenzie.

"Don't you think it's a little odd that a Soviet fighter would stray this far south, attack a Chinese gunboat, and then take off?"

"I'm glad he did."

"That's not the point. Why would he do it? No reason for it."

"Maybe he was protecting innocent fishing boats on the high seas."

"Except that we weren't innocent. We were attempting to smuggle goods into China. I don't like this."

"Well," said MacKenzie. "I fucking love it."

EN ROUTE RIYADH, SAUDI ARABIA

Marie Frankowski sat in the copilot's seat of the C-141 Starlifter and wished that they were on the ground. It had been a long flight from the United States, and although she hadn't had to sit there strapped in the whole way, she was getting tired of being in the cockpit of the aircraft. When she was flying, she was aware of the confined spaces of an aircraft.

The aircraft commander, Richard Hansen, had done most of the flying. He'd made the takeoffs and landings and had set the autopilot to suit himself. He'd left the task of dealing with the various towers, ground controllers, and flight service agents to Marie. She preferred flying to talking, but Hansen was a new AC and afraid of making a mistake. Frankowski, as one of the senior pilots, had been given the task of flying with him to keep him out of trouble.

She took a deep breath and asked, "You going to make the approach into Riyadh?"

"I think I'll let you handle this one," he said.

"Well, thanks. We're what now, thirty minutes out?"

The navigator, Captain Elizabeth Shawn, leaned forward and said, "Twenty minutes is closer."

"Thank you," said Marie. She reached forward, touched the controls, feeling them move in her hands as the automatic pilot made slight course and altitude corrections. "I'm going off autopilot."

"Go ahead," said Hansen.

Marie adjusted herself in the seat and then flipped off the autopilot. The controls suddenly felt solid in her hands. She searched the sky outside the aircraft but couldn't see any other traffic. She turned her attention to the instruments, looking for a sign that the engines were still operating properly. All the gauges were in the green. The airspeed was steady and the altimeter was pegged.

"Need to come right three degrees," said Shawn.

"Three degrees," echoed Marie. She thought about the correction, moving her hand ever so slightly. Before she felt the big jet begin to move, she tried to level out. The correction was so small that it was impossible to let the instruments catch up to show it. There was a lag time in them. She had to guess, but when she glanced at the compass, she saw that the three-degree correction was in. "You going to make the radio calls?" she asked.

Hansen, a tall, thin man, was sitting with a foot propped up. He shrugged. "If you want."

"I'd appreciate it. I'm tired of trying to make myself understood to most of the Third World. I'd love to have someone else try to decipher them."

"Fine," he said.

"We're getting closer," said Shawn.

"I know," said Hansen.

"Just thought you'd want to alert them," she said.

"Okay." Hansen sat up straight and reached over for the radio control.

To Shawn, Marie said, "I'll be glad to get on the ground. I'm looking forward to relaxing for a few moments. I'm looking forward to not having to listen to the rumble of jet engines."

"I sometimes wonder about your attitude," said Shawn. "Shouldn't a pilot be excited about flying."

"You're thinking of the barnstorming days when a pilot was sitting in the open air and the autopilot didn't do a better job of flying. I mean, sitting in this seat for ten or twelve hours isn't the same as flying a fighter at treetop level."

"You're not instilling confidence in me," said Shawn.

"Oh hell, I can land an airplane."

"Yes. Well, we'll see," said Shawn.

"We need to come around to fifteen degrees," said Hansen, "and begin the letdown."

Again Marie scanned the instruments and made a few adjustments. She watched the compass swing with the turn. The altimeter began to unwind, and the rate of climb slipped to minus five hundred feet a minute. Everything was smooth and easy.

"There's no other traffic in the vicinity," said Hansen.

"Well, that's something," said Marie. "Now, if the Iranians don't go crazy and try to shoot us down . . ."

"We're four hundred miles from Iran," said Shawn.

"I know that, but there's always the chance that an Iranian suicide squad has taken up a position around the airport with an SA-14 to shoot down an American airplane. Or maybe the Iraqis will try. They don't like us either."

"You hear something during the intel briefing?" asked Hansen.

"No. I'm just saying that the Arabs are all crazy."

"Thanks for the in-depth analysis of the national psyche of the Iranians and Iraqis."

"Glad to be of assistance."

Hansen mumbled into his microphone again and then said, "We're cleared in number two behind a 747. Winds are light and variable."

"Roger that," said Marie.

"Who's buying the dinner tonight?" Shawn asked.

"I think Hansen," said Marie. "He's the aircraft commander and it's his responsibility to make sure that the crew is properly fed and housed.''

"Right," said Shawn. "I'd forgotten about that."

"A drink," said Hansen. "I'll buy everyone a drink, but I can't afford to buy dinner for everyone."

"The hell," said Shawn. "It's only fair."

They fell silent as they worked to get the aircraft on the ground. Marie had the airport in sight and finally spotted the 747 three or four miles in front of them. There was some military traffic. A couple of jet fighters taking off, but they were headed in the other direction.

"What's that?" Hansen said suddenly. He was pointing to a point to the north of the airfield.

"Low-flying aircraft," said Marie.

"Helicopters," said Hansen. "Flight of ten, eleven, twelve of them. I don't recognize them."

"Look like Hinds," said Marie. "Shouldn't be Hinds, though. Saudis don't have any Hinds." She pulled her attention away from the helicopters and looked back at the airfield. The 747 had crossed the threshold and touched down.

"We're cleared to land," said Hansen. "Take the third taxiway."

"Understood."

They were now close to the ground, lined up on the runway with the wheels down and locked. The flaps were down and the airspeed was bleeding off. Now Marie was concentrating on the controls, on the instruments, on the approaching runway. She was holding off the landing as they crossed the overrun area and then let the aircraft settle to the thick concrete, trying to grease it in so that no one would know when they were on the ground.

The instant they touched down, Marie stepped on the brakes and Hansen hit the thrust reversers. Energy that had been directed at keeping them in the air was suddenly channeled into slowing them down. The forces on the body changed as the aircraft decelerated radically.

They reached the taxiway and turned onto it, now traveling slowly. They saw the terminal in front of them. Not a military terminal on a military base, but an international terminal announcing to the travelers that they had landed in Riyadh, Saudi Arabia.

As they rolled to a stop, directed into a parking place by a man holding colored paddles in his hands, one of the helicopters they had seen flashed overhead. The dying noise of the engines couldn't suppress the sounds of the Hind turbine or the popping of the massive rotor blades.

"Jesus," said Hansen. "That asshole shouldn't be over-flying us that way." He twisted around in the seat, trying to look up into the sky. "Anybody get that asshole's tail number?"

Then, as they began to turn off the radios and other electronics, someone screamed over the air. It sounded as if there was a burst of machine-gun fire behind the voice. A single short burst that was cut off quickly.

"What the hell?"

There was a rumbling from outside punctuated by a series of crashes. Hansen threw off his seat belt and shoulder harness and forced himself out of his seat. "What in the hell?"

The loadmaster stuck his head in, looking up at the flight deck. "Something's happening out there."

"What?"

"Hell, sir, I don't know. Looks like the guys in the helicopters are attacking the airfield."

"Don't be stupid," said Hansen.

Marie sat in the seat, her eyes on the control tower above the terminal. She could barely see it from where she was. Something or someone flashed by the glass and then one of the windows shattered. Glass exploded outward, showering down and twinkling in the setting sun.

"Jesus," she said. "We got any weapons?"

"Negative," said Hansen. "We're not authorized weapons."

"I've a pistol," said the flight engineer.

"Good Christ, Williams. What the fuck do you have that for? We don't need weapons here."

"Just in case, sir."

Marie twisted around in the seat. "Get it and bring it up here."

"Yes, ma'am."

Now the air was filled with the sounds of fighting. Bursts of machine-gun fire. Detonations from grenades. Hind helicopters had positioned themselves at the end of the runways facing in, toward the terminal, as if daring any of the aircraft there to take off. Others hovered overhead like eagles, waiting for prey to show itself.

"We've got to get out of here," said Hansen.

"I think we'd better sit tight," said Marie. "We're safer sitting here than trying to get out."

Hansen turned and looked out the windshield. He stepped across the flight deck and knelt down as Williams returned with the pistol. Hansen held out a hand and said, "Give that weapon to me."

"Sir?"

"Let me have that weapon."

Williams hesitated. "Do you know how to use it?"

"I've qualified with the pistol every year just like the rest of you."

"Yes, sir." Williams ran a hand through his short, gray hair. "You ever been in combat, Major?"

"That has nothing to do with it."

"Has everything to do with it, sir. How do you know you could pull the trigger when facing another man? You don't get time to think about it. You just have to open fire or you get dead yourself."

"Give me the goddamned weapon," Hansen shouted.

There was a burst of fire. Machine-gun bullets slammed into the side of the aircraft and punched through the thin skin with audible snaps.

"Jesus, they're shooting at us." Hansen dived off the flight deck, sprawling on the deck of the cargo compartment.

"Let's get the fuck out of here," Shawn yelled. "I mean right now."

Marie felt sweat bead on her forehead and drip down her sides. They'd shut the engines down. They were low on fuel and now they had combat damage. There was no way they could safely take off, not without an opportunity to look at the damage that had just been done.

"Out," she said. "Let's get out of the aircraft." She

threw her seat belt out of the way and scrambled for the ladder.

Outside, there were more explosions. The firing increased in tempo. Machine guns and automatic weapons. Pistols and rifles. Now she could hear shouting. Commands in Arabic. And screams. Sudden screams of surprise and pain.

"We've got to get out of the aircraft," said Marie.

"No," Hansen screamed. "We have to stay with it. Protect it. That's what we have to do."

"No way. I'm not going to get blown up sitting here waiting for the situation to stabilize."

"Williams," said Marie, "hide that pistol."

He looked at it and then nodded. There was nothing that he'd be able to do with a single pistol. It would only get them all into trouble.

Marie was trying to open the front hatch. Williams moved toward her to help. They shoved the door up and out of the way. The hot, desert air filled the aircraft immediately.

"Let's go," she said.

With the door open, the sounds of the battle roared around them, screams and orders and the firing of weapons. Marie dropped down to the concrete and crouched, using the aircraft as cover. She slipped toward the nosewheel and looked up at the terminal building. Smoke was pouring from a hole in the roof. Flames were visible behind the tinted glass. Men and women were running.

Williams joined her. "What's happening?"

"I thought it might be a terrorist attack, but there seem to be too many people involved. Besides, there was no warning over the radio. I don't know."

"What should we do?"

"Stay here," she said. "Until something happens or someone comes to get us."

On the right came a wild burst of firing. Three men retreated from the terminal, firing back at it. One of them turned to run and was hit in the shoulder, lifted from his feet, and thrown through the air. He hit the ground, rolling. His weapon fell from his fingers.

Watching it, Marie felt as if she was seeing a film,

men dying make-believe deaths. In a moment someone would yell "cut" and everyone would get up, shake hands, and head off for the next scene.

The firing was slowing down. Smoke was pouring from the terminal, staining the evening sky black. Flames shot into the air and roared.

Hansen appeared. "What do we do now?"

Marie shrugged, figuring that Hansen should be making the decisions. He was in charge, even if it was his first overseas flight as an aircraft commander.

"Stick with the airplane." She glanced around. "Where's Shawn?"

Williams said, "She stayed on board."

"Let's get everyone off the plane," said Hansen.

Williams turned, duck-walked from under the fuselage, and then leaped up into the airplane. Suddenly he leaned back out. "Hey! We've got someone hurt."

"Shit."

Marie pushed herself away from the nosewheel and ran around to the hatch. As she climbed back into the aircraft she spotted the loadmaster lying on the deck with Shawn crouched over him. Her hands were bloody.

"We need some help."

Marie ran back and knelt by the wounded man. His face was chalky white. Sweat had beaded on his forehead. Shawn had pressed a bandage from the first-aid kit against the man's ribs. It had turned crimson.

"I can't stop the bleeding," said Shawn.

"Okay," said Marie. "The situation has changed. We need to get some medical assistance in here now."

"I'll go," said Williams.

"You sure?" Hansen asked.

"Ryerson needs help," said Williams. "I'm sure."

Marie glanced at Williams's flight suit and noticed the small American flag sewn to the sleeve. It was obvious that he held no weapons and he wouldn't be mistaken for anyone of Arabic origin. "Go. But be careful."

Williams disappeared through the hatch, and Marie turned her attention to Shawn and the wounded man. "Keep the pressure on," she said. "Stop the bleeding is the first rule of first aid."

"I'm trying," said Shawn. Her voice was shaking and there were tears in her eyes.

"We've got to do something," said Hansen.

"Shut up," snapped Marie. "We're doing everything that we can." Then she thought about it. "We'd better get ourselves identified as Americans. We don't want to get dragged into this thing."

"How?"

"If we've got a flag, we better get it displayed."

"I've got one," said Shawn. "In my kit."

"I'll get it," said Hansen. He turned and headed back to the cockpit.

Marie looked down at Ryerson. His eyes were closed and his breathing was ragged. She reached out and took his hand, squeezing it in her own. The skin was cold and clammy.

"Hang on," she said. "Help is coming."

Ryerson opened his eyes, looked up at her, and tried to smile but coughed instead. Blood poured from his mouth. His eyes rolled up into his head and he died.

"Oh God," said Shawn. "Oh God."

Marie let go of his hand and tried to close his eyes. Shawn turned away from the dead man and threw up. She turned, looked at Marie, and was sick again.

"I've got the flag," Hansen yelled from the cockpit.

Marie stood up and stepped over the body. She helped Shawn to her feet. "You did everything you could, Liz," she said.

"No," she said, her voice quiet.

"Come on." She led Shawn away from the body, toward the aircraft. "Come on."

Hansen leaped from the cockpit as Williams stuck his face in the hatch. "We've got to take Ryerson into the terminal. There's an aid station set up in there."

"Too late," said Marie.

Williams was about to say something and then realized what she meant. "Oh."

As they reached the front of the plane Marie realized that the firing had ended. There were two quick shots and she amended that. Almost ended. She let go of Shawn, who slumped to the deck, crying quietly.

"What was happening inside?" Marie asked.

"I didn't see much. There were soldiers all over the terminal. I think some of them were Russians, though they weren't in uniform. The passengers had been herded away for their protection. They tried to get me to go with them, but I told them we had a badly wounded man."

"Russians?" said Hansen. "You sure?"

"Hell, no, sir. But those helicopters at the ends of the runways are Russian. And there were a bunch of tall, white Europeans giving orders in there and it sounded like some of them were speaking Russian."

"Okay," said Marie. "From this point on, we don't recognize anyone as Russian. We just keep our mouths shut, we try to get refueled and the hell out of here."

"Yeah," said Hansen. "We didn't see anything and we don't know anything."

"What about Ryerson?" Shawn asked.

"He caught a stray round," said Hansen. "No one to blame for that. It was an accident."

"They should have warned us," Shawn accused.

"Who?" Marie asked. "The airfield? They didn't know they were going to be attacked. Our intelligence? Maybe they should have known something, but they didn't. It was an accident."

"A plan," said Hansen. "We need a plan."

"We need to get refueled and the hell out of here," said Marie. "We probably should try to contact the American embassy and let them know what happened. Let the air-force attaché alert our people at home."

"What about the body?" Hansen asked.

"Let the embassy worry about that," said Marie.

"He was one of our crew," said Shawn. "We can't desert him here."

"No one said a thing about deserting him. We'll get him taken care of before we depart."

Hansen sat down on the ladder that led up to the cockpit and rested his elbows on his knees. "If we'd been two minutes late, we'd have avoided this."

"Can't live with the ifs," said Marie. "I think one of us had better try to find an officer and demand to be taken to the embassy."

"Yeah," said Williams. "Things were a little wild in the terminal."

"That's it, then," said Marie. She looked at Hansen. "There's your plan."

He shook his head. "Not much of a plan."

"At least we have one."

A shadow passed the hatch and then a man with a rifle looked in. He seemed surprised to find anyone in the aircraft. He jerked his weapon up and snapped off something in Arabic. When no one responded, he said, "You are prisoners. Now. You come. We go."

"Great," said Marie.

"No talk. You come." He stepped back to let them exit the aircraft.

Hansen stood. "We'd better go."

"Why am I not thrilled with this?" said Marie.

"You no talk. You come."

"Right," said Hansen. He moved forward and dropped to the concrete. The others followed him.

THE KREMLIN
MOSCOW

General Stepanov sat in one of the four high-backed chairs, a glass of vodka in his hand. The air was filled with thick blue smoke from Havana cigars. It was a brightly lit room done in deep browns and reds. Along one wall was a series of tall, thin windows that looked down on the darkened square.

In the room with Stepanov was the Soviet president, the head of the KBG, and the foreign minister. Each was seated in one of the high-backed chairs, with a small table on their right that held their vodka glass or an ornate ashtray.

The president, Andrei Popovsovich, sat leaning his head against the soft leather. Popovsovich was an old man, nearing eighty, but still had the energy and strength of a man thirty years younger. His hair was now solid white, but his eyebrows remained thick and black.

The president blew out a stream of smoke and said,

"You handled the situation in Tartu quite well, Comrade General."

"It worked well," said Stepanov. "Captain Kurlov's soldiers carried out their mission brilliantly."

"Yes," Popovsovich agreed, nodding. "We knew that you'd handle the problem quickly, efficiently, and discreetly. Our confidence in you was justified. You'd demonstrated the resourcefulness that we expected.

"But there are other problems looming on the horizon. Delicate problems that if handled with the same skill, the same discreet aplomb, will result in a rapid advancement for all those involved."

Stepanov wasn't sure what the president meant. Tensions in Europe had seemed to evaporate as the Berlin Wall crumbled and the two Germanies became one again. Poland had thrown off the Communist yoke and other once-solidly Communist states were no longer the puppets of Moscow. The Soviet Union had survived those changes because the United States had not been willing to exploit the sudden weaknesses.

"Our dream," said Popovsovich, "has not changed with the shifting of the world policies. The fascists must be destroyed and the revolution must be carried to the rest of the oppressed peoples. But warfare, with its threat of complete destruction of the world, is not the means. The revolution must be carried out slowly, carefully, subtly."

"Certainly, Comrade," said Stepanov, still confused.

"I believe it is now time to strike," said the president. "The world is ready for it, but it must be as subtle as the operation you organized in Tartu." The president stood up, revealing that he was a short man. Short and fat. Not stocky as some would say kindly, but fat from years of living higher than the rest of the Soviet people. He didn't mind the privileges of high status.

"First," he said, turning to stare at Stepanov, "I'd like to employ Captain Kurlov's troops again. We have a special mission for them. One that must be handled quietly and carefully."

"I'm sure that Captain Kurlov would respond to any challenge handed him."

Popovsovich nodded. "I'm afraid that our friend in

Cuba has become a burden for us. A drain on our resources as our people demand more consumer goods and a higher standard of living. They have tired of decades of sacrifice for the good of the state.''

He stopped talking and looked at the head of the KGB. ''We have been hoping that Fidel would retire, but he doesn't seem inclined to surrender the reins of power.''

''And Captain Kurlov might be able to persuade him to,'' said the KGB man.

''Captain Kurlov has a unique argument.'' Popovsovich faced Stepanov for a moment without speaking. He let the silence grow and then asked, ''Do we understand each other?''

Stepanov realized what the order was. He wasn't surprised that Popovsovich hadn't said it directly. If anyone should ask, he could deny that he'd given the orders. It was the doctrine of plausible deniability.

With that order given, Popovsovich changed his attitude. Now he was lecturing, as if standing in front of students. He waved his cigar like a pointer and said, ''The problem, the real problem, is the lack of oil. For the near future, the energy of the world is going to be oil. We can put reactors into large ships and we can power cities with the atom, but we cannot drive our cars with it. Oil is the key, and the Middle East is the place to get it.''

He looked at Stepanov for a moment and grinned. ''You're thinking about the Americans and the Chinese. You're thinking that any move we make will be countered by the Americans and the Chinese. And the Europeans. You believe that, don't you?''

Stepanov sipped his vodka and then shrugged. ''Both would oppose any overt move into the Middle East by us. Any threat to the world oil resources would be met with a counterstrike from the rest of the world.''

''Of course,'' said the president. He looked at the other two men, who sat quietly sipping their vodka and smoking their cigars. ''But the Americans are in the middle of a war themselves. Drugs flow into their cities, rotting them from within. Drug dealers and police are in pitched battles for the cities. The American military might is being drained to fight a war against drug dealers." Now he grinned. "Capitalism is rotting from the inside."

"The Chinese," said Stepanov.

"Ah, yes, our brothers in China." He smiled. "The true keepers of the revolution. They have yet to learn that times change and people change and governments must change. Lenin could not, did not, envision a world with satellites in the sky." Popovsovich waved an arm at the high ceiling. "Satellites that reveal the whole world to the people. What we say here, in Moscow, can be challenged by those in New York or Washington or Tokyo. Comrade Tetkorov?"

The head of the KGB stood up, looked at Stepanov, and walked to the window. Without turning, he said, "The Chinese have their own internal problems. They believe that the state is everything and that individuals mean nothing. They still massacre their own people if they disagree. They kill those who think for themselves."

"Until radical ideas are dead," said Stepanov.

"There are ways to keep ideas alive," said Tetkorov. "In today's world it is much easier to keep ideas alive, and with the help of the Americans, we have been doing that."

"The Americans?"

"They have an interest in undermining the ideals of the Chinese state. We simply supply them with some covert assistance."

"What General Tetkorov is saying," Popovsovich interrupted, "is that internal problems are keeping both the Americans and the Chinese occupied for the moment. They will not notice a few minor changes in the wind." He lifted his glass and took a drink. "They especially won't notice if it seems that the changes are the result of internal politics in various Middle Eastern countries."

"The Chinese," said Stepanov again. There were over a billion of them and they had common borders with the Soviet Union. The Chinese still did not have the technical capability to attack the United States. The Pacific Ocean was the best defense there. But the Chinese, with their limited-range missiles and bombers, could invade the Soviet Union. Aloud, Stepanov echoed the advice of an

American general: "Do not get into a land war with the Chinese."

"The Chinese have many traditional enemies," said the Soviet president. "They hate the Japanese and the Japanese hate them. They have fallen out of favor with the Koreans, and the Vietnamese have been fighting with them, forever."

"A little push here and there," said Tetkorov, "a few quiet suggestions from us, and the tensions with the West increase. We assist, covertly, the American effort to slip information to the Chinese people." He grinned. "And we alert the Chinese to the American effort. Such moves only heighten the tensions between the two while we sit back and watch the action."

"And," Popovsovich added, "we use the Koreans, the Vietnamese, and the Japanese to keep the Chinese off balance. Asia becomes a chessboard with only one party making the moves. Us."

"The Japanese are now capitalists," said Stepanov. "They will not risk their industry and they have no standing army. The Americans have seen to that. And both the Koreans and the Vietnamese would not be able to stand up against the full force of the Chinese."

"True," said Popovsovich. "But we have seen, in the last thirty years, the mightiest fought to a standstill by the weakest. The key here is that the Chinese would not commit their full force to the fight. They would do the same thing the Americans did in Vietnam and we did in Afghanistan. Use a limited response."

Tetkorov spoke again. "Besides, the Vietnamese, still believing they defeated the Americans in battle, would attack the Chinese if the incentives were there, if they felt they had a chance to win. Disputed lands between China and Vietnam would be the perfect wedge."

"The Vietnamese would like an air-mobile division. Such a gift might suggest a plan to them," said the president, smiling.

"So many things," said Stepanov.

"No, only one thing. One goal. And if we're careful, we will see that goal achieved."

"What will be my role in this?" asked Stepanov.

"The North Vietnamese have invited a delegation to Hanoi for discussions about the development of such an air-mobile division. We'd like you to head that delegation."

"Certainly, Comrade President. It would be an honor to do so."

"But you must remember, as always, that these negotiations must remain discreet. Although the Americans are more concerned with activities in South America, they have an eye cast on the rest of the world. We do not want to raise their suspicions now."

"I understand."

"The world situation is unique at the moment," said Popovsovich. "The world remembers what Germany did, and for those who try to forget, there are the Jews to remind them. There are those who are now more afraid of the reunified Germany than they are of us. It is the Germans who are the evil empire now. Not the Soviet Union."

"Yes, Comrade."

"And the world is appalled at the Chinese and what they did to their own people. For the moment, eyes are focused elsewhere and we must take advantage of that."

"Yes, Comrade."

"Your delegation leaves for Hanoi in two days. Briefings have been prepared for you." The president looked at Stepanov. "You will be ready?"

"Certainly, Comrade."

Stepanov waited in the lighted entry until the black Lincoln Town Car slipped out of the shadows. When it stopped near him, he reached out and opened the rear door himself rather than wait for the driver. As he climbed into the backseat he said, "To my headquarters."

"Yes, Comrade General."

Stepanov sank back into the soft leather seats. To one side a small bar held a fresh stock of vodka and a pepper grinder as well as bottles of scotch, bourbon, and even corn liquor. On the other side a small console held radio equipment. He could talk to his headquarters, to aircraft overhead, or listen to a music broadcast. When the conditions were right and the ionosphere cooperated, he could listen to rock and roll from Germany.

They rode through the streets of Moscow. Stepanov was pleased with himself. He'd dodged the pitfalls that had swallowed so many of his friends, stayed out of the line of fire during the purges, and managed to grab the assignments that brought him to the attention of the Politburo without compromising his ambition. Over the years, he'd been on the right side in each of the various activities and power struggles and now he was in a position of power.

Tetkorov didn't realize that the Spetsnaz troops were loyal to Stepanov. They would obey his orders and not those of the KGB. If he ordered his Spetsnaz troops to seize the KGB headquarters, they would do it. If he ordered them into the Politburo, they'd probably refuse. A fine line divided hatred of the KGB and loyalty to Mother Russia.

But Stepanov realized the difference. If the KGB decided he was too dangerous, it would be an interesting fight. Stepanov believed that his soldiers, trained in the traditional military arts as well as covert operations, small-unit tactics, assassination, and escape and evasion, would be more than a match for anything the KGB could field. The Spetsnaz were better trained and more loyal. Of course, Stepanov told himself, it would never come to that.

"Headquarters coming up, Comrade General," said the driver quietly.

"Thank you. You are free to return to your quarters once you drop me off."

The car pulled up in front of a modern brick, steel, and glass building. One man ran down the steps and opened the rear door of the limousine, saluting as he stepped back.

Stepanov climbed out, returned the salute, and asked, "Who's the duty officer tonight?"

"Major Duropov."

"Please ask him to join me in my office."

"Yes, Comrade General."

Stepanov entered the building. He noticed again the giant crack that ran the length of the hallway floor next to the wall. It had developed shortly after the building had been completed. Stepanov had complained and demanded that it be fixed, but everyone blamed everyone else and no one would fix it, believing that such repairs were tantamount to claiming responsibility. A few officers had suggested that they tile over it, but Stepanov vetoed the idea. He wanted the daily reminder of the result of lousy workmanship and a lack of pride.

Stepanov reached his office and entered. With only a skeleton staff on at nights, no one was waiting for him. He turned on the lights, passed the reception area and entered his office proper. After turning on more lights, he put his hat on the rack, and removed his uniform blouse.

There was a knock on his door as he sat down at his desk. "Come on in," he called.

The man walked briskly across the carpeted floor, stopped in front of the desk, and said, "Major Duropov reporting as ordered, Comrade General."

Stepanov smiled and waved at one of the visitor's chairs. "Why so formal tonight, Fyodor?"

Duropov dropped his salute. "Because it is so late, Comrade General."

"It is nothing to worry about. Please bring me the latest message traffic and current briefings on Vietnam, China, and North Korea."

"Everything?"

"No, the capsule versions. I'm not interested in the troop strengths and orders of battle, although some military information on Vietnam would be most beneficial."

"I'll have the current fact books brought in for your convenience, sir."

"Fine. And where is Major Salnikov?"

"He has gone home for the night."

"Then please call him and ask him to come back. I'm afraid our intelligence officer is going to find himself very busy for the next few days."

"Yes, sir."

Duropov left the office. Stepanov leaned back in his chair and wished that he'd avoided the vodka in the first meeting, but knew he couldn't have. If President Popovsovich wanted a drink, then the only smart thing was to drink with him. If the president hopped on one leg, then everyone hopped on one leg.

Stepanov opened the middle drawer of his desk, took out a notepad, and began making notes. It was going to be a long night and then a longer day. He could think of no way to avoid it.

MOSCOW

Stepanov sat at his desk, a tall glass of vodka near his left hand, hoping that the doctrine of plausible deniability applied to himself as well as his leader. He held a gold pen in his hand as he scanned one of the reports he'd asked for. When there was a knock at the door, he said, "Come on in."

Major Boris Salnikov, wearing a full uniform, stepped through the door, stopped three feet from the front edge of the general's desk, and saluted. "I am reporting as ordered."

"So formal?"

Salnikov shrugged and then grinned. "One can never tell with generals. Some stand on ceremony. Others are so busy that they want to get the meeting over with."

"Sit down, Boris." Stepanov pointed at his glass of vodka. "Care for a little refreshment?"

"It's early for me, General."

"I've been at it all night. I need a little kick to keep the juices flowing."

"Yes, sir."

Stepanov capped his pen and set it on his desk. "I've a delicate problem here. One that will take some finesse. And discretion."

"Yes, sir," said Salnikov carefully. He crossed his legs and sat back in the chair.

"Our friend in Havana is creating new and interesting problems for us."

Salnikov nodded but didn't say anything. He just wished he's taken the vodka when it had been offered to him. Now it was too late.

"I have been directed to ensure that the situation is changed radically. Everyone feels that if our friend were to retire suddenly, our position here would be better."

"Yes, sir," said Salnikov cautiously.

"Of course, a leader who has retired will often be consulted by those who replace him. Elder statesmen are often as unpredictable as young men."

"Castro is becoming a burden," said the major.

"Let us say that the Soviet economy is not in shape to continue the unrestricted assistance that Cuba has enjoyed for the last thirty-five years. Changes are necessary."

"Certainly," said Salnikov.

Stepanov stood, walked to the window, and stared down at the open plaza. "But there are additional problems. The financial support is secondary. There is the exporting of revolution."

"A noble cause."

"A decade ago, yes. But the world has changed radically. A destabilizing influence, even with the most noble of aims must sometimes be stopped."

"Yes, sir."

Turning, Stepanov looked into the eyes of the young major. "I hope that you understand what is being said here."

"Yes, sir."

Stepanov returned to his chair and sat down. "You and your team will be available for a mission into Cuba in the next week to ten days. It will be a covert operation. It will not be discussed with anyone outside of this office. No one, absolutely no one, will know that you're going to Cuba.''

''How will we get there?''

Stepanov grinned. ''Those operational details will be worked out in a few days. You'll be informed.''

''Yes, sir.''

Stepanov leaned forward, elbows on the desk. ''This is one of those missions that could kill us all. Anything goes wrong and all of us will be looking at the firing squad. If it's handled properly, no one will ever know, and that's the way we want it. No one must ever know what we've discussed here.''

Salnikov didn't speak for a moment, his mind racing. ''I understand, General.''

''There is one thing that I haven't made clear here. You are not required to accept this mission. It is a volunteer operation.''

''I'm afraid that it's too late for that,'' said Salnikov. ''I know too much about it.''

''That you do.''

''Besides, this is not something that you and I cooked up by ourselves. There are good reasons for it. The benefit to the Soviet Union, and to the world, is obvious. We must do what we must.''

Stepanov nodded slowly. ''I'm glad to hear you say that. Our contact will be limited from this point. The fewer people who know, the better off we both will be.''

Salnikov got to his feet. ''I understand.''

''Major,'' Stepanov said. He hesitated, unsure what to say. Almost everything seemed inappropriate. Finally he settled on, ''Good luck to you.''

''Yes, General.''

Martinez and his team sat in the briefing room, which resembled a small theater, and watched a series of officers take places at the rostrum, give them information, and then vanish. Half of them had slides projected on a screen built into the rear wall. One showed a brief movie. The remainder just handed out the information. None of Martinez's team looked as if he'd slept any during the last twenty-four hours. Reclining in the chairs, some with their knees braced on the seats in front of them, they looked as if they were about to drift off.

It had been a grueling twenty-four hours. One minute they were fighting their way out of a hot PZ and the next they were in Panama, being told to hop a plane to Florida. And when they could have been sleeping on the plane, they'd had debriefing officers at their sides, taking down their every word.

At one point, over the roar of the engines, while sitting in the red webbing of the troop seats, Martinez had asked, "You learn anything special from the documents?"

It was a worthless question because everyone on the team could read Spanish as well as a native. They hadn't needed anyone to translate the information for them. During the flight from Colombia, they'd shared the documents they'd found. They knew what they said.

The briefing officer shook his head and yelled back, "Can't tell you that. Be contaminating the source."

Martinez laughed at that. They'd seen the Cuban soldiers, had fought them, and they had read the orders from the Cuban army to the locals, giving them training schedules and instructions. No doubt that the orders had been written in Cuba and transmitted to the Cubans in the field in Colombia.

And there was no doubt that it was all going on with Fidel Castro's knowledge. No one in Cuba made policy decisions without consulting Castro. To do so would be death.

But the debriefing officers carefully avoided saying anything about it. They just kept pushing, asking questions, taking notes, as the aircraft crossed the Caribbean, skirted the territorial waters and airspace of Cuba, and then landed at Homestead Air Force Base in southern Florida.

It had been as hot and humid on the airfield in Florida as it had been in Panama. Martinez stood at the rear of the aircraft and watched as a crew van approached from operations. It stopped near him but the driver hadn't spoken as he and his men climbed into the rear, each man with his personal gear, and were driven straight to the briefing room. Now, after a series of briefings, breaks, and an hour for breakfast, they were getting to the heart of the matter. Apparently it had taken intelligence that long to digest the information collected in Colombia and get it to the Pentagon, where the proper orders could be issued.

The atmosphere in the room changed. The doors were locked and an armed guard posted outside. The briefing officer was wearing jungle camouflage fatigues, but there was no insignia on them. No identification at all. The uniform was bright green, looking as if it had been issued no more than an hour earlier.

"Gentlemen," he said. "This briefing is classified top secret and none of it will be discussed outside the confines of this room. Are there any questions?" He looked down at Martinez.

"That's clear. We understand."

"Fine." He turned and said, "First slide, please." The screen brightened and resolved into a poor picture of the top of one of the documents that Martinez and his team had captured. "What we have here is an operational order, issued at the highest level of Cuban command and found in the jungles of Colombia by a Special Forces team."

Martinez laughed. Apparently the briefer didn't know that they were the ones who'd found the documents.

The briefer moved away from his podium and extended a pointed to the screen. "Up here we have the designation of the issuing headquarters. That puts the originator of this order in Cuba." He turned to face them. "As you know, there are American mercenaries operating in various arenas. They do not have the backing of our government. The argument that the soldiers in Colombia were also mercenaries and not under the control of the Cuban government has been eliminated by this document. Castro and his government are fully cognizant of the activities in Colombia."

He touched the screen again. "Here, we have a statement linking these soldiers, Cuban soldiers, to the drug cartel. It is an authorization for training and later equipping, with Cuban arms, the guards used to protect the shipments from the fields to the processing labs and then onto either the coast or airfields in the interior before being sent to the United States.''

Martinez spoke up. ''That single document, proving everything that we wanted proved, is amazing. It could be said that it was a planted document. Or one created in the labs of the CIA for the purpose of swaying public opinion.''

The briefer collapsed his pointer and moved to the front of the stage. ''The document originated in Colombia. Or, I should say, was discovered in Colombia. There is no doubt about it. Source was a drug camp hidden in the jungle.''

Martinez said, ''Is there supporting intelligence for any of this?''

''Certainly,'' said the briefer. He turned again. ''Next slide.'' He pointed out sentences in that document, went to a third and then a fourth, drawing a parallel between the drug cartels and the Cuban government each time.

When he had finished reviewing the documents, he returned to the lectern. ''There can be little doubt that Castro and his government are behind these operations. It is our belief that Castro, knowing he could never win a war with the United States, is doing everything in his power to destroy us from within. Erode the society, create a world of fear in the country based on drug abuse, and the United States will collapse, leaving him as the real power in the Western Hemisphere.''

''Crap,'' said Martinez.

The briefing officer shrugged. ''If you are the little guy and you have a way of defeating the big guy, even if that method is as complicated as this, you grab it. If it works, fine. If it doesn't, you've lost nothing.''

''That's still a little nebulous,'' said Martinez.

''You've just seen the documented evidence,'' said the briefer. ''Castro is controlling, at the very least, forty percent of the drug traffic into the United States. These are the conservative figures based on classified sources. They are confirmed, reconfirmed, and double-checked.''

Martinez nodded but didn't respond. He'd seen the Cuban soldiers in Colombia. He'd seen the camp. And if there were other teams in Colombia, they'd probably seen similar things. No doubt about it: Castro was involved.

"Gentlemen," said the briefer, "now that you've seen the intelligence uncovered in the last year or so, I'll bring on the second half of the briefing team."

The door at the rear of the small auditorium opened and a Special Forces officer entered. He wore a green beret, the flash centered above his eye, jump boots, and a new set of fatigues. Martinez studied him intently, looking for signs that the new man was a CIA agent posing as a Special Forces trooper. And then he got a good look at the man's face and recognized him. The man was definitely Special Forces.

He climbed the three steps to the stage, glanced at the briefer, and said, "That'll be all."

"But . . ."

"You are dismissed. Make sure that the door is locked after you exit."

For an instant the briefer stood flat-footed, looking as if he was going to protest. Finally he gave up, gathered his notes, and left through the rear door.

The Special Forces officer watched him go and then moved forward to the edge of the stage. He sat down there, his feet dangling. He looked at Martinez and asked, "Do we need to carry on this charade?"

"I can't see any point in it," said Martinez.

The officer rubbed his face. "They've handed you a real gem. Let me say that it is volunteer, but if you don't volunteer, you'll be held in isolation until the mission has been completed. And naturally, everything is top secret, so that a mention of it will get you thrown in jail."

"Do you really need to threaten us?"

"No, I guess not. But this is a very important mission."

Martinez stared at the officer for a moment. He knew what it was going to be. He'd just watched a parade of men giving him all the good reasons for it. He'd seen the documents. He and his team had been briefed, repeatedly, on the drug problem. They had been told that it was the biggest problem facing the United States. The Japanese and the Germans, during the Second World War, had failed to destroy the country. This could do it.

And then they'd made the tie to Castro. They drove that point home. Repeatedly. That left a single conclusion. And the officer confirmed it.

"Gentlemen, what I'm about to say cannot leave this room. Ever. Too many lives are involved. It is too important for us to let any of it leak. Is that understood?"

"We can keep secrets," said Martinez.

"Fine. Your mission is to take out Castro."

The words hung in the air for a moment. Martinez had known it was coming but still couldn't believe it. Such an order was impossible to believe.

"You mean kill him," said Alvarez. His voice was quiet, almost inaudible.

"That's exactly what I mean."

ABOARD THE USS *CUTLER*
NORFOLK, VIRGINIA

Commander Kelly Raymond Dees sat in the captain's chair aboard his ship and wondered how it had all happened. It seemed like only yesterday that he was struggling in a high school that didn't like having black students except on the football team, struggling to earn an appointment to Annapolis because he wanted to be in the navy, and then struggling to get through the courses that were designed to teach him everything he would ever need to know about being a naval officer.

Dees liked having a command, although everyone had always said it was the loneliest job in the world. Now he had it and it wasn't lonely. There was always someone around, someone who had to listen to his flights of fancy, if that's what he wanted them to do. His exec was a good man, as was the first lieutenant. All the officers were well trained and dedicated, and if there was ever a question they couldn't answer, one of the chiefs could. A good crew. His crew. And not one of them seemed to care that he was black.

Sitting there, looking out, he could see a beautiful, deep blue sky with only a few fluffy white clouds to mar it. But Dees was elated because he was sitting on the bridge of a naval vessel that he commanded. An American warship. One of only four hundred and eight still in commission thanks to the peace dividend from Eastern Europe.

Dees knew everything about his ship, a Spruance-class destroyer. It was lightly armed with only two single five-inch MK-45 guns, an ASROC missile launcher, and two triple torpedo tubes. His ship also carried Sea Sparrow short-range missiles, Harpoon antiship missiles, and two Phalanx 20-mm CIWs.

But the real danger from the ship was not its weapons, but the helicopters it carried. Those helos could see enemy subs when other systems were blind and could kill the subs before the other weapons could be used. His ship could find the enemy and rid the sea-lanes of it before the enemy could get into range to attack. That was why the traditional weapons were missing. In the days of silent subs and antiship missiles, big guns were not needed.

The exec, Henry Randolph, appeared beside him. Randolph was a big man with broad shoulders, very short brown hair, wide-set features, and large, round, brown eyes. "We're about ready to get under way."

Dees looked at his watch. "Twenty minutes early."

"Aye, sir. Didn't want you to look bad in front of all the visiting brass."

"Never could understand the thrill of standing on a dock to watch ships sail off."

"Maybe the thrill is knowing that the poor bastards on the ships might vanish under the sea while you get to go back home to the wife or girlfriend and not have to worry about disappearing."

Dees smiled. "I believe what you said is akin to heresy. No one could possibly prefer to stay on shore when the real men are sailing off to glory."

"I wouldn't call a routine patrol glory," said the exec.

"No, I suppose not." Dees stood up and moved forward so that he could look down at the bow. Sailors were working below him, getting ready to cast off. Dees watched the activity for a few moments, then turned and watched the staff on the bridge. He let them do their jobs, do what had to be done. Everyone had been well trained and knew what to do. He would stand to the side and say nothing and the ship would sail on time.

"We're set, Captain," said the exec.

On the pier, a band began to play. People cheered. Wives and mothers and brothers and fathers stood waving. Sailors lined the rail waving back at their families and friends.

Dees, feeling the power of the engines, gave the orders. Lines fell away. Whistles and horns sounded and the band kept playing. Another order and the screws began to turn, pulling the ship away from the dock with the assistance of the tugs, while he stood there and watched. He was a big man, burly, almost an exact match for the exec, with short-chopped hair, and a thick, black cap. His features were fine, however, and his eyes large and bright. The sleeves of his khaki uniform were filled. There were rows of ribbons above his breast pocket, there to remind the others that he was not a desk jockey given command for political reasons. Dees had earned his way up the ladder by serving in the line navy.

The ship turned slightly and then began to pick up speed. They maneuvered through the harbor and were suddenly in the open ocean, the land falling away behind them.

Dees stayed on the bridge, circulating, watching as the men worked. He walked out onto the port side. The sea air seemed cooler. A fine spray blew up. He stood looking out over the ocean.

The exec joined him on the wing and said, "Everything's running smoothly."

"This is what it's all about." Dees looked toward the sun and then closed his eyes. The sea was calm. There was nothing around them except open ocean.

"It's always a little depressing. We're what—twenty minutes out now and won't be back into port here for a long time."

"That's not the way to look at it," said Dees. "You have to see this as an opportunity to prove your worth. An opportunity to serve."

"That's what they all say." Randolph grinned. "You're beginning to sound like the recruiting pitch I heard in college."

Dees looked at him for a moment and then stepped back onto the bridge. "I'll be in the wardroom if anyone wants me in the next twenty minutes."

"Aye, sir," said the officer of the deck.

Dees left the bridge. He still felt that he was unnecessary but knew this would change when something happened. It was the captain's duty to make decisions. It was the captain's duty to take responsibility when something went wrong.

As he left he heard one of the sailors say, "Captain's off the bridge."

Captain First Rank Mikhail Inber sat in his tiny cabin and listened to the sounds of his boat as it pushed its way slowly through the ocean. He was working on his log, but not paying attention to the task. Instead he was staring at the blank pages, listening to the creaking of the boat.

They had been submerged for most of the day. The air was being circulated and cooled, but it was beginning to smell canned. Inber could surface at any moment, but he wanted to stay submerged, to get a feel for the boat as it ran underwater for extended periods of time.

He sat back, his eyes on the bulkhead, and tried to shut everything out of his mind, to pretend that he was on shore, sitting in his small apartment, listening to the sounds of the city outside.

There was a quiet tap outside his cabin. "Comrade Captain."

Inber recognized the voice of his exec. He opened his eyes and said, "Yes?"

"It's fourteen hundred hours, local time."

Without a word, Inber moved to the base of the bulkhead where a private safe had been installed. Only Inber had the combination, but if something happened to him, a copy of the combination was locked in the main boat's safe. The seal on the envelope could not be broken unless Inber was incapacitated.

He punched the code into the safe, turned the stainless-steel handle, and took out the sealed orders that had been handed him before they had departed Arkhangelsk a week earlier.

He returned to his chair, glanced up at the exec, and then broke the seal. As he pulled out a packet of papers, he said, "They are getting verbose. Complicated instructions for us. Looks like it includes an intelligence summary, charts, and reporting times."

The exec stood quietly. He wanted to say something but couldn't find the right words.

Inber spread the papers out on his small desk. "Looks like we're going south and west. To the Caribbean." He grinned. "We're to watch our brothers in Cuba and to monitor capitalist shipping in the area."

"Not the mission for our boat," said the exec.

"Ah, you are wrong, Comrade." Inber leaned back in his chair. "Think of the position we'll be in. Cuba is but ninety miles from the United States. Many of their important military installations are situated in the south. Air-force bases and naval facilities and even their space center."

"You are not suggesting that we're going to attack their space center?"

"Attack?" said Inber. "Who said anything about an attack. Monitoring American military activity and watching our brothers in Cuba suggests nothing of an attack."

The exec shrugged. "Rumors, Comrade Captain. There have been rumors through the fleet for weeks."

Inber, fully aware of the rumors, asked, "And what did these rumors tell you?"

"A boat would be sent south to watch the Americans lift equipment into space. An expert marksman with a high-powered rifle is supposed to fire on the American launch vehicle just as it begins to lift off. The resulting explosion would force the Americans to shut down their space program, giving us the lead in space."

"You have been reading too many spy novels," said Inber, laughing. "Such an act would trigger a war between us and the Americans."

"Which we would win," said the exec confidently.

"But at what cost?" Inber asked. "The Americans might be weaker than us, but they have the strength to lay waste to much of our homeland. In a nuclear confrontation, being number two is as good as being number one."

"Aye, Captian."

Inber glanced at the papers and then said, "Such rumors must be stopped now."

"But we did take on a detachment of marines," said the exec. "Expert riflemen with very accurate, high-powered weapons."

Inber pulled the patrol chart from the papers and showed it to the exec. "Do you see anywhere on the course where we'll be in a position to shoot at a launching American spacecraft? I want it fully understood. We are taking no action against the Americans."

"Aye, aye, sir."

"Now," said Inber, "I have sealed orders for the commander of the marines, but I am not authorized to give him the instructions until we're on station, south of Cuba. Not off the coast of Florida."

"What are our orders?"

"We patrol the sea-lanes and watch the shipping," said Inber. "Certainly nothing as exciting as shooting an American spacecraft."

"But think," said the exec. "We could wreck their plans. After their *Challenger* exploded, they did not launch any manned craft for more than two years. Missions backed up while we raced ahead."

"I would hope," said Inber, "that you are not advocating a course of action here."

"No, sir. Merely commenting on the situation and the power that we have."

Inber pulled the first chart from the papers and said, "Take this forward. I want the course laid in immediately."

"Aye aye, sir."

As the exec took the chart Inber was again tempted to tell him to forget the rumors but decided against it. He didn't want to push the subject too far.

When the exec was gone, Inber thought about what he had said. He was wrong on one point. They did not have great power. All the power rested in his hands. If he, Inber, decided to launch his missiles, there was nothing to stop him. The men would follow his orders, assuming that he had authorization from Moscow. He had enough nuclear power to wreak havoc on the Americans, or anyone else he decided to attack.

Now he grinned. He could defeat smaller nations. Beat them to submission in a matter of minutes. They would have no power to resist because most nations had no weapons with which to retaliate. If he attacked Cuba, the Cubans could launch an attack on Moscow, but the planes and missiles the Cubans had didn't have the range, and Soviet fighters could destroy the threat.

No, thought Inber. He was now a world nuclear power. He could attack Cuba and make it look as if the Americans had done it. The Soviet Union would then either retaliate or not, as the old men in Moscow thought fit.

Of course, Inber had no desire to do this. He wasn't going to launch his missiles unless ordered to do so by Moscow. He was not going to flaunt his position as a world nuclear power because so many others had equal power and no man in his right mind was going to initiate a nuclear war.

Inber rubbed a hand through his short, now sweat-soaked hair. He wondered if the air-conditioning had failed again. If it had, he'd be forced to surface. Computers and delicate electronic equipment required a cool, dry environment.

Deciding that he'd wait for the maintenance chief to contact him, Inber returned to reading his instructions. There was a packet for his eyes only. He ripped it open and glanced at the instructions quickly. He felt his heart begin to hammer and his face grow cold.

The exec hadn't been far off. The detachment of marines did have a special mission that involved long-range sniping. Inber couldn't believe the orders, but there they-were, signed and countersigned. The instructions were explicit and were obviously real.

Stunned, Inber returned the material to his safe, locked it, and began to work his way forward. He had to speak to the marine officer. The man had to know what was happening in the real world. Inber felt as if he was no longer a resident of it.

Major Richard Brizzola sat in the air-conditioned office in the building at Eglin Air Force Base and read through the overnight intelligence traffic. Although he was the assistant operations officer for the brigade and not the intelligence officer, he liked to know what was going on in the world. It helped to have one of the operations officers as knowledgeable as the intelligence officer.

When Brizzola finished with the secret messages, he stood up and stepped to the safe, a heavy file cabinet with a combination lock on the second drawer; it wasn't locked. Brizzola opened it and stuffed the messages into the folder marked "current."

Sitting down at his desk, Brizzola wondered what to do next. At the moment the brigade was little more than a paper unit. Most of the battalions had been stripped away in the economy moves called peace dividends. Units attached to the Rapid Deployment Force had returned to their bases or had been deactivated. With the Eighteenth Airborne Corps just up the road at Fort Bragg, there wasn't much need, in the eyes of Congress, for a fully charged Rapid Deployment Force. Now they had rosters of units and men who could be called if a mission came to them, but they had very few marines or soldiers assigned permanently.

He had to laugh about that. Even if they had the mission, there was a possibility that they wouldn't have the transport. The C-17, designed to use small fields, to operate at the forward edge of the battle zone, to ferry troops and equipment, had been cut back, too. Most of the dedicated aviation assets were ancient C-130 Hercules that were older than the pilots flying them.

No, Brizzola had said many times, if the president decided he wanted to deploy a force rapidly, he'd have a difficult time finding that force, because there was nothing more than a skeleton staff working out Oplans and marshaling orders for a series of paper units.

In his fifteen years as a marine, Brizzola had seen nothing like it. He'd entered the corps during Reagan's administration when it seemed that all the military had to do was ask and the president would see that the requests were granted. The public had forgotten about Vietnam. Soldiers, sailors, and marines were no longer considered second-class citizens. People respected the uniform again. He knew men and women who had served in Vietnam, real heros with rows of combat decorations who had been ignored by the public. Now men and women with nothing other than meritorious decorations were reaping the benefits bought by the blood of others.

Of course, the collapse of the Warsaw Pact had made it more difficult to get equipment and manpower. People didn't want to spend five hundred million dollars for a bomber that could elude Soviet radar. They wanted to see their taxes trimmed. They wanted to see the infrastructure repaired.

And they wanted to see the great reservoir of manpower in the military reduced, which threatened Brizzola. From the moment he'd seen John Wayne crossing the beach at Iwo Jima, all he'd ever wanted to be was a marine and when he read about Jimmie Howard, a sergeant who had spent a long night fighting the Viet Cong and saving the lives of most of his men while winning the Medal of Honor, it removed any lingering question.

It was getting harder to do. With the corps shrinking, the number of slots available were shrinking, so the competition for them was getting tougher. Brizzola, now the assistant operations officer for a brigade that existed only on paper, saw his chances of being promoted approaching zero.

Lieutenant Colonel William Bloch entered the office without knocking. "Anything in the intel traffic this morning?"

"Nothing of interest."

Bloch pulled the visitor's chair around and sat down. There wasn't much in the office except a desk, the safe, a couple of chairs, and a short bookcase holding black binders.

"You seen today's training schedule?"

Brizzola shook his head. "I try to avoid that whenever I can."

"You're due for a refresher on chemical warfare."

Brizzola had to laugh. "They take away our units and equipment because the Soviets are no longer considered a threat, but we maintain the old training schedules, including this nonsense about chemical warfare."

"Chemical warfare is the poor man's atomic bomb. Chemical weapons can be as deadly as atomic weapons but not nearly as destructive."

"I don't need a lecture on the subject. And I don't need to spend the afternoon in that stupid chemical warfare suit either."

Bloch nodded. "You don't have to accomplish the training this afternoon. I just wanted you to know it was on the schedule so that you could plan accordingly."

Brizzola looked at his watch. "What I'd rather do is find a Coke and a sandwich."

Now Bloch grinned. "Why didn't you say so? I could be persuaded to eat something."

Brizzola moved to the safe, closed the drawer, and then spun the lock. He tried to open each drawer in turn to make sure that it was properly locked. That done, he turned the sign around and slipped it through the handles on the front of the safe. It announced to anyone who could read that the safe was "locked."

Brizzola grabbed his cap, set it on his head, and said, "Lead the way."

Together they left the small, brick building and walked out into the stifling heat of the Florida panhandle. Before they could reach Bloch's car, both men were sweating from the hot sun and the high humidity.

"I hate this weather," said Bloch. "After Vietnam, I swore that I'd stay in the north, where it would snow on me, and if the weather was too hot, I knew it would change soon.''

He opened the door to his car and then stood to the side, letting the hot wind blow into it before getting in.

As they pulled out onto the street Bloch said, ''Heard some interesting things this morning.''

''Classified?''

''Momentarily. There's going to be a new marine battalion coming through here sometime in the next couple of months. They want us to set up a training schedule for them. Whole routine.''

''We don't even have enough men assigned for the cadre,'' said Brizzola.

''Not right now, but think about it. We've got to get them jump-qualified. Okay. Army school at Benning can take care of that.''

''We can't send a battalion down there for jump training,'' said Brizzola. ''Even if the army would allow it.''

''But they'll take one company. We'll get another going through a rifle refresher and give them a chance to use the new official weapon. Put another company through extensive hand-to-hand and we've got it made.''

''Except we have no instructors.''

Bloch grinned as he pulled into a lot. ''No problem there. Army'll supply the rifle instructors and we can get the hand-to-hand instructors from Parris Island. Not to mention we've now got an excuse to bring some of our people back in. Maybe as many as a company.''

''That's something,'' said Brizzola.

Bloch parked the car. He left the engine running so the air conditioner was working. ''Everything I've just said is confidential. Nothing has been finalized and there is nothing on paper. Yet.''

''It sounds to me,'' said Brizzola, ''that someone is expecting trouble and they're quietly getting us back into shape.''

''That's a hell of a lot to be reading into the situation. All we've got is a single, untrained battalion coming in for upgrade training.''

''Yes, sir. And it provides us with an excuse to bring in our top people and form a hard-core cadre from them.

Makes it very easy for us to go back up to full strength without anyone realizing what we're doing.''

"You have a point?'' Block asked.

"No, sir. I was just wondering.''

Bloch turned off the ignition and grinned. "So am I, Major. So am I.''

KAGOSHIMA, JAPAN

Reisman had forgotten about being sick as the fishing boat limped back to port. There were new bullet holes in the wood and one round had hit the engine. It had taken the mechanic a couple of hours to get it repaired so that they could make the run back to the Japanese coast. There was no talk of pretending to fish as they headed to the east; they just wanted to get back as quickly as possible.

As soon as they had tied up, Reisman raced down the gangplank. He was glad to be off it.

A moment later, MacKenzie walked down and joined him. "Well, you got to see the operation."

"Didn't work well," said Reisman. "You didn't make it to China."

"No, not this run. But we've made it in a dozen times."

"Was there a leak?" Now that they were away from the Japanese crew, Reisman could ask those questions.

"Leak? No. The Chinese patrol their territorial waters well. With radar and patrol planes, they probably spotted us moving toward them and headed out to intercept."

"Still, we were quite a ways from the coast when they arrived. And they started shooting right away."

MacKenzie stood facing the boat. He reached a hand up to shade his eyes. "Just one of those things. We lost—what, two, three hundred dollars' worth of supplies and video tapes? And a little time. They lost their boat."

"Uh-huh," said Reisman. "It was fortunate that the Soviets arrived when they did. Interesting, too."

"Coincidence," said MacKenzie.

But Reisman wasn't buying that. A Soviet plane would not have flashed out of the sun to save a Japanese fishing boat unless there was something else going on. And the fact that the Su-27 was available to save the boat was also significant.

"That was a Soviet aircraft, wasn't it?"

"Soviet-made would be a better description."

"Look," said Reisman, "I'm not that familiar with the insignia of the Soviet air force, but I got a good look at the aircraft. Won't take long to verify it."

"Then do so. You're not going to get me to verify something when I'm not sure that I can make such a claim."

"Don't dance with me, MacKenzie. I know what I saw. You've got Soviet-Japanese cooperation directed against the Chinese."

"That's quite a conclusion to draw from a minor incident which no one, not the Chinese, Japanese, or the Soviets, will confirm. Report it and you're going to look like a dummy."

"No," said Reisman, "I report it and people are going to wonder just what in the hell is going on over here. They're not going to think I'm crazy. You'll end up with a dozen, two dozen reporters trying to find out what is going on." He turned to walk off the dock.

MacKenzie grabbed his arm. "You can't report this. It's too important for you to report. I should have never allowed you on that boat, but I figured we'd sneak in just as we have in the past."

"What in the hell is going on here?"

"Can we make a deal?"

"Depends. I'm not an unreasonable man. Hell, I served in Vietnam. I understand that the story sometimes has to take the backseat to security. I just want to know that I'm doing the right thing here."

"Let's go someplace where we can talk," said MacKenzie. "Too much open territory out here."

"Lead on."

They left the dock and returned to the car. MacKenzie started the engine, turned on the radio, and then turned it up loud. Over the noise he said, "The best equipment can filter out all the noise. But the radio playing, especially the random sounds of the words, the commercials, and the breaks, makes it difficult to record the conversation."

"Who's going to be recording?" Reisman asked.

"Whoever," said MacKenzie. "I just don't want to make the job any easier for them."

He backed up, turned, and entered the traffic. He glanced up at the mirror, turned, checked the traffic behind him, turned again, and made another check. After the third turn, they were approaching the main road again. MacKenzie pulled out on it.

"What was that about?"

"Nobody is going to do that unless they're following us. It's an easy check."

"Sure."

As they drove back toward Tokyo, Reisman tried to organize his thoughts. He wanted to be prepared for any story that MacKenzie might try to push off on him.

After thirty minutes MacKenzie said, "That was a Soviet fighter. An Su-27."

"Looked like a MiG-29 to me."

"They've updated the avionics packages, improved the fire control systems, and enhanced the radar. When we do it, we put a letter after the aircraft designation. The Soviets redesignate the aircraft."

"I'm not interested in the Soviet reasons for naming aircraft. I want to know what in the hell is going on."

"It's nothing, really. Soviets and the Japanese have an unofficial mutual defense pact. Soviets trade in Japanese electronic goods, computers, radios—hell, even televisions. Pay good money for them, but as a way of paying off some of the debt, they provide protection for the Japanese."

Reisman was silent for a moment. "Why is this being kept quiet? What difference would it make?"

"The feeling is, after what happened during the war, a Japanese-Soviet pact would not be welcomed."

"The war? You mean the Second World War?"

"Exactly."

Reisman laughed. "That's the dumbest thing I've ever heard. No one gives a shit about that anymore. No one's worried about the Japanese becoming a major military power. Hell, they dominate the region with their wealth. They can buy everything they tried to conquer."

"I'm just telling you the reason behind the silence. It just doesn't seem to be the right moment to let the world know that the Soviets and the Japanese are friendly."

"You're going to have to do better than that," said Reisman. "I mean, I don't know of anyone who'd view an economic relationship between the Soviets and the Japanese as dangerous. Hell, the Japanese will probably end up owning the Soviet Union. Why fight when you can buy?"

"That's a simplistic view," said MacKenzie.

"Simplistic or not, I'm afraid that there is more here than you're telling me. I want the truth."

MacKenzie shot him a glance, touched the brake, and then hit the horn. "Fucking assholes."

"You cut him off," said Reisman.

"You know everything about driving, too."

"Hey. Don't get hostile because your cover story is full of holes."

"I just want you to know that this is something that shouldn't come out right now," said MacKenzie. "It's important that it be kept a secret."

"Why?"

"Just because."

"That won't wash. I'm going to file a story that says

a Japanese fishing boat, under attack by a Chinese gunboat, was saved by a Soviet fighter.''

"I really wish you wouldn't," said MacKenzie. That was the last thing he said.

Reisman reached down and let his seat recline. He closed his eyes and thought he could feel the rocking of the boat. He tried to ignore it, but it was beginning to make him sick. He opened his eyes and stared at the road. The feeling of sickness evaporated.

He watched the scenery pass. He'd thought of Japan as a rural place, filled with rice farms and water buffalo. Tokyo and a few cities were built up and land prices near them were sky-high. A hundred miles from Tokyo things were supposed to be better. But all he saw was an endless string of buildings, businesses and residences. Every square inch near the road had been taken. It was an incredible scene and it explained the Japanese drive to own land in other parts of the world.

For an instant he had a worldview that was ridiculous. Everything was owned by the Japanese. They'd learned that war couldn't get them the resources they craved. But money could, so they used it to conquer the world. It worked because no one was paying attention.

When they finally entered Tokyo, MacKenzie asked, "Is there some place I can drop you?"

"The hotel will be fine."

They arrived there, and Reisman started to get out of the car. MacKenzie stopped him and said, "This shouldn't be broadcast. There are lives at stake."

"I'll think about it," said Reisman. He got out, crossed the sidewalk, and entered the hotel, a glass, steel, and tile structure that had no warmth at all; style and human needs were sacrificed. You got a clean room that cost too much and that was all.

Reisman picked up his key at the desk and walked to the elevator, watching the people circulate through the lobby or sit on the furniture arranged around a goldfish pool. He saw nothing out of the ordinary. He didn't see any spies or enemy agents. No one seemed to be interested in him.

As he reached his room the phone was ringing. He

pushed the door closed, threw his key on the bed, and grabbed the instrument. "Reisman here."

"What in the hell are you doing up there?" screamed the voice at the other end.

"Carmichael."

"Damn right it's Carmichael. Christ, Reisman, I've been getting phone calls about you for the last two hours. Everyone and his brother is in on it. They're calling you everything in the book from a liar to a sloppy reporter. That you don't know a thing about investigative journalism, that you distort, lie, and invent."

"You don't believe that, do you?"

"If I did, you'd be unemployed right now. What I want to know is what in the hell you've been doing up there." Carmichael's voice was tinged with anger.

"This is an open phone line," said Reisman. He sat down on the bed, cradled the phone between his shoulder and his ear, and reached down to take off his shoes.

"I know it's an open line."

"Then you know that I can't talk."

"Doesn't matter," said Carmichael. "You can brief me on it when you get here."

"Okay," said Reisman. "I've a couple of things I want to check out here first. Two, maybe three more days and then I'll hop a plane."

"You don't seem to understand," said Carmichael. "You're to come back now."

"But I'm onto something important here. I can't describe it now, but it's big."

"I'm sure it is. But you're still to return now. Before anyone else makes any more phone calls. Tomorrow morning at the latest."

Reisman sat up and looked at his reflection in the mirror. He was quiet for a moment and then said, "But . . ."

"Listen," said Carmichael. "This isn't a point for debate. You come back here and we'll find you another story. Something that will interest you."

Reisman was going to protest and suddenly realized what was happening. Either someone was in Carmichael's office, listening to his side of the discussion, or someone was monitoring the entire conversation. That meant that Carmichael was putting on an act for someone.

"I can't," he said suddenly. "There's too much to do here. Too many leads that need to be followed."

"This is not a request," said Carmichael.

"But it's one hell of a story," said Reisman. "Pulitzer Prize stuff. A real, gut-busting story."

"All you reporters talk about gut-busting stories no matter what they are. You're off it now, and I expect you back tomorrow. You call the office when you get in. I want to know the minute that you're back in Hong Kong."

Reisman grinned at himself in the mirror and wondered if he'd played his role well enough yet. Should he make another stab at it. Shrugging, he said, "Tomorrow. But I can come back to Japan later?"

"We'll see when you get here. I just want you out of Japan in the morning."

Reisman nodded. "Yes, sir. Tomorrow." He hung up. Then he slipped back and lifted his feet from the floor.

It was obvious that the story was bigger than he thought. They had wasted no time in calling his boss to try to get him out of Japan. Someone on the boat must have talked to someone in Tokyo who called Hong Kong. A well-run organization, able to bring pressure to bear on a worldwide scale.

Reisman couldn't help laughing. They'd betrayed themselves by making those calls. Carmichael wouldn't be bought off that easily. He just wanted Reisman out of Japan so that nothing would happen to him.

"Then tomorrow," said Reisman, "I continue to push."

OFF THE COAST OF CUBA

Inber stood with an eye pressed to the periscope and slowly scanned the ocean around his submarine; to the east, west, and south it was empty. To the north was a black mass with a few lights on it. That was the Cuban coast. The triangle of lights, visible only from the ocean, was the signal that Inber had been looking for.

"Down scope," he said as he turned away from it.

Major Boris Salnikov stood close and waited. He was dressed all in black, with black greasepaint smeared on his face. He carried no equipment and had no weapons except a small, silenced automatic pistol hidden under the uniform.

"We're three, four kilometers from the beach," said Inber. "The water is deep enough that we can maneuver in closer to the shore."

"The closer the better," said Salnikov.

"How long will it take your men to get ready?"

"Ten minutes," he said. "Five minutes to get up on deck, get the raft launched, and then move away."

Inber turned and said, "Right rudder and ahead slow. Give me a reading on the depth."

"One hundred fathoms."

"We'll be ready to launch you in about twenty minutes, Major."

"Then I'd better get down to see how the men are doing. We'll be ready as soon as you can put us out."

"Fine."

Salnikov left, using a ladder to descend deeper into the sub. As soon as he was gone Inber's exec, Yuri Yegorov, asked, "What are they doing?"

"I'm not supposed to know," said Inber.

"Which means that you do."

Inber shrugged.

Yegorov glanced at the men at their stations around them. The ratings were concentrating on their jobs and their equipment. There was a quiet pinging as the sonar searched. One of the chiefs was standing behind a sailor talking to him. No one was watching the captain and the exec.

Leaning close, Inber said, "They're an assassination team."

"Who are they after?"

"Castro."

"Holy Mother of God! Are you serious?"

Inber shot him an angry glance. "Hold your voice down. They have orders straight from Moscow."

Yegorov shook his head. "I'm afraid I do not understand global politics."

"We do not need to understand. We only need to do our jobs and ignore that which does not concern us."

"We are approaching the line of departure," said the chief.

"Fifty-two fathoms."

Inber glanced at the chart on the plotting table. "We're getting very close." He leaned over to use the intercom. "Major Salnikov, we are nearing the departure point."

There was a moment's hesitation. "Understood."

For a few minutes there was silence and then the officer of the deck said, "We've reached the line of departure."

"Up scope," he ordered. Again he surveyed the sea around him, searching for Cuban patrol boats. He knew that he would have a good shot at avoiding detection because they were south of Cuba. Castro concentrated his efforts on the northern shore. Not many people tried to escape to the south, and most of the infiltrators came from the north. The distance between Florida and the Cuban coast was so small that it made sense.

But then, most of the infiltrators didn't have an Oscar-class sub to help them. Inber was sure they had avoided Cuban detection, and even if they were spotted, the Cubans wouldn't say much about it.

He turned slowly and studied the shoreline. The triangle of lights was still burning. There was nothing moving on the shore. They had made it.

"Let's surface," said Inber. Again he used the intercom. "Major Salnikov, have your men prepare for departure."

This time there was no response. Inber waited as the boat slowly rose. He stood near one of the hatches, and as soon as they broke the surface one of the sailors ran up the ladder, spinning the wheel. He hesitated, waited for the lights to be turned down, and then pushed the hatch open. Water trickled in, soaking the sailor's shirt.

The man pushed his way up and out. Inber followed him up into the humid air of the tropical night. He moved to the side and uncapped the binoculars he wore around his neck. Slowly he scanned the shoreline. Other lights were burning, but they were hidden back among the trees and bushes away from the beach. There still was no sign of any movement on the shore.

The exec joined him and then two lookouts came up. They were studying the shore, the sea, and the sky. The sonar and radar operators were searching electronically. Before Cuban planes or patrol boats could appear, the boat should be able to sink beneath the waves.

The forward hatch opened and shapes began to appear. They spread out, helped stack the equipment, and then moved away. There was a quiet hissing as the inflatable raft was activated. Using ropes attached to the eyeholes, the men dragged the raft to the side and let it down into the water. Two men followed it as the rest of the team passed the equipment down to the men in the raft.

Finally the last of the men worked their way down into the raft, taking up positions round it, sitting on the large rubber sides. The lone man on the deck turned toward the bridge and threw a salute up at Inber. He then disappeared over the side. As that happened two sailors appeared, gathered up the nets and ropes, dropped them back down, and then vanished. The hatch clanged shut.

Inber used his binoculars to measure the progress of the raft. It was bobbing in the waves as the men paddled toward the shore. They had brought a small, electric motor that ran with a quiet buzz, when they could get it operating. Salnikov had decided that it was more trouble than it was worth and had left it on the boat.

They fought the waves, moving closer to the beach. At first Inber could see the movement as they paddled, but as the distance increased, the shapes merged into a single, black lump floating on the surface of the water.

"Let's reverse course here. All back dead slow."

"Aye, sir."

Inber watched the raft for another few minutes, until it disappeared into the gloom, he lowered his binoculars. "Let's clear the bridge."

The lookouts came down and disappeared through the hatch. Yegorov was next. For an instant Inber stood staring into the inky blackness of the night before turning and climbing down. As he reached the deck a sailor scrambled up the ladder and sealed the hatch.

"Let's get out of here," said Inber. "Left standard rudder at two-thirds speed."

"Aye, sir."

"Give me a depth reading."

"Sixty-three fathoms."

"Make preparations to dive," said Inber.

"Aye, sir."

Another voice said, "We have a green board."

"Dive. Level off at thirty meters."

"Aye, sir. Twenty-degree down on diving planes."

There were several minutes of silence broken only by the pinging of the sonar gear and the hiss of the electronic equipment and then, "Leveling at thirty meters."

"Let's come around to zero-nine-zero degrees at ten knots," said Inber.

"Aye, sir."

To Yegorov, Inber said, "You have the conn. I'll be in my cabin."

"Aye, sir."

Inber made his way to his cabin, sat down at his desk, and took out the boat's log. For a moment he didn't know what to write. Finally he glanced at the time and wrote simply, "Patrolling forty nautical miles off the southern coast of Cuba." That was all he had to write.

He put the log aside, stood, and stretched. He unbuttoned his shirt and then sat down on his rack. It had been forty minutes since the raft had been put into the water. They should have reached the shore. They should have crossed the open beach and found cover in the dense tropical vegetation growing there . . . if everything had gone right and the Cubans hadn't discovered them.

Of course, Inber had no way to learn what was happening. The men on the shore would not make a single radio call unless the situation changed radically. They were on their own. They would either be at the rendezvous or they wouldn't. Inber wouldn't know until he arrived at that point and the raft appeared near his boat. Until then, there was nothing for him to do. There was nothing for him to worry about. He would stay submerged and remain on station. It was easy.

Commander Dees liked the nights in the Caribbean on a ship. With enough forward speed, a good breeze over the decks kept things cool. The skies overhead were a deep, rich black filled with stars. The Milky Way was a bright band of light. The moon, a fingernail crescent, hung low in the sky. He wished he knew more about astronomy. Because there was no light pollution, it would have been the perfect place to study the heavens if he'd had a stable platform for the scope.

Dees was enjoying himself, just standing there, feeling

the power of the engines as they pushed the ship through the sea. There was a faint vibration in the deck, something that wasn't noticeable, except when it suddenly stopped.

Randolph appeared next to him and said, "Message up from the CIC, Captain. Guantanamo picked up something on one of their scans and wants us to check it out."

"They say what it was?"

"Sub of some kind, according to the information they have. Figure it might be Soviet."

"They sure it's not the Midnight Express?" That was the name given to a huge shark that lurked in the waters of the bay. Each night, as the sailors flushed the waste from their base, the shark entered, searching for food. It was large enough to be detected during the various scans they ran.

"They say it's a sub."

"These are international waters," said Dees. "Soviets have as much right to sail them as we do."

"Yes, sir. They just wanted us to check it out. Satellites won't be in position for another twelve hours. Might be too late then."

"You have the coordinates?"

"Aye, sir."

"Then get a course plotted and head for it. Make twenty knots. Full alert. Sonar, radar, sound."

"Aye, sir." Randolph retreated toward the bridge. He began giving orders, getting the information that the captain wanted, and getting the men set to complete their tasks.

Dees was a little annoyed with the intrusion. He'd rather just remain on his ship, on station, cruising the Caribbean without a real destination. He wanted to remain on patrol, calmly maneuvering without having to worry about a submarine and what it was doing.

He turned and left the wing, entering the bridge. He glanced at the helmsman who was standing behind the wheel, staring out over the bow. The exec and the OOD were bent over the plot table, a couple of charts spread out in front of them. The ASW officer was standing behind them, watching them work and commenting periodically.

"What you got?"

"We're probably five hours away. Maybe more," said Randolph. "That's if he stays right where he is."

"We get any indication of the direction he's taking?" asked Dees.

"No, sir. They had a target on the surface. Just popped up there."

"Why didn't they send in one of the EC-3s. He could have done everything we could."

"Plot shows the sub inside the Cuban territorial waters," said Randolph.

"You have our helo crew standing by?"

"Haven't alerted them yet," said Randolph. "Hell, sir, they can't operate inside Cuban territory either."

Dees studied the chart. "I think we'd better get them airborne. They can stand off the coast and see if they can pick up the sub."

"Aye, sir."

Dees looked at the ASW officer. "Why don't you brief the flew crew now. Let them know what we know, or the little we know, and get them into the air. Get a spread of DISCASS out there? I want to know everything I can about this guy."

"Aye aye, Captain."

Dees turned back to the charts. "What in the hell was he doing close to shore there? No port facilities. Just some deep water right off the shore."

"Well, if it was one of ours," said Randolph, "I'd say they were putting a team ashore. But the Soviets can just land when they want to go to Cuba."

"It's five hours into the search zone," said Dees. "Not much for us to do here." He glanced at his wristwatch. "I want that helo airborne as quickly as possible. Let the crew earn their flight pay for a while."

"Aye, sir."

The captain moved back to the bridge wing. Placing a foot on the bottom of the railing and his forearms on the top, he stared out into the darkness, knowing that he'd never be able to see the enemy, or rather the Soviet sub, while it remained submerged.

The enemy sub. Soviet sub. He'd have to get those thoughts out of his mind. The Soviets were not the enemy. They never really had been the enemy, though they had supported countries that were. North Korea and North Vietnam. But American soldiers had never knowingly faced Soviet soldiers. The two superpowers stood off and let each other maneuver throughout the world, trying to maintain a shaky peace and avoid a confrontation that could escalate into an apocalyptic thermonuclear exchange.

He had heard that American fliers had engaged Soviet pilots over North Vietnam in the 1960s and early 1970s. He'd heard stories of Soviet advisers with Viet Cong units. And he'd heard of American advisers with the Afghans, fighting the Soviets, but all of it was covert. Nothing to accuse the other side with. No evidence. Or if there was evidence, both sides ignored it. It was safer that way.

So the Soviets weren't automatically the enemy. There was a sub, operating in international waters. As was he. He could track the sub. It could track him. No one cared as long as no one fired.

From the stern he heard the growl of an APU and the beginning whine of a turbine. The sound built gradually until it was the roar of a jet engine and the popping of rotor blades. He glanced to the rear but couldn't see the helicopter.

"Helo's ready to rotate, Captain," the OOD announced from the hatch.

"Tell them to go ahead and launch. Maintain radio contact with us at all times. This isn't a secret mission."

"Aye aye, sir."

A moment later the sound of the helo's engine changed. It lifted off, climbed out, and then headed around toward the front of the ship. It circled once, the nav and anticollision lights flashing brightly against the dark backdrop of the night sky, then straightened out and headed off to the west, climbing rapidly. Dees watched it as it became a shapeless black lump with bright flashes near it and then vanished completely.

"Helo's away, Captain," said the OOD.

"I saw." Dees straightened up and stretched. "Guess I'll head down to the CIC and see what's happening."

"Yes, sir." The OOD waited until Dees had crossed the bridge. As the hatch closed he said, "Captain's off the bridge."

RIYADH, SAUDI ARABIA

Marie Frankowski, still dressed in the gray Nomex flight suit she had been wearing when captured at the airport, was leaning against the cool stone of the cell. It was dim inside, with just enought light for her to see the floor, the metal door, her cot, and the one used by Elizabeth Shawn. In the corner was a bucket that took the place of a toilet. The accommodations were not the luxurious ones that she had envisioned as they had begun the approach into the Saudi capital so long ago.

Both of them had protested their treatment, but that had done no good. Both had demanded that someone call the American embassy, but apparently that hadn't been done because no one from the embassy had interviewed them. They had demanded much, but the only concession they had received was that someone had taken the handcuffs off them after a couple of hours.

"I wish you'd sit down," said Shawn.

"Why?"

"Because seeing you standing there bothers me, that's why."

"Well, sitting on that heap of straw called a cot does nothing for me. I have to stand."

"Fine. Stand there, then."

"Hey, who jerked your chain? I'm not hurting anything by standing here. I'm not making any noise."

"Yeah," said Shawn. "Sorry. I just don't like this. Nobody knows where we are."

"Air force knows that we landed in Riyadh about the time someone started a war at the airport. They'll find the plane sitting there. Satellite imagery will show the plane sitting there. They'll know that we're here somewhere. We can't just disappear."

"I don't know about that. It wouldn't be the first time that someone from the West disappeared into the Middle East. Remember all those hostages that were taken in Lebanon. And then Hussein grabbed all those people in Kuwait."

"That wasn't Saudi Arabia."

"Then what about when the Iranians took over our embassy in Tehran?"

"Still wasn't Saudi Arabia," said Marie.

"I don't care. I don't like this." She stood up and walked to the steel door, bending at the waist to look out into the dim corridor. "If I was still in college, this would be a kick. A little Dungeons and Dragons to break up the monotony of the school year. But this is a real dungeon."

"You see anything out there?"

"Nope. Just an empty corridor with a torch, a fucking torch, hanging there. Just like the movies."

Marie pushed herself away from the wall and sat on the edge of her makeshift cot, elbows on her knees. She didn't like what she was thinking. She was feeling lucky because no one had burst into the cell to rape them yet. There had been no beatings, no demands for unimportant information or for false confessions to nonexistent war crimes.

So far the only indignity had been the treatment at the airport. They had been searched by their captors, dirty men in rags who had carefully felt them to make sure they had no concealed weapons. A little pawing like that wasn't so bad, considering that Ryerson was dead in the back of the aircraft.

With that thought in mind, she hadn't protested as her hands were pulled behind her and cuffed, though Hansen had demanded that someone call the American embassy immediately. They'd been transported through part of the city. There wasn't much in the way of combat damage there, but she heard the sounds of fighting elsewhere, and thick clouds of black smoke hung in the air, suggesting that fighting was going on somewhere.

"I want to get the fuck out of here," Shawn shouted suddenly.

"That won't help," said Marie. "It'll only call attention to us, which is the last thing we want." She rubbed a hand over her face and stared at the floor. "A lot of things could happen to us. A lot of bad things. Right now I think we're okay because no one wants to annoy our government, but that can change."

"Then we've got to get out of here," said Shawn. Her voice was higher, tighter.

"Right now we've got to keep a grip." Marie stood and walked across the cell. She bent and looked out into the corridor and saw nothing of interest there. She returned to her cot. "We've got to remain cool and rational."

There were distant sounds then: a metal door opening and leather on worn stone, a quiet murmur of voices. Marie turned her face toward the door but didn't move. She wasn't sure what attitude to present, quiet surrender or indignant outrage; which would get her back to her airplane; which is what she wanted most?

"Hey!" Shawn shouted.

"Shut up!" Marie snapped. "Don't draw attention to yourself. Survival is the key here, not making noise."

Shawn jumped to the rear as a key rattled in the lock. The door was flung open so that it slammed back against the stone wall with a loud, resounding clang. "Jesus."

Marie stood up and watched the door. A man in a khaki uniform with a Sam Browne belt, silver insignia on his collar, entered. He had a dark complexion, a black beard that covered most of his face, and he wore a Kaffiyeh He held a pistol in one hand and a set of keys in the other.

"We demand to be taken to the American embassy," said Frankowski.

"You demand?" said the man. His voice was rich and deep, no hint of an accent in his English.

Marie shrugged. "We request, then. We are American citizens who were caught in the, ah, activity at the airport. We were innocent bystanders."

"You are American soldiers. You are not innocent bystanders. You assisted a corrupt regime exploit the people."

"We have no quarrel here," said Marie. "We are neutral and we request permission to contact the American embassy."

The man laughed. He threw back his head and roared. "Your embassy is under siege. They have fired on innocent, unarmed civilians."

Marie realized that whatever she said would only get her in deeper. She had no idea what was going on. The briefings had mentioned turmoil in Saudi Arabia but nothing about armed revolt, and that was what she had seen. Now anything she said would be turned against her. In all the briefings she had sat through, intelligence officers telling her to remain silent if captured, she had not believed it. Now she knew those officers had been right.

"We have the right to contact our embassy," said Shawn.

"You have the right to die now," said the man. "You have no other rights except for those granted by us."

"I have—"

"Captain," snapped Marie. "You will keep your mouth shut."

"But—"

"Now," said Marie.

Shawn shot her a hostile look but didn't say another word. She retreated to her cot.

"On your feet," said the man. "The revolutionary council has decided to grant you an interview."

Marie moved to the front of the cell. She glanced at

Shawn but didn't say a word. The man stepped aside and let the two women walk past him.

The corridor held another four men. All were armed with old AK-47s and wore khaki uniforms like that of the leader. They stood in a semicircle by the door. They weren't going to let anyone bolt from the cell and escape.

"Follow me," said the man. He moved past his soldiers to walk up the corridor.

They reached the stairs and began to climb. They were narrow steps with steep risers. They reached a metal door with a metal slide in it. That opened and the man on the other side peered through at them. His face disappeared and the whole door opened.

They were taken across a narrow courtyard. There was a high, stone wall to the left. It was pockmarked and there were rust-colored stains on the stone. To Marie, it looked as if more than one person had been stood up against it and shot.

They entered another building through a wooden door, walked down a hallway, stopping at an ornately carved, heavy wooden door. It was five feet wide and ten feet tall with what looked like bronze hinges; armed guards stood on either side.

"You wait here," said the leader. "You will be called for your interview." He opened the door and walked in.

Shawn leaned close and whispered, "What do we say?"

"Name, rank, serial number, and date of birth. That's it. Nothing else."

"We're not prisoners of war," said Shawn.

One of the men motioned at her with the barrel of his weapon. He grunted something in Arabic. The leader emerged and said, "You will follow me."

They entered a huge room. There were red banners around the perimeter and one hanging from a thick wooden beam that was twenty or thirty feet above them. A long table ran across one end of the hall. A dozen men sat behind it, all wearing uniforms. There were weapons on the table in front of them, and a huge picture of a man in flowing robes and a turban behind them.

The man pointed to a spot on the floor. "You will

stand here and answer the questions. Be very careful how you answer. Your lives depend on it."

"Where are our friends?" Marie asked.

"They have already been here. Their fate has been sealed. See that yours is better." He then said something to the men sitting behind the table. Their discussion went on for several minutes, then the man turned and said, "The council would like to know what unit you fly for and what spy mission you were on before your arrest."

"Frankowski, Marie. Major. United States Air Force. Four one two, six seven, four eight nine nine. June twelve, one nine six three."

"What was that?" asked the man.

"Under the terms of the Geneva Convention, as a prisoner of war, I am required to give only that information."

"You are not a prisoner of war."

"I will not provide information of a military nature to those not authorized to receive it."

"Failure to cooperate could result in your being named as an enemy of the revolution. You could be shot as a spy, if the council decides." He turned his attention to Shawn. "The questions remain."

Shawn didn't answer right away. She looked first to Frankowski and then at the men of the revolutionary council. She took a deep breath and gave the same answer. Just her name, rank, serial number, and date of birth.

The man relayed the information to the council. They talked among themselves for a moment and then addressed the man. He looked at the woman and said, "The questions remain. If you answer them, you will be returned to your cell. If you do not, you may be shot."

Frankowski shook her head. "There is nothing I can do about it. The answer must remain the same. You are offering us nothing except an opportunity to return to our illegal imprisonment."

"The consequences are out of my hands."

"It's not vital military information," said Shawn. "It doesn't matter. We shouldn't have to die over this."

"Shut up," said Frankowski. "You give them anything and you'll be lost. We must stand firm."

The man turned his attention to the tribunal. He spoke

to them for a moment. Then, suddenly, the man in the middle slammed his hand to the table, the sound echoing in the huge hall. He half stood and shouted in Arabic, then picked up his rifle and waved it in the air.

"Answer the questions," said the man. "Answer them now or suffer the consequences."

"No." Marie's voice was calm.

"Major, we have got to cooperate," said Shawn. "It's not worth it."

Marie didn't look at the navigator. "Shut up!"

One or two members of the tribunal shouted and then the head man looked at the prisoners. He shouted something, pointed at them, waved a hand, and then fell silent.

The man shook his head slowly and said, "You have been condemned to death."

"Oh my God!" Shawn wailed. She felt her knees go weak and started to slump to the floor.

Marie grabbed her under the arm and lifted her. Leaning close, she whispered, "You are an officer in the United States Air Force. Try to remember that."

"We're going to die."

"We are not going to die. Now stand up like an officer. Remember who you are."

Shawn straightened up. She shrugged off Frankowski's hand and stared at the tribunal. She started to speak, thought better of it, and said nothing.

"Come with me," said the man. He bowed to the council and then headed toward the door.

Shawn was right behind him with Frankowski following her. They left the huge hall, and as they started down the corridor, the remainder of the guards fell in behind them.

As they reached the tiny courtyard Frankowski was afraid that they were going to be stood up against the wall right then, but they walked by it. They reached the other building and worked their way down to the dungeon.

When they reached the open door of their cell, the leader bowed to them and gestured. "Your quarters await you."

Marie stopped outside and looked at the man. "I think you had better allow us to meet with the rest of our crew."

"Do not make things worse for yourselves. Enter."

"Your actions here are illegal. There will be repercussions to these acts."

"In."

She entered the cell and watched the men pull the door shut and lock it. As soon as they were gone she said, "Jesus."

Shawn collapsed to the floor. "Oh God. Oh God."

Marie knelt beside her. "Listen, don't worry about that. It's all psychological warfare. Condemn you to death to soften you up and then you spill your guts. Nothing we do can make a difference."

"We've got to tell them what they want to know. We've got to do something."

"No. We do nothing. We sit here, we ask for our rights under international law, and we wait for the air force to get us the hell out of here."

Shawn began to cry then. "I just wanted to fly airplanes, and when I couldn't do that, I just wanted to navigate. I've done nothing."

"Keep that in mind," said Marie. "We've done nothing." She looked at the other woman. She was young. She had never been out in the real world. She had gone from high school to college and then into the air force. It was a protected life. There had always been someone in charge, someone in a position of authority who had all the answers. Now Shawn was learning that sometimes things didn't work out.

"Listen," said Marie, "there's a chance they'll split us up."

"Why?"

"Because they're smart enough to see that I told you what to do. Had you been alone, you would have reacted differently. You might have given them the answers to the questions they asked."

"The information isn't that important."

"Didn't you listen to anything said in any of the code-of-conduct classes? First they get you to talk to them. Maybe argue with them. Then you give up some unimportant information. The next thing you know, you'll be telling them the things they really want to know."

"We're not at war."

"Right now we have to act like we're at war. We have to remain strong. You have to promise me that you'll do nothing to harm us."

Shawn was quiet for a moment. "I'll try."

"Our lives are hanging in the balance here. Right now it's all bluster." She reached down and touched Shawn on the shoulder. "They condemned us to death but they didn't shoot us. Remember that. Remember that cooperation will make things worse. You've got to be strong."

"I'll do my best."

The door swung open suddenly. They hadn't heard the sound of the men coming down the corridor or the noise of the key in the lock. The door slammed into the wall, the clang scaring both of them.

The man they'd seen before pointed at Shawn. "You come with me."

"No," said Shawn.

Marie reached down and lifted Shawn to her feet. "You go. You show them you're strong. You tell them nothing."

"I can't."

Marie looked her in the eyes. "You've been taking the pay of an officer for four years. You demanded that you be treated with respect. You have demanded the privileges of an officer in the air force. Now it's time to earn that pay. Show that you deserve that respect."

"Yes, ma'am."

"You come with me," said the man.

Shawn straightened up, her shoulders back. She looked at Marie. "You don't have to worry about me."

Frankowski grinned. "I know I don't."

"You'll be next," said the man. "Don't think you'll get off scot-free."

"I'll be here."

The man pushed Shawn from the cell. He then ducked out and one of the guards reached in for the door. He pulled it shut and the key rattled again.

To the empty cell Marie repeated, "I'll be here."

HOMESTEAD AIR FORCE BASE, FLORIDA

Martinez, Chavez, and Alvarez sat in a small office and studied the maps, photos, and personality profiles spread out on the table before them. There was hot coffee nearby and a couple cans of Coke. Other than their three chairs, the room was empty. No pictures on the walls, no file cabinets or safes, and no phones or radios.

Martinez leaned back, picked up a Coke, and popped the top. He drank deeply, then set the can down. "There's no need for the whole team on this."

Chavez nodded. "Two guys. A shooter and a spotter."

"Security?" Alvarez asked.

Martinez stroked his chin. "I think putting more than two guys into this isn't going to be beneficial. Each time you double the size of the unit, you increase the odds of screwing up by four. Two guys should be able to do it. Anything more is going to be a waste."

"What two guys?"

Martinez glanced at Chavez. "I would think that we'd leave you here, in charge of the team. Be ready to roll if we need you. Hell, it's only what—two hundred miles from here to our target. You could be there in under an hour."

"I don't like this," said Alvarez.

"I'm sorry, Steve, but I can't see any reason to put the whole team on this. The Cubans are going to be madder than we were when our president was shot. They're going to be swarming, hitting anything that looks suspicious. I think two of us have a better chance of getting clear than the team would."

"Not to mention," said Chavez, "that Banse, Davis, Jones, Brown, and Cline do not look Hispanic."

"Then leave them behind and use the rest of the team. A good cover squad will help you get out."

"He does have a point there."

"No," said Martinez. "I think just the two of us, working carefully, will have a better chance. I don't want to risk lives we don't have to risk."

"How you going to get out?" Alvarez asked.

"There are two good routes," said Martinez, pulling a map around. "One is overland, right into the clutches of the United States Navy at Guantanamo. That'd take a couple of days, maybe a week or more. The other would be to the coast, to be picked up by a navy ship or sub. That might take only a couple of hours."

"There's the possibility of an air extraction," said Chavez. "A helicopter, from a navy ship, or from one of the islands, and we could be out within minutes."

"But we don't want the Cubans to know who did the shooting, so we have to be careful," said Martinez.

"Hell, they're going to know," said Alvarez.

"No," said Martinez. "They might think they know, but we've got to be careful so that they can't prove it. That's another reason to leave certain members of the team at home. Don't want anyone who is obviously an American."

Alvarez rocked back in his chair and picked up a cup of coffee. "I think this is the dumbest idea that anyone has ever come up with regardless of the rationale for it. I mean, shooting Castro isn't going to end the drug trade."

"But if the cartel members see that even Fidel Castro isn't safe, they might begin to think of other methods of making money." Chavez shrugged. "Besides, it's the mission assigned to us at the moment."

Martinez rubbed his face again. He was getting tired. Too much had been crammed into the last few days. He was operating on Coke and coffee and sandwiches, and it was beginning to get to him.

"When do they want you to deploy?" Alvarez asked.

"As soon as possible."

Chavez rocked back, glanced up at the ceiling and then back at Martinez. "I don't like this, Captain."

"What?"

"This whole thing. They want it done too quickly, without giving anyone a chance to think about it. We pull it off and our butts are going to be hanging out. They're going to seal off that island in a matter of minutes."

"I'll go in his place," said Alvarez.

"No," said Martinez.

"Oh, I'll go, Captain," said Chavez. "I just wanted it known that I think this one stinks."

"Most of them do, Master Sergeant. Most of them do."

Martinez stood at the edge of the airfield and said, "Infiltration. That's the key. Sneak in and then we have a better chance of sneaking out."

The navy aircraft, painted gray, stood on the ramp, the engines running. It was a twin-engine cargo plane on its normal run into Cuba.

The gear was piled behind them: enough food for a week in the field. Radio equipment so that they could stay in contact with net control, personal weapons, and finally the sniper's rifle that had been zeroed by Martinez. He'd decided that he would make the shot. If Chavez was uncomfortable with the mission, Martinez would see that he had as little to do with the actual pulling of the trigger as he could.

"They're ready, Captain," said Chavez.

"Not too late to back out. Both Alvarez and Ortega are prepared for this."

"No, sir. You need someone to take care of you. Liable to get lost in the woods."

Martinez turned and picked up his share of the gear. Then, carefully, he lifted the sniper's rifle. Because, if things worked out, he would be shooting at Castro from more than half a mile, he had to be very careful of the weapon.

"Nice of the Cubans to provide us with a base on their own island. Makes the infiltration so much easier."

The aircraft taxied toward them and stopped. The hatch near the cockpit opened and a man wearing a flight helmet that was attached to the plane appeared. He pointed at Martinez and Chavez and then waved them forward.

Ducking his head into the wind to hold his beret in place, Martinez ran forward. He reached the ramp, handed most of his gear to the crewman, and then followed him up into the interior of the plane, Chavez right behind him. He dropped his gear to the deck, and then turned, looking at the red web seating strung along one side of the fuselage.

Over the roaring of the engines, the crewman shouted, "You're going to have to buckle in."

Martinez set the sniper rifle on the canvas seat, carefully strapping it in. Then he sat himself, pulling the seat belt around his waist. He held a thumb up to let the crewman know that they were ready to go.

For a few moments it seemed quiet, then the roar of the engines increased and they began to taxi out toward the active runway.

Chavez leaned closer. "I'd feel better if we had the whole team with us."

"So would I, but it's better this way."

"Yes, sir."

They reached the runway, pulled up on it, and turned. The pitch in the engines changed again and the roar built quickly until it overwhelmed all other sounds. The aircraft vibrated for a moment and then they began to roll. The speed increased and suddenly the aircraft rotated and lifted, pulling itself into the sky.

Alvarez had thought that with Martinez and Chavez gone, the team would be allowed to sit around their rooms in the visitors' quarters, watch the ballgames on TV, drink beer, go to the PX, and do little else. He alerted net control and the base operations that he and the team would remain close in case they were needed.

Sitting in the small room that had been assigned to him, he tried to concentrate on the tiny black-and-white TV. The movie didn't interest him and his mind kept slipping from the show to the mission. He knew that nothing could have gone wrong yet. They were on an airplane heading toward Cuba. Unless the airplane crashed, there'd be no news from there.

The knock at the door took him by surprise. Alvarez pushed himself up and opened the door.

"Lieutenant Alvarez?"

"Yes."

"Would you sign for these, please?" The messenger extended a clipboard.

"What is it?"

"Message, sir."

He signed his name and took the envelope, watched the messenger disappear, and then closed the door. As he turned he ripped open the envelope. He read the message and said, "What in the hell is this?"

He sat down, glanced up at the television, and then read the orders again. They were ordered to Eglin Air Force Base on the first available transport. They were not authorized a leave en route, not authorized to use commercial air or POVs, and were given a single travel day. They had to report the day after tomorrow, meaning that they had only a day to put things in order.

"What a crock," said Alvarez.

And then he thought about it. Maybe it was the cover. They couldn't have been in Cuba creating trouble if they were on orders to Eglin Air Force Base.

The only thing he could do was delay the transfer as long as possible and then hope that Martinez didn't need any help while they were traveling.

"No," he said, grinning. The drive from Homestead to Eglin couldn't take more than a couple of hours. If he split the team, half of them heading to Eglin tomorrow and then the other half the next day, they could report on time and not leave Martinez and Chavez uncovered.

He wondered how he was going to explain that the team commander and the team sergeant were missing. And then he noticed that neither Martinez nor Chavez was mentioned on the orders. Someone was paying attention.

He'd have to let Gibson know what was happening and the two of them would have to get things organized. It wouldn't take long and it would be better than watching old movies on the black-and-white TV.

The plane touched down, rolling to a stop, but neither Martinez nor Chavez moved. They sat quietly, waiting for someone to come get them.

The hatch was opened by the crewman, letting in the hot, humid tropical air. Bright sunlight filtered in. A shape appeared, and then came at them.

"Either of you Martinez?"

"Yeah."

"If you'll come with me."

"What about my sergeant?"

"He necessary for the upcoming mission?" the man asked.

"If he doesn't accompany me, I doubt that we'll have any luck. He's fully briefed."

"Fine. And bring your gear, too."

They got up and exited the aircraft. There was a car parked near the nose of the plane. The trunk stood open. Chavez tossed his ruck into it and then Martinez's. Martinez held on to his rifle and climbed into the backseat. The man got behind the wheel, and Chavez joined him in the front.

"Name's Boyel," said the man. "I'll be functioning as liaison while you're here."

"We should be able to get out tonight, sometime about one or two in the morning."

"That's fine."

They drove off the airfield, turned a corner, and drove to the base proper. Martinez looked at the one- and two-story buildings, many of them painted gray. There was lush vegetation around some of them. Newer buildings, of brick and glass, had small lawns around them. White posts, two or three feet high, lined the roads.

"Where are you taking us?" Chavez asked.

"Got a secure area for you. Guards on the gates. You can relax, or whatever."

"Food," said Martinez. "We'd like a lot of food brought in. Steaks. Potatoes. A little beer. Salads. Anything you'd like, Art?"

"Iced tea. For some reason I have a craving for iced tea. Lemon and sugar."

"Okay," said Boyel.

He slowed for a guard on a gate. It was a small compound, buried deep in the base. The guard nodded, saluted, and waved them on through.

"Who knows we're here?" Martinez asked.

"The commander, me, and a few of the staff. The rest of the people know that someone came in but don't have a clue about who it is."

"Let's keep it that way," said Martinez.

"Goes without saying."

"Tonight," said Martinez, "I want a covered truck to take us to the fence."

"Certainly. There will be a quick briefing to cover the contacts inside Cuba. The truck is set about two klicks from here. A driver'll be waiting to take you toward the jump-off point."

Martinez slumped down in the seat, resting his head on the rear, and closed his eyes. Too many people were involved in this already. And even if they didn't know what the mission was, once it had been completed, they'd be able to figure it out. Too many people with too much knowledge. On something like this, someone would eventually talk.

The car stopped and Martinez opened his eyes. The building was isolated from the rest of the base by a fence, wall, and strategically placed bushes and trees. Whoever had planned it knew what he was doing.

"Your home for the next several hours."

Martinez forced himself up and opened the car door. "Thanks."

EGLIN AIR FORCE BASE, FLORIDA

Bloch knocked on the door and stuck his head into Brizzola's office. "Close up your safe," he said. "We've got some kind of emergency briefing in five minutes."

"What's going on?" Brizzola asked.

"Hell, I don't know. Old man called down and said to round up the staff. In the conference room."

"He want anything from us?"

"Nope. Just get your ass up there."

"Yes, sir." Brizzola stood up and locked his safe, turning the little sign around. He surveyed the office to make sure everything was where it was supposed to be and then walked out.

The building was one of the newer ones, but still had cinder-block walls, tile floors, and an unpredictable air-conditioning system. He walked down the hall, ignoring the color photos of the president, vice-president, and the other civilian members of the chain of command.

Brizzola used the stairs, arrived at the second floor, and turned to the right. He saw a captain disappear into the smaller conference room.

Bloch had beaten him. He was sitting at the far end, near a vu-graph projector. He pointed at the empty chair next to him. "Over here."

Brizzola worked his way around. The conference table almost filled the room. The dozen chairs around it were about half-filled by marine officers. Only one of them was a woman. There was a buzz of conversation as everyone tried to figure out what was happening.

A moment later the door opened and Brigadier General Porter Gleason entered, a grim look on his face.

As the assembled staff started to stand he waved them down. "Remain seated. We've got some real problems here." He looked over his shoulder as Captain Diane Carpenter followed. She closed the door and sat down next to the general.

"Our situation has changed radically in the last thirty minutes and I'm not sure what we can do about it." He glanced at Carpenter.

She stood up and said, "I have the preliminary reports of an attempted coup in Saudi Arabia. The information I have is from classified sources and will remain classified, though I'm sure the local news will have taped reports before any of us can get home."

"Get on with it," said Gleason.

"Aye aye, General." Carpenter looked down at the papers she held and began reading. "Iraqi soldiers, assisting local Communist forces, engineered a takeover in Saudi Arabia. With the recent death of the Saudi king, controlling factions have vied to force their man to the top. Apparently the Iraqis, with some assistance from the Soviet Union—though that assistance has not been confirmed—decided that now was the time to make their move. They have taken the airport in Riyadh, two radio stations, a television station, and control several government buildings."

"Jesus," said Bloch.

Carpenter looked up at him. "You have a question, sir?"

"No. Well, yes. What has our response been?"

Carpenter looked at Gleason. The general held up a hand. "As of this moment, our State Department has sent strongly worded messages to the governments in Baghdad and Moscow."

"Messages," said Bloch, shaking his head. "As if Baghdad is going to pay any attention to messages. Especially after our response in 1990."

"Captain," said Gleason.

Carpenter said, "As of now, it seems that the radical forces in Saudi Arabia, backed by the Iraqis and Russian support, have the upper hand. It seems likely that if they consolidate their successes and claim the country, that Saudi Arabia will suddenly realign itself with the East. Our bases, treaties, and oil will then be jeopardized."

Gleason held up a hand. "Thank you, Captain." As Carpenter sat down the general continued, "That is the bare bones of the situation. I assume we'll be able to learn more as the various news organizations begin to file their stories, complete with pictures of the military units involved in the operation."

Gleason then looked around the room at the assembled officers. "Here comes the real kick in the head. We've been put on alert."

"What?" said Bloch.

"We are to be prepared to move at a moment's notice and we're to report our readiness to move in the next twelve hours."

"With what?" Brizzola blurted.

"A very good question, Major." He looked at Carpenter.

She looked a little nonplussed. "I haven't had much chance to work the problem, General."

"Preliminaries are fine."

"Well, I've checked the computer and there are a couple of companies that we could get in here sometime in the next day or so, as long as the transport is available. We might be able to field a battalion but certainly not a full brigade. More than that and it'll be a week."

"You're sure of the figures?"

"Yes, General. Fairly sure. I might be able to find something a little faster, but not with the training that we require."

"Peace dividend," Bloch snapped.

Gleason ignored the comment. "We're required to report readiness in twelve hours. Not a couple of companies that might arrive, but the brigade."

"There's nothing I can do," said Keller.

Bloch spoke up. "When the units were assigned to us, each man was required to be prepared for deployment in twenty-four hours. Once the units were released to other controlling agencies, that requirement was lifted."

"I understand that," said Gleason. "But I have orders, too, and they require a full force."

"The public wanted to save money and they stripped us of our brigade," said Brizzola. "They even questioned the need for the marines, claiming that our mission was outdated. They pointed to the Eighteenth Airborne Corps. We were redundant. Now they want us ready to deploy in twelve hours."

"That does us no good, Major," said Gleason. "I want some answers."

Bloch nodded. "Just talking off the top of my head, sir, but if we can get three companies of trained marines, and a company of regular line troops, we can field a force in twelve hours. Once that has been accomplished, we can begin organizing the rest of the brigade."

"There are some army troops who've been through the various schools, too," said Brizzola. "Maybe a call to the Eighteenth Airborne Corps at Bragg would shake some troops loose for us."

"Nope," said Gleason. "I'd thought of that, though I wasn't thrilled with the idea. Eighteenth Corps is on alert, too. They have no one to spare."

"Special Forces?" said Brizzola.

"No, let's not get into that," said Gleason. "Bloch, how long to get that cobbled-together short battalion ready?"

Bloch looked at Keller. She said, "Depends on the transport, General. We can have the first of them arriving tonight."

"Logistically," said Brizzola, "that's going to be a nightmare. Quarters have been put into mothballs. We don't have the messing facilities, or the support companies we'll need."

"Air force can supply the clerk typists," said Gleason. "Grunts can bring their own weapons, shelter halves, and their MRE rations."

"You had any of those, Meals, Ready to Eat?" Brizzola asked.

"Not recently, but then they can't be any worse than the old C rations." Gleason looked back at Keller. "These companies are going to have to have support from their parent units. We don't have the resources and I don't see those arriving for a week, maybe two."

"Rapid Deployment Force. Shit!" said Bloch.

"Colonel," said Gleason, "we have been given an opportunity to shine here."

"Yes, sir. I was just thinking that it's typical of Congress. Give us a mission, but don't give us the resources to accomplish that mission. After this is over, we'll have to fight off the men with the money."

Gleason grinned and looked at the assembled staff. "Anyone else have a comment?"

"Air transport," said Carpenter.

"That'll be arranged through the air force. I understand that they'll call up some of their reserve units. I don't think air transport is going to be the problem."

"Billeting area?"

Gleason shrugged. "You people are going to have to answer some of these questions. All we need is an open field here on the base. They can post their guards. Bloch, you or Brizzola call the base commander and have him give us something."

"Yes, sir."

"We have plenty of work to do. Let's get at it." Gleason stood up and turned. Carpenter leaped to open the door for him they remained behind as he vanished.

When they were gone, Bloch looked at Carpenter. "What can you tell me about the troops coming in?"

"Right now, nothing."

Bloch turned to Brizzola. "You've got a master roster on the cadre?"

"I can put my hands on it."

"Do so, and then pass it along to Diane. Get orders cut bringing those people in here. Individually there might be enough of them to form another company."

"Billeting and supply," said Brizzola.

"Air force has transient quarters and messing facilities. I can't believe that a hundred and fifty or two hundred new guys coming in would overtax those systems. They'll be able to handle that."

"I'll get right on it," said Keller.

Brizzola said, "If we include ourselves in the cadre, that adds another forty-five or fifty people."

"Good. We're pushing two thousand."

"On paper," said Brizzola.

Carpenter ignored this and said, "We don't have the supplies on hand for two thousand."

"Again, everyone will have to bring his own gear. Those forced into commercial air travel might have trouble with weapons, but the number should be small enough that we can handle it."

Bloch pushed his chair back and stood up. "We'd better get at it."

Carpenter gathered the papers she'd spread out in front of her and said, "I'll let you know just as soon as I have something concrete."

"Good. Dick," said Bloch, "let's head down to the operations office and get things moving there."

"Aye, sir."

They walked out of the small conference room. As they headed down the hall Brizzola said, "It strikes me that someone ought to put together a complete briefing on the situation in Saudi Arabia, the territory around it, and the history of the peoples involved in the conflict."

"Right," agreed Bloch. "That's the function of intelligence. I'm sure that Carpenter, when she's finished with the roster, will be putting that information together."

They reached the main floor and headed toward the operations area. The sergeant was sitting at his desk, his feet up and a magazine on his lap. He glanced at the clock periodically, waiting for the minute hand to drop to the six so that he could go home. He thought the day was about over.

"Sergeant Taber," said Bloch. "I have good news and I have bad news. The good news is that it looks as if we're going to be revitalized. The bad news is that we're starting right now."

Taber dropped his feet to the floor and closed his magazine. He didn't seem to be disappointed that his plans had been changed. Instead he asked, "Where we going?"

"Right now, nowhere. Get on the horn and whistle up as much help as you can. Administration as well as operations. We'll need people cleared for top secret."

"Aye aye, sir."

Bloch looked at Brizzola. "You know what to do?"

"Dust off a couple of the Oplans. We'll need to get an assessment of the airfields in the area. We'll need some idea of how much transport is available, flight times, and the locations of any navy task groups that can supply direct support and air cover."

"There should be some marine air wings available. I think we'll need them to be carrier-qualified."

Brizzola ran a hand through his hair. Even in the air-conditioning, it was sweat damp. "I suppose I'd better call Trudy and let her know that we'll be working late."

"Right." Bloch turned toward Taber and then turned back. "You have to be very careful what you say to her."

"She's on our side."

"Yeah, but the wrong word . . ." said Bloch. "We don't want anyone to realize what's going on here."

"Hell, Bill, you can't hide it. We've been quiet for months, everyone going home at sixteen-thirty with everyone off on the weekends, and suddenly we're burning the midnight oil with a parking lot full of cars."

"I hadn't thought of that," said Bloch. "Soviet agents might notice and report it."

Brizzola couldn't help himself. He laughed and then asked, "Report what? That we're busy one night out of the year. Besides, we're buried in the middle of the base. There's no one around to see us."

"I'm getting paranoid. We've been running at half

speed for so long, I sometimes get lost." Bloch grinned. "We've got a hell of a lot of work to do before we get any sleep."

"Yeah. I hope somebody thought about getting some coffee in here."

"And hot food," said Taber. "We're going to need it before the night is over."

"Right," said Bloch.

Brizzola turned and left the operations office, heading for his own office. For the first time in months he felt good. For the first time in months he felt that he was going to be earning his pay.

Reisman stood in his editor's office, facing Carmichael. He turned so that he could look out into the city room. He watched the activity, the men and women moving around. One man jumped up suddenly, screamed into a telephone, and slammed it down.

"Source must have just dumped on him," said Reisman.

Carmichael said, "You want to have a seat?"

"Sure." Reisman slipped into the chair. He reached over and pushed the door shut. "I have to assume that someone was here, listening in."

"That makes no difference."

"What I didn't tell you was that it was a Soviet Su-27 Soviet, not just manufactured by the Soviets, but flown by them. Protecting a Japanese fishing boat."

"I don't see anything in that."

Reisman laughed. "You've got the Soviet Union protecting a Japanese fishing boat that is attempting to smuggle videotapes about the good life in America into China. Come on. Even you must see the significance of that."

"No reason to get snotty."

"Okay. Sorry. I think the place to go now is Tibet."

"What? I can't see a connection between Japan, the Soviet Union, and Tibet. Sounds more like you're joining one of those 'I've been in every country in the world' clubs."

"China annexed parts of Tibet and there has been unrest there ever since. Chinese troops have attacked locals, suppressing riots. It's the same story in a different location. I'm wondering if the Soviets and Japanese might not be in Tibet causing troubles for the Chinese."

"That scenario sounds absurd to me. Besides, I can't see this as being important to people back at home. Just another example of the Chinese and their satellites fighting it out. It's just not as significant as the Soviet satellites breaking away. The Chinese never posed a threat to the United States. Not the way the Soviets did."

Reisman glanced skyward, as if searching for assistance from there. Looking at Carmichael, he said, "Wouldn't the fragmenting of the last great Communist empire be considered a major story?"

"No. We ignored the Chinese for twenty years, and then paid little attention to them. The people don't give a shit about the Chinese. And they don't care that the Soviets and the Japanese have teamed to aid in the destruction of China. Now, if the Russians and the Japanese invaded, that would be one hell of a story. You think that's going to happen?"

Reisman was quiet for a moment and then shook his head. "No reason to invade. China is falling apart."

"Then there is no reason to go to Tibet," said Carmichael. "But there is reason to go to Saudi Arabia."

"Oh hell," said Reisman. "Everybody can see what's going on there. You don't have to be a rocket scientist to figure out a story in Saudi Arabia. Tibet takes finesse. Tibet requires some digging."

"Tibet is out, and I don't want to discuss it further," said Carmichael. "It's Saudi Arabia or you stay here for the next month or so. Period. But, I would think that someone of your talents would be able to find the story that the others have overlooked."

Reisman laughed. "And I'm a little too smart to fall for such transparent manipulation."

"Well, it's up to you."

"What's the status of journalists in Riyadh?"

"Right now, they're being welcomed by the revolutionary council. I think they want to show that things in Riyadh are normal. It's not like it was in Kuwait in 1990."

Reisman laughed again. "I've always wondered about

the wisdom of pushing into a hostile country. Seems to me that they could change their minds and I'd be stuck in Riyadh.''

"Then you'd have one hell of a story.''

"Stop selling," said Reisman. "I'll go. I think Tibet would be better, but I'll go to Riyadh.''

"I knew that you'd see the light. Catch the first flight you can.''

Reisman stood. "I still think this is a stupid idea.''

IN THE DESERT NEAR RIYADH,
SAUDI ARABIA

Captain Kurlov stood in the dung-colored tent while the hot desert air ripped at the flaps. His pistol held one corner of the map on the table. A canteen sat on another, and the magazine from an AK-74 held the third. Sergeant Yerikalin stood right behind Kurlov, studying the map with him.

"The Saudi lines of resistance kept retreating," said Yerikalin. He was wearing a light-colored tan uniform that closely matched the color of the desert. His web gear, ruck, and holster were all the same light tan. Nothing that would contrast with the desert around them.

"No way to get behind them to interrupt them. Makes our task so much more difficult. Can't catch them to disrupt them."

"I would guess," said Yerikalin, "that they'll make a stand here at this small town. Good position, crossroads, water, and food."

"Are you suggesting that we head there first?"

Yerikalin shrugged. "We could create some havoc there and then drift away."

Kurlov took off his soft cap and wiped the sweat from his forehead. He settled the cap on his head as he continued to study the map. "Maybe it's time that we joined the Iraqis."

Yerikalin moved around so that he could get a better look at the map. "We'll need airlift into the zone. Maybe touch down here?"

"No," said Kurlov. "Nothing going on there and it's firmly in the hands of the Iraqis."

Yerikalin laughed suddenly. "I think I got lost on that last turn somewhere."

"Does get confusing, doesn't it?" said Kurlov. "But with the Saudis out of the picture, too busy worrying about their internal problems and the attacks from the outside, we have a perfect opportunity to gain support in the area."

"Of course," said Yerikalin. "A warm-water port, and Iran is the only thing sitting between us and those port facilities. Not to mention the oil reserves."

"You're very well versed for a mere sergeant," said Kurlov.

"A sergeant who studies his history and can look at a map."

"Here," said Kurlov, pointing at the map. "The Iranians have stockpiled a great deal of equipment, arms, and food. They're building a base from which to launch a push into Iraq to retake some of the disputed lands. Treaties of the last five years notwithstanding."

"Of course," said Yerikalin. "The destruction of those supplies would certainly inhibit an invasion."

"And it might induce the Iraqis to attack to the east. Move the Iranians back."

"But won't that also cause the Iraqis to pull back from their attacks on the Saudis?"

"So. The dissidents in Saudi Arabia have taken control of the government. They have power for the moment. The Iraqi assistance is no longer as important."

"These are decisions that should not be made by a captain and a sergeant," said Yerikalin.

''No, they should not. However, there are orders that have been issued that allow me a certain degree of latitude in what we do.''

''Ah.''

''I think that we should get the team ready to move. Two hours to get the men set and then on board the helicopters. A short flight into Iran, a landing and attack, and then a short flight right back out.''

''Yes, sir.'' Yerikalin turned and moved through the tent's entrance.

Kurlov stayed a moment longer, examining the map. He had to agree with Yerikalin. The strategy didn't really make sense. They should push at the Saudis until that prize was firmly in their hands. Then it would be time to stir the stew again. Let the Iraqis and the Iranians get into a fight. Support of the Iranians, if handled properly, would give Moscow its direct access to a warm-water port.

Shrugging, Kurlov picked the pistol off the corner of the map and stuffed it back into his holster. He pulled the map from under the two other objects and then rolled it up so that he could push it back into the map case.

Finished, he stepped out into the blazing sun and searing heat of the late afternoon. He hated it, preferring the cold of a Moscow winter. That was weather he was used to, not the constant heat of the desert that sucked the fluids and the life from the body.

He walked toward the small, cinder-block building that held an array of radio antennas on the top. Air-conditioning rumbled from behind the building. Computers and modern radio equipment demanded coolness. A modern army needed its computers for all sorts of point defense.

He opened the door and stepped into the dimness of the commo room. For a moment he couldn't see and then his eyes slowly adjusted; he could make out the shapes of men hunched over their equipment and he could see the dancing needles on the vu meters of the various pieces of radio equipment. There was a quiet hiss of air-conditioning, a hum of the radios, and the smell of electricity in the air.

The radio watch officer stood behind the men operating the equipment. Kurlov moved to him and said, "In the Zebra Code, alert Moscow that we go tonight."

"Yes, sir. Will there be a reply?"

"No. Just an acknowledgment."

"Shall I relay that to you?"

Kurlov shook his head. "I do not need to know that. Only that the message has been transmitted."

"We'll do that now."

"Thank you." Kurlov turned and reluctantly left the cool radio shack. He walked toward the main squad tent erected at the edge of an oasis. Shadows from a couple of date trees fell across it but did little to protect it from the sun. The front and rear flaps were open in an attempt to catch the breeze, even though the wind resembled a blast of hot air from a furnace. Inside, the men were sitting on a wooden floor, attempting to get their equipment ready for the upcoming mission. He stopped at the tent flap and watched the men at work, cleaning weapons, sharpening knives and the edges of their infantry spades.

The spades were small, simple tools that had a variety of uses. With their razor-sharp edges, they were efficient weapons. The could be used to silently split the skulls of the enemy or to disembowel or decapitate him. They could be used to measure distances because of the precise length of the handle or the distance across the flat of the blade. And if necessary, they could be used to dig fighting holes.

Kurlov watched the activity for several minutes and then stepped into the tent. The men glanced at him but continued to work. Had they been in the Soviet Union, or had there been another officer with Kurlov, they would have risen to greet him. But alone, with work to be done, they ignored the formality.

"How's it going, Sergeant?"

"Finishing up," said Yerikalin. "Would you care to inspect the equipment?"

Kurlov knew that it would all be in the best of shape. The men knew that their lives depended on their equipment, but he also knew they wanted him to inspect it. When there was nothing wrong, when no fault could be found, the men wanted the officers to look at the gear.

Kurlov moved into the tent and picked up one of the

AK-74s. He worked the bolt, listening to the smooth click-
ing of the weapon. He held it up and looked down the
barrel, seeing the light reflecting from the well-cleaned
sides.

Next he picked up one of the infantry spades and used
his thumb to test the edge. As sharp as any combat knife.
He wondered how the man would feel if he was forced to
actually dig in the sand with it.

He crouched near the radio operator and lifted an eye-
brow in question. The man nodded and said, "Ready to
go, Comrade Captain. Two sets, one as backup. Battery
packs good for a week and a small hand generator to con-
serve or rebuild the batteries. New printed circuit boards."
He pointed to an array of them on the blanket beside him,
each sealed in clear plastic. "A gift from the Americans."

"Gift?"

"Sold to us in the interest of world peace," said the
RTO. "Our amateur radio operators can communicate with
their amateurs."

"Fine," said Kurlov. He looked at Yerikalin. "Have
you briefed the men on the operation?"

"No, sir. I thought you'd like the privilege."

Kurlov sat on one of the cots set along the edge of the
tent, his hands clasped. "This is going to be a simple
mission. We go in, destroy as much of the equipment and
supplies as we can, and then get out. We'll hit the western
end of the camp, sweep through to the east, and then get
the hell out of there."

"Rules of engagement?" asked one of the soldiers.

"We do not allow ourselves to be killed or wounded.
We shoot to defend ourselves and we kill any guards who
are in our way."

"Yes, sir."

Kurlov pulled the map from the case he carried and
spread it out on the floor. "This is the target."

The men crowded around, Kurlov kneeling with them.
It was a detailed map of the Iranian camp, based on intelligence reports and satellite imagery.

"We'll hit them just after one in the morning," said
Kurlov. "We'll infiltrate, here, here, and here. We tear up

everything we see, setting it on fire or blowing it up. In and out as quickly as possible.''

"Exfiltration?" Yerikalin asked.

"Helicopters," said Kurlov. "That's been arranged from the top.''

"Good. We don't have to walk."

"Or steal a truck," said Chuykov.

"All right," said Kurlov, "let's get down to the specifics. I want to go over the operation in detail before we board the helicopters later.''

Kurlov was satisfied with the plan. He'd have liked three or four days to review and refine it, but time didn't allow that. They had to move before the Iranians could launch their assault on the Iraqis. That had been clear. So he'd walked though the plan with his men, listened to their comments, and then worked through it some more. When they had something that looked good, Kurlov told them to finish their preparations and to meet him at the helipad at twenty-two hundred hours.

Now they sat in an Mi-26 helicopter that carried everyone Kurlov had assigned for the mission and still had room for another thirty-five soldiers. Spread out in seats that tilted so that the soldiers could exit quickly, they mentally rehearsed the plan, each man going over his role in the upcoming fight over and over again.

They took off with two Mi-24 Hind helicopters as escort. They stayed low, fifty or sixty feet off the ground, so that the various radars in use would have trouble spotting them. With all the activity going on in the region, they'd probably get lost in the clutter. The pilots wore night-vision goggles so that they could search the ground for obstacles. Through the windows Kurlov could sometimes see the two gunships. They had their running lights on.

Over the noise in the aircraft Yerikalin yelled, "According to my calculations, we're getting close.''

Kurlov checked the time and then moved forward. He looked into the cockpit. To the navigator he yelled, "How much longer on this?''

"Thirty minutes."

Kurlov returned to the men. He looked at them. Some were sitting quietly, their eyes closed, perhaps sleeping. Another was cleaning his rifle over and over, ramming a rag down the barrel to make sure that no dust, dirt, or fine sand had accumulated in the ten minutes since he'd done it before. Two men were talking, their heads close together. Each man was passing the time in the chopper as best he could.

"One last time," Kurlov yelled. "Let's review the plan one last time."

They crouched on the open deck at the rear of the chopper, near the ramp that would allow them to swarm from the rear. They'd be out and moving within fifteen seconds of touchdown. The helicopter would be climbing out as they ran toward the first of the attack points on the ground.

Kurlov went over those again. They needed to be eliminated in seconds, before an alert could be sounded. Once that was done, the men would fan out and begin the real work. When they finished, they would head into the desert. The exfiltration would be covered by the Mi-24s. They'd pile into the rear of the Mi-26 and everyone would return to their camp.

Kurlov and then Yerikalin pointed out the primary targets, as identified by the satellite imagery Finishing, Kurlov said, "Any last-minute questions?"

"No, sir," said one of the men.

"Okay. We leave no one behind, we leave no equipment behind, and we destroy as much as we possibly can." He glanced at his watch. "Ten minutes or less. Let's get ready."

He turned and reached back into a crate that held bandoliers of ammo. He pulled one free, slipped it over his shoulder, and then got another. He took a single magazine from it, shoved it into the well at the bottom of his AK-74, and worked the bolt, chambering a round. After flipping the safety on, he pulled the other bandolier over his shoulder. He now had nearly three hundred rounds, more than he thought he'd need, but he'd always believed that it was better to have too much than not enough.

The rest of the men picked up their equipment and got

ready for the landing. Most of them had smeared black greasepaint on their faces so that they wouldn't be easy to see in the dark.

"Five minutes," the navigator yelled. The information was relayed through the rear of the chopper.

Kurlov moved back, so that he was crouched at the edge of the ramp. When it was dropped, he wanted to be among the first off the chopper. He glanced over his shoulder. The men were all there, waiting.

The sounds of the turbines changed and the rotor system began to pop like a machine gun. The nose of the aircraft came up as they slowed suddenly. As the wheels were leveled the servos began to whine and the ramp dropped.

They bounced once as they contacted the ground. Kurlov was up, stepping toward the ramp. As soon as the opening was big enough to get out Kurlov leaped forward. He dropped to the ground and spun, looking back at the black smudge that was the Iranian camp.

The ramp came fully down and the men were running from the chopper. It lifted, the nose diving as the pilots used the collective to maintain altitude. It was gaining speed rapidly, climbing straight out as the gunships circled once and then joined it.

Kurlov, with half a dozen of the men, was running across the soft sand, heading toward the enemy camp. An Iranian stood up, looked at them as if he couldn't believe what he was seeing, and was then cut down by a Soviet with his infantry spade. There was a quiet noise, like a baseball bat against a ripe melon, and the enemy was gone.

In seconds the soldiers were at the edge of the camp. There was no fence, nothing to protect it or establish a perimeter. Kurlov and his men rushed forward and in seconds were among the tents, buildings, and supplies.

Kurlov pointed and yelled, "Go. There." One of the soldiers nodded and his men turned, disappearing into the darkness. Another group ran in the other direction, spreading out so that they could infiltrate the entire camp.

Kurlov moved in deeper, no longer running, using the shadows as he worked his way among the tents. He crouched near the entrance to one and listened. Men were sleeping inside; he could hear them snoring. Taking a grenade, he pulled the pin and rolled it into the tent. Flattening himself to the ground, he slowly counted, ducking his head and closing his eyes when he hit five.

The grenade detonated with a loud, flat bang. There were shrieks from inside. One man roared in sudden pain. Another, blood covering his face, staggered out. Kurlov stood and clubbed him.

Grenades began to detonate all over the camp. An AK fired a short burst. That was answered by two weapons. One burned through a thirty-round magazine. Another only fired a couple of shots. Kurlov left the tent, ran around it, and joined Yerikalin.

"Nothing in there," said the sergeant.

Before he could move, a shape loomed out of the darkness. Kurlov fired a single shot from the hip. The man collapsed without a sound.

"Let's go," said Kurlov.

Together they ran toward another tent. This one held boxes. Kurlov tossed in a thermite grenade, and then both of them ran off, diving for cover as the grenade exploded. It showered flaming debris on the boxes and set the tent ablaze. Flames spread rapidly, and suddenly they could easily see the enemy soldiers.

A dozen were running toward the fire. Kurlov kneeling and Yerikalin standing opened fire on them. Green tracers flashed. Two of the enemy fell. Another staggered, screaming. A couple turned to flee and the rest opened fire. Kurlov aimed into the muzzle flash, flipped the selector to full auto, and pulled the trigger. Another of the Iranians died.

Firing erupted around them. More of the Iranians were in the battle now. Grenades were going off around them, some of them thrown by the Iranians. Kurlov didn't care. One way or another, the battle was destroying equipment, and that was the mission.

The last of the Iranians in front of him died. He fell to his side, tried to get up, and was hammered down by Yerikalin pumping rounds into him.

"We move now," said Kurlov.

The Russians ran forward, Kurlov hesitating long

enough to make sure all the enemy soldiers were dead, to a small, stone building. In the flickering firelight bleeding through the open door, Kurlov realized they'd found the powder magazine.

"Timed explosive. Five minutes."

"Of course." Yerikalin moved in and set his weapon down against a stack of wooden boxes.

Kurlov knelt at the door, watching the shapes moving through the cap. An Iranian, obvious in his robes, ran toward the powder magazine. Kurlov let him get close and then fired once. The enemy dropped and didn't move.

"Ready," said Yerikalin. "Set it for five and tossed it toward the rear. They'd have to start searching now to find it."

"Then let's get out."

But as he stepped through the door the stones around him seemed to erupt. Bullets whined off into the desert night, bits of rock clipping him. Kurlov dived back into the magazine.

"Four minutes," said Yerikalin.

Kurlov rolled to the other side of the door and got up on one knee. He searched the area outside, but couldn't see the Iranian who had fired. He squeezed off a couple of rounds, aiming into shadows, but there was no return fire.

"About three minutes," said Yerikalin.

"Okay. You go right, I'll go left. There's one guy out there, maybe more. On my mark."

Yerikalin crouched at the door, waiting. He held his weapon in both hands and was searching for signs of the enemy soldiers.

"Go," Kurlov yelled. He leaped out, sprinted a dozen meters, and threw himself to the ground. Rifle fire erupted, the rounds snapping over his head. He rolled to the left and tried to spot the sniper but failed.

Yerikalin was up then, firing. He ran at the corner of a tent, shooting as he ran. Kurlov turned, saw a shadow pass in front of the burning tent and equipment and fired at it, missed, and fired again. The Iranian spun around, tossing his weapon away.

"Down," Yerikalin yelled.

Kurlov looked at him and then hit the dirt. There was firing from around the camp. It was sporadic. Single shots and short bursts. Kurlov glanced to the rear, at the magazine, and then pushed himself lower.

There was a quiet explosion from inside the building that was followed by a second, louder one. Then the building seemed to collapse in on itself and finally exploded with a single, long, loud rumbling. A fireball erupted as the walls blew out. For a moment it was as bright as noon in the camp. Heat washed over it like waves on a beach. Debris began to fall, some of it white-hot, setting a thousand small fires.

Kurlov felt weak. He wanted to get up and run but couldn't force his muscles to respond. The concussion from the explosion had stunned him. He'd been too close to it. Slowly, feeling returned to his body and he stood, shakily.

The firing had died out. There was shouting and a couple of random shots but no organized resistance. Kurlov took a staggering step, regained his balance, and began to move.

Yerikalin appeared next to him. "You hurt, Captain?"

"No. Stunned. Let's get the hell out of here and get the pickup zone established."

"Yes, sir."

They ran forward and reached the other end of the camp. Kurlov turned. Everything was in flames. The tent city was gone, now nothing more than glowing embers of the wooden floors. Flames from equipment stockpiles shot a hundred feet into the night sky. Ammunition was cooking off, the rounds detonating in the heat of the fires. Tracers were tumbling into the night sky, giving the attack a festive look.

The rest of the attacking force began to appear. They fanned out, turned back to the camp, looking for the enemy force, but they didn't materialize. They were lying scattered in the camp, dead or wounded or in hiding.

Kurlov brought his hand down in a chopping motion and the men opened fire again, everyone shooting into the camp on full auto, burning through the magazines. Tracers flashed, ripped into the few remaining structures, and shredded the last of the night.

Finally satisfied, Kurlov ordered, "Cease firing. Cease firing." As the men stopped shooting he said, "Get me a count. Let's make sure everyone is out. Chuykov, take a dozen men and get a PZ established half a klick from here."

"Yes, sir."

"Umarov, I want five men to remain here as a rear guard. When the choppers are inbound you can break off and join us on the PZ." To Yerikalin he said, "Where's the RTO?"

"Over here."

Kurlov turned toward the sound of the voice. "Get the choppers coming in now. We're a good thirty minutes ahead of schedule."

"Yes, sir."

As the RTO made his coded call Yerikalin approached. "We've got four dead and three wounded. But we got everyone out of there."

"That means we pulled it off," said Kurlov.

"Yes, sir. That we did."

"Let's get the men moving toward the PZ."

"Yes, sir." Yerikalin ran off to get the squad leaders organized.

Kurlov turned and looked back at the burning camp. There was no doubt that the raid had been a success.

VIETNAM

G eneral Stepanov decided that he didn't like being in Vietnam on a diplomatic mission. Such things should be left to the politicians, who understood the subtle maneuvering necessary for negotiations. It was not the job of a general.

They rode through the streets of Hanoi that showed no signs of the war that had been fought twenty years earlier, except for the circles in the sidewalk. Stepanov knew that under each cover was a hole that people had once used for protection from American B-52 raids. One person to a hole. There were dozens of them along the sidewalk, left as a monument to the people who had braved the falling bombs.

They came to a modern building in the center of the city. It could have been in Moscow or Berlin or New York; a glass-and-steel structure surrounded by buildings that looked as if they belonged in another age in another place, tan buildings with small balconies under the windows and red tile on the roof.

"Comrade Tan is waiting inside."

They entered the building and then walked to the third floor. Here the halls were wide but poorly lit and the tile floors dirty. On either side were offices, the doors to them open, as were the windows opposite them. This provided no relief from the stifling heat or the oppressive humidity.

They reached a closed door, but didn't knock. One of the Vietnamese opened it and gestured at Stepanov. He entered and recognized the Vietnamese premier sitting behind a small, worn desk in a Spartan office: wicker chairs for the visitors, a ragged bamboo mat on the floor, and a small ceiling fan turning slowly.

Tan Tri Van stood. A small, thin man in black pajamas, with gray hair and a Ho Chi Minh beard, he bowed slightly and said, in passable Russian, "Welcome to the People's Republic of Vietnam."

Stepanov bowed and made his speech in Vietnamese. Tan grinned, waved at a chair, and sat down. He switched to French and said, "Shall we stop trying to impress each other with our ability to learn phrases in the other's language?"

Stepanov was uncomfortable with French but could speak it. He nodded. "It is an honor to be able to meet one of the great leaders of the world."

"Your words are kind but untrue, I'm afraid. Welcome to our country."

"Thank you, Comrade." Now they were suddenly into a diplomatic situation and Stepanov didn't know how to proceed. He wanted to mention the Chinese and the Thais and what the Soviets were prepared to offer, but didn't think he should launch into that, especially with his aides and staff at a hotel rather than in the office with him.

"Would you care for some tea?" Tan asked.

Stepanov nodded. "That would be most refreshing."

Tan waved a hand and one of the men disappeared quietly. Smiling, he asked, "What did you think of our little ceremony at the airport?"

"Quite nice. Very impressive. Your soldiers are well disciplined."

"You saw, of course, only our very best."

"Still, it was most impressive." Stepanov waited.

Tan sat behind his desk, nodding slowly like an old, skinny Buddha. "There is so much that needs to be done and so little time. And there are those who would like to see us fail."

"The Americans?" Stepanov asked.

"Of course. They promised aid when they were thrown out, but they have not provided it. And there are the Chinese. Communist brothers, but men who would like to see the end of the Vietnamese state. Like others, the Chinese once ruled here, but we pushed them out, too."

It was an opening. Maybe it hadn't been intentional, but it was there. Stepanov said, "We are prepared to assist in that arena."

The door opened and the man returned with a tray with several small cups on it. First he served the premier and then Stepanov. Again, Stepanov recognized the gesture for what it was.

Tan tasted the tea and then set the cup on his desk. "The Chinese believe that they are invincible. They believe that their numbers make them strong, but only so many can be sent to fight at once."

"There are those of us who believe we can help," said Stepanov cautiously.

"At what cost?" Tan asked.

Stepanov shrugged. "We are providing aid for a friendly nation, just as we did during the struggle with the French and the Americans."

"Are you claiming the victory as your own?"

"No. The fighting, the bravery, the dying was done by the Vietnamese in the interest of us all."

Now Tan smiled and picked up his teacup again. He drank and then said, "What are you suggesting?"

Stepanov sipped his tea and then said, "If we learned anything from the Americans in Vietnam, it was to move troops rapidly on a battlefield. If the enemy can be cornered and contained, even if his force is numerically superior, then air mobility can negate the numbers. The enemy can be defeated."

"Air mobility?" said Tan.

"I have heard American estimates claiming that as many as a million and a half additional troops would have been required to fight in Vietnam if it hadn't been for air mobility. In days past, a soldier fifty kilometers from the battle was as useless as an untrained soldier. But with air mobility, that soldier could be a hundred, two hundred kilometers from the battle when it began and could get there to fight in a matter of minutes, rested, and ready to kill."

"The Americans demonstrated that to us many times," said Tan grudgingly. "But we do not have the capability, the industry, the resources, to produce an air-mobile force."

"No," said Stepanov. "And you did not have the industry or the resources to produce an air force or the surface-to-air missiles that you used to fight your war with the Americans. These were gifts from my people to yours."

"And we thank you." Tan sipped his tea slowly, rocking slightly and smiling. "Why are you suddenly offering us this gift?"

Stepanov would have preferred to have his advisers around him, not that he needed them. They would have provided him with some security, some confidence, but he knew exactly what he was to say and what he was supposed to forget.

"The Chinese have been pushing at your borders. There are disputes over important territory. We would like to see those resolved."

"In whose favor?" Tan asked. "Are you suggesting that we surrender land to receive machines?"

"No," said Stepanov. "No. We'd like to see the dispute resolved in your favor. Our assistance will allow you to become more vocal in the matter."

"Why are you so interested in this? Why should our brothers in Moscow care about a few hectares of land in the Far East?"

"We have similar disputes with the Chinese. A solution to one may force the solution to another."

"You would like us to fight your battle for you," said Tan harshly.

"No one said anything about fighting a battle. I only suggested that air mobility would increase the impact of your military forces and that we were willing to assist the great Vietnamese people in creating that force."

"To attack the Chinese," said Tan.

"Comrade, we are not advocating hostilities with our brothers in China. We are attempting to see conflicts resolved."

"Through armed forces."

"A strong military will allow you to bargain from a position of power."

"Comrade," said Tan, "we are rushing into something that doesn't need solving this afternoon. You are probably tired after this long journey. We should allow you the opportunity to rest. We can meet again tomorrow."

"I confess to some strain from the trip," said Stepanov, "but if we can get something settled today, then I am prepared to work on it."

"There is no need; we have plenty of time. Our dispute with our Chinese comrades is centuries old. We won't resolve it this afternoon."

Stepanov saw his advantage slipping through his fingers. He knew other Soviet plans were being set into motion. Their timetable was critical, but the Vietnamese would not be pushed. To try would make them suspicious, and a suspicious ally was a dangerous one. He could only grin and nod, finish his tea—and hope that things would go better during the next meeting.

He nodded toward Tan. "The tea is excellent."

"I'm glad you like it, Comrade." He hesitated and said, "We will meet again tomorrow, then."

Stepanov stood. "Certainly, Comrade."

Using his binoculars, Stepanov scanned the open plains and wide, shallow valley far below him. Low-hanging clouds and fog obscured some of the rice paddies and farms; a single, two-lane highway bisected the valley, disappearing into the hills at the far end.

"That is China," said one of the Vietnamese officers. "The soft rice paddies on either side of the highway limit the value of the road." He grinned. "And we have artillery ready to interdict the road, if necessary."

The bunker where Stepanov stood was built into a hillside. It was concealed among the vegetation, giving the defenders an unobstructed view of an oncoming enemy, but hiding them from that enemy. The interconnecting trenches, bunkers, and fighting holes were in the best traditions of the Soviet military. Stepanov was impressed with the job the Vietnamese had done emulating the Soviet doctrine.

"A reinforced regiment could hold off a concentrated attack of a division for a week or more. Plenty of time to reinforce our men," said the Vietnamese, "especially if we had air-mobile capabilities."

Stepanov handed back the binoculars. "A very impressive work." The comment about air mobility hadn't been lost on him.

"The Chinese would not be able to penetrate here."

Stepanov thought of the French Maginot line, built to stop German invasions; each time the Germans invaded they ran around the end, through the Low Countries. Fixed fortifications were of little use in a world of air mobility, lightning warfare, and huge artillery pieces that could reduce them to smoking craters in a matter of minutes.

As a temporary defensive position, though, the line was good. It could stop the enemy tanks on the road and force a massed attack across open ground. If the enemy wanted it, he would be able to take it. Stepanov hoped the Vietnamese, who had beaten the French in their defensive position at Dien Bien Phu, had not forgotten that lesson.

"General Stepanov," said a man, ducking down and dropping into the bunker.

"Yes?"

"I have a message for you, Comrade General. You are asked to cut your tour short and return to Hanoi."

"Is there a reason?"

"No, Comrade General. I understand that your embassy asked for your immediate return."

Stepanov looked at the small delegation of Vietnamese officers. They were proud of their bunker line, constructed without concrete or steel. It was an effective defensive line, but it would not stop a concentrated attack. They seemed to understand that, too.

To them, he said, "Thank you for allowing me the privilege of seeing these facilities. Most impressive." He then moved toward the tiny square entrance at the rear. He levered himself out, put a knee on the soft, wet soil, and stood up. He brushed off his hands and began the steep walk up the hill toward the waiting cars.

"There was more to see, Comrade General. We have a SAM site hidden in the jungle to the east. The command post is buried under ten meters of earth, and the radar, both acquisition and targeting, is almost a klick away. Makes it difficult for the enemy to destroy the facility. It's a trick we learned during our struggle with the imperialist Americans."

Stepanov was leaning into the steep climb. "I'm sure it is an impressive facility, but I must return to Hanoi. I'm truly sorry."

"Certainly, Comrade."

They reached the top of the hill and then started down to the parking area. The road was built fifteen meters below, rather than on top of, the ridge, on the military crest. It would block the Chinese from seeing the troop movements. As they approached the general's car the driver leaped from behind the wheel and ran around to open the rear door.

"Would you like me to accompany you to Hanoi, Comrade General?"

Stepanov looked at the Vietnamese colonel. Ngo Tri Tran was a small, old man with a white beard and a very wrinkled face. He had been fighting for the Communist cause in Asia for his entire life.

"That's not necessary," said Stepanov.

"Then I shall remain here, with our soldiers." He bowed. "Thank you for coming."

Stepanov returned the bow. "I appreciate your kindness in showing me your facilities." He climbed into the back of the car, and the driver slammed the door.

Another Vietnamese officer, a young man who had not fought the Americans, but had fought the Cambodians, the Thais, and the Chinese, got in beside the driver. He had been told to keep Stepanov company and to accommodate him in every possible way. The theory was that anything a man promising to bring them air mobile capabilities wanted was not too much to ask.

Turning in the seat, the young officer asked, "Are you comfortable, Comrade General?"

"Certainly. Let's get going."

"Yes, General."

The engine started and there was a quiet hiss as the air-conditioning was turned on. Two vents blew at Stepanov, drying the sweat on his face. He leaned back in the seat and closed his eyes momentarily, trying to figure out what was so important that he would be recalled.

He felt the car bounce along the road and then turn sharply as they began the descent. He'd been told, on the way up, that the Vietnamese had purposely kept the road rough and narrow in case the Chinese attacked. Stepanov didn't tell them that doing so also inhibited the Vietnamese from reinforcing the area. In the day of helicopters, roads weren't that important. The Americans had taught that lesson in Vietnam and the Soviets had learned it well in Afghanistan. Roads were for the old-fashioned and the poorly equipped.

"Missiles," one of the Vietnamese had said. "Missiles and antiaircraft weapons."

Stepanov remained silent. Helicopters, because of their maneuverability, could defeat most missiles. A helicopter could stop and hover, or back up or suddenly climb straight up. A missile, which slashed through the air like a bullet, couldn't do that.

If the helicopter stayed close to the ground and used the terrain to mask its position, antiaircraft became useless. But the helicopter was vulnerable to the man with a rifle. It was an interesting twist on an old problem, but the point was, simply, that helicopters could defeat the sophisticated weapons systems and move hundreds of troops hundreds of miles in a very short time. Roads and bad terrain were no longer problems.

But then, Stepanov wasn't in Vietnam to teach the Vietnamese modern tactics, not when they were experts in guerrilla warfare. They'd have to learn their lessons on their own. All he cared about was the Vietnamese irritating their Chinese neighbors. If the Vietnamese pushed at them the Chinese would be, momentarily, out of the arena. Several million Vietnamese could not defeat a billion-plus Chinese, but they could make a huge dent—if they were willing to fight. And with the new toys supplied by the Soviets, they would be willing to fight.

Stepanov opened his eyes as they reached the bottom of the mountain and turned onto a paved highway that cut through the thick jungle. Here, there was no room for tanks to maneuver. They could run down the highway, or they could stay behind, sitting on the ridge line, waiting for the war to return to them. The bridges were narrow and the Vietnamese could drop them into the rivers quickly, if they wanted. Nothing would hold up an armor attack better than a narrow road with no bridges. The tanks would be sitting ducks for the Vietnamese air force.

That was, of course, if the war between China and Vietnam heated up. Stepanov looked out the window. The jungle was thick and dark. He could hear animal cries from the interior and was glad that he didn't have to fight a war in it.

They crossed a bridge that was a good thirty meters above a river. If the bridge was gone, there would be no easy way to get across. A Chinese attack could be halted right there. Vietnam had many natural barriers.

As they drove on, Stepanov began to wonder what was happening at the embassy. Why had he been recalled? The news couldn't be good. He thought about asking, but knew the Soviets at the embassy would never confide in the Vietnamese. Besides, if his Vietnamese aide knew anything more, he would have said something. There was nothing to do except wait.

They crossed a second bridge and turned onto another highway, this one wider. The jungle faded away and they were driving through country that could have been anywhere. Stepanov was surprised to see corn growing. He thought that the Vietnamese only grew rice. As they raced along, passing military cars and trucks and old fashioned ox carts, the cornfields gave way to rice paddies, and he saw men with oxen in the paddies. It was strange to see modern military equipment mixed among farmers who still relied on animal power.

Finally they reached Hanoi. Stepanov was glad that his car had air-conditioning; it kept out the stench of the city. Not the diesel stink or clouds of pollution created by a million slow-moving cars, but the odor of raw sewage dumped in canals. The one thing he would remember about Vietnam was not the juxtaposition of old and new technologies but the stench.

They pulled up to the gate of the Soviet embassy. Apparently they were expected; a guard opened the gate and waved the car through.

"Do you wish me to wait, Comrade General?" asked the Vietnamese driver when they reached the main building.

"No. If I need a ride, I'm sure that I can find one here." He reached for the door.

"General," said the Vietnamese officer, "would you like me to accompany you?"

"Totally unnecessary. Thanks for your help." Stepanov got out of the car and slammed the door. He watched it retreat before he turned to enter the building.

A military guard waiting for him inside the door announced, "General, the military attaché is waiting for you in his office."

Stepanov climbed the huge semicircular staircase that led to the second floor. The bright red of the carpet here was in contrast to the white marble of the entrance. A small receptionist's desk sat to one side; unseen guards were there in case she needed help. Stepanov found the office of Colonel Nikolai Chevcheskov, tapped on the door, and entered without waiting for an invitation. Being a general provided certain privileges.

Chevcheskov stood as Stepanov entered, smiling broadly. "Comrade General, how was your trip to the border?"

"Tiring, Nikolai. Very tiring and not too productive. They live in the nineteenth century, when forts and cannon were enough."

"Please, General, sit down. Can I offer you a drink?"

"Vodka would be nice." Stepanov fell into the closest leather chair.

Chevcheskov leaned toward his intercom and ordered the vodka. He then came around his desk and sat in the second leather chair. "Can the Vietnamese stop the Chinese?"

"No. If the Chinese decide to roll over them, they would be lost, but it would cost the Chinese dearly. I think that's why the Chinese have not made an offensive move. The cost would be too high."

"The Vietnamese stopped the Americans," said Chevcheskov.

"Yes, that's the popular myth. But we know the truth. The Americans stopped themselves. They weren't committed to see the war through to its end."

"Yes, Comrade General."

There was a knock at the door and Chevcheskov turned. "Come in."

A soldier brought in a silver tray that held the vodka, two small glasses, and a pepper grinder. He set the tray on a small table and then escaped. Chevcheskov poured the vodka, ground the pepper, and handed a glass to Stepanov.

"Thank you, Colonel." Stepanov sipped the vodka. "It was suggested that I return here quickly."

"Ah, yes. Down to business right away. I have a communiqué in the safe for you." He stood. "I'll get it." He moved across the narrow office and crouched near the safe concealed in the corner. He opened it and took out an envelope, handing it to Stepanov.

"Have you read it?" the general asked.

"No, Comrade. I do not know the contents."

Stepanov ripped open the envelope and extracted the single, folded sheet. He read it quickly and then said, "I'm required to return to Moscow."

"Arrangements can be made through the Vietnamese."

"No. A military aircraft is waiting at the airport. I need transportation there immediately."

"Before you finish your vodka?"

Stepanov held the glass up and examined it. He tasted it and then said, "A few moments won't hurt."

"Back to Moscow," said Chevcheskov.

"Which I won't complain about." Stepanov finished the vodka and set the glass down. Suddenly he had nothing to say to the colonel. He couldn't get interested in small talk and he wouldn't mention the details of the recall order.

"I'll get a car arranged," said Chevcheskov, sensing that the general had other things on his mind.

Stepanov stood and left the office. When he reached the main floor, a soldier escorted him to the waiting car. Stepanov climbed into the rear without a word. As they left the embassy in Hanoi he wondered what had gone wrong. The North Koreans were expecting a visit from him. All that would have to be explained.

He ignored the sights of Hanoi, the museum erected around the remains of an American B-52, the monument to celebrate the defenders of the city, and the new buildings constructed by the Vietnamese with Soviet money. He didn't want to see any more of the Vietnamese. He decided that he didn't like them, that they were arrogant and disgusting. He didn't like their city and their pretensions and he would be happy as soon as the airplane took off.

But that joy was tempered by the mysterious recall order. If he was in some kind of trouble, there would have been hints before. There had been no changing of power in Moscow, no secret plans to overthrow the current regime. All he could do, sitting in the back of the big, black limousine, was wonder what in the hell had happened. And the only place they could be in trouble was in the Middle East.

But as he thought of that he realized that others plans might have been uncovered or might have failed. He needed more information. The only intelligent course of action was to relax until he had it.

They reached the airport and Stepanov saw an Aeroflot Il-76 sitting on the tarmac. The ladder on the side of the aircraft was down, and Soviets, in white coveralls, were standing at the base, as if waiting for him.

The Vietnamese waved them onto the airfield and then allowed the limousine to drive to the aircraft. As the car stopped, one of the men in white opened the rear door and said, "Comrade General Stepanov?"

"Yes."

"We are ready when you are, Comrade General."

Stepanov climbed from the car and looked back toward the buildings of the airfield. Suddenly he felt like a criminal sneaking away in the dead of night. A group of Vietnamese stood near the operations building, watching. None of them came out to say a word.

"If you'll board, Comrade General, we will take off."

"Of course," said Stepnov. "The sooner the better."

GUANTANAMO BAY, CUBA

Martinez had slept for a couple of hours in the air-conditioned comfort of the isolated building and awakened feeling better than he had in days. He'd then found Chavez sitting in a small room, working on the gear they would take with them, making sure nothing on any of it could identify them as Americans. Chavez had changed into civilian clothes, an old, faded work shirt, khaki pants, and sandals. He hadn't shaved.

"Afternoon, Captain."

Martinez flopped into a chair. "Afternoon."

"Clothes for you are over there. I'd suggest you shower, using the local soap so that you don't smell like an American."

"And forget to shave, too, I would imagine."

"Certainly. I like to think of it as camouflage."

Martinez nodded and looked at his watch. That was

something that he'd have to leave behind. There weren't many Cubans with digital watches.

"We've got about four hours."

"Yes, sir. Time enough for a decent meal. And a little rest."

There were things Martinez wanted to say, but this wasn't the time. An officer was not supposed to tell his NCOs that he was not as enthusiastic about a mission as he could be. Never communicate ambivalence to subordinates.

"I'll take a shower," he said.

Chavez pointed. "Right around there. You'll find everything you need. I might suggest that you ignore deodorant, after-shave, and perfumed soaps."

Martinez grinned. "I'm not stupid."

"Yes, sir."

Martinez took a long, slow shower, letting the water run off him. It would be the last time he'd have that luxury for a couple of days. He used a large yellow bar of soap that smelled of lye to lather, rinse, and lather again, and then used it to wash his hair. Finished, he put on the civilian clothes, hoping he would now look like one of the natives.

He entered the room to find Chavez sitting quietly, his eyes closed. He opened them, glanced at Martinez, and said, "Now you blend in with the rest of us."

"Weapons give us away," said Martinez.

"Only if they're seen."

Martinez moved around and sat down. "I wish they'd get here with the final briefing package."

Almost as if to answer him, the door opened and Boyel entered. "Last intel on your mission."

Martinez leaned forward and took the thick envelope, then glanced up at Boyel. "Anything else?"

"No."

"Then thank you."

As soon as Boyel was out of the room Martinez pulled the documents from the envelope. Showing them to Chavez, he said, "This sets it up." He pointed to the map. "Castro will be there. No problem."

At midnight, Martinez and Chavez turned off the last

of the lights in the building. They waited in the shadows at the front door until a covered truck backed to them. Chavez climbed up into the rear, and Martinez handed up the gear to him. He retrieved the sniper rifle and gave that to Chavez, too. After he closed the door, he climbed up into the truck.

They rode along the deserted streets of the base, past dark barracks, empty offices, and silent warehouses. Except for those on guard, those monitoring the electronic gear or servicing the equipment, the men and women were asleep.

They turned toward one of the fences, stopping in a small park that was hidden from the road. The driver turned off the engine and the lights.

Chavez jumped out, crouched, and watched the street for a moment. There was no movement, no sound coming from anywhere.

"Let's go, sir."

Martinez pushed the gear toward him and then handed him the sniper rifle. Together they strapped on the gear, and Martinez moved to the cab of the truck.

"I'll wait here for thirty minutes before moving," said Boyel. "You want to hit the fence right over there."

"Thanks," said Martinez.

He turned, watched as Chavez crossed the road and disappeared into the high grass. Martinez joined him and they climbed a slight rise, sliding down the far side. A drainage ditch led to the fence; a metal culvert kept the sides from eroding away. A gate barred the entrance, its padlock hanging open.

"Someone was paying attention to the details," said Martinez.

"Yes, sir."

"Let's lose that 'yes, sir' crap now." He swtiched to Spanish and added, "In fact, let's just use Spanish."

"Of course."

Chavez opened the gate, slipped through, and worked his way to the other side of the culvert. Martinez followed, closed the gate, and then duckwalked through the pipe, holding the sniper rifle in both hands so that it didn't hit either side.

Once out, Chavez asked, "Now where?"

Martinez used his compass and stared into the star-filled night. There was a black clump about a hundred yards in front of them. Their path ran right through it.

"That way."

Chavez led. They followed the ditch for forty yards, climbed the sides, and then, staying with the shadows, worked their way into the jungle.

They stopped for a moment, Chavez crouching on one knee, Martinez standing, and examined the jungle. It looked like the jungle in Panama or Colombia. Thick trees, bushes, ferns, and dead vegetation. Insects swarmed around them, buzzing. There were calls of the night animals and a rustling to the right that might have been a snake.

"About a mile to the road," said Chavez.

"Go."

Chavez began to walk forward slowly, getting used to the jungle. They felt their way through it, and then reached the road.

"Now what?" Chavez whispered.

Martinez knew they couldn't walk down the road with their packs and weapons showing. If the Cuban police happened along, there would be no way to explain that equipment.

"Stick to the trees and we'll follow the road."

"Fine."

For an hour they paralleled the road. They stopped frequently, listened to the jungle and for sounds of cars or trucks, and then moved on. There was no one out late. Too easy to disappear late at night, too hard to explain what you were doing, even if it was only sneaking out to see a woman in the next village.

The truck was sitting next to the road, the hood up. A man sat on the bumper, smoking a cigarette. The orange glow of the tip marked his location.

Chavez stopped. "That our man?"

"I would imagine." Martinez handed him the rifle. "You wait here and I'll approach. If it's okay, I'll call you Esteban. If not, I won't use your name. If things go bad, you're on your own."

"Understood."

Martinez took a deep breath, stood up, and walked out of the jungle like a tourist on a main highway. He sensed rather than saw the smoker turn toward him. He walked up slowly, held a hand up, and called out in quiet Spanish. "Looks like you've broken down."

"Just my luck."

"Want me to take a look at it?"

"Be my guest."

He worked his way to the truck and then took a position so that a fender was between him and the man. If something went wrong, if it was an ambush, there would be some protection.

Keeping with the code, Martinez said, "Looks like a wire has worked loose."

"If you fix it, I'll give you a ride wherever you want to go."

"Even Los Baños?"

"Sure." The man was silent and then asked, "Martinez?"

"Yes."

"Good. I was told there would be more than one."

Martinez hesitated, giving the trap a moment to spring. But there was no movement anywhere around. The ground was open on the other side of the road. The only hiding place was in the jungle where Chavez waited.

Turning, he called, "Come on in, Esteban."

Chavez, carrying the sniper rifle and the remainder of their gear, left the jungle. He walked slowly, giving those in ambush a chance to jump, if they were around. But nothing happened. There was no ambush.

"You can put your gear in the back," said the man.

Chavez tossed in the rucks but kept the sniper rifle. He walked around to the front of the old truck and waited.

The man slammed the hood and opened the door on the driver's side. "Climb in."

The interior was a mess. The dashboard had holes where the radio, ashtray, and oil gauge would have been. The seat was covered by a dirty blanket with the springs pressing up. The windshield was starred and bits of glass were missing.

The engine sputtered, coughed, and then backfired, but it caught. They made a U-turn and began to bounce up the road before the driver turned on the headlights.

"Be about two hours," he said. "Get you there sometime about sunup."

"Thanks," said Martinez.

They didn't talk. Martinez wanted to know nothing about the driver so that he couldn't tell the Cubans anything about him if he was caught. And he wanted the driver to know nothing so that he couldn't betray them.

With the noise of the tires on the gravel and the pounding of the engine, it was impossible to hear anything on the outside. The lights flashed across the jungle, showing nothing of interest. Once, there had been an animal on the road, its eyes glowing red in the headlights, but as the truck got close it ran for the tall grass.

They slowed once and the driver turned off the lights, rolling up to a paved highway, checked both directions, and then shot across it. There was no evidence of military patrols.

Chavez leaned forward. "I would have thought that the military or the police would be out searching for people."

"Not often. Only when they suspect something."

Now the road was little more than a single track, barely visible in the headlights. The jungle seemed to come down to the side of the road; branches scraped the side of the truck. They slowed, bouncing along. Martinez rode with one hand braced against the roof.

"Little farther," said the driver.

Chavez nodded, cradling the sniper rifle in his lap. He didn't want anything to jar it.

Suddenly the jungle opened up; it ended abruptly, looking as if someone had mowed everything down, creating a straight edge. There were farm fields beyond.

They stopped and the driver turned out the lights. "You need to go on, across this. Jungle again about a klick away. I have to go home."

Chavez pushed open the door. There was a sound of scraping metal.

Martinez said, "Thanks for the ride."

"I wish you luck with your mission, whatever it is."

"Thank you for everything."

Chavez got out and walked around to the rear. He set the rifle down, propping it against a tire, then reached into the bed of the truck, grabbed a ruck, and handed it to Martinez as he joined him.

Quietly, Chavez asked, "How far now?"

"Two klicks at the most. We'll be in position when the sun comes up. Then we can move toward the house and set up."

"Good." Chavez shouldered his own ruck, buckled it down, and then picked up the rifle.

Martinez slapped the rear of the truck. The driver pulled forward onto the field, turned, and reentered the jungle, driving back the way he'd come.

They waited for fifteen minutes, letting the jungle settle down again. Now they could hear the sounds of the creatures around them, calls of the hunters and hunted. The screams as the animals searched for mates. Insects dived out of the dark; neither Martinez nor Chavez had used insect repellent. That was something that a farmer in Cuba would not have. Instead, they crouched and rubbed dirt on the exposed areas of their skin. That worked, after a fashion.

"I guess we're alone here," said Martinez, finally.

"I guess."

"Let's skirt the field then."

They started off, afraid of looking too military. If they strolled along together, like two friends heading for the fields, any police or army patrol that saw them might reveal itself in time for them to get away. Appearances became important.

But they managed to circle the field and then head into the jungle without seeing or hearing any sign of another human being. The jungle was deserted.

They stopped an hour later. Martinez glanced up through a hole in the canopy, saw that the stars were fading. There was just a hint of gray now. The sun was beginning to rise.

"Nearly dawn," he said.

Chavez nodded. "We should be close."

"There's a stream about a hundred yards away, if we're right. Let's find it."

"Certainly."

It didn't them long. They came to the bank and then halted. Martinez sat down, his back to a tree. He stared down at the water, now easily visible in the growing light. He lifted a hand and wiped the sweat from his face. He wanted to sit right in the middle of the stream, but that would stir up the silt, showing anyone waiting downstream that something was happening.

Chavez leaned close and touched his shoulder. Then, quietly, his lips no more than six inches from Martinez's ear, he said, "There's someone close."

CUBA

Major Boris Salnikov crouched in the thick mud next to a palm tree and watched the plantation house at the far end of a manicured lawn. The men of his team were scattered through the swamp, forming a thin skirmish line, with two men behind them so that no one could sneak up on them. Salnikov, his deputy, Senior Lieutenant Sergei Avchinsk, and his senior sergeant, Alex Zinoviev, were in the center of the line, watching the house more than a kilometer from them.

Salnikov had been studying it since they had gotten into position three hours earlier. That hadn't been a difficult task. Once they were launched from the sub, there was nothing about them that would give an effective radar return. They stayed low, paddled to shore, and then dragged the raft across the dark sand of the beach.

They had reached the jungle quickly and easily. One man had walked back to the waterline and carefully concealed all evidence of them coming ashore, backing up as he obliterated the evidence. They'd then moved deeper into the jungle, avoiding trails and roads and clearings. They'd wormed their way through the thickest portion of the jungle, staying close together so that they didn't get separated.

Before dawn, they'd found hiding places, spread through the jungle. Half the men were alert, just in case the Cubans were patrolling, the other half of the team trying to sleep; every few hours they switched. Two hours after dusk they started forward again, making their way deeper into the interior until they had reached the edge of a swamp. The last thing that Salnikov wanted to do was work his way through a swamp in the tropics, but there was no choice. He had to put up with leeches and poisonous snakes and the danger of a dozen other animals.

They'd spent a night in the swamp, but near dawn reached the edge of it. On the dry ground to the north was the plantation where Castro was supposed to be. Or where he was going to be. Where one of his mistresses, a young, blond woman who had been sent to Cuba to assist in modernizing some of Havana's aging equipment, was waiting for him. As soon as she had his itinerary, she had given it to her case officer, who passed it along to Moscow.

Now Salnikov was waiting in the tepid water, the sun creating a steambath. He kept his binoculars on the plantation house, waiting for the official car that would bring Castro. Once the car was spotted four men, outfitted with Dragunov sniper's rifles with a special, heavy barrel and a built-in silencer, would spread out. When Castro appeared, the man who had the best shot would take it.

Zinoviev finally moved slightly, the water stirring around his knees. Quietly, he said, "There are cars coming now."

In the distance Salnikov could see dust rising above the palm trees. He turned his binoculars on the gate and saw, for the first time, a half-dozen guards. They were in starched uniforms and carrying brand new rifles. Salnikov thought they were the AK-74.

"Got to be our boy," said Salnikov.

"Should we move into position?"

"No, let's get confirmation."

The first of the cars appeared near the gate. It was a small, black car that was highly polished. Salnikov didn't know what the make was. He'd never seen anything like it. Following it was a larger car, also black, but with a pennant on the front fender.

"This could be it." Salnikov raised the microphone of the tiny radio to his lips. Its range was just over two hundred yards. The odds that an unauthorized party would pick up the signal were slight. Using the intrasquad set, he said, "Let's all go to red."

A series of one-word replies acknowledged the new orders. Salnikov stood up slowly, letting the water drip from his uniform. He picked up his sniper rifle and checked the case. He'd been careful, as had all the others, that the water did not saturate the case. He'd kept it high and dry during the trip from the sub and then the travel through the swamp.

"I'll slip to the right," said Zinoviev. "Maybe two hundred meters and then work my way down to the small outcropping of rocks. I'll have a clear shot at the front door of no more than six hundred meters."

"Looks like a good spot. You'll take two men for your backup?"

"Yes, sir."

"I'll move to the right maybe a hundred and fifty meters where that finger of jungle reaches down onto the plantation. I'll be able to cover the front door, the porch, and the side garden."

"That's five hundred meters to the garden," said Zinoviev. "Maybe five fifty or sixty to the front door."

"Yes. First man to get a good shot takes it."

"Yes, sir."

Salnikov moved to the rear, away from his spotting position, and found two men, both sergeants. They would be his cover team. Each of the shooters had a two-man cover team, whose job was to allow the sniper to get clear once the shot was made. They would deal with the initial response if one was made, fighting a holding action and then breaking off, fleeing into the jungle.

A half dozen of his soldiers were scattered in the

swamp behind the shooting teams. Their job was to eliminate a threat from that direction if one materialized before
the shot was made. Once it was over, they would provide
security for the snipers as they escaped.

Into the radio, Salnikov whispered, "Let's go to position now. Report ready."

Again the snipers reported in sequence. With that finished, Salnikov took his two men and worked his way
through the swamp to the finger of jungle. They came up,
out of the water and onto the dry land. The vegetation
wasn't as thick as it had been, and they had an unobstructed view of the plantation house.

Salnikov studied the blind for a moment, figuring the
angles of response and the probable locations of enemy
soldiers on the ground below them. That was one of the
tricks. If he placed his security team properly, they would
be able to take out the first of the Cuban soldiers. Stopping
the initial pursuit was critical.

He placed one man on the southern side of the finger,
looking back toward the gate where two guards waited.
He placed the second man on the northern side, in the
crotch where the jungle and the swamp met. He could
hose down anyone coming from the house, the guard
shacks behind it, or any vehicles that might try a cross-
country trip from the looped driveway.

Satisfied, Salnikov began the slow process of working
his way to the tip of the finger. He stretched out on his
stomach, the Dragunov in its case on top of his hands to
keep it out of the dirt and decaying vegetation. With one
hand he touched the wet leaves, pushed a knee up, and
lifted himself forward. The last thing he wanted was to
disturb the animals and insects that lived in the jungle. He
needed to slide through it like a ghost, moving with the
speed of an aged snail. He didn't want anyone to be able
to see his movement.

Sweat stung his eyes, but he refused to wipe it away
as he pulled himself forward with agonizing slowness. One
hand, opposite foot, other hand, other foot. His face was
inches from the rotting jungle floor. He could smell every
odor, almost taste the rot. But still he moved on, feeling
insects landing on him and then taking off. He'd been in

the jungle and swamp long enough that he was no longer
an attractive target for the mosquitoes. Too much dirt and
crusted salt on his skin.

Forgetting about everything, he kept the pace smooth
and even. He concentrated only on reaching the tip of the
finger where he would stop and then watch, carefully
checking his rifle to make sure that the markings he'd put
on the scope, the breech, the barrel, and the stock had not
moved. Shooting at a human-sized target at over five or
six hundred meters was a difficult task. He had to allow
for the wind, the rise of the bullet and then drop. He had
to think about squeezing the trigger rather than pulling it.
Sniping was not the simple, hide-in-the-trees-and-kill-as-
many-of-the-enemy-as-you-can task that many believed it
to be. It was a precise, military operation that if handled
correctly, could disturb the enemy more than an atomic
bomb.

He stopped for a moment, settling to the ground. He
felt the moisture soak his uniform again. Nothing he could
do about that. With the sun hidden behind a thick overcast,
there would be no chance to dry out until they made it
back to the sub. Then there would be hot food and hot
showers and no more danger.

After a short rest, he started forward again. Glancing
to the right, he spotted a lizard that was watching him.
The creature didn't seem worried about the slow-moving
mammal. Salnikov thought then of snakes, venomous
snakes that hid under rotting logs or that dangled from
trees to bite the unsuspecting. During the briefings, they
hadn't talked of many venomous snakes.

Putting all that out of his mind, Salnikov crept forward, rifle off the ground. Finally he reached the tip of
the finger and rested for a moment. Now he needed to find
a stable bench rest for the rifle.

Slipping to the right, he found a log. He used his knife
to cut away some of the rot until he reached a solid core.
He moved behind it and looked down at the plantation.
He could still see the front door, the garden on the western
side, and even a few of the structures in the rear. He'd
found the perfect position.

Now it was time to get ready. Slowly, he opened the

rifle's case and extracted it. He checked the marks, found that each was lined up, and then pulled the caps off the scope. He sighted on the front door of the plantation. He moved it around, checking the sight post in the scope. Satisfied, he loaded the weapon and chambered a round. A sniper had to be ready to shoot when the target appeared.

He glanced right and left, checking the open fields that led down to the plantation. The two guards at the gate sat there, watching the road. They rarely ventured from the small hut near the wrought-iron gate.

Salnikov touched the button for the intrasquad radio. "One is ready," he said.

There was no response from any of the others.

For a moment Salnikov studied the plantation house. Through his binoculars he could see that the curtains in a few of the rooms were open. A light flashed in one and he focused on it. A naked woman entered and stepped to the window. She stood there framed, her head, shoulders, and upper body showing. The sight surprised Salnikov. He'd rarely had the opportunity to see an undressed female in such circumstances. He wondered briefly if she was the spy planted by Moscow.

She raised her hands over her head, stretching, leaving nothing to the imagination. If she could get Castro to stand in the window for that long, he would be able to put a round into him. If.

The radio came alive for a moment. "Two's in place."

Salnikov didn't acknowledge. Now they would stay as quiet as possible. Everything was ready. Castro was there and the snipers were in position, or almost in position.

"Three's in place."

Salnikov nodded to himself. He reached to the right and touched the rifle, keeping his binoculars on the house. The woman had disappeared. A shadow passed behind another window, but it was only a shadow.

He turned and looked down into the garden. French doors opened onto it. There were lush, tropical plants, the flowers bright reds, oranges, and yellows. Brightly colored umbrellas stood above tables. A man armed with an AK stood near the door. There was no sign of Castro.

Now he looked at the four cars parked on the driveway loop in front of the house. All were passenger cars. Salnikov suspected Castro's was heavily armored. None of them held machine guns. There were no tanks or military vehicles. No more than twenty guards had arrived with Castro. It wasn't much of a bodyguard for the man.

"Four's in position," said the radio.

Salnikov nodded. That was good news. Everyone was ready. Now the task was to wait for Castro to show himself. That could be anytime. It could be ten minutes or ten days. All they could do was wait and watch.

He kept the binoculars moving, searching for signs of the Cuban leader. Two men exited through the French doors on the western side of the house and seemed to inspect the garden. They looked up into the trees of the jungle, then turned and walked back into the house.

Salnikov couldn't contain himself. He used the radio. "Get ready, three."

"Roger."

Salnikov picked up his weapon, set it on the log, and used the scope to watch the doors. He felt his heart began to hammer. This was one of the things that he had trained for. This was the culmination of their planning of the last six weeks.

"Got him," said number three.

"Wait for it," said Salnikov. "I see him."

Fidel Castro, accompanied by two bodyguards, exited through the French doors. He stopped and looked up into the sky, as if wondering what had happened to the sun. He stepped down and then turned, waiting. The woman, blond and thin, joined him then. Together they moved to one of the tables and sat down. A man in a white coat, carrying a tray, exited the house.

"Take him," said Salnikov on the radio. "Count of three." Salnikov aimed at Castro, the sight post on the center of his chest. The wind was blowing almost straight at him and was slight. "One." He took a deep breath and let half of it out. "Two." He let Castro turn slightly, to address the waiter. "Three." Salnikov pulled the trigger.

Seconds later the first round struck Castro in the chest, tossing him rearward. He threw his hands up in surprise.

The second round caught him in the head, snapping it back. The rear of his head exploded, splattering blood and brains over the French doors.

Salnikov turned, saw a Cuban look toward the jungle where the other sniper was hidden. Salnikov dropped him with a single shot, then scrambled around and leaped to his feet. He ran back through the jungle, passing the men he had stationed as his security.

Sound erupted from the plantation. A siren began to wail. There was firing, one or two weapons on full auto, but the rounds didn't come close.

One of Salnikov's security men opened fire, a long burst from his AK. That was answered by the Cubans. A twelve-seven began to hammer. The rounds slammed through the jungle overhead, but Salnikov, now at the edge of the swamp, paid no attention to them. Through the gaps in the trees he saw a half-dozen Cuban soldiers running at the jungle. An instant later his second security man began to shoot. Four of the Cubans fell, bullets hitting them. The remaining two threw themselves to the ground to return the fire.

Over the radio Salnikov said, "Let's pull out. Now." With that, he plunged into the swamp, moving south.

Now there was the sound of an aircraft overhead. A single engine aircraft that buzzed the trees, skimming the tops. Salnikov stopped and turned, but the interlocking branches of the swamp trees and the hanging Spanish moss created an effective canopy.

Three men came at him from the left. The security force turned, but it was one of the other sniper teams. Salnikov used the radio. "Report all teams clear."

"Two's clear."

"Three's clear."

"Four's clear."

"Rendezvous point four. One hour. Let's do it."

There was no acknowledgment of that. Salnikov pushed his way deeper into the swamp, away from the plantation. He wanted to ask the others what they had seen, what had happened after Castro's head and chest had exploded, but there wasn't time. They had to get out as quickly as possible.

The aircraft overhead buzzed down once and then the sound of its engine retreated. Salnikov didn't believe that the pilot or pilots had been able to see anything. The overhead canopy was too thick.

"Jets," said Avchinsk on the radio.

The sound of the engines was a distant, insectile hum, growing rapidly. Salnikov stopped to listen. He didn't believe that the jets, if they were fighters, would find a target. All he could do was ignore them, though he wished he'd thought to bring a couple of SA-14s. The shoulder-fired antiaircraft weapon, with a better acquisition system than the old SA-7 Grail, would provide some protection against an air attack.

Suddenly one of the jets slashed through the air overhead. Salnikov ducked and then looked up. There was a rumble and the top of the canopy began to shake. Bits of leaf, bark, and wood fell into the swamp.

"Recon by fire," said Salnikov. "Don't shoot. Rendezvous as quickly as possible."

Another jet attacked the trees, this time using a cluster bomb. The solid case hit the canopy with enough force to shatter it. The explosion showered four dozen bomblets into the swamp. They detonated in a series of low, quiet pops too far away to hit him or his men with shrapnel.

To the security team with him, Salnikov said, "Keep moving. As long as they're firing blind into the swamp, there won't be any other pursuit."

But running through the thigh-high water was like running in syrup, requiring a slow-motion stride that sucked at strength and stamina. Sweat poured from him and his mouth filled with cotton. He was surrounded by water, but none that he could drink. All he could do was try to force his way through the swamp, his men behind him, listening for the Cubans.

They reached some high ground, a series of low islands covered with cyprus and mangrove trees. Salnikov pulled himself out of the water and collapsed against the roots of a mangrove that looked like the gnarled hand of a giant.

The jets were firing into the canopy more than half a klick away. They were ripping up the vegetation, and the water under their strafing runs was a boiling mess of mud and foam.

One of the men knelt near Salnikov, his head down, the breath ragged in his throat. "Now what?"

Salnikov pushed himself to his feet. "We have got to get moving. Suvorov, take the point. Leschukov, in the rear. Let's go."

The men began to run across the island, splashed through a shallow and up onto another long island. Patches of sky showed through the canopy. They could run faster on the dry land. They raced across it and plunged back into the swamp. Now the water was waist-deep and they slowed to walk, always pushing forward, away from Castro's plantation.

Then, suddenly, they were out of the swamp and into jungle. A thick jungle with an undergrowth that tugged at arms and legs and hands and feet. Sharp thorns tore at the thick material of the black uniforms. Vines managed to tangle ankles, slowing progress. But Salnikov didn't care now. They had to put distance between themselves and the Cubans. The death of Castro would cause a huge search. They had to get off the island before soldiers were brought in.

They came to a shallow depression in the jungle floor. The earth fell away in a large dish-shaped area. In the center of it, weapons at the ready, was part of the assassination team. Salnikov grinned as he moved down toward it. Somehow Zinoviev and his security team had gotten there first.

"We have secured the area," the sergeant reported.

"Good. The others?"

"On their way."

Salnikov bent at the waist, his hands on his knees. He sucked at the air. They would have to try some conditioning in the water next time. Once they were back in Moscow, he would design a series of exercises to be accomplished in waist-deep water. When he caught his breath, he looked back at the jungle. The Cuban jets were still firing into the swamp near the plantation. The sounds of the battle were almost inaudible now. The Cubans still thought the assassins were close.

He looked up at Zinoviev and blinked rapidly. "What'd it look like?"

"It was beautiful. He was dead before he hit the ground. Just beautiful."

"Then half the mission is complete."

"Half?"

"Yeah. Now we have to get the hell out of here."

CUBA

The shots had not caught either Martinez or Chavez by surprise. They had watched as the snipers had slipped into position. Then, realizing that they could not get close to Castro's plantation without revealing themselves, they had stayed where they were. Martinez figured they would either move in after dark, or they would get out, depending on what the others did.

A moment later, there had been a burst of machine-gun fire and then another. That was answered by single shots, coming from the jungle.

"What happened?" Chavez asked.

"I think they just took a shot at Castro. Maybe hit him."

"We've got to get clear."

"Wait," said Martinez.

They heard someone running through the jungle. The

firing had not tapered off but had increased. Machine guns were shooting. A siren was wailing.

"Forward," said Martinez. He was up and running, hunched over, his rifle in his left hand. He dodged to a tree, then around it, and to another. He slipped to a knee and now had a better view of what was happening on the plantation.

The cars had scattered. Two were down near the gate. Another had charged across the lawn, tearing up the grass as it spun around the corner of the house. Cuban soldiers were attacking a finger of jungle to the south of Martinez. Machine-gun fire was directed at it. There were bodies scattered on the ground, looking as if the Cubans had tried to rush it and had been pushed back.

Machine guns were firing into the jungle. A man on the roof of the house, standing behind a weapon mounted on a tripod, was firing in short bursts.

Martinez grinned. Someone else had taken the shot for him. He hoped that whoever it was, he had been able to kill Castro.

Martinez pulled his weapon from the case and aimed at the machine gunner on the roof. He leaned back, into the side of a tree to steady his aim, and then fired. A moment later the machine gunner seemed to jerk upright and then fell back, holding down the trigger. The weapon, pointed upward, fired into the clear sky.

One of the guards at the gate turned and looked up toward the house and then whirled, searching the jungle. He fired his AK, the rounds snapping by Martinez. An instant later there was another shot, and the Cuban soldier dropped.

Now Martinez began searching for targets. A man in a black uniform ran from the front of the house. Martinez fired, missed, and shot again. The man sprawled on the driveway.

From the north came the sound of aircraft engines. Chavez joined Martinez and said, "Aerial search."

"Our boys must have done some good," said Martinez.

"Let's get the hell out of here," said Chavez. "It's not our worry."

Martinez noticed that the Cubans had gained the finger of jungle. Now they would be searching the other areas. Anything he did would draw attention to himself, and even if those others had shot Castro, it was not his responsibility to protect them. He'd done more for them than he should have.

As he turned, there was a flash of movement at the side of the house. The big car slipped around the corner. The driver gunned it, ripping up sod as it lurched for the driveway. When it reached there, the tires smoked as they fought for a purchase. The car rocketed toward the gate, slowed as one of the guards opened it, and then shot through it.

"Has to be Castro," said Chavez. "Wouldn't use his car for some inferior."

"I'd like to confirm it," said Martinez.

The car disappeared over the horizon.

"No way to confirm. We'd better get the hell out of here."

Martinez reached out and slapped him on the shoulder. "Go. I'm right behind you."

A jet streaked over and then suddenly climbed, the engines roaring. A moment later there were explosions in the jungle, far to the south, and more shooting. AKs on full auto, but nothing was directed at Martinez or Chavez.

Chavez led the way, running along an old game trail, leaping a log and then diving off to the side. He slipped to a stop, whirled, and waited for Martinez.

"Anything?" asked Martinez, his voice rasping.

"No. Just listening."

It sounded like a fierce battle to the south. Machine guns, jets, and bombs. The jungle vibrated with the sound. Periodically, they could still hear the wailing of the siren.

"Doesn't sound like they're going to give up easily," said Chavez.

"But they're heading south. Away from us."

"For the moment."

"Right. As soon as they get more people in, they'll march through shoulder to shoulder. We'd better get the hell out of here first."

Chavez was up and moving again. He shoved his way

through the jungle, came to a stream, and leaped it, slipping on the bank. He scrambled up, his feet cutting into the soft earth, leaving telltale marks.

Martinez caught him there and shook his head. "Leave it. We've got to make some time."

Without looking back, Chavez was up and running. He found another game trail and dodged down it. If they had been in a combat environment, they would have avoided the trail, but for now it was important to put distance between themselves and the Cubans. At the moment they had to run.

Martinez felt the pain in his chest. The air seemed to be hot, and then hard. It felt as if it was cutting his throat as he breathed. He wanted to stop and rest, but there wasn't time.

The sounds of the battle faded. Chavez stopped, stepped off the trail, and looked back toward where the plantation would be.

"I think we're clear."

Martinez stopped, bent at the waste, and sucked at the humid, hot air. He stared at the jungle floor. "We need to keep moving. I don't want to get caught in the net."

"Neither do I." Chavez was silent for a moment. "I think they got Castro."

"So do I."

Chavez slipped to the jungle floor, keeping his back to a tree. He pulled his canteen from the holder and took a deep drink. He wiped the sweat from his face with his sleeve. He took another drink.

"What are we going to say to the debriefer?"

Martinez shook his head. "I guess just what happened. We got close, someone started shooting, and we had to get the hell out. If Castro's dead, it's going to be obvious in the next week or so."

Chavez, still breathing hard, grinned broadly. "How many attempts have there been on Castro's life?"

"By Americans or everyone?" Martinez asked.

"Everyone."

"Two dozen? Four dozen? A hundred? Who knows?"

Chavez glanced up into the canopy of the jungle. "We've got a few hours of daylight left."

Martinez straightened. "I'll take the lead for a while, if you want."

"You got it."

Martinez moved out, following the game trail until it turned to the south. He entered the jungle, reaching out to push a fern out of the way. He stepped over a log and then slipped down a gentle slope. At the bottom the ground was soggy. The water covered his foot.

He moved through there, reached the other side, and then climbed up into the jungle. He stopped, turned, and listened carefully. There was a quiet, distant rumbling that sounded like falling bombs.

"Sounds like they're catching hell, whoever they are," said Chavez.

"The Cubans are probably concentrating on them. We should be in the clear."

"Sounds like wishful thinking," said Chavez.

"Maybe. But it sounds good. Let's rest for a few minutes and then get going."

"Back to Guantanamo?"

"Yeah," said Martinez. "I think that's best."

IN THE CARIBBEAN

Dees was now haunting the CIC, watching the electronic displays and listening to the radio messages from the helicopter that was actively searching for the reported submarine. The computer screens flickered as the information on them changed when the reports were updated.

"What's the latest from the helo?"

The watch officer, Lieutenant Patrick Conlon, bent over the shoulder of one of the ratings and read the computer screen. "He's got buoys in the water and is now patrolling the area. He has yet to report any contact."

Dees wanted to scream. He wished there was some way to make things happen. He wished he could order the helo to make contact but he knew the crew was doing everything they could. It was getting ridiculous. They'd had fleeting contacts with the sub over the last day, but they had been unable to pin him down. Each time they got close, he somehow slipped through the net of LAMPS dipping sonar, sonobuoys, and MAD detections.

"Captain," said Conlon suddenly, "helo reports a sonar contact. Faint, heading nearly due south. He's pushing toward it now."

"Right. I'll be on the bridge. You keep me informed."

"Aye aye, sir."

Dees moved from the darkened CIC into the red-lighted corridors of the ship and toward the bridge. As he opened the hatch to enter, one of the sailors announced, Captain's on the bridge."

"What's our course?" Dees asked as he approached the exec.

"We're steering two-one-zero."

"You have our helo plotted?"

"No, sir. Haven't gotten a good report from them in the last twenty minutes."

"Contact CIC and get a plot on the helo. He reports the sub south of him. I want an intercept course."

"Aye, sir."

Dees stepped back and let the men work. He watched Randolph plot the position of the helo, make a single line, and then called out, "Helm, come about to two-two-five."

"Two-two-five, aye."

Randolph turned to Dees. "We're now four hours from the enemy sub."

"Soviet sub," Dees corrected, not sure that it was a Soviet sub.

"Soviet," said Randolph.

"Captain," said antisub warfare officer, "helo reports strong contact now. Sub is making fifteen knots, steering one-six-five."

"Mr. Randolph?"

The exec turned to the plotting table, picked up a pencil and a handheld calculator. "We come around to two-one-zero degrees and we should be able to intercept."

"Do it."

"Helm, two-one-zero."

"Two-one-zero, aye."

"We're still four hours from getting into this thing," said Randolph.

"We've got the helo on station. He can scatter some more sonobuoys. That should help us keep track of the sub unless their captain suddenly starts to maneuver to evade us or to get clever."

Dees looked at his watch. Four hours. The Soviet sub could get a hundred and twenty nautical miles from its current location. He looked at the charts. The sub's course was taking it toward the Cayman Trench. That could make it easier for them to track him. No bottom echos to clutter the sonar. No hulks of sunken ships to give them false readings. But he could dive deep and get lost in the currents and cold-water pockets of the trench.

"How much longer can the helo stay on station?"

"With the sub heading south, we can get a relay going with Guantanamo Bay. They can send another helo or one of the EC-3s."

"Let's get that taken care of. We'll need . . ." Dees shook his head and stopped to think. The problem was becoming bigger than he had anticipated when alerted so long ago. Routine, he had thought. Now the chase had stretched out over more than a day with the sub seeming to maneuver to lose him. Finally he said, "I'm going back down to the CIC. I'll see what other ships we've got in the area."

"Why so hot to track this guy?" Randolph asked.

Dees shrugged. "I'd just like to keep my hand in. Someday we might have to do this for real and it's not the same tracking our subs when we play games. I know our submarine doctrine as well as the sub commanders. Going after a Soviet sub teaches me something about their thinking." He wasn't sure that was the real reason, but it sounded good.

"Don't you tell their captain something about your thinking, too?" Randolph asked.

"It's a trade-off. I learn what they can do. What they do do when confronted by a destroyer. I think I learn more about them than I reveal about myself." He studied the chart a moment longer. "I'll be in CIC."

"Aye, sir."

As Dees left the bridge he heard one of the sailors call out, "Captain's off the bridge."

Back in CIC he told Conlon, "Give the location of all our ships in the area."

"Aye, sir."

The computer screen shimmered, the displays faded and then came back. Each ship in a two-hundred-nautical-mile radius appeared complete with a short track that gave its direction.

Dees said, "Give me ID on the ones we have."

The ship IDs appeared. Dees took a step forward and pointed. "That a Soviet trawler?"

"Yes, sir. But he's not catching many fish."

"He monitoring us?"

The sailor studied the screen for a moment. "I don't think so, Captain. He's positioned much closer to those two destroyers. I would think he's shadowing them and not paying attention to us."

"That the only trawler around?"

"Aye, sir. That's the only one we've got spotted and plotted. I don't think there are any others at sea, but that doesn't mean that one or two might not be in port in Cuba. And we're close enough to Cuba for them to monitor our transmissions if they decide."

Dees looked at Conlon. "What's intelligence say?"

"We don't have any indication that the Soviets have any other trawlers around."

"We'll need to keep watch."

"Yes, sir."

"The Soviet sub?"

"Right there," said Conlon, pointing. "Don't have him labeled because we don't really know who he is and the plot is based only on the last information we got from the helo."

"Well, we've got him spotted. I wonder if he knows that we're looking?"

Inber sat in his cabin, writing a letter to his wife that he knew he would hand to her rather than mail to her. It was impossible to mail letters back to the Soviet Union from most of the world. In the West, there was a chance of spies opening and reading it, and in the East there was the very real possibility that it would get lost. So he wrote home faithfully and then handed the packet to his wife after he'd been home for a couple of hours.

Yegorov appeared and said, "Comrade Captain, we have been detected again."

"Meaning?"

"Our equipment shows that we have been pinged by enemy sonar."

"Enemy?"

"Americans," said **Yegorov**.

Inber capped his pen **and** set it down on his tiny desk. "We have been spotted by the Americans. This is a problem?"

"They know we're out here."

"We are in international waters," said Inber. "There are no laws to prevent us from sailing international waters."

But even as he said it he realized the fallacy of his statement. Once Salnikov's team had completed its mission, they would be heading for the coast. It was imperative that the sub retrieve them. They had to get away clean. And if the Americans tracked his sub into Cuban territorial waters, they would know the identity of the assassins. They wouldn't be able to name the man who pulled the trigger, but would know the name of the man who pulled the strings. It was the reason that he had attempted to avoid detection and the reason he had worked so hard to break the contact once it had been made.

"Maybe we should go forward," said Inber.

"Aye, sir."

Inber glanced down at the letter, blew on it to make sure the ink was dry, and then put it in the drawer along with his pen and the boat's log.

As they entered forward plot a sailor announced, "I have weak sonar on the port side."

"Come about to one-nine-zero," said Inber.

"Aye, Captain."

There was a moment's hesitation and then, "We're steadying on one-nine-zero."

"Lost the active sonar," said the plotter.

"It couldn't be so easy," said Yegorov.

"These Americans are not aware of the importance of

the game," said Inber. "They are tracking us because we are here. We must lose them for the mission."

"Weak active sonar to the stern," said the plotter.

"You see, Yuri, the American wasn't fooled that easily. Increase our speed by ten knots."

"Aye, Captain."

Inber suddenly felt hot. He wiped his face with his hand and then rubbed it on his chest.

"Hard right rudder," he said. "Steady on a course of one-four-five."

"Hard right rudder."

It was suddenly quiet in the boat. Each of the one hundred and thirty men of the crew knew that they were being tracked by the Americans. None of them realized the importance of shaking the pursuit. They simply wanted to beat the Americans at the game they were now playing.

"Slow to five knots," said Inber.

"Aye, sir."

Whispering, Yegorov said, "The Americans will be able to figure this out, too."

"Maybe they won't care. Maybe they'll give up if it becomes too difficult to detect us."

"Weak active sonar on the stern. Strength fading," said the plotter.

"He'll turn again," said Yegorov.

"Of course, coming around to this point. We won't be here when he does."

"We're clear of the sonar," said the plotter.

Inber stood for a moment with his eyes closed, visualizing the ocean around him. The American's signal had disappeared to the rear of the boat. Almost any turn he made would put him back into the American sonar dome. The only move he could make was to one-eight-zero. Due south. If the American swung back, he would sweep the ocean where he'd lost the signal, expanding the search from that point. That would take some time.

"Come about to one-eight-zero at full speed."

"Aye, sir."

"That should buy us a little time," said Inber. "But

we have to get out of this deep water. Too easy for the Americans to see us here.''

Conlon glanced skyward, a pained look on his face. "Helo's lost him."

Dees thought about recalling the helo and abandoning the search. It was just a silly game, played by the captains of the two vessels for their own amusement. It was the sailors who did the real work. The hard work.

But then he thought better of it. The sub's captain had worked very hard to lose himself in the ocean. Worked harder than was normal. That made Dees curious. He decided that he would stay with the game awhile longer.

He glanced up at the computer screen that showed the plots of the sonobuoys the helo had dropped. They were tiny devices, four or five inches in diameter and about three feet long, that radioed information from a hydrophone to either the helo or the ship. Information also came from the DISCASS, which used sonar to find the subs. By studying the pattern of sonobuoys, the DISCASS information, and the plottings from the helo, Dees suddenly understood what was happening. The computer display laid it all out, so that the lowest ranking sailor on the ship would be able to see it clearly.

"He's heading to the south," said Dees. "Advise the helo to swing to the south."

"Aye, sir."

To Conlon Dees said, "Do we have a fix on the type of submarine?"

"Information is limited. Our best guess is an Oscar class. The LOFAR reading was made under less than ideal conditions, so we could be wrong on that. We're still working that problem, though it hasn't been a high priority."

Dees reached up with his left hand and wiped his lips. Even in the air-conditioning of the CIC, he was uncomfortable. Heat seemed to be radiating from his body. Sweat beaded and dripped as he concentrated on the task.

"Helos got him again."

"Yeah," said Dees, his voice rising. "Yeah. I want the helo to drop a standard pattern on the sonobuoys. We've got him corralled now and I don't want him to get away again.''

"Aye, sir.''

Conlon, watching the computer displays, said, "He's running for the open ocean. Nothing there but water.''

"There's something else going on here,'' said Dees. "Besides, there's no reason for us not to keep an eye on him now that we've found him. We'll just escort him out of our patrol zone. He should turn for the Atlantic soon.''

"Why?''

"Because we found him,'' said Dees.

"Weak contact,'' said the plotter. "Moving toward us.''

"Damn,'' said Inber. "All stop.''

"All stop, Captain.''

Inber saw the questioning look on Yergorov's face. "Let him overrun us. Let him get in front of us, and then we'll turn back the other way.''

"Strong contact to the stern,'' said the plotter. "Getting stronger.'' And then suddenly: "Passed over us. Signal strength weakening.''

"We move now?''

"Let him keep going,'' said Inber. "Give him a chance to lose us completely.''

"Signal gone.''

Inber smiled. The American had anticipated his move to the south. Of course it had been the only logical one. Now he had to think of something that was not logical and that would keep him from sailing into the buoys the American had most certainly deployed. He had to outfox the American this time. The game was taking too long.

"Deploy a decoy,'' said Inber. "Right standard rudder. Come around to three-six-zero degrees.''

"Decoy away.''

"Right standard rudder.''

"Now we'll see if he can find us again. Maybe he'll chase the decoy for a little while and allow us to slip away.''

"Weak contact to the port,'' said the plotter.

"Come to zero-two-zero degrees," said Inber. "Ahead two-thirds."

"Steadying on zero-two-zero, Captain."

"Now we must wait," said Inber. "It's his move."

"Helo reports strong contact," said Conlon.

Dees nodded and looked at the plots on the computer screen. The sub was running due south. Sonobuoys and the dip sonar from the helo were both showing the sub.

"I want the search area expanded," said Dees.

"We have him pegged, Captain," said Conlon. "He's running south, toward the deep water."

"If you were a sub captain trying to avoid detection or break contact," said Dees, "would you head due south with no turns, especially after we had you painted?"

"But we don't know that he's trying to avoid detection," said Conlon. "There's no reason for him to want to avoid detection."

"Then why not just turn and run for the Atlantic?" asked Dees. "He's in these waters for a reason. Therefore, I want him watched."

"We have him," said Conlon.

"Expand the search area anyway," said Dees. "I want a spread of sonobuoys across his path."

"Aye, sir."

Dees looked at the chronometer; a couple of hours had elapsed since they had first started hunting for the sub the second time. They were getting into the area where they could now begin searching for the enemy themselves. If the sub had turned back to the northeast, then he would be heading right at the destroyer. With their larger array of equipment, it would be that much harder for the sub to evade them.

"Captain, we've got two more helos in the area now, both off Guantanamo."

"Once they're on station, recall our helo. And show me the location of the new helos."

"Aye, sir."

The computer image flickered once and the two helicopters appeared, heading nearly due east from the American naval base in Cuba.

"Order one of them to sow sonobuoys in a line, north to south twenty miles from the sub's original path."

"Aye, sir."

"Have the second sow buoys east to west twenty miles south of that last plot."

"Aye, sir."

"Now, if he's moving at all, we're going to find him again," said Dees.

"Our helo still has a strong lock on him," Conlon said.

"I think we've been decoyed. Do we have a MAD reading on the new plot?"

"No, sir."

"Then get one now." Dees stood quietly for a moment with his arms folded, staring at the computer screen. He knew where the sub had to be. Not where the instruments put it, but to the north and east of that point. He was zigzagging his way into the shallower water where he could hide better, where he could stop his engines and screws and turn off his electronic equipment so that he would become invisible.

"The Americans have taken the decoy," said Yegorov. "They are moving off to the south."

"Then we shall stop here," said Inber. He ordered the helm to slow to dead slow. He needed to maintain a slight speed to hold his position below the surface. It was much like the shark that had to keep swimming to force water over its gills so that it didn't drown.

With everything shut down, they were emitting no discernible signals. Sonar, radar, radio, all emitted electronic beams that could be detected and traced by the Americans. With all that shut down, Inber was blind and dumb, but not deaf. The hydrophone was a passive system. It listened to the sounds of the ocean, to the sounds of the American's ships. A good operator could tell the type and sometimes class of the ship by the noise the screws made. Other instruments could receive the electronic signals sent out by the surface ships, and by studying those, more information could be gained.

But Inber was not interested in the type of American

ship. He was interested in the number and the location. That would help him determine which direction to take. It would provide him with the clues he needed to avoid further detection.

"Comrade Captain, I believe they are using helicopters in the search for us."

"Location?"

"I have one spotted to the east, at twelve nautical miles, and a second to the south, thirty nautical miles. I get soft returns from the closest."

"What's the range of their sonars?" Inber asked.

"No more than fifteen nautical miles, Captain."

"Change course to three-five-zero for five minutes, then a hard turn to zero-zero-five degrees and accelerate to twenty-five knots. Ahead now at ten knots."

"Aye, sir."

"Captain," said the radioman, "I have a coded message from our team on shore. They are requesting immediate pickup at the first designated rendezvous."

"Do not acknowledge them," said Inber. "No radio transmissions at all."

"What will they do if we don't respond to their call?" Yegorov asked.

"They will assume that there is a problem with us and attempt to make the second rendezvous automatically. Everything slips back by twenty-four hours."

"The signals are fading," said the plotter.

"Tell me when you've lost them completely."

"Aye, sir." There was a hesitation as the sailor held up one hand. "They've faded, Captain."

"Hard right rudder," said Inber. He hoped that the sudden maneuver would create a knuckle of turbulence for the Americans to detect. While his boat was hiding in it, a momentary thing, Inber ordered, "Release another decoy."

"Hard right rudder," echoed one sailor.

"Decoy away," said another.

"Now, if they take the bait, maybe we can slip their detection and get those men at the second rendezvous."

It was a big if.

EGLIN AIR FORCE BASE, FLORIDA

The C-141 touched down with a squeal of tires and a burst of smoke. It decelerated rapidly and turned onto one of the high-speed taxiways to clear the active runway. It continued to slow, turned again, and rolled to a stop on the tarmac a hundred yards from the edge of the flight line.

Standing in the operations building, Brizzola watched the plane shut down its engines and three dark blue buses drive out toward it. There wasn't the mass exodus of passengers that he had expected. In fact, it began to look as if the plane was empty.

Turning, he asked the operations sergeant, "That the C-141 in from Guantanamo?"

"Yes, sir. On time, too."

Brizzola turned his attention back to the aircraft, and when no one seemed to be exiting, he moved to the door. He opened it, letting the bright, afternoon sun spill in.

The humidity washed over him like the surf on a beach, and before he'd taken a half-dozen steps, he was bathed in sweat, his underarms soaked and a stain spreading down his back.

His hummer was parked at the side of the operations building, but didn't have the stickers or the authorization to drive onto the flight line. He wished that he'd ridden out on one of the buses.

He walked toward the aircraft, wondering what in the hell was going on inside. Still no one had appeared. After the flight from Cuba, he would have been fighting to get out of the aircraft. When the ramp in the rear dropped, Brizzola started around toward it, thinking that the soldiers had been lined up to march out. But the first two men down the ramp weren't marching in any kind of formation. They had shouldered their equipment and were getting off as if they were passengers on a commercial flight.

One of them, a short man with black hair and olive skin in camouflaged BDUs, an M-16 slung over his shoulder, stopped at the bottom of the ramp. He moved toward Brizzola. He stopped short and violated the precedent of not saluting on the flight line.

"Captain Martinez, Major."

"I've brought buses for your men, Captain. How many of you are there?"

Martinez glanced at the three buses and grinned. "Two."

"What?"

"Just the two of us. How many were you expecting?"

"Two? I thought the plane was loaded with soldiers. A reinforced company at least."

"No, sir," said Martinez. "Just the two of us, with orders to report to Brigadier General Porter Gleason as soon as possible after our arrival. And to meet with the rest of our team here. They came in earlier."

"Damn it," said Brizzola. He looked at the Special Forces trooper. "I guess I won't need the buses. You can ride with me if you like."

"Sure," said Martinez. "You don't seem to be real thrilled to see us."

"It's not that." Brizzola wasn't sure how much he was supposed to say and how much was considered classified information. Troop strengths, given the world situation, were probably classified information, but there was no one around to hear. "We were expecting two hundred men."

"Well, it wasn't too long ago that I was in the field, living in the jungle and eating MREs rather than real food. I point this out only so that you understand that we have no idea about the situation here." Martinez laughed. "I suppose I also mention it so that you realize you're not stuck with garrison troopers but real soldiers."

"Again," said Brizzola, "let me say that it's not your fault. I had higher hopes. By that I mean hopes for a larger number of soldiers."

"Well," said Martinez, "there is the story of the Texas Rangers sending a single man to end a riot. One riot, one ranger. Maybe they figured we're all you need."

It was Brizzola's turn to laugh. "You're not part-marine are you?"

"Army Special Forces, but hell, Major, we're just as tough as they come."

Brizzola stopped and shook his head. "I believe there are going to be more people prepared for the in-processing than there are of you."

"Great," said Chavez. "Should go smoothly then. Will the rest of the team be there?"

"Possibly. Probably."

Brizzola, Martinez, and Chavez walked back across the ramp. Behind them the buses rumbled to life, backfired, and then drove out the gate, leaving clouds of diesel smoke and stench behind.

"You'd think," said Chavez, "that the military could find better buses in their rush to improve everything."

"You think they've improved things?" Martinez asked. "Hell, I prefer the old C rats to these new Meals, Ready to Eat. And the hummer is an expensive joke."

"Hey," said Brizzola. "You're talking about my wheels here."

"Sorry. Didn't know that you were attached to it."

They walked out the gate and stopped behind the replacement for the jeep. Chavez opened one of the backdoors and shrugged his gear off his shoulder. He tossed it in.

Martinez handed him his gear and then opened the passenger's door. Brizzola climbed behind the wheel and then waited as the two Special Forces officers got in.

With the doors shut and the engine running, Martinez asked, "Can you tell us what the hell is going on here?"

"You'll have to wait. General Gleason isn't going to be happy. We ask for a battalion and we get two guys."

Brizzola backed up, turned, and then drove across the base. He didn't say much; there wasn't much that he could say to the Special Forces men and he didn't know what the general would do. He might just tell them to spend the night and return them to Cuba. Two men, no matter how highly trained, would not make a difference to their requirement to field a brigade.

He pulled up in front of the Rapid Deployment Force building and shut off the engine. "We're here."

"Looks almost deserted," said Martinez.

"Well, it is late in the day, but then, we don't have a complete force yet, either."

"We're cadre?" Chavez asked.

"No," said Brizzola. "I'll let the general brief you on this."

"Our gear?" Martinez asked.

"Safe enough in the hummer."

Chavez got out and then leaned back, grabbing the rifles. He handed one to Martinez. Brizzola led them down the corridors, past a radio room that could be used to contact any unit in the field anywhere in the world. It was just like every other building on every other base in the world: cinder blocks and green tile with photos of the chain of command hanging on the wall.

As they neared the general's office Brizzola slowed and said, "General Gleason is of the old school. Massed assault across the enemy's beaches. He's a stickler for discipline and customs and courtesies."

"Seems that a man in command of a Rapid Deployment Force would also see the need for finesse," said Martinez. "World War Two tactics won't always work. A modern soldier has to remain flexible, ready to either fight the newest war with the newest weapons or be ready to return to the Indians of the Old West.''

"Well," said Chavez, "I'll try not to spit on the floor."

"Just remember that he's a general."

"I'm sure that we'll be fine," said Martinez, a little annoyed. "We might be Special Forces, but we're still in the army."

"Sorry. Too often I'm dealing with people who are not as familiar with the military as they could be."

They reached a door and stopped. Brizzola said, "Here we go."

"Why does it sound like we're about to jump into a combat zone?" Martinez asked.

Brizzola opened the door. The air inside was cooler than it had been in the corridor. Brizzola let the two Special Forces troopers in first and then followed them.

"You wait here and I'll see if the general is ready to meet with you."

"You going to let him know that there are only two of us?"

"No. I think I'll let you drop that bomb on him."

"Thanks."

Brizzola knocked on the door, opened it, and spoke to the general. Finished, he turned and said, "Go on in."

Martinez walked in briskly, stopped three feet from Gleason's desk, and snapped off a salute, running through the ritual again. Gleason grinned at him and waved him to one of the leather chairs opposite him. Chavez took the other one.

"That probably was a little annoying, wasn't it?" said Gleason.

"General?"

"Saluting an officer who wasn't Special Forces."

Martinez grinned. "Well, you're a marine and that's close. The worst are leg officers who haven't seen a shot fired in anger."

"When I was a young officer, I didn't like to have to salute anyone in the navy. It seemed sacrilegious. Now I realize the navy officers have their place, and often they're as well trained in their jobs as I am in mine."

Martinez could think of a dozen things to say but decided he'd better just keep his mouth shut. Sometimes generals showed a human side, and once they had a response, they chopped the feet off.

"Yes, sir," he said.

Gleason nodded, was quiet for a moment, and then asked, "How many of you are there?"

"Two," said Martinez, grinning. Then he added, "But we're supposed to have an additional ten here somewhere."

"Yeah," said Gleason. "I thought the Southern Command let us have assistance too easily."

"Well, General," said Martinez, "we're well trained and have some combat experience. . . ."

"You look too young to have been in Vietnam."

"Yes, sir. I was thinking of some of the lesser-known activities in Central and South American. Combat operations against the drug lords. And I was a sergeant in Desert Storm."

"Ah."

"Anyway, we have combat experience and can be useful in a variety of functions."

"But there are only twelve of you, and I can't think of a thing that would help us out. My job is to find a brigade that can be fielded at the whim of the president and the Congress. And the media."

Now Chavez spoke up. "I thought you commanded the Rapid Deployment Force."

"I command a paper force that doesn't exist. Now we're scrambling for troops."

"We've had some experience in covert operations. We're used to operating what would be considered behind the enemy lines. We're self-sufficient," said Martinez.

Gleason nodded and then smiled. "I appreciate your enthusiasm."

"I have a fully equipped, fully trained team here in Florida. Somewhere," said Martinez. "We've specialized in Central and South American operations, are fluent in Spanish and a few other languages, can work behind the enemy lines, and know Cuba as well as anyone outside of

Alpha Sixty-six. We're here and at your disposal. We don't need a lot of direction.''

"Right now I just don't have a mission where twelve men would be enough. I will keep your unique qualifications in mind as the op orders come down. You have any questions?''

Martinez shrugged. "I don't know how long we're supposed to be here.''

"I'll try to get your status clarified for you. I'd like to thank you for coming.''

"Didn't have much choice,'' said Martinez. "Orders were issued, orders designed to get us out of Cuba as quickly as they could.''

"Of course,'' said Gleason. "But again, thanks.''

Martinez stood. "It was nice meeting you, General. Too bad you wasted your time in the marines. You'd have made a good Special Forces trooper.''

"I was thinking the same thing about you, Captain,'' said the general.

Martinez saluted, waited for it to be returned, and then did an about-face. With Chavez right behind him, he left the general's office.

"Well?'' said Brizzola.

"Well nothing,'' said Martinez. "He thanked us for coming, but doesn't see the advantage of having only twelve men. He might not fully appreciate the role we can play.''

"I'm sure he does,'' said Brizzola. "Anyway, nothing more to do here. I suppose we need to let you go find the rest of your men.''

"That would be nice.'' Martinez stifled a yawn. "If there is anything you need us to do, just ask. We're here for something.''

"That's it, isn't it?'' said Brizzola. "We're all here for something.''

"That's what I'm afraid of,'' said Martinez.

THE CARIBBEAN

"We've lost him, Captain."

Dees turned and looked at the screens arrayed around the CIC. He touched his forehead, found it beaded with sweat even though CIC was air-conditioned. He wiped it away.

"Bearing on last contact?"

"Zero-one-zero, skipper."

Dees looked at the electronic display of his area of the ocean. Cuba was a mass at the top, and deep water was at the bottom. The cold blue water, with its varying currents and pockets of warm or colder water, made detection that much more difficult. Modern subs could dive to two thousand feet, run at forty knots, deploy a variety of decoys, and create dozens of false targets.

"Everything dead?" Dees asked.

"No contacts, skipper," said Conlon.

Dees stood for a moment listening to the electronic

pinging around him, listening to the whisper of the fans for the environment control and to the soft talk of the men in the CIC. He was uncomfortable there. Hot. He wished that he was on the bridge, where the captain belonged. He wiped the sweat from his face again.

"Damn it," said Dees.

No one responded. They continued to search for the sub. The helos were dipping the LAMPS and the MAD was activated, but the Soviets had eluded detection.

"Final heading on the sub?" Dees asked again.

"Zero-one-zero."

"Expand the search area to the south," he said. "Advise the helos."

"Aye, sir."

"Buoy number seven is hot."

Dees turned. "Report hot bearing. Put it on the screen."

"Two-four-zero degrees. On the screen."

"There he is," said Dees. "I'll be on the bridge."

"Aye, sir."

"They've found us again," said Inber. "Right full rudder. Steady on course one-seven-zero."

"One-seven-zero, aye."

Inber looked at Yegorov. "He anticipates us well, this American. Let's make the game a little tougher. We'll run straight to the deep water and then dive deep."

"He'll anticipate that," said Yegorov.

"Captain, we have a second transmission from the beach. They are demanding pickup."

"There will be no response," said Inber. "They'll just have to evade until the American is gone."

"Sounds like they're being pressed by the Cuban security forces."

"They knew the risks," said Inber. "We have other problems at the moment."

"Aye aye, Captain."

"Strong contact, Captain," said a sailor. "They have us solid."

"Stay on this heading."

Inber turned and looked back toward the glowing electronic displays. The bright lights contrasted with the dim running lights. Bright areas of greens and reds and yellows, showing the Americans, their buoy patterns, and the occasional LAMPS dipping sonar.

"He's got our path blocked," said Yegorov. "We can't get back into Cuba."

"At the moment it doesn't matter."

"Our problem," said Conlon, "is this frontal area moving in. There's a squall line about a hundred and fifty nautical miles to the west, moving toward us at thirty knots. That's going to force the helos out of the area."

"Shit," said Dees.

"Water temperature changes radically, too," said Conlon. "We're beginning to get false echos."

"Keep me posted," said Dees.

"Aye, Captain. Conlon turned back to look at the information displayed around the CIC.

"Watch supervisor, I believe I have sub contact."

"How's your echo quality?" Conlon asked.

"Sharp and strong."

"Put it out. CIC observe V-scan." Conlon contacted the bridge again. "Captain, we've got the sub."

"Bearing and heading?"

"He's two-two-zero heading one-seven-zero."

"Thank you."

"Sonar has active V-scan contact. Sub is low."

Conlon moved around the CIC, watching the various screens, searching for more information about the sub. False echos were beginning to appear from the cold-water front. The sub was heading directly into it.

Conlon called the bridge again. "Captain, we need to move the helos farther to the south or we're going to lose him again."

"Understood. Do you have MAD contact?"

"We have sonar."

"Understood."

Conlon watched as his men stayed with the contact, tracking it as the sub launched another decoy. They realized what it was immediately and didn't respond to it.

Conlon thought they had him now. It would be hard for the enemy to evade.

"I've got a surface contact. High-speed screws."

Conlon turned. "Type of ship?"

"Patrol boat."

"Bridge, CIC. We've got high-speed screws coming at us. Patrol boats."

"You have an identity on the patrol boats?"

"Negative, Captain. I would assume they're Cuban."

There was a moment's hesitation and then: "We're well outside Cuban territorial waters."

"Aye, sir. Castro has announced in the recent past that his territorial waters in this area extend for three hundred miles."

"Keep me informed of the progress of the patrol boats."

"Aye aye, sir."

Inber stood quietly, listening to the sounds around him. The American destroyer was steering directly toward him. They were running from it at nearly thirty knots.

There was nothing else he could do at the moment. The events were conspiring against him. And the American destroyer captain was very good. He stayed with the sub, he anticipated the moves, tracking him as he tried to sneak back in toward Cuba. If it weren't for the team on the beach, he could make a high-speed run to the south and disappear into the deep, cold waters of the Caribbean.

"Destroyer's closing on us, Comrade Captain."

Inber turned to face his exec and then relaxed. The man was not criticizing him but merely reporting information. Everyone knew they needed to get their men off the beach.

"Where's the bottom here?" Inber asked.

"Three hundred fathoms."

"Take us down to three hundred meters. Full speed."

"Aye, Captain."

Inber was sure he could feel a rumble in his feet as the speed increased. Scientists had told him that it was his imagination, but he didn't believe it. As the sub approached full speed he knew that he could feel the reactors laboring to maintain it.

"We've got high-speed screws."

"Another destroyer?"

"No, sir. Sounds like a smaller boat. Something that just entered the picture."

"Cubans?" Yegorov asked.

Inber grinned at the irony. If the new contact was a Cuban patrol boat, it might chase the American away. The Americans tried to avoid confrontation with the Cubans.

"Course?"

"On an intercept for the American destroyer."

Inber nodded. This was what he needed. A little diversion. Let the Americans worry about the Cubans, and while they were doing that he would slip away.

"Right standard rudder."

"Right standard rudder," repeated the helm.

"All stop."

"All stop."

That would create a knuckle of water, an area of disturbance that could be detected by sonar. As the water settled down, the contact would change slowly and the sonar man would detect it. He might think that the sub had slipped away into the deeper water and ignore the contact.

Inber felt the sweat bead and drip. The air inside the sub felt oppressive. They'd been submerged for days. He knew the air was fairly fresh and it was cool, but he believed it to be recycled. Sometimes, thinking of that made it hard to breathe. The air he was taking into his lungs was the air that someone else had breathed out. He thought of germs and bacteria and the insides of the human body, and wanted to vomit. He wanted to hold his breath or demand that the boat surface.

He closed his eyes for a moment and tried to think of something else. All air was recycled, even that at home. Living in a house with someone meant breathing the air they had breathed. Underwater it seemed more intimate.

"Destroyer's turned."

Inber snapped his eyes open. "Hold steady now."

"Contact fading. Losing him completely."

"Sonar? Buoys?" Inber asked.

"Sonar is fading. Screws are retreating. He's moving out of the area."

"I want to move forward dead slow," said Inber. He'd see if the destroyer would turn back to the search.

"High-speed screws are turning to meet the American destroyer."

Inber nodded but didn't speak.

"Captain," said Yegorov, "we have got to rendezvous with the team on the beach."

"In good time, Comrade," said Inber. "In good time."

"Patrol boats closing rapidly, Captain."

Dees nodded and stepped out on the starboard wing. He raised his binoculars and scanned the ocean behind him, searching for the Cubans. Near the horizon he caught a flash of light.

"Come to course one-eight-zero," said Dees.

"One-eight-zero, aye."

Randolph stepped out with him. "We going to abandon the search for the sub?"

"No reason to keep at it," said Dees. "It's only an exercise anyway."

"He was trying awfully hard to avoid us."

"Sure. Maybe he was just practicing his skills, too. We don't get that many opportunities to track a Soviet sub."

The XO reached up and tugged on an earlobe. "You sure he was Soviet?"

Dees grinned. "I doubt that our navy would have us track one of our own subs."

"Why not? They could feed information to both of us. See how well we do without telling the other one who was being tracked."

For an instant Dees was going to buy that and then shook his head. "CIC said that it was an Oscar-class sub. Our guys wouldn't miss on that."

"True."

"Got to admit, though," said Dees, "the guy was good. Seemed to know his business."

Randolph turned, facing the horizon where the patrol boats were. "Still, we stayed with him."

"We'd have lost him," said Dees. "Once the squall line grounded our choppers and he got into the deep water, we'd have lost him."

"Captain, CIC reports they've got a strong contact on the sub. He's moving dead slow to the west."

"See," said Randolph. "We've picked him up again."

"But it does us no good now." Dees leaned toward the hatch. "Have CIC secure the search."

"Aye, Captain."

"No reason to do that," said Randolph.

"It's getting late. We've played this game a hell of a long time. Let's give our boys a break."

"Yes, sir."

"He pinged us again."

Inber shook his head. He didn't want to hear that. Didn't want to know it.

"Contact weak and fading. Going, going. That's it. He's faded."

"Full speed. Course two-seven-zero."

"Aye, Comrade Captain."

"If he doesn't pick us up in the next hour," said Inber, "we'll head in for the coast."

"I hope it's not too late," said Yegorov.

"Yuri, you are an old woman. The men on the beach will either be successful or they will not. The danger to our sub is what was important."

"The Americans would not attack us."

Inber shook his head again. It was the reason that he had not recommended Yegorov for a captaincy. He didn't think ahead. He didn't see the whole picture. The big picture. He was a slave to his orders, not realizing that orders were given to captains to be interpreted by the captain. If there was a good reason to ignore or disobey the orders, then that was the course to be followed.

It wasn't the Americans they had to worry about, it was the Cubans. The American destroyer might be enough to alert the Cubans to the presence of the sub. If the Americans were searching for a sub, it was probably Soviet, and the location, so close to the recent landside activity, might provide clues to the Cuban intelligence service. They might not understand the clues, but still, there was no reason to provide them. The big picture meant they had to evade the Americans and the Cubans. Yegorov did not understand that.

"All screws fading to the stern. High-speed screws are following the destroyer."

"There," said Inber. "Just as we suspected. Maintain this course for one hour."

"Aye, Captain."

Inber looked at the exec. "We must maintain secrecy, Yuri. One hour will tell us if the search is over."

"The men on the beach," he said again.

Inber looked at the man but didn't respond. Instead he said, "I will be in my cabin. If the American comes back, you alert me."

"Aye, sir."

"And if we are not found in that hour, turn to the north and plot a course for rendezvous number two. Our men will just have to hide a little longer."

"I hope that will not be too late."

Inber shrugged and then walked away. He would either rescue the men on the beach or he would not. It would do no good to worry about it now.

CUBA

They had reached the coastline after a couple of hours of pushing through the jungle, and fanned out, staying in the thick vegetation but looking across a white beach to the deep azure of the Caribbean Sea. Billowing clouds floated overhead, some of them blocking the sun. When they did, the temperature on the ground seemed to drop ten degrees.

The only sounds were natural: the buzz of insects, the call of animals, and the rattling of the bushes, trees, and leaves as a light breeze blew. The Cubans who were searching for them had slipped far to the rear, staying close to Castro's plantation. Aircraft, helicopters, and soldiers on flat-bottomed swamp boats searched the swamp, apparently believing that the assassins had been trapped there.

Salnikov slipped to one knee and tried to see the beach through the gaps in the vegetation without touching it.

Sweat stained his uniform, so that it looked as if he'd just stepped from the shower. Sweat dripped down his face and matted his hair. He didn't move to wipe it away. The slightest motion could give away his position.

In a barely audible voice, he said, "Make contact with the sub. We're ready."

The RTO slipped away from the beach and into a thicket of trees and shrubs. He set the radio on the ground and attached an antenna to it. The antenna was little more than a long wire, which he looped over a low-hanging branch; then he pulled himself up into the tree with the antenna. It would be impossible to see the wire and it extended the range of the radio.

He dropped back to the ground, picked up the keypad, and touched it. Setting the earphones, he opened the key, tapped it a couple of times, and then listened.

He wanted to do nothing that would allow the Cubans to triangulate. A short message, on a narrow band, would be almost impossible to detect. Even if the Cubans heard it, they might not recognize it, and if they did, they shouldn't be able to get a bearing.

There was no response from the sub. The RTO wasn't worried. He tried again, listened, and then shut down the transmitter and receiver. There was no reason to run down the batteries.

"Negative contact," he said.

Salnikov nodded and turned toward Zinoviev. "We might as well stay here. No search in the area."

"I'll get the men scattered."

Salnikov nodded. He crawled toward the beach. There was no sign of human life anywhere. He wondered if it was a scene that the explorers might have witnessed when they first came to the New World. No transmission towers, no military ships made of steel and iron. Nothing except a few primitive people who didn't realize their reign was over.

Zinoviev slipped close and said, "We're set. Men are spread in a wide circle with each man in contact with the one on either side of him."

Salnikov took a deep breath. "The hardest part. Mission is over, the enemy is searching, and we've got to lay low here. Seems like we should be running or digging in or something.''

"We can dig in if you want, Comrade Major.''

"Don't be ridiculous, Sergeant. The infantry digs in to hold ground. We hold nothing. We get the hell out as soon as possible.''

"If the sub comes for us.''

"No reason for it not to come," said Salnikov. But even as he said it he could think of a dozen reasons for the sub not to come. Two dozen. But he put those out of his mind. His job was to wait patiently, make contact when possible, and get off the island as soon as he could.

"I'll take the first watch," said Zinoviev.

"All right," said Salnikov. "I'll relieve you. Two hours.''

"Yes, sir.''

Salnikov laid his head on his arms. He tried not to think of the dangers of the jungle and tried not to notice the odor of rotting vegetation. He closed his eyes and pretended he was in Moscow, lying in the grass in a park, trying to catch a nap.

Salnikov snapped awake when Zinoviev touched his shoulder. He didn't move and didn't speak. Not until he knew what was going on. But it was nothing other than his turn to watch.

He let Zinoviev go to sleep and watched the beach and listened for signs that the enemy was searching for them. As Zinoviev slept Salnikov realized that he never heard anyone snore while in the field. Men's barracks often were loud with snoring, but not in the field. It was as if each man knew his life depended on silence. If he could understand this, he could pass it along to the doctors and solve a major problem for married couples.

He passed the time watching the surf crash into the beach, the clouds drift by. He thought about home and then the sub and finally about a dinner with all he could eat. Food quickly took the place of sex in his thoughts.

Zinoviev came awake on his own. He hesitated, listened, and then looked at his watch. "Time to make contact again."

"Let's do it."

They moved to the rear, deeper into the jungle. The circle collapsed inward. The RTO slipped back to the area where he'd strung the antenna, found it again, and hooked it into the radio. Again he tried to make contact and again he failed. He waited ten minutes and tried again.

This time he got an acknowledgment. He tapped the key and shut down the set. He pulled the antenna lead free, picked up the radio and moved back to the rest of the team.

"We're set," he said. "Midnight."

Salnikov looked at his watch. "Eight hours, gentlemen. That's all we have to stay clear."

Zinoviev looked back toward the beach. "We just have to be careful. No sign of the enemy. Let's not do anything stupid."

"Full alert," said Salnikov. "We'll get ready to pull out at ten."

It was darker than he thought it could get. Clouds had moved in. First, high cirrus clouds looking like wisps of ice blown around by a strong wind, and then thicker, darker clouds that threatened rain. Lightning flashed in the tops of them, creating dancing patterns as the sun faded and the ground became as black as the darkest of caves.

The distant thunder rattled like all the artillery Napolean had used against Moscow. The rain fell on the ocean and then drifted to the land. At first it was a dizzle that soaked the already wet soldiers but didn't cool them. Rain began to fall, sounding like frying bacon. Communication was suddenly difficult. The jungle was alive with the noise of the storm.

Zinoviev stood up, wiped the rainwater from his face, and said in a normal tone of voice, "They'll call off the search for us now."

Salnikov nodded. He knew that searchers didn't like bad weather any more than those attempting to evade. But evaders were told to travel in bad weather, at night, over the worst possible terrain.

"Avchinsk, get the men on their feet," Salnikov called. "Down to the water. Get the raft deployed and wait there. Wait at the water's edge."

"You're not worried about the Cubans?"

"They won't be able to see us in this weather. They're probably all inside by now."

"Yes, Comrade."

To the RTO he said, "See if you can get the rendezvous moved up. This is perfect weather."

"Yes, sir."

Salnikov pushed himself out of the jungle and stepped onto the beach. The sound of the surf, of the falling rain, of the thunder, covered any sounds that he made. No one more than ten feet away would hear anything.

He slipped to one knee and scanned the horizon, looking for the light from the sub, a single white light that flashed twice, once, and then twice. After a break, the sequence was to be repeated.

Zinoviev came up to him. "Nothing on the radio. Makes sense." Rainwater washed down his face and cascaded from his chin. It looked like he was standing in a shower.

"Doesn't matter. Cubans won't be out."

Avchinsk and the rest of the team burst from the jungle, dragging the raft with them. They ran down to the water's edge and stopped. They were outlined in stark relief each time the lightning flashed.

"You'd think the Cubans would be so mad about the death of their leader they'd be out searching no matter what."

"Maybe that's it," said Salnikov. "Maybe they don't care."

"Then let's go."

Salnikov nodded but then grabbed the sergeant's arm. The flashing lightning had just revealed something. He pulled the sergeant back into the cover of the jungle.

"What?"

"There."

"Shit."

A half-dozen men were running down the beach, armed with the old AK-47s. They spread out and then shouted, lowering their weapons into firing position.

Salnikov's men turned and then slowly, one by one, raised their hands.

"We'd better take them now," said Zinoviev.

Salnikov knew the sergeant was right. Once the two groups were mixed, there would be no way to free his men without someone getting killed or injured. He pulled his weapon from his shoulder and flipped it around, touching the safety. "On my command."

"Ready."

"Take 'em." Salnikov, sighting over the top of the barrel, pulled the trigger, hosing down the Cubans.

As he opened fire his men scattered, leaping for cover wherever they could find it. Two men dived into the surf, others just dropped, and one rolled behind the raft.

The Cubans hadn't been well trained. Rather than shooting the men in front of them, they turned, opening fire as they did. One man went down. Then a second. Zinoviev fired, his rounds flashing out. Another two Cubans fell, dropping their weapons.

Now some of the Soviets on the beach got into the firefight. Two more Russians opened fire. Tracers crisscrossed as the muzzles strobed. Lightning streaked and the scene became a muddled mess of orange and blue white. The men moved in the jerky motions of a silent movie. A Cuban backpedaled, waving his hands as if trying to keep his balance. The last of them fell to his side, rolled toward the surf, and was hit a dozen times.

"Let's go," Salnikov yelled. He took off running across the beach. Zinoviev held back.

When he reached his men, they were checking the bodies, making sure that the Cubans were all dead. Salnikov crouched near one of them; his chest was wet, but he couldn't tell if it was from the rain or blood. Lightning flashed and he saw the gaping wound in the side of the man's head. Part of his skull was missing and his brain had a hole in it.

"Any of our people hurt?"

"No, sir."

Salnikov stood up and looked down the beach. "There'll be more of them somewhere close. We'd better get out of here."

Zinoviev appeared and touched Salnikov on the shoulder. He was still talking in a normal tone of voice. The rain and thunder covered the noise.

"There, sir," yelled one of the men.

Salnikov turned and saw the single light bobbing on the water five hundred meters out. It flashed the sequence and then went out.

"Let's go." He reached down and grabbed the rope that was strung through eyelets on the side of the raft. He tugged on it as the rest of the team joined in. They hauled it into the surf.

"They're coming," yelled a man.

Salnikov turned and saw more men on the beach. Maybe a dozen, maybe more. There were lights bobbing along with them as they ran.

"Hurry it up," he shouted. He pulled, leaning forward, the water now up to his waist. He turned and tossed his weapon into the bottom of the raft. Letting go of the rope, he grabbed the side and hauled himself up, landing sideways and then twisting around so that he was riding the raft like a bronco-riding cowboy.

In moments the men had joined him. They were paddling, fighting the current and the wind. The rain was slapping them in the face. Salnikov heard something snap by his head and turned toward the beach. It was alive with fireflies.

One of his men groaned suddenly and fell to the right, into the water.

"Grab him," Salnikov yelled. He tossed his oar away and reached back, snagging the arm of the man. "Help me."

Two others leaned over and hauled the wounded man out of the water. They dumped him into the bottom of the raft.

Now they were spinning around. Too many men paddling on one side but not the other. Bullets were hitting the water around them, snapping past them, ripping at the ocean and the raft; another man was hit but fell into the raft.

Salnikov dived off the side, lost his grip on the raft, and came up sputtering. He could see nothing in front of him but heard the men behind him. He grabbed the rope and began to swim.

There was a loud, slow hammering. Tracers the size of watermelons floated over him, heading toward the beach. He watched the tracers disappear into the surf and then walked out of the water. Somebody on the sub had opened fire with a twelve-point seven-millimeter machine gun.

"Yeah!" screamed one of his men. "Give it to them."

"Swim," Salnikov ordered. "Swim!"

He pulled at the water, his eyes now on the sub. He didn't have to see the signal light; the strobing of the machine gun muzzle was enough. Ignoring the men on the beach, who were busy trying to save their own lives, he kept swimming, a hand on the raft, the other digging at the ocean. He closed his eyes and opened his mouth, sucking in air and rain. He shook his head, trying to throw the water off it, but it was raining too hard.

The machine gun stopped firing, but now he could see the sub as a low black shape sitting in the water. It was somehow blacker than the night around it. An ominous shape that threatened death and promised life. A distant object that seemed to be slipping away at the same speed as he paddled toward it.

And then, suddenly, they were there. Sailors were running along the deck. Someone tossed a line. Salnikov caught it, looped it through the rope on the raft, and let the sailors do the work.

As they got close, he yelled, "We've got wounded men here."

"Hurry it up," came the response. "We've got patrol boats closing on us."

"Help us."

More lines hit the water. A couple of his men dragged themselves up the side of the sub. They reached back, trying to pull the raft with them. Salnikov scrambled out of the water and onto the deck. He dropped to his knees and gulped air. For a moment he couldn't move. His muscles felt like rags and his lungs like miniature balloons unable to suck in the air he needed to live.

"Patrol boat two klicks to the stern."

"We're aboard," Salnikov yelled, and that was true. They had hauled the raft out of the sea. They held it in place as sailors fought to get the wounded men out of it.

"Fuck the equipment," said Zinoviev. He was standing over the raft and just let go. The rest of the team did the same and the raft slipped back to the water.

"Come on," ordered a sailor. "We've got to get out."

They ran up the deck to a small hatch. The wounded men had been handed down and were out of the way. A couple of soldiers stood waiting for a chance to get down.

There was a distant boom, like a quiet pop of thunder. "They're firing on us," said a sailor.

A moment later there was a splash far to the starboard and then another quiet pop.

"Out of range."

But then it was Salnikov's turn to enter the sub. He crouched, felt with his foot, and found the ladder. He entered and scrambled down. The last of the sailors came down after him. As he did he pulled the hatch shut with a loud clang and spun the wheel on it. He then seemed to step into space, sliding down the ladder to hit the deck with a quiet thump.

"Hatch secure."

"Let's dive," said a new voice. "Dive. Dive. Dive."

A horn sounded as the sub began to sink. The voice yelled, "Left standard rudder. Full speed."

"Left standard rudder. Aye."

Salnikov felt his knees begin to tremble, and his legs would no longer hold him. He slipped to the deck, a grin on his face. He wiped a hand over his face and looked at it. The black camouflage paint stained it.

"Are you hit, sir?" Zinoviev asked.

"No. Tired. How are our injured men?"

One of the sailors said, "I'm afraid both of them were dead when they were brought on board."

Salnikov nodded and said, "The mission had been perfect until that point. Just perfect."

"It was still a success," said Zinoviev.

"We clear?" Salnikov asked.

"Close," said the sailor. He hesitated and then added, "We're at two hundred meters, pulling away at thirty knots. The patrol boat has lost us."

"Now," said Salnikov. "It's a success."

RIYADH, SAUDI ARABIA

Marie Frankowski sat on the side of the straw-filled stone platform that served as her cot. She knew that she was in trouble. The flight suit she wore was now ragged, stained, and reeked. She touched her cheek. The skin was tender from the last blow. Her captors were getting rougher with each passing day.

She got up and touched her side, sure that one rib was broken. She let the pain subside and then sat down again.

At first they had been questioned and sentenced to death. But no one had touched them. Frankowski was convinced that their status as American military pilots and aircrew was what saved them. The Arabs, whoever they were, didn't want to bring the wrath of the United States down on them as Hussein had done five years earlier.

But then they had started with the beatings. First just stinging slaps to the face and then rocking slaps that sometimes drew blood. She'd watched them punch Hansen, finally knocking him to the stone floor and kicking him. His face had swollen, so that he was nearly unrecognizable. Blood had crusted in his hair and on his uniform.

When they finished with Hansen, they had started on her, but not as violently. At least not at first. She was punched a couple of times, knocked down, and then dragged from the room to be thrown, alone, into her cell.

They had separated them in the hopes of breaking them singly. Marie wondered how Shawn was holding up. She'd been about ready to crack when they had been condemned to death that second day, and the one time she'd seen Shawn recently, it looked as if she was suffering the same fate as the rest of them.

The door rattled and was flung open. Two men stood there, one of them holding an AK. The other was unarmed.

"You come now."

Marie stood up and tried not to show the pain that flashed through her with the movement. She walked forward slowly and then waited for the men to step back. They shoved her once and she took a running, stumbling step, but caught her balance quickly. The last thing she wanted to do was fall down. She wasn't sure she would be able to get up again.

They dragged her through corridors, up the steps, and out of the main building. She was taken to another building and shoved into a small room. There were only two chairs in it, wooden chairs that had seen better days. The stone floor was dirty and there was nothing on the walls.

For a moment she stood there and then sank into one of the chairs. She was an officer in the United States Air Force and didn't have to ask permission to sit. The Arabs could do anything they wanted, but they weren't going to make her ask permission to sit down. When she heard a noise at the door, she had to force herself to sit still, pretending that she wasn't interested. She kept her eyes on the floor and tried not to hear what was happening behind her.

Someone entered and sat down in the other chair. He said, "My name's Morris Reisman."

Marie snapped her head up. "You're an American?"

"Yes."

"From the embassy?"

"Well, yes and no. The embassy knows I'm here, but I'm a reporter."

"Oh."

Reisman glanced at the door, saw that it was closed, and asked, "How have they been treating you?"

She ignored the question. "Has anyone notified my husband that I'm here and alive?"

"I don't know. I would assume that he has been notified now that we know where you are."

"Right," she said disgustedly. "Have you seen the other members of my crew?"

"One or two of them. They're fine."

She snorted. "Fine? You call this fine?"

"They're alive," said Reisman. "A little worse for wear, but they're not in any danger of dying."

"Why are we here?"

Reisman held up a hand. "I'm a reporter, not a representative of the revolutionary government. I'm here to learn a little about what's happening to you. A story in the right place might get you out of here."

"Bullshit," snapped Frankowski.

Reisman shrugged. "Couldn't hurt."

"Sure it could," said Marie. "You could write something to piss off the revolutionary council. They don't have you in custody but they have us. They'll take out their anger on us while you're safe in the embassy or wherever the hell you're staying."

"My question still stands. How have they treated you?"

"Can't you figure that out?"

"Hey. I'm on your side."

"Then get us the hell out of here. These people have no right to hold us. We did nothing to them and nothing illegal. All we did was land five minutes too early."

"The country is in a state of flux," said Reisman. "There are two, maybe more groups claiming that they're in command, that they're the legal government here. You've been captured by one of the more moderate ones."

Marie looked at Reisman and shook her head. She felt

the frustration bubble through her. She wanted to cry, but suppressed her emotions. "What's the embassy doing to get us out of here?"

Reisman rubbed his forehead. "They're in negotiations. One of the things we were able to gain was this interview. Doesn't cost them anything." He was quiet for a moment. "How are you doing?"

"I've been condemned to death as an enemy of the revolution," she said. "You're the first contact I've had with the outside world since I was thrown in here, and you're a goddamned reporter."

"I can carry a message out," said Reisman.

"Tell my husband that I'm fine and that I miss him. I'll be home as soon as I can."

Reisman nodded. "Where are they keeping you?"

She nodded toward the dungeon. "Down one flight of stairs. I'm in a cell by myself. Captain Elizabeth Shawn was in there with me for a while."

"Shawn? I haven't seen her."

"She was the navigator on the flight. A young woman. I'm worried about her."

Reisman nodded and then asked again, "How have they been treating you?" This time he stressed the word *they*. He winked as he spoke.

Now she understood what was happening. "The treatment has been all right. Food could be a little better, but there really isn't anything to complain about."

"Uh-huh. What will you do if you're released?"

"Return home as quickly as possible," she said.

Reisman looked at her carefully. "I'll report your condition to the people at the embassy. They're working around the clock to see that you're released."

"I appreciate that."

"Anything I can get for you?"

Marie shrugged. "I don't know. I'd love a Coke or a steak, but those will have to wait."

"Okay." Reisman stood. "If there's anything else . . . ?"

"No."

Reisman turned and left the room. Marie watched the door close and then wondered what in the hell was going on. She had wanted to see someone from the embassy. Hell, she'd wanted to see the marines come through the door with their guns blazing. She wanted to see Arabs splattered all over the closest wall. Instead all she got was a reporter who didn't seem to know very much.

The door opened again and her guards appeared. "You come with us now."

"Surely," she said. She stood up slowly and sucked in a breath. Her rib hurt her, but she tried to hide it. She wouldn't give them the satisfaction of knowing that she was in pain.

They walked out of the building, across the courtyard and the wall where more than one person had been shot. She knew they meant to scare her with the sight of the wall. They entered the prison building, descended to the first level, and then walked to her cell. She stopped in front of the door.

"Do not get your hopes up. The council has placed a death sentence on you. Do not expect them to grant any enemy of the revolution a reprieve." He turned and walked out. The door was pulled shut and locked.

Marie stood for a moment and then moved to the cot. She carefully sat down on the edge, a hand over her ribs. She prodded them carefully, felt a white-hot flash of pain, and sucked air through her clenched teeth.

She slipped to the rear, lifted her feet, and lay back. There was another flash of pain, but then she was on her back. Staring up at the ceiling, she wondered how much longer the council would hold them. She wondered why her government wasn't doing more for her. She wondered what her husband was doing. Questions swirled in her mind and she didn't have an answer to any of them.

Major John Frankowski wandered through the empty house, first into the bedroom, then into the living room, and finally into the kitchen. He sat down at the kitchen table, staring at the dirty dishes sitting on it. He'd thought, because he was a fighter pilot and Marie was a transport pilot, that if anything happened to one of them, it would be him. Transport pilots were rarely over the FEBA, where the real fighting was taking place.

Of course, there wasn't really a war going on. Or rather, not one that involved American forces. Tiny conflicts in the far corners of the world were boiling, but the American role in them was one of a neutral bystander.

The telegram he'd received so long ago lay on the floor where he'd dropped it. He stepped around it for a week, afraid to touch it again, afraid to acknowledge its existence. If he ignored it, the nightmare would end.

The phone rang and John looked at it. Marie had insisted on having a phone in the kitchen, hanging on the wall near the stove. It had an extra-long cord so that she could move around the kitchen as she had talked on it. She claimed that it made the tasks in the kitchen easier if she could use the phone.

It rang again, the bell intruding on his thoughts. That was something else that Marie had wanted. A phone that rang rather than chirped or buzzed at her. A wall phone like those from the sixties.

It kept right on ringing and John pushed himself up. He didn't want to answer it because he knew it would be bad news. Nothing good ever came over the phone. And then, as he crossed the kitchen floor, he realized that bad news would not come by phone. A delegation of officers from the base would come with his friends, and a chaplain, and maybe a couple of his neighbors.

He grabbed the phone and growled into it. "Yeah."

"John, this is David. We've gotten some news. A reporter in Riyadh managed to get in to see Marie. She's all right. Tired and dirty, but she's all right."

"He saw her?"

"Yeah. Talked to her for fifteen, twenty minutes. Said that she, like the others, was a little worse for wear, but they're alive and in no real danger."

"Thank God." He felt the relief flow through him, then suddenly felt weak in the knees. He backed up to the table and jerked around one of the chairs.

"Apparently one of the crewmen was killed during the fighting at the airport, but that was an accident. Marie was not hurt."

"Okay," said John, somewhat breathlessly. "Okay. Now what do we do?"

"We? I don't think there's anything that we can do."

"You mean that some foreign government can take our people hostage and there's not a damned thing we can do about it?"

"Hostages have been taken for the last ten, twelve years, and we've done nothing about it. We've had to grin and bear it because there was nothing we could do."

John felt rage burn through him. A helpless rage because there was no one to attack. And then he realized the fallacy of that. They knew, in general, who had taken the hostages. They could attack them. Hit them hard to prove that taking Americans hostage would not work. Kill members of the groups taking the hostages; if you didn't get the men and women who had actually committed the outrage, you'd get their friends.

"Why don't we burn their fucking city?" he said.

"Would that help Marie?"

John thought about it and knew that it wouldn't help her. If they retaliated, it was a given that the captors would kill the hostages. But his rage had gotten the better of him. "Maybe not, but they sure as hell wouldn't do it again."

"The situation is fluid," David said. "She's in no danger now. You wouldn't want us to try something before we have all the facts, would you?"

"Why the fuck not?" His voice low, the anger obvious. "We let these ignorant fuckers get away with this and they'll do it again. Stop them now. Kill them all!"

"We can't do that," said David.

"And that's our problem. We can't do it. Or maybe you should say we won't do it."

"We don't want to come down to their level. We're civilized. We do not attack the innocent to get at the guilty."

"Jesus, what bullshit."

"I'm sorry about Marie," said David. "Real sorry, but right now there isn't a damned thing we can do about it."

John slammed a fist onto the tabletop, rattling the dirty dishes. A fork jumped to the floor. He gripped the phone tightly and felt like screaming.

"You should be happy to hear that she's alive and well.

She might be held in a cell, but she hasn't been abused. The government is doing everything it can to free her and the rest of her crew.''

Before John could respond, the anger burned out of him. He seemed to collapse in on himself and stared up at the ceiling as tears formed and fell from his eyes.

''She'll be okay, John. Once the situation over there is stabilized, they'll release the prisoners. We're lucky that they're talking to our embassy people.''

''But when?''

''Soon, I'm sure. The fact they've allowed our people to see them is a positive sign.'' He hesitated and then asked, ''How are you doing?''

''Fine.''

''You need anything? Want someone to come over there for a couple of hours?''

''No. No, I'm fine. I'll be fine.''

''You know that we're here for you, if you need it. Anytime. Day or night.''

''Yeah. I appreciate that.''

Again the line was silent. Finally David said, ''I just wanted to pass the news along to you. Wanted you to know that it wasn't as bleak as it could have been.''

''Thanks,'' said John. He stood and walked across the kitchen to hang up. He took a deep breath, sighed, and then took a bottle of bourbon from the cupboard near the phone. It had been in the house ever since they had bought it, neither of them drinking that much hard liquor, but now he felt he needed a drink. A real drink.

He walked back to the table, sat down, twisted the cap, and lifted the bottle to his lips, letting the liquor run down his throat. He felt the bourbon pool in the pit of his stomach like so much liquid fire.

It didn't help.

EGLIN AIR FORCE BASE, FLORIDA

Brizzola read the intelligence report that had just been handed him. It didn't contain much in the way of hard data, but it did have a few surprises in it. He used a marker to highlight the portions that interested him and then left his office, heading next door to where Bloch was sitting with Carpenter. They were drinking coffee and neither seemed to be working very hard. Brizzola entered and waved the intelligence report like it was a banner.

"Either of you seen this?"

Carpenter set her cup down and nodded. "I'm the one who retrieved it from the message center."

"You seen it, sir?" Brizzola asked.

Bloch held out a hand and scanned the document. "I've seen it. So what?"

Brizzola couldn't help himself. He grinned broadly and asked, "Didn't you see anything significant in it?"

Bloch glanced at the highlighted places. "Obviously you think this is important."

"Look at it," said Brizzola, letting the impatience creep into his voice. "Look at it closely."

"It says that several Americans are being held by the revolutionary council at the prison in Riyadh. It says they're all alive and well, or as well as can be expected considering that they've been beaten."

"Damn it," said Brizzola, "do I have to draw you a picture?" He glanced at Carpenter. "Don't you see it, Diane? You're supposed to be the intelligence officer here."

"What are you talking about?" said Bloch, getting angry.

"It tells where our people are being held. Gives us the location and says that someone from the American embassy has visited them."

"I can read," said Bloch.

"Tells where they are," said Brizzola again, and when no spark of recognition appeared, he added, "It means that we can go get them."

"The hell you say," said Keller.

Brizzola glanced at her and then at Bloch. "The problem in the past was that these groups had always taken the hostages to secret places. They were held in houses or the basements of houses with only a few people knowing the exact location. We have that now. The exact location."

Bloch shook his head. "The general will never go for it. We don't have the right people here to do it."

"But we know where they're being held illegally. We can go get them. Just like that raid on Son Tay."

"It took months to plan," said Bloch. "Took months and failed anyway."

"You're just throwing out problems without thinking it all the way through," said Brizzola.

"And you're talking without thinking at all. You'd need a battalion to do it and we don't have a trained battalion. You'd need a month to plan and you don't have the month. No, there is just no way to do this."

"Let's go talk to the general," said Brizzola.

Bloch deliberately picked up his coffee cup and took a deep drink. He set it down carefully, as if afraid he'd spill some of it, and took a breath. "I suppose that we should bring this to the general's attention, just in case."

"Just in case," Brizzola echoed.

Bloch stood and looked at Carpenter. "Maybe you'd better put together a briefing on this. Everything you can find about the prison and that section of Riyadh. Don't forget to check the weather patterns in that area for this time of year. That's how they screwed up the raid into Iran."

"I know how to do my job," said Carpenter.

"I know you do, Diane," said Bloch. "The general may want something fast on this. Or he might tell us all to get the hell out of his face."

"Yes, sir," said Carpenter.

Bloch left his office with Brizzola. As they neared Gleason's office Bloch said, "I don't know why we're doing this. There's not a thing we can do with the information."

They reached the office, opened the door, and saw Gleason's aide standing looking out the window. He heard them enter and turned.

"The general in?"

"Yes, sir," said the aide. He glanced at the phone and saw all the buttons were dark. "Knock first."

Bloch rapped on the door. When he heard Gleason speak, he opened it. "If you have a minute, General, Major Brizzola and I have something to discuss with you."

"Come on in." Gleason pointed at the leather chairs. "Have a seat."

Bloch sat down, as did Brizzola. The general looked at them and asked, "What can I do for you?"

Brizzola leaned forward and set the intelligence report on Gleason's desk. "I've highlighted the important points."

Gleason took the document and flipped through it. "This information good?"

"We had a man in the prison," said Brizzola. "He's still at the embassy in Riyadh. I would think the information is still good."

Gleason closed his eyes. "This is a somewhat unique situation."

"Yes, sir," said Brizzola. He glanced at Bloch.

Without opening his eyes, the general asked, "What kind of force do we have standing by?"

Bloch shrugged. "We've only a single company that was originally designated as a part of the Rapid Deployment Force. But this is a specialized mission."

Brizzola broke in. "I hate to say this, General, but we do have that Special Forces A-detachment. This is just the sort of thing they do."

"You're talking heresy, Major," said Bloch. "The marines are capable of doing this."

"Yes, sir," said Brizzola.

But Gleason opened his eyes and said, "That's not a bad idea. They're trained to infiltrate, act, and get the hell out. We use our company of marines to back them up and we might have something."

"Sir!" said Bloch. "*They* back *us* up. The marines go in first."

"Let's not get hung up on image," said Gleason. "The important thing is getting those people out of there." He turned his attention Brizzola. "You want to get the commander of that Special Forces unit over here. Let him look at it and see if there's anything he can think of."

"General," said Bloch, "this should be a marine operation. You want to relegate us to a subordinate role. The marines go in first."

"I might remind you, Colonel," said Gleason, "that it is air-force people being held. Maybe you think we should stand back and let the situation continue because they aren't marines."

"No, sir."

"We're all Americans," said Gleason. "There's too much fighting among the services. Each protects its own little empire regardless of the effects on others. Should we have our own air force? Should the navy have one? And the army?"

"Sir, the point is that we're marines. . . ."

"No, Colonel. The point is that we're Americans. I've been handed an opportunity to solve part of the problem and I've been given forces other than marines to do it. I'll use everything at my disposal."

"You want to get in touch with that Green Beret captain?" Brizzola asked.

"Yeah," said Gleason. He held up a hand to stop Bloch from saying a word. "Let's meet with him and see what he has to say. That can't hurt."

"Yes, sir," said Brizzola. He stood up and saluted. "I'll get right on it."

Martinez had been sitting in his quarters watching afternoon television. He had flipped past a half-dozen talk shows, reruns of game shows, a music-video channel, and found an old western. John Wayne was about to shoot the shit out of the bad guys while Walter Brennan threw dynamite at their hideout. It was one of the better westerns but not quite as good as *The Man Who Shot Liberty Valance*.

The knock at the door came as no surprise. What had been a surprise was that he'd been allowed to sit there and watch as much of the movie as he had. He got up and opened the door.

"Captain Martinez. Mind if I talk to you?"

Martinez stepped back. "Come on in, Major . . . ?"

"Brizzola. We met briefly."

"Yes, sir. When I was politely informed that there wasn't a need for me or my team." Martinez grinned as he shut the door. "Not that we're complaining. It's good to be in the land of the round eye and the all-night generator."

"Things that rough in Panama?" asked Brizzola, keeping up the charade. He sat in the only chair.

"No, sir." Martinez thought briefly about Cuba but didn't want to say anything about it. If Brizzola wanted to believe he'd come directly from Panama, that was his business. He added, "But then nothing really beats the States, does it?"

"I suppose not." Brizzola looked at his watch. "Listen, I don't have much time and General Gleason asked if you might come by his office."

"When?"

"Now."

There was a cackle from the television as Walter Brennan tossed another of the sticks of dynamite. It blew the porch off the front of the building. Martinez stepped over and swatted the front of the TV, darkening the screen.

"Now would be fine," said Martinez. "You want me to round up Lieutenant Alvarez or Sergeant Chavez?"

"Not right now," said Brizzola.

"Then I'm at your disposal."

They left the VOQ and walked down to the front door. Brizzola stepped out into the muggy, Florida afternoon. Martinez wished he'd stayed in his room. He'd grown fond of the air-conditioning in the few days he'd been there.

They climbed into a hummer with Brizzola driving. As they pulled out of the parking lot Brizzola said, "I don't suppose I have to mention that everything you're about to see and hear is classified, do I?"

"No, sir," said Martinez. "I'm used to dealing with classified material."

They drove on in silence for a few moments. Brizzola glanced at Martinez and then back at the road. He wanted to say something else but didn't. Finally they pulled up in front of Rapid Deployment Force building.

Martinez climbed out, waiting for Brizzola, and then they walked into the building. In a few moments they were in Gleason's office.

Martinez saluted. Gleason returned it and then pointed at a chair. "Have a seat."

"Thank you, General."

Gleason picked up the classified intelligence brief and said, "Take a look at that."

Martinez read the document quickly. He scanned the highlighted parts again and then handed it back to the general. "Interesting."

"That all?"

Martinez shrugged and waited.

"Can we do anything?" Gleason asked finally.

"Yes, sir. I believe we can."

Gleason waited again, scratched a cheek, and when Martinez didn't speak, asked, "What?"

"Well, General, we know where the hostages are being held. If we had a map, a good map, of the city, and one of the building, then we might be able to do some-thing.''

"We have a man who was in there at our embassy," said Gleason.

"I don't believe he was down in the cell area. That'll be a problem. If we had someone who had been inside there, it would help."

"How long?" Gleason asked.

"For what?"

"Before you could hit the field."

"Hell, General, take us two, three days just to get a workable plan designed, then I'd like a week of rehearsals and mock-up raids. We need the current intelligence, maps of the area, the buildings, the size of the enemy forces, the guard strength, and their level of training. Transport will be a problem. We've got to get in without them know-ing we're coming. And then we need an extraction plan. A month at least. Two months would be better."

"That's useless," said Gleason.

"You want a plan that'll work."

Gleason took a deep breath and shook his head. "Three days before you hit the prison."

"No, General."

"Can't do it?"

"Use the marines," said Bloch. "You won't get a bunch of excuses why it can't be done."

"General," said Martinez, "I'm talking about a plan that will eliminate the danger for us. You want us to suc-ceed. If we fail, we'll be dead and the hostages will be dead, too."

"Captain Martinez," said Gleason, "the enemy is holding several of our people illegally. They have not re-sponded to governmental pleas and pressures. Each of these people has been condemned to death. Any positive action will be applauded by the American people."

"Not if we fail," said Martinez.

"There's no way that you can do it faster?" Gleason asked.

"Not with the resources I have," said Martinez. "I've only got a single team. We'll need assistance."

Gleason nodded and looked at Bloch. "You have a company of marines available?"

"Yes, sir."

Gleason looked at Martinez. "Does that change your mind?"

"The level of enthusiasm seems to be right for this. Still, the time frame is the problem. Without a good, solid plan and time to work through it, we could run into trouble."

"But you'll have a company of marines," said Bloch.

"And a company of marines can correct a lot of mistakes and cover our butts. The risk will be high, though."

"You didn't expect to live forever, did you?" Gleason asked, grinning.

"Well, sir," said Martinez, "I had planned on it, or to die in the attempt."

"I want something done," said Gleason. "I want a plan and I want you to be ready to go in three days. By this time on the fourth day, I want those people to be free."

Martinez studied Gleason's face and realized that it had been very difficult for the marine general to ask for his help. He realized that the man was frustrated with the hostage situation and now had a chance to do something about it. He knew that Gleason wasn't going to let go of it.

"General," said Martinez, "if there is a way to get those people out of that prison, by God, we'll find it. We'll find and get them out."

Gleason looked at the young army officer for a moment and then said, "I wish to hell you were a marine."

"General, I wish to hell you were in Special Forces."

EGLIN AIR FORCE BASE, FLORIDA

Martinez sat at a table in a small conference room with the rest of his team. They had passed around copies of the intelligence reports, the maps of Riyadh, and the information about Saudi Arabia that Keller had prepared. It included the latest estimates of the strength of the enemy forces holding the capital, the size and distribution of the government forces, and the current attitudes of the Saudi people.

Information on the prison facilities was less well documented. They had the report written by a man named Reisman who had been in the prison, but Reisman wasn't a soldier looking for military information. He was a journalist who happened to be assigned the task of interviewing the prisoners.

Chavez, who had been studying the plan of the prison, pushed the paper away and said, "That doesn't tell us much of anything. How thick are those walls? Are they really stone, or is something like reinforced concrete behind them? He thought the outer walls were twelve feet high. Could they have been fifteen feet? I'm sorry, Captain, I just can't buy it. We don't have the information we need.''

Gibson, the intelligence man, added, ''We don't even know where our people are being held. How can we free them if we don't know where they are? We don't know how many levels there are in this place.''

Martinez looked into the faces of the men around the table. ''Maybe I didn't make it clear. This is not a normal Special Forces mission. We are the only team involved and we have three days to make this work. Four days from now we're to be back here with the mission completed.''

''Shit,'' said Chavez. ''That's not the way it works.''

''Sometimes,'' said Martinez, ''it's the only way it works. We have no choice.''

Chavez pulled a bunch of papers back and studied them. He wiped a hand over his nose and mouth as he thought. ''We might be able to get in there. With a little luck, if it's not heavily guarded, we might have thirty minutes inside. But we're going to need better information than this.''

''What you want,'' said Martinez, ''is an aerial photograph of the prison.''

''That would be perfect.''

Martinez grinned. ''We'll have that in an hour. I was promised anything that I wanted to make this work. I asked for the 101st Airborne. That was denied, but the maps shouldn't be.''

''And the surrounding city,'' said Chavez.

Martinez stood and moved to the door. He waited as the men covered everything or turned it over so it couldn't be read. He then opened the door and looked at the three marines standing outside.

The senior man moved toward him. ''Yes, sir.''

''I want you to get with either General Gleason or one of the operations officers. I want the latest aerial photos of the prison area and Riyadh. Now, tell him I only want stuff that is no more than ten hours old. Satellite imagery would be best.''

"Aye aye, sir."

"Report to me as soon as you've talked to them and find out when we can expect that information."

"Aye aye, sir." The man spun and hurried from the area.

Martinez closed the door and returned to his chair. He folded his hands in front of him and said, "We'll get those pictures in a couple of hours."

Alvarez flipped over the rough map of the prison. "We could parachute into it. There are enough large areas to allow for that."

"No," said Martinez. "We're too vulnerable in that confined a space."

"Then we must penetrate the wall," said Chavez. He looked at the map. "I'd suggest hitting it here, only because it looks to be the place where there will be the fewest guards. I think it's the back."

Martinez found himself getting bored with the planning. They could stay at it all day and not accomplish anything. But then, as they brainstormed, each saying the craziest things, a viable idea would evolve. That was how things were done.

But he couldn't get fired up for the mission. He didn't like the circumstances. He didn't like having a marine general running the show, only because the general wouldn't understand the finer points of the Special Forces. Officers locked into traditional ways of thinking often ignored the special requirements of covert military operations. And when it was an interservice operation, egos got in the way. That was why the navy Seals had died during the Grenada operation. It was why a Pathfinder squad was dropped onto a ZSU-23 antiaircraft battery and why they couldn't get reinforcements.

Martinez had seen that happening already. The marine colonel, for example, who didn't like the marines calling on help from the army, no matter how much training and how expert those army troopers might be. Martinez was afraid that attitude would get in the way of the wisdom and lead to bad decisions.

There was a knock at the door. Conversations stopped in mid-sentence. Martinez glanced at his men and then opened it. The marine stood there holding a sealed envelope marked "secret" top and bottom.

"The photos you requested, sir. I signed for them."

Martinez raised his eyebrows and glanced at his watch. "Already?"

"Yes, sir. They had some on hand." The marine grinned as if to say that not all marines were stupid.

Martinez accepted the package. "Thank you, Sergeant."

"Yes, sir." The marine stepped away from the door so that Martinez could close it.

As he returned to the table he pulled open the envelope and extracted the pictures. He looked at the black-and-white images that had been taken from an altitude of over a hundred miles and marveled at their clarity.

Tossing one at Chavez, he asked, "That what you wanted?"

Chavez examined it and nodded. "This is perfect."

Martinez dropped into his chair, leaned back, and closed his eyes. He listened halfheartedly to the conversations swirling around him, hearing snatches of ideas and counterplans. Suddenly a single voice knifed through the banter. "Jesus H. Christ in a hammock. We can do this!"

Martinez opened his eyes and then straightened slowly so that he was facing Chavez. The sergeant flipped a photo toward him and asked, "You see anything there?"

"I'm not in the mood for games, Sergeant," said Martinez harshly.

"Sorry, Captain. On the left side of the prison there's some kind of water discharge area. It's concealed from the surrounding area and appears to lead right into the prison. We can use that to gain access. No indication of any major barriers on the other side."

Martinez looked at it and shook his head. "This makes no sense. It means that prisoners could escape easily."

"Yes, sir," said Chavez, "if the prisoner knew about it. I think it was put in by the designers of the prison just in case they found themselves as inmates. It's separated from the rest of the prison, so that they'd probably have to break into a few rooms, but it allows an access to the outside, or in our case, to the inside."

Martinez took a magnifying glass and bent over the picture. He had to remind himself that he was looking down on it. Straight down. But he could see what Chavez was talking about. A narrow, shallow channel that led to the interior of the prison. He was sure that there would be bars across it, but that would be no trouble for soldiers with the proper equipment. They could burn through it in seconds.

"The only problem is radar facilities at Riyadh," said Martinez.

"No, sir," said Chavez. "Elint* shows radars are all down as a result of combat damage. We hit the airfield late enough, we should be able to get in without trouble."

"Okay," said Martinez. "I think we've got it. Let's put together an assault plan, remembering that we've got to include that marine company, and I'll take it to General Gleason."

Gleason had approved the plan immediately and told Martinez to have his men draw the equipment and weapons they would need. He wanted them in the air within twenty-four hours. No excuses. They were a "go," with presidential approval all the way. The hostages were all military personnel who understood the risks of being military personnel. The civilian world might not understand, but such people would take any losses stoically because they had always accepted military losses. Gleason could not contain his excitement as he yelled, "It's a go."

Martinez had met with the marine officers—a captain, two first lieutenants, and four second lieutenants, and outlined their role. They would create diversions in the city as well as provide cover for Martinez's team, providing a rear guard as Martinez and the freed hostages made their break for it. The marines didn't seem pleased with the role but said they would do their best.

That left one problem. How were they going to get into the city without alerting the enemy? Once they were in and had completed the mission, the obvious method of extraction was helicopters from the American fleet still on station in the Persian Gulf.

*Elint-Electronic Intelligence

They had argued that point, first suggesting the helicopters bring them in, that a C-141 put them down at the airport and that they drive hummers and trucks into the city, and then that they parachute in. No one wanted to trust his life to a hummer. They weren't bad for tooling around a base in the States, but no one wanted to have to depend on them in a life-or-death situation. Everyone preferred the old reliable jeeps, and one man suggested they requisition some of the old jeeps mounted with either the new SAW-249, old M-60s, or the Browning M-2 .50-caliber machine gun. Martinez wasn't sure they could find enough of the vehicles fast enough.

They had finally decided on a parachute jump and a quiet infiltration. The marines would land at the airport twenty minutes later and start a firefight, with one platoon breaking out and heading toward the prison. They would quietly take up positions around the prison and not move until Martinez and his people either called for help or had broken out.

The last thing Martinez had asked for was air support. He wanted fighters standing by in case they needed them. And with a carrier task group in the Persian Gulf, no one saw that as a major problem.

Within twenty-four hours of presenting the plan to Gleason, they found themselves in a C-141 Starlifter en route to an Israeli air-force base near Dimona. From there they'd fly in a C-130 to the drop zone. The marines, in a second C-141, were to take off from Dimona long after they were gone.

Now, sitting in the back of the C-141, Martinez wasn't sure that the plan was all that good. There were holes in it that the time had not allowed them to plug. Timing was critical, and if they were even a little off, a lot of good men could end up very dead. Chavez was pointing at men and asking them what they would do if the enemy appeared as they were crawling through the channel that led into the prison, if they were confronted as they exited it, if they found jailers in the corridors of the prison.

Finished with that, Chavez looked back to Martinez. "All right, sir."

"We'll have thirty minutes inside," he said. "I want two-man teams and one of you has to keep an eye on the time. If you have not cleared your whole area in thirty minutes, you have to get out. That's it.''

"Yes, sir.''

"Now, does anyone have a preference for who they work with?'' Martinez asked.

Banse said, "I'd like to work with Munyo. He likes to blow things up.''

"Fine,'' said Martinez.

"I would think that we should make sure that the medics get down into the prison, just in case,'' said Chavez.

"Alvarez,'' said Martinez, "why don't you go with Jones.''

"Yes, sir.''

"Espinoza? You want to work with Brown?''

"Fine, sir.''

Gibson spoke up. "I'll go with Ortega.''

"Okay.'' Martinez looked at the rest of the team. "Cline, why don't you and Davis set up a position near the wall to cover us as we pull out.''

"Yes, sir. Happy to do it.''

"Does that mean I'll be working with you, Captain?'' Chavez asked.

"Unless you've got a problem with that.''

"No, sir. Just checking.''

"Okay,'' said Martinez, "those of you who are going to hit the prison cells, review what we know about that. Cline, study the prison map and let me know where you want to set up.''

"One problem, Captain,'' said Banse. "I'm not sure how good our radio communications among the teams is going to be. The transmitters won't have the power to push through all that stone.''

"We'll do what we cán.''

Martinez looked at his watch. They still had a long flight in front of them. They could take a break for an hour or two, catch some sleep, and then have another briefing. And the flight from Israel into Saudi Arabia would be a long one, too. Maybe it was time to relax a little. If that was possible.

Chavez touched Martinez on the shoulder. "You awake, Captain?"

He opened his eyes. "Yeah."

"We're about to touch down in Dimona."

Martinez took a deep breath, stretched, and then swallowed. "You have anything to drink?" He glanced at his watch.

"Coke or bourbon?"

"Give me a shot of bourbon. I need to kill this taste in my mouth."

Chavez produced a small flask and handed it over. "Don't drink it all."

"You know that this is against regulations," said Martinez. "Transporting spirits on a military aircraft can get you into a great deal of trouble."

"Will the court-martial be before or after I participate in the illegal action in a sovereign foreign nation?"

Martinez took another swig and handed the flask back to Chavez. "Probably after."

"Great. I'm looking forward to that."

Martinez leaned forward and rubbed his eyes. "Okay, we know the drill here?"

"C-130 should be sitting on the runway close to us, the engines running. We run from this aircraft to the C-130 and it takes off without us having time to piss or complain about anything."

"I think I'll just go back to sleep," said Martinez. "You seem to have everything under control."

"Yes, sir. That's my job."

The loadmaster walked past them, checked to see that they were wearing their seat belts, and then kept on going.

Martinez said, "Just like a real airline. Make sure we're all strapped in so that the bodies will be easier to identify if the plane crashes."

The noise in the plane changed slightly and Martinez worked his jaw, making his ears pop. "Feels like we're beginning the descent."

Chavez twisted around and saw that the rest of the team was sitting up and was strapped in. There was nothing for them to do until the plane touched down.

"You know," said Martinez, "I always worry about this. Something goes wrong now and the pilots don't have a chance to correct it. We just pancake in and turn into a glowing ball of spinning gases."

"Lovely thought, Captain. I'd like to thank you for sharing it with me."

"Don't mention it."

They listened to the muted growl of the servos as the flaps were extended and then the wheels were put down. They heard the roar of the engines change as the power was reduced so they could slow for the approach. In an airliner, they would have been able to watch the progress from one of the windows, but this was a military aircraft, its seats facing the rear and small portholes near the various doors instead of windows. From where they sat they could see nothing outside the aircraft. They could only tell that it was daytime, and if they hadn't worn watches, they wouldn't have known if it was morning or afternoon.

"I think we're getting close," said Chavez.

Martinez nodded. The sounds around the aircraft had changed again. It seemed that the buffeting they felt was the ground effect. An instant later they touched the runway, bounced, and settled back.

"We're down," said Chavez. "We're not a spinning ball of hot gases."

"Air force did it again." Martinez threw off his seat belt and stood up. He moved toward the equipment pods that the loadmaster had strapped down and began working at the buckles as the rest of the team joined him.

Chavez walked to the porthole and looked out. "Other aircraft is on the ground, engines running."

"Saddle up," said Martinez. He grabbed some of the gear and shouldered it.

The loadmaster moved to the rear of the aircraft and touched the button that worked the rear ramp. It started down.

"Wait one," Martinez yelled. He watched as his men picked up their gear, and when everything was ready, he nodded at the loadmaster. "Now."

The ramp descended. The hot, dry desert air filled the rear of the aircraft. Martinez moved to the edge of the ramp, waited for it to touch the concrete, and then ran down it.

Martinez ran toward the waiting C-130, the sound of the turboprops filling the air. He stopped behind it and looked back at the other aircraft. His men were strung out, heading to the new plane. Behind that was a small, dun-colored building. Two men in khaki uniforms stood near the door watching. Neither moved, smiled, or waved.

Chavez ran up the ramp into the rear of the C-130, dropped his gear to the deck, then grabbed Gibson's arm to pull him up. The others were right behind them.

As soon as they were all aboard the loadmaster touched the button and the ramp began to close. Martinez stood looking at the two officers by the operations building until they vanished as the ramp closed.

The loadmaster shouted, "Welcome aboard, sir. Would you and your men please strap in?"

Another crewman tossed a net over the gear, fastened it all to the floor, and moved back to buckle himself in.

Once the ramp was up, the second man glanced at Martinez and his team, saw that everyone had strapped in, and then sat down himself. He touched a button on the long cord that was fastened to his flight helmet. A moment later the aircraft jerked once and they began to roll.

Martinez leaned close to Chavez. The noise inside the C-130 was louder than it had been in the C-141. He shouted, "That's got to be some kind of record."

They were suddenly thrown toward the rear as the aircraft left the ground, beginning a steep climb, the engines screaming. Martinez reached out, grabbed the reb webbing, and pulled himself upright.

"On our way," he yelled.

"Yes, sir," said Chavez. "On our way."

SAN ANTONIO, TEXAS

The order had caught Sandi Paulding by surprise. She'd been sitting in her faculty office, her feet propped up on her desk with her shoes off. She looked at her slightly swollen ankles and wished that she didn't have to stand in front of the classroom lecturing. Some teachers were comfortable sitting on the desk or among the students, but she believed that she lost some of her authority by sitting with them. Therefore she stood, even when her feet hurt and her ankles were swollen.

The phone rang and Paulding leaned forward, trying to get it without putting her feet down. Her skirt slid up her thighs, but since there was no one in the office with her, she ignored it.

"Paulding, this is Major Hawks. We have been alerted."

"What?"

"We are being called to active duty, effective immediately. You have one week to settle your affairs and then report for extended active duty."

"What?"

"I believe I have made the situation clear, Major," said Hawks coldly.

Paulding dropped her feet to the floor and opened the middle drawer of her desk, searching for a pad. She wanted to say something to Hawks, but nothing came to mind.

"Are you there?" asked Hawks.

"Yeah." She felt herself begin to sweat. "I can't just drop what I'm doing here and report for active duty."

"I'm afraid you have no choice. If you do not report on the designated day," said Hawks, "you will be arrested and jailed. Either way, you'll be coming."

"There's so much to do here."

"You'll have to arrange for whatever you need. And I want to caution you to keep this as quiet as possible. You are not to give the real reason for your sudden departure, if you can avoid it. All applicable laws and regulations are in effect."

"Now what in the hell does that mean?" She picked up her Coke and drank from it. It was simply something to do to cover her agitation.

"Simply that upon your return, the law states that your job will be returned to you with no loss of salary or standing."

"Damn it," she said, and felt the tears burn her eyes. She didn't want to be a real soldier. It had been the prestige that had induced her to join the reserves. They had told her that no one was called to active duty anymore, especially with the laws passed after the Desert Storm call-up. She could resign anytime she wanted. There was no obligation. They had all smiled and nodded as they mentioned that if they were called up, all bets were off. Then she would have to go. But that just wouldn't happened, not now.

"If there are no questions, Major," said Hawks, "I have a dozen others to call."

"When do I have to report?"

"One week. You'll be receiving orders by mailgram."

"Christ," said Paulding.

Hawks softened slightly. "Yeah. It caught us all by surprise. Good luck."

"Wait," she said. She almost asked if it had anything to do with the suspected assassination of Castro, but then remembered that most of the information was still classified. The media was speculating about the rumors coming from Cuba, but had no hard information. She didn't know how to ask the question over the open line.

"Is there something else?" Hawks asked.

"No. I guess not."

"Then I must make those other calls." Without another word, he hung up.

Paulding sat there staring at the window. The building was nearly a hundred years old; men who had had her office in years past might have been called to fight in World War I or II or Korea. Dozens had sat where she now sat and looked out onto the treelined campus. Students hurried between the buildings, going from one class to another.

She shifted around, tugged her skirt down, and then checked the class schedule. She didn't know what she would do about her Tuesday seminar. There was just no one available to take it over. The rest of her teaching duties could be split up among the rest of the staff. Students could be transferred into other sections for the remainder of the year.

There wasn't much she could do. Her only course was to see the chairman of the department and let him know that she was going to be missing for a couple of weeks.

And then a thought hit her. How did she know it was going to be only a couple of weeks? It could be a couple of months or a couple of years. Suddenly she wished she could remember what she had been told about that. Could they hold her in the service for a couple of years? She seemed to remember the men and women of Desert Storm hadn't remained on active duty more than a few months.

She stood up, having to move. She walked to the window and looked down on the sun-drenched campus. A couple sat next to a huge rock carved with the date of the class that had moved it to campus. It had been there for more than a hundred and ten years. The couple, holding hands, seemed oblivious to everything around them.

"Damn," she said. She wanted to cry or throw up or scream but knew it would do no good.

There was a tap at her door, but she ignored it. She didn't want to see anyone at the moment. Not some student with his or her trivial problem or a colleague with his or her equally trivial problem. The knock came again and then someone rattled the doorknob. She'd failed to lock it.

"Just a moment," she snapped.

"Sorry."

She automatically brushed at her skirt and tugged at the bottom of her jacket. Glancing in the mirror, she noticed that her face was pale and her eyes puffy, but it was nothing obvious. She returned to her desk. "Come on in."

Sinclair Chommers stood there in his immaculate suit, tightly knotted red tie, and carefully combed hair. "How are things going?"

"Funny you should ask," said Paulding, "but I find that I must desert you in a week."

"Oh?"

"Something came up and I find that I have to leave here."

"I'm afraid that is just not possible."

She pointed at the couch opposite her. The bookcase behind it was loaded with old, leather-bound books. A Navaho rug hung on the wall.

"I have no choice," said Paulding.

"You have a contract with us."

Knowing that she was violating the order she had just been given, she said, "My unit, or rather a few of us with specialized knowledge, are being called to active duty. I have to report in one week."

Chommers's face paled slightly. "Good God, what's happening?"

"Nothing too extraordinary, I would imagine. Otherwise we'd have heard something on the news."

"Could this have something to do with the trouble that's brewing in Cuba?"

Paulding cocked her head slightly, thinking about it.

"My guess would be no. But who can tell?" She didn't like lying about it. But she did like knowing what the trouble was when Chommers could only guess.

He ran a hand through his hair, forgetting about how carefully he combed it. "I suppose there's no one I can call about this?"

"Believe me, if there was a way around it, I would have tried it. I'm stuck."

"I was going to ask you to take over one of Davidson's sections next week, only for the week, but I guess that's now out. I don't understand why everything has to happen at once."

"Neither do I," said Paulding. "This happens sometimes. Usually we spend a week or two playing at war and then come home."

"I don't remember you having to go before."

"Normally during the summer months," said Paulding quickly. "When I'm off doing my research or traveling."

"Ah," said Chommers. He stood up. "Well, I'd better go to my office and begin to organize things."

"I'm really sorry about this."

He waved a hand. "It's not your fault. It's one of those things that can't be helped." He moved to the door. "Still, it is unusual."

"Not all that unusual. Remember Desert Storm."

"Of course." Chommers opened the door. "See me a little later on this."

"Sure." As soon as his footsteps faded she moved to the door and locked it. Then she walked to the couch and sat down.

"It's not fair," she told the floor, knowing that it didn't care about her assessment of the situation. She took a deep breath, thought she was going to cry, and then didn't. Army officers do not cry when the situation doesn't meet with their approval. They plunge ahead and make the situation work for them. Paulding knew that was all she could do.

Stepanov sat in a small, plush room with Popovsovich and Tetkorov and two intelligence officers. Stepanov had briefed them on his findings in Vietnam. Told them of the desire of the Vietnamese to take the disputed lands from the Chinese. To have an air-mobile division modeled on those of the superpowers.

"Their response was nearly Pavlovian. They couldn't wait to agree to our terms."

"Then they will attack the Chinese?" Popovsovich asked.

"Attack might not be quite the right word," said Stepanov, "given the differences in size, but I think we can look to the Vietnamese as allies. There will be more armed conflict between the two."

"Good," said Tetkorov.

"Now," said Popovsovich, "I want you to analyze what has been happening in the Middle East." He nodded at one of the two intelligence officers.

The man stepped forward, glanced at the general, and said, "Everything said in this room is classified as most secret. It must not be discussed outside the confines of this room with anyone."

"We don't need to be reminded of the necessity of secrecy," said the Soviet president.

"Certainly, Comrade," said the officer. He opened his folder and began: "At the moment, the revolutionary council in Riyadh has made no additional gains. They retain control of portions of the capital, two of the radio stations, and the television. The gains in other areas have been neutralized, and without additional assistance from us, covert assistance to include some elements of General Stepanov's Spetsnaz, the Saudis will probably reverse the revolution. All gains there will be lost."

The briefing officer glanced at his three listeners, waited momentarily for questions, and when none was asked, continued. "Our support of the Iraqi invasion is progressing well. They have made gains all along the line, and the Iranians have resorted to their old human-wave tactics." The officer grinned. "They threw away nearly twelve thousand lives to stall an armor advance near Khorramshahr."

"Did it work?"

"Momentarily. Four tanks were lost and the advance stalled for five hours, but the column then pressed for-

ward, overrunning several Iranian defensive positions
along the main road.''

The briefing officer turned the sheet over and then
glanced at his audience. "Our Spetsnaz raid into Iran destroyed much of their stockpile of antitank weaponry and
blew up a significant store of ammunition, killing more
than a hundred Iranian soldiers.''

"Your figures are confirmed?'' Tetkorov asked.

"Yes, sir. The Iranians have downplayed the event to
the world press, of course.'' He stopped and grinned. "But
in secret meetings with our representatives in Tehran, they
confessed that the Iraqi bandits were very successful in
destroying the Iranian warmaking capability. They have
asked for more aid to stop the invasion.''

"And are we going to grant it?'' Stepanov asked.

"Oh, most assuredly,'' said Popovsovich. "With
strings attached, of course. We are not a rich nation like
the United States. There must be a return for our invest-
ment.'' He looked up at the intelligence officer so that he
would continue.

"Iraqi surface-to-surface missiles have been used in a
terror campaign against the population centers, including
Tehran. The Iranian government is asking for defenses
against these weapons as well as surface-to-surface missiles to be used in retaliation.''

"The war escalates,'' said Stepanov.

"Certainly. Each turn of the screw makes the Iranians
more dependent on our assistance. We are negotiating for
oil and port facilities now, as payment,'' said Popovsovich.

"The Iraqis,'' said the briefing officer, "have used a
great deal of their weapons stockpiles. They have fired the
majority of the surface-to-surface missiles we supplied
them. Most of them were used to reduce Iranian resistance
along the attack fronts. They are clamoring for more
weapons, both heavy, long-range weapons and small arms
and ammunition. They are also being drained by their assistance to the revolutionary council in Riyadh.''

"The air war?'' said Stepanov.

"Limited engagements,'' said the officer. "The feeling on both sides is they must retain their air forces. The

Iraqis feel they'll need air power to crush the last of the Iranian resistance, and the Iranians believe they'll need their planes to fight off the last of the Iraqi attacks.''

"Both sides have asked for additional planes," said Tetkorov, "and we have promised aid to both."

"Won't we have Soviet pilots flying against Soviet pilots?" Stepanov asked.

"Our mission is training," said Popovsovich. "Soviet pilots will be used in combat roles only with the permission of the Supreme Soviet, and we will not issue such a permission if it would involve Soviet pilots facing one another."

"At the moment," said the officer, "the war is going in favor of the Iraqis. They have the momentum and are driving hard into Iranian territory. They have increased their demands for our assistance." He turned another page and said, "Iranian defenses are toughening. They have slowed the Iraqi progress."

"So," said Popovsovich, "no matter who is victorious in these conflicts, we will be in the best position to demand . . ." He stopped, glanced at colleagues, then continued: "Demand what we want. It is our aid that gave the Iraqis the power to attack and the Iranians the power to resist. We cease our support to either side and it will collapse."

"Yes, Comrade," said the briefing officer.

"Then the real problem," said Tetkorov, "is Saudi Arabia. The revolution is not going well there."

Now the second intelligence officer came forward. He didn't tell the assembled men that his briefing was classified. Instead, he launched into his assessment of the situation, telling them that without massive support, the revolution would soon collapse. The Saudis had too much military might left. The surprise attack had led to impressive early gains, but once the surprise was over and the attack sputtered, the gains would soon be lost.

"General Stepanov?" said Popovsovich.

Stepanov was quiet for a moment, stroking his chin as he thought. Finally he asked, "What do we gain in Saudi Arabia?"

"They have the world's single largest reserves of petroleum."

"And the Iranians have the second?"

"Or third," said the intelligence officer, waving a hand.

"And our scientists are working to replace oil with other forms of fuel. Solar, geothermal, nuclear . . ."

"The point?" asked Popovsovich.

"We don't need Saudi Arabia," said Stepanov. "It is a thorn in our side, with a hostile population and no direct access for us, except through other countries. Warm-water port facilities are available in Iran, as are major oil reserves. We do not have the demand for petroleum products that the West has. We could find ourselves pouring troops, equipment, and funds into Saudi Arabia to prop up a revolutionary council we do not control."

"You are suggesting that we abandon the revolution in Saudi Arabia?" the head of the KGB asked harshly.

"We have no soldiers in Saudi Arabia, we have no direct link to the revolution there. Let the Americans have a small victory," said Stepanov. "They will be celebrating the defeat of global communism in Saudi Arabia as we slowly expand into Iraq and Iran."

Popovsovich nodded. "That seems to be a sane course and it costs us nothing."

"Except the support of the revolutionary council in Saudi Arabia," said Tetkorov.

"A few of them, yes, but only those who knew that we pulled some of the strings," said Popovsovich. "Handled properly, the setback will not be great, but the advantages will be."

"I'm not so sure," said Tetkorov.

"I am." Popovsovich glanced at Stepanov. "Is there anything else?"

"I did not have a chance to visit North Korea."

"Not important now. Representatives of North Korea are on their way to Moscow. They will ask for military aid—aircraft and tanks and artillery. We'll supply some of it and they'll place it either close to the Thirty-eighth Parallel or on their border with China. The Chinese will respond with more troops and equipment, weakening themselves elsewhere.''

Stepanov then shrugged.

Popovsovich studied the two briefing officers. "Do either of you have anything of importance to add?''

"No, Comrade President.''

"No, sir.''

"Then you are dismissed.''

Both men gathered their folders and papers and left the room. When they were gone, Popovsovich stood up and walked to a small bookcase. He touched the back of a forbidden book, *Huckleberry Finn.* The line of books seemed to swing open and a small bar was revealed.

But before he offered a drink, he asked, "Now, what about Cuba?''

Tetkorov grinned. "The mission was a complete success. The Cubans had no clue who fired the shots, and they have refused to admit that their leader is dead. Quietly, through coded messages to us, they are blaming Alpha Sixty-six.''

"What is that?'' Stepanov asked.

"Cuban dissidents living in Miami. But officially they are only saying that Castro has taken ill. Nothing serious. Overwork.'' The grin spread on Tetkorov's face. "A permanent condition.''

Popovsovich nodded and glanced at Stepanov. "Our marines are very good.''

"Very well trained,'' said Stepanov.

Holding a glass up to show the others, Popovsovich said, "I believe that calls for a drink. A shot of vodka?''

"Certainly,'' said Tetkorov.

"Always,'' said Stepanov.

Popovsovich filled three glasses, sprinkled pepper, and then gave one to each man. "To the Spetsnaz.''

"To the Spetsnaz,'' Stepanov repeated.

Brizzola had been haunting the message center for hours, listening to the radio communications with units around the world and reading the computer and teletype messages as they came in. He asked the same questions a dozen times, annoying the clerks, technicians, NCOs, and

watch officers. They all wanted to tell him that they had
better things to do, but none of them did. All knew that
General Gleason had sent him and no one wanted to annoy
the general.

He found an old beat-up desk in the rear of the cavernous, air-conditioned room and watched the activity
swirl around him. It was amazing to see so many people
working so hard to accomplish so little. The machines
transmitted the messages automatically. The computers
analyzed the data, distributed it, and sent it on. A computer alerted the proper agency that a classified message
had arrived. And if it was Flash Priority, it could signal
that as well. Only a few people in the message center
actually worked at typing messages into the machines.
Most of the traffic arrived so that an OCR could read it,
type it, and dispatch it.

He watched a young woman in a short light, print dress
as she moved among the dozens of desks, handing out
papers and picking up others. Brizzola decided that if he
hadn't been fifteen years older than she was, he'd be in
love. Even so, he decided that he was in love in much the
same way that someone could love a painting or a sculp-
ture. He was afraid that his attitude was sexist, but as long
as he kept it to himself he decided that he was safe.

She dropped one of the papers and bent to pick it up.
It was a show that Brizzola wished he hadn't seen. He was
embarrassed at watching but didn't pull his eyes away. He
decided that it figured she'd be wearing black lace panties.

"Major Brizzola?"

He looked up at an intense young second lieutenant.
He looked so young, but was the right age to ask the
woman for a date. Brizzola would have traded places with
the man, if it could have been arranged.

"Yes," he said.

"Got a message. Think it's the one you've been waiting for." He held it out like an offering to a god.

Brizzola scanned it. It was short but to the point.
"Several units transmitted our location at nineteen hundred hours Zulu. No problems."

"Thank you," said Brizzola. "Please log that in and
file it."

"Yes, sir."

Brizzola took a final look at the young woman. She was sitting at a desk with her legs crossed, showing a lot of thigh. He shook his head and moved to the vault door of the message center, feeling very old.

ABOARD THE C-130

They were getting close to the drop zone. For the first few hours, the time had seemed to drag. Martinez almost believed that they were caught in a time warp, destined to stay for all eternity in the back of airplanes heading toward destinations they would never reach. But now, suddenly, it seemed as if there wasn't enough time. They were racing to the destination before they had a chance to plan. This was the first time that he hadn't felt confident about a plan and he knew the reason. The planning hadn't been adequate.

Martinez examined his weapon, what in the old days had been called the CAR-15. It was a chopped-down version of the M-16 but had a short metal stock that could crush a skull if the fighting turned hand-to-hand. The M-16, made of plastic, was useless for that sort of thing.

Each of the men had sound suppressers for their weapons. Unlike the short metal tubes one sees on television,

these silencers were nearly two feet long and reduced the
muzzle noise to a quiet hiccup. The problem was the operating of the bolt and the supersonic speed of the bullets.
Both produced noise.

In fact, all of the men had opted for something other
than the new individual weapons pushed on the military
by a Congress that didn't understand that killing people
was an inhumane business. The new weapons fired a thin
fléchette that penetrated the body without creating additional trauma. Martinez and his team wanted the targets
to know they had been shot. The M-16 round tended to
tumble once it struck someone, and that broke bones and
tore up flesh. The hyperstatic shock of impact was often
enough to kill, even if the wound was to a hand or foot.
Blood was forced back up the vessels to explode the heart.

Martinez set his weapon on the deck beside him and
took one of the flash grenades. Detonated in a confined
area, it could temporarily blind the occupants. There were
also fragmentation grenades, gas grenades, and smoke
grenades. Banse had an M-79 grenade launcher, as did
Davis. Neither man figured to need it, but Martinez was
happy to have them.

"Radios working?" Martinez yelled over the noise in
the interior of the plane.

Espinoza nodded and then looked at Banse. "They
checked out before we boarded the plane. Got extra batteries just in case, but we're not going to be on the ground
that long."

"Let's get them passed out. Each team is to have one."

"Yes, sir. I drew enough so that everyone can have his
own."

Banse pulled a metal container close and popped the
top. He removed the small Styrofoam boxes that contained
the radios. They were small units that had a wire mike,
an earplug, and a small, self-contained antenna. Range
wasn't great, but it would allow the team to communicate
with one another after they split up.

Handing one to Martinez, Banse said, "Captain."

"Thanks." He accepted the box and extracted the radio. He put it on and then donned his helmet, a high-

impact plastic model painted a light tan and shaped somewhat like the Nazi helmets of the Second World War.

"Are we going over it again?" Chavez asked.

Martinez looked at Gibson and yelled, "Hey, Tomas,
what is your role in this?"

"Sergeant Ortega and I hit the southern wing of the
prison, taking out all the guards there. Once that is accomplished, we work our way lower, emptying cells as we go.
After thirty minutes in the prison we return to the rally
point regardless of results."

Martinez looked at Chavez. The sergeant shrugged.
"Never hurts to run through it again. Make sure that everyone understands his role here."

"Not now," said Martinez. "We're close now. I think
we all know what we need to do."

"Yes, sir."

They sorted through the equipment the lightning raid
demanded: radio equipment, weapons, grenades, ammo,
water, and medical supplies. They carried no food, nothing that wouldn't be needed in the raid. It meant they
could jump with more ammo, and Martinez always liked
to carry as much as possible.

He took out the aerial photo and studied it again. There
was nothing about the prison as seen from the air he didn't
know. They had pinpointed the guard towers, the doors,
the buildings, and the entrances. In a few of the pictures
there had been some strange-looking lumps that had short
shadows. No one could figure them out until they realized
they were looking down on people seen from directly
above.

Martinez stood up and yelled at Chavez. "I'm going
to check on the progress of the second aircraft."

"Yes, sir. I'll get the men ready to jump."

Martinez walked forward slowly. He stepped over the
rails that had been installed on the deck of the C-130 to
allow one man to push heavy pallets if the aircraft was
being used for resupply. He veered to the left and then
looked up into the cockpit. He climbed the short ladder.

The navigator saw him and leaned close. "You need
something, Captain?"

"The second plane. Is it on time?"

"Wait one." The nav turned and said something into the mike at his lips. One of the pilots looked over his shoulder and then held a thumb up. The nav said, "Everyone is on course and on time. We're about twenty minutes from pushing you fellows out the door."

"Thanks." Martinez returned to the rear of the aircraft. His men were shifting around, making sure the straps of their chutes were secured properly, that the equipment was tied down so that the sudden rush of wind wouldn't tug at the chute and flip it around, injuring them. They had their helmets on, the chin straps buckled tightly.

Chavez and Alvarez moved toward him. "How's it look up there?" Chavez asked.

"About fifteen minutes," said Martinez.

Alvarez looked at his watch and grinned. "Looks like it's all going to come together."

Martinez nodded. He didn't like pregame pep talks before a jump. What he needed was a couple of minutes of silence to think, and then something to keep him busy until it was time to launch himself into space.

"I want team members to jump together," he said. "Each team member is responsible for his buddy."

"Yes sir." Chavez whirled and began checking the troopers carefully, giving them last-minute instructions.

"This isn't going to be a cakewalk," said Martinez. "Not with the planning that didn't go into it."

"Yes, sir."

"We've got to be ready to react to the changing situation. It's not going to be easy."

"Yes, sir."

Martinez looked into the eyes of his second in command and knew that the young lieutenant didn't believe him. He was sure they would blast in, free the prisoners, and blast out, all before the enemy could react. Martinez hoped he was right.

The loadmaster moved in and yelled over the engine noise, "We're getting close. I'm to advise you that the second aircraft is still on course and on time."

"Thank you." He moved among his men and shouted, "Let's get it ready."

The men spread out in the back of the plane, waiting

for the ramp to be extended. Martinez stood near Chavez as the sergeant again reminded the men of what they all knew already.

The plane slowed then and began a gradual descent. The loadmaster moved to the side and touched a button but didn't push it yet.

"We're getting close," said Chavez unnecessarily.

"Yeah," said Martinez, wishing that the jump was over. He always felt that he was going to chicken out at the last instant. He always debated about jumping, telling himself he didn't have to if he didn't want to, but when the time came, he always leaped into space.

The descent stopped and the loadmaster touched the button to open the ramp. The lights behind them, which had been white for most of the trip and then had gone red, suddenly went out. Only a couple remained on so the men would be able to exit the aircraft in safety.

The ramp locked down and the cold, dry desert air swirled into the rear of the aircraft. Martinez could taste the dust. He could feel the dryness. He was surprised that he could tell so much about the desert so far above it.

The loadmaster shouted, "One minute."

Outside the aircraft, Martinez could see nothing. There were no lights in the desert. Nothing. The city was in front of them and they were facing the wrong way. Nothing to see except the endless waves of desert sand. Nothing to mark their progress.

"Thirty seconds."

The men moved up on the ramp. The swirling slip-stream curled around, ripping at their uniforms and their equipment. Still there was nothing to see on the ground.

"Go!" yelled the loadmaster. "Bailout. Bailout. Bailout."

Martinez rushed forward, stopped at the very edge of the ramp, and looked down. Then, without thinking about it, he stepped into space.

As soon as he was out of the aircraft he rotated and looked toward the front. The darkened city was easy to see, as was the prison, because of its distinctive shape. The air-force photos had put them right on the money. He pulled the ripcord and felt the chute spill from the pack on his back. He let himself begin to spiral in toward the prison. He glanced up and saw the rest of the team.

And in the distance was the C-130, having begun a turning climb, taking it away from the city. He couldn't hear the rumble of the engines, just the air as he dropped toward the desert.

An instant later he was down, the sand soft under his feet. He hit a quick release, dropping the chute from his body. On a covert mission, he would have gathered it up and buried it. Now, by the time anyone found the chutes, they would have gotten out.

Chavez came at him, his weapon held at the ready. Martinez nodded and pointed. Chavez moved off to take the point. Martinez, crouched on one knee, touched the safety on his weapon, making sure that it was on. Gibson appeared, and then Chavez. Without a word, the men fell into position, moving across the open desert toward a short, dun-colored wall about fifty yards in front of them.

Two more of the soldiers ran by him in a low crouch. They hit the wall and moved along it, just black shapes next to the light-colored stone. Martinez stayed where he was, holding his weapon, until he counted each of his men. He turned, saw the black shapes of the discarded chutes, but ignored them. Over the tiny helmet radio, he heard Chavez.

"In position."

Martinez ran forward, staying down. He hit the wall and knelt there. He pulled the camouflage cover from the face of his watch and checked the time. The marines should be getting close, if they were on schedule. Their portion of the initial attack was not that critical, but if Martinez got into trouble, they would need the help.

Chavez slipped along the wall until he came to the end, where he stopped and looked around. There was a wide street with nothing, no buildings, signs, or poles, along it and no traffic using it.

The marines were supposed to check in the moment they touched the ground, but Martinez heard nothing from them. The airport was close enough that he should have heard the plane landing or the firefight beginning. The city was quiet, almost as if it was deserted.

"Proceed?" Chavez asked.

Martinez knew the sergeant was as aware of the problem as he was. He touched the wire mike and whispered, "Go." They could get into position. If the marines didn't land, they could fall back on Plan B.

Chavez stood up, put a hand on top of the short wall, and vaulted over it. When no one opened fire and no one shouted an alarm, he moved on. The rest of the team climbed the wall and then crouched near it. In the distance they could see the high walls of the prison.

They all moved out, staying five to ten meters behind Chavez. In the moonlight they could see each other easily, seeming to stand out against the lighter background. No one had thought of that as they rushed to complete the planning for the mission. When Chavez disappeared into a shadow and followed it, moving toward the east, the rest of the team followed him and then closed up the interval as it became harder to see each other.

When they were twenty yards away from the prison compound, Chavez halted them. Martinez used his night binoculars to scan the top of the prison wall and the guard towers at the corners. He detected no movement; no one manned them.

Using the radio, he said, "Go."

Chavez sprinted from the shadows to the base of the wall. At that point someone on it, or in the guard tower, would be unable to see him unless he leaned over the railing and looked down.

As Chavez slipped along it the team joined him, one by one. They fanned out and then moved farther to the east. He rounded the corner and moved forward. The team did the same, and Chavez stopped short of the channel that led into the prison.

Martinez joined the sergeant. Chavez, leaning close, whispered, "Do we go?"

They could hear the quiet sound of a distant jet. It had to be the marines. The air force had missed the TOT by five or six minutes. Nothing critical.

"Yeah," said Martinez. "We go."

Chavez waved and Munyo moved forward. He dropped into the shallow channel and began to crawl. Banse slipped in the channel behind him without a word. When they reached a covered portion that looked as if flat stones had been laid across the top to protect it from the sun, Munyo rolled to his back and pulled himself deeper, lifting his shoulders and back as he moved. With one hand he reached out, over his head, feeling his way along.

"Bars," he said over the radio.

"Burn them," said Martinez.

There was no reply. Martinez knew that Munyo and Banse would be doing their job. The rest of the team spread out slightly in a half circle against the wall. They were searching for the enemy, providing security. It seemed that no one knew they were around.

At that moment there was a distant ripping sound, barely audible. Martinez recognized it as the firing of a SAW-249. The marines were down and working to secure the airfield. The diversions had begun.

From the channel came a quiet sputting sound as the bars were burned away. The odor of hot metal and cordite filled the air. Light flickered and one of the bars fell against the stone with a quiet, dull clank.

"Bars cleared," said Munyo.

Martinez nodded and whispered, "Cline, you've got it up here. Let's go," then dropped into the channel and began his low crawl along it, Chavez right behind him. The rest of the team followed as quickly as they could.

Martinez reached the bars. Some of the metal was still glowing from the heat. Munyo had thrown an asbestos shield over the bottom pieces. Martinez scrambled over that and suddenly found himself in the open again. Twisting around, he looked up at the inside of the wall.

He climbed to his knees and then out of the channel, joining Munyo at the base of the wall. Now he could see a few of the buildings. Dark shapes. No light showed in any of the windows. There was no movement, other than that of his men. He watched them fan out, breaking up into the two-man assault teams. Everyone stayed close to the wall. The interior of the prison was still quiet, but the fighting at the airport had intensified. More weapons had joined in and there was a series of concussions. Explosives of some kind.

"We're ready to go," said Chavez.

Martinez nodded. Over the radio he said, "Thirty minutes from this point. Everyone back here."

He didn't expect anyone to say a word. Their acknowledgment was their sudden movement toward the various buildings around them.

As the men disappeared Martinez slapped Chavez on the shoulder. "It's time for us to get going."

Together they were up and moving, running across the open field toward a small door in the closest building. Martinez hoped that the interior plan they had seen was close to correct. He was afraid that it wasn't.

Chavez hit the door, reached down, and touched the latch. "You ready?"

Martinez nodded, not sure if he wanted the door opened or not.

RIYADH, SAUDI ARABIA

Captain William A. Ramey, Wild Bill to his men, sat in the rear of the C-141 looking like he was John Wayne about to assault Iwo Jima. The difference was that his uniform was tan, to match the sand, his weapon was a fully automatic individual rifle that fired a fléchette round, and he wore a vest of light Kevlar designed to stop an AK round from four feet away. He wore a harness to hold his spare ammo, had a razor-sharp knife taped upside down on the left side, and had smeared tan-colored grease-paint on his face so that the ambient light would not be reflected from his skin.

Wild Bill was a young officer who had selected his nickname himself and then insisted that his NCOs use it until the enlisted troops had picked up on it. Wild Bill figured it was better than letting the men think of something like Iron Ass or Horse's Ass. Besides, if his superiors heard his men using it, they might be impressed.

Bruce Jenkins, his company gunnery sergeant, a big man who looked as if he played tackle professionally, whose huge hands nearly engulfed the nine-millimeter pistol that had replaced the trusty .45, crouched on the deck of the aircraft in front of him. Over the roar of the jet engines, the man shouted, "Company's ready to deploy."

"Okay," said Ramey. He pushed himself out of the seat and moved to the hummers that were parked in the center of the aircraft. The recon platoon would use them to get to the prison; they'd speed off the airfield as soon as they landed. Ramey and the remainder of the company would attack the security forces at the field, eliminate them and the men in the control tower, and then hold the field until the operation was over.

He moved to Lieutenant Jeremy Harris, a young man who looked to be eighteen but who was twenty-three. If he'd gone to Hollywood instead of Parris Island, he might have ended up playing some of the roles now given to Tom Cruise. Of Ramey's officers, Harris was the one he trusted the most, and that explained his assignment.

Harris was leaning against the front fender of the lead hummer. He held his rifle in his right hand, trying to look like a warrior about to go in harm's way. He looked more like a frightened kid about to face the principal.

"You ready?" Ramey asked.

"Yes, sir." He touched the fender of the vehicle. "I'm not thrilled with the transportation."

"The Pentagon paid good money for that vehicle, Lieutenant. They tested it, approved it, and purchased it so that you wouldn't have to walk. Twenty-five thousand a copy."

"For that kind of money, it better have one hell of a stereo," said a voice from the back.

Ignoring that, Harris said, "I wish I believed that they bought them for my convenience."

Ramey laughed, but it was nervous laughter. "Anyway, you've got the easy task. Cover those Green Berets."

"Aye, sir."

"You understand the rules of engagement?"

"Return fire for fire received. I am to initiate no ground

action, but I am to protect the lives of my men and those of other Americans.''

Ramey shrugged and leaned closer. ''Be a little liberal in the interpretation of those rules. I don't want one of my men dying because we were a little slow on the trigger.''

''Aye, sir.''

''Well,'' said Ramey. ''Good luck.'' He wanted to say more, but couldn't think of anything. In the movies the officers always had words of encouragement, but in real life that didn't happen. He just nodded and turned, returning to Jenkins.

''We're on the approach.''

Wild Bill acknowledged the information and felt his stomach turn over. Butterflies as big as vultures launched themselves, the flapping of their giant wings tickling his belly. The adrenaline was beginning to flow. He gripped his rifle so tightly his knuckles were white.

''We ready?'' he asked.

''We're set, Captain.''

Ramey wiped at the sweat on his face, smearing the camo paint. He rubbed his hand on the thigh of his BDUs, took a deep breath, and told himself to calm down, but he knew the only way was to burn off the adrenaline with action.

The sounds in the back of the aircraft changed and the pressure increased. Ramey worked his jaw to pop his ears and then touched the side of his rifle, making sure the safety was on. He didn't want to shoot holes in the airplane.

He turned and watched Harris's men climb into the hummers. They would roll off the aircraft as soon as the rear ramp was down and be gone before the enemy could attack them.

''We're about to touch down,'' yelled the loadmaster. Normally he'd have made the marines strap in, but this time he wanted them off as quickly as possible. They were lined up along both sides of the fuselage, crouched and hanging on, the hummers in a line between them.

The pilot greased the aircraft in so smoothly that Ramey wasn't sure they'd landed. But then he heard the engines roar as the pilot reversed the thrust, and they were

DAWN OF CONFLICT   403

all thrown around as he stood on the brakes, trying to stop.

The loadmaster was lowering the rear ramp as the plane continued to slow. Warm desert air invaded the aircraft. Ramey could see nothing outside except the darkness. Then, suddenly, the plane was stopped and the ramp was down. The engines of the hummers began to crank, the starters whirring. Wild Bill didn't wait for them, he was up and moving, shouting at his men, "Let's go. Move it. Move it."

Ramey ran down the ramp toward the terminal building. It was dark, the only lights on in the control tower far above them. Without waiting, he sprinted toward the closest door. A man loomed in front of him, holding an AK. Ramey swung upward with the butt of his weapon, striking the man on the point of the chin. He went down without a sound. Ramey ran by the sprawled figure and reached the first door.

Glancing to the right, he saw marines reaching the building. A dark shape appeared, running at them. One of the marines dropped to a knee, aimed, and fired a short burst from the Squad Automatic Weapon. The running man collapsed, disappearing behind a short wall.

Ramey grabbed at the door, found it locked, and kicked at it. The glass shattered. He reached in, worked the lock, and pushed his way through, his feet crunching on the broken glass, then ran up a short flight of stairs. Now, from the outside, he could hear shouting and shooting. His marines were clearing the enemy soldiers from their posts around the airfield.

Behind him were more of his men. Some would head in the other direction. His job, along with a couple of squads of marines, was to seize the control tower. He was running down the center of the concourse, tinted windows on either side, showing the airfield. To the right were the flashes of the brief firefights as his men overran the defenses.

Someone popped up from behind a desk, fired two quick shots, and disappeared again. Ramey dived to the left, behind a row of chairs. He rolled and fired at the base of the desk, not sure if the fléchettes penetrated the wood there.

Across the corridor another of his men fired a burst into the desk. As he did so a third marine tossed a grenade, throwing it like a man trying sink a thirty-foot basket in a championship game, and Ramey flattened himself and closed his eyes so that his night vision wouldn't be ruined by the flash as the grenade detonated. Silently, he counted to himself, reached two, and the grenade went off, the explosion echoing through the concourse. Shrapnel cut through the air. There was a sudden, quick scream and then nothing.

Ramey was on his feet immediately, running forward. He leaped around the desk, his weapon leveled, but the man was dead. Blood from a dozen wounds stained the floor.

"Go," yelled Ramey, running down the concourse. The windows on the right shattered suddenly. He dived for the floor as a machine gun began to hammer. Shards of glass blew inward.

Ramey crawled toward the windows. The enemy had a machine-gun nest built in the angle of a wall. It controlled the airfield directly in front. He pulled a grenade, yanked the pin, and let the safety spoon fly. He counted to three quickly and then tossed the grenade through the broken window. It bounced on the top of the wall and then fell into the machine-gun nest, exploding as it hit. Shrapnel ripped through the air and shredded the enemy soldiers.

As the machine gunners died marines swarmed over the nest, pressing on to the next objective. Ramey was on his feet again, running along the corridor. He came to a door and slid to a halt; the stairs to the tower had to be behind it.

He reached out but it was locked. That didn't surprise him. He stepped back, glanced at the marines who were with him, and fired. The fléchettes stuck in the frame of the door, in the door itself, and around the lock. They didn't blow holes in it as the rounds from an M-16 would have done.

"Stand back, Captain." A marine with a shotgun

pushed forward, aimed at the knob, and fired. The force
of the double-O buck ripped it from the wood. The marine
jacked another round into the chamber and with the
weapon pointing up at the ceiling, stepped forward and
kicked. The door gave way.

Ramey, disgusted with the new rifle, threw it to the
side and drew his pistol. He flipped off the safety and then
kicked the debris that had been the door out of his way.
With the wall against his back, he began to work his way
up the steep, narrow steps. At the top was another door.
He leaned forward carefully and reached for the knob. He
would have been surprised if it had been unlocked.

The marine with the shotgun moved up closer so that
the knob was eye level with him. He glanced at Ramey
and, when the captain nodded, fired. He jacked another
round into the chamber as a burst crashed through the
door. The AK rounds hit the marine in the top of the head.
He pinwheeled back, tumbling down the stairs.

Ramey dropped to the steps as several men behind him
opened fire. The sound was deafening in the confined
space; he couldn't hear a thing over the pounding of the
weapons. The narrow steps smelled of cordite and blood
and bowel.

Under the rain from the weapons, the door slowly disintegrated. Dust and smoke hung in the air, stinging the
eyes. Ramey found it difficult to breathe.

"Grenade," yelled one of the marines.

The grenade flew through the air, landed in the space
behind the door, and exploded. Without thinking, Ramey
was up and running. He stumbled on the debris and fell
to the left. As his shoulder hit the wall someone fired.
Ramey shot back, firing into the center of the enemy's
muzzle flash.

He fired again and again until the pistol was empty,
the slide locked back. He reloaded it hurriedly, dropping
the empty magazine to the floor. His men were up there
with him, shooting at the enemy soldiers. There was a
long-drawn-out wail of pain and the machine gun fell silent. Two men rushed it. A third stopped near Wild Bill.

"You hit, Captain?"

"No," said Ramey, climbing to his feet. "No. Let's get going."

They raced down the hallway and came to the last door. This one led up into the tower. Ramey leaned against the wall and was suddenly aware of his own fear and his own sweat. It was dripping down his face and tickling his sides. It was the damned vest. The desert was hot enough without a wrapping of material so densely packed that it didn't allow the air to circulate.

This door, to his surprise, was unlocked. He pulled on the knob and it opened, revealing a twisting staircase. Ramey suddenly didn't want to lead anymore. He'd led the charge down the concourse and up the stairs and then down the hall. Now there was another obstacle, and Wild Bill wanted to do something tamer.

But there was no one else. He leaned back against the wall and looked up at the tower. He could see dim lights at the top of the stairs but heard no sounds. He was positive the tower would be manned.

He glanced at the small group of men with him and nodded. With that, he moved around the corner and started up the stairs, his men following. When they reached a narrow landing, they stopped and listened, but heard nothing. Ramey continued on, keeping his head down. When he was near the top, he threw himself to the floor, rolled, and twisted, swinging his pistol right and left, but there was no one up there. No one visible.

"Clear," he called, and his men scrambled up into the tower.

Ramey moved to the panels that held radios, radar, controls for the field's lighting and telephones. Through the windows he could look down at the entire airfield. He saw one machine-gun nest that was still occupied. He snapped his fingers and pointed at the RTO.

"Bullyboy Two-Six, this is Bullyboy Six. I have one nest identified directly in front of you."

"Roger."

A moment later there was a small explosion as a grenade from a launcher landed in the nest. Small fires erupted, but the machine gun was gone.

DAWN OF CONFLICT 407

"I've taken care of it, Six."
"Roger. Out."

Harris, in the lead hummer, had a map in one hand and his military flashlight in the other. He kept glancing out of the windshield as they raced from the rear of the aircraft, along a taxiway, and then turned, heading toward the city. As they drove through the gate and out onto a main street he pointed and said, "To the left."

"Got it."

Harris sat up and twisted, looking right and left. At first there wasn't much to see: low buildings set back from the road, no street signs. Harris had to count the streets so that he didn't get lost.

"Straight," he said.

The driver nodded and kept going, keeping the speed down. The radio was on, but no one was broadcasting. They were staying off the radio.

Harris pointed to the right and they turned again. They sped up as the road widened and they could see better. Harris looked down at his map and said, "We should be able to see a hint of it somewhere on the left." He bent down and tried to spot the prison through the windshield.

"There," said the driver.

Harris nodded. "That's it. Slow it down."

They slowed as they approached a low wall. Harris studied that and the prison behind it. This was the perfect place to set up the platoon. They could see two sides of the prison easily and, if he sent out one squad, could cover three sides of it. There was a half-dozen escape routes for his men, if they needed them, and they had protection for them behind the wall.

"Stop," he said.

As soon as the vehicle halted Harris was out. He ran around the front, crouched near the wall, and took out his light-enhancing binoculars. Using the LEB, he scanned the area at the base of the wall and then searched the top. There was no movement; the only sounds were from the engines of the hummers. He straightened and waved a hand, signaling the drivers to shut them down.

The platoon sergeant ran over and leaned close, waiting for instructions.

"Put one squad at the far end to watch that side of the prison. Scatter the rest along the wall and a final squad here to watch this side. Drivers to remain with their vehicles."

"Aye aye, sir."

The sergeant turned and headed back, bent low so that his head was not above the level of the wall.

Harris spotted his radio operator and walked toward him. He held out a hand and took the handset. "Bullyboy Six, this is Bullyboy One-Six. I'm in position."

"Roger that."

Harris surrendered the handset to the RTO, turned, and looked back at the prison. There still was no activity around it, although he could hear firing from the airfield, a distant sound that didn't disturb the night. No sirens, no alerts, and no response. So far, so good.

The platoon sergeant dropped to one knee near him. "Platoon's in position, Lieutenant."

"Thank you, Sergeant. Now everything is up to someone else. We wait."

RIYADH, SAUDI ARABIA

Martinez opened the door and then jumped out of the way. The interior was dark and there was no sound or sign of movement inside. Martinez pointed at two men and then waved them through the door. They disappeared, diving in. Martinez and the others waited until one of the men stuck his head out and told them it was clear inside.

They worked their way through the room. It was long, narrow, and empty. The floor was stone and the walls were bare. On the other side, Martinez hesitated, an ear against the door.

"Nothing," he whispered. He opened that door and found an open courtyard. There were other buildings around them and a couple of doors. "Sergeant?"

Chavez ducked back and used a penlight to study his map. "Two to the left should lead down into the cell area. One directly opposite might lead into some kind of great hall. Doors on either side will lead into other cells."

"Banse, take the door opposite on the right. Alvarez on the left. Gibson, you've got the one closest and I'll take the farthest."

Each man nodded at his assignment. Before they could move, Martinez reminded them, "Thirty minutes."

"Yes, sir."

Martinez took a deep breath and said, "Go."

Banse and Munyo ran out the door and crossed the open area. Right behind them were Alvarez and Jones. As soon as they were out of the way Martinez took off. He stayed close to the wall, ducked under a darkened window, in front of the one door and then to the second. He waited and let Chavez run around him.

Chavez reached for the latch and pushed. The door swung open. He nodded and Martinez dived through, rolling to the left. He came up on one knee and saw that the room was empty. It was a hell of a way to run a prison.

When Chavez joined him, they moved to the next door. It was made of steel with a small sliding peephole. Martinez looked at it. It needed a key.

"Burn it," he said quietly.

Chavez packed the keyhole with thermite, stuck a fuse in it, and stepped back after igniting it. He heard quiet hissing and a plume of blue smoke curled up. The metal turned cherry red and then began to melt. Using his foot, Chavez pushed on the door. It swung open slowly.

"Let's do it."

Martinez touched the safety on his weapon to make sure it was off. Keeping his back to the wall, he slipped along the corridor. He listened for sounds of occupants. It was as if the prison was deserted. For the first time since they got in, he wondered if the information had been faulty.

They came to a barred gate. Beyond it was another darkened hallway. Martinez listened closely but could hear nothing from beyond it. He pushed on it, but it wouldn't open.

"We go deeper?" Chavez asked.

"Yeah." Martinez touched the button to activate his radio and then didn't use it.

Chavez moved closer, used a penlight to examine the

lock. He grinned and said, "This'll be a piece of cake."
He crouched down and pulled out a stiff piece of wire and
his knife so that he could pick the lock. A moment later
the gate swung up. "After you, Captain."

Martinez stepped through and then hurried down the
stone steps that led into the dungeonlike lower level. He
peered into one of the open cells. The stench from the
interior was overpowering. No one had bothered to empty
the waste bucket.

They worked their way down the corridor, listening for
the signs that someone lived there. Martinez heard a
scraping of leather against stone and turned in time to see
someone following them down the steps. He stopped and
waited as the man continued forward. A flashlight beam
stabbed out suddenly and the man called in Arabic.

Martinez raised his silenced CAR-15 and fired once.
There was a quiet clatter of the bolt and the cough from
the muzzle. The man grunted in surprise and took a stumbling step to the rear before falling. He dropped his flashlight and weapon, tried to sit up, and then slumped to the
stone floor.

Chavez ran back to him, crouched, and touched his
throat, looking for a pulse. Then he reached over and
turned off the flashlight.

Rejoining Martinez, they began working their way
deeper into the prison. The radio crackled once, but the
message was badly garbled.

"No one's here," said Chavez finally, quietly.

Martinez stood for a moment, thinking. He couldn't call
out because that would give him away. Some of the cells had
solid doors with only small covered squares that operated as
peepholes. Martinez opened one, looked in, but in the dark
couldn't tell if the cell was occupied or not.

He pulled his own flashlight and shone it in. Nothing.
It looked as if no one had been housed there for weeks.
He moved to the next one and went through the procedure
again. Again he saw nothing.

That began to bother him. In the wake of a revolution,
he would have thought that hundreds, thousands, would
have been imprisoned. But this wing of the prison was
deserted. No sign of guards or inmates. They'd seen no

one except the man Martinez had shot. Looking into another cell, he again saw no one. Just an empty, yawning space filled with nothing but darkness.

Chavez hurried to the end of the corridor and found another door that would take them down even lower. No one had provided any information about how many levels were underground. The prisoners, their fellow Americans, could be hidden far from the surface.

Martinez looked into another cell and caught a flicker of movement in the straw. He peered in and saw a face. "Hey!" he whispered.

The person sat up and Martinez could see the tattered remains of an air-force flight suit. The person put a hand up to shield the eyes.

"Who're you?"

"You an American?" Martinez asked.

"Frankowski, Marie."

Martinez felt himself grin. "Well, stand back, Frankowski, Marie. We'll get you out."

"The others?" she asked.

"We've seen no others yet. Get on back." He watched her retreat to a corner of the cell, snapped off the light, and moved away. As he did so he realized how well disciplined she was. She'd told him nothing but her name, and she had obeyed his orders without question. She didn't even complain when it looked as if he might be leaving. She was waiting patiently for him to get her out.

Chavez had heard the whispering. "You find someone?"

"Frankowski. Need to open the cell."

Chavez nodded. "No sweat." He held up a ring filled with keys. "Found these on the body."

"Great."

They returned to the cell and Chavez used the keys until the lock turned. He pushed open the door and stepped inside. He flashed his light around until he found Frankowski standing in the corner.

"Who're you?" she asked.

"Master Sergeant Arturo Chavez, United States Army Special Forces. You can call me Art."

With that, she launched herself at him, wrapping her

arms around him and hugging him tightly. Her breath was hot on his neck, and he wrinkled his nose. She needed a bath, but he didn't say anything about that. Instead he asked, "Where are the others?"

"I don't know."

He looked at her closely. "You okay?"

"Got a cracked rib. Hurts a little bit when I move."

"We got a couple of medics with us."

"Please. Don't worry about it. Just get me the hell out of here."

Martinez turned and looked at the line of cell doors. Their voices had been carrying along the corridor. If there were guards nearby, they would have already heard. He raised his voice slightly. "Anyone here?"

After a moment of silence, he heard, "Yeah."

"That's Elizabeth Shawn. One of ours."

Chavez moved toward the sound. He heard someone knocking on a steel door, shone a light up at the peephole, and saw the pale face of an American.

"Get me out of here."

Chavez unlocked the door. As he pushed it open the woman sagged toward the stone floor. He caught her and lifted her up. She clung to him.

Chavez half carried her into the corridor. He bent down and let her sit on the floor, her back propped against the rough stone wall.

"I think the men were held somewhere else. A different wing," said Frankowski.

Martinez tried the radio again but got no response. Chavez glanced at his watch and said, "Time to get out of here anyway."

Frankowski was crouched over Shawn. "Liz? You okay?"

Shawn opened her eyes and nodded. She struggled to sit straighter and then climbed to her feet. "Please. Just get me out of here."

Martinez nodded and said, "Let's go." He started to work his way back up the corridor toward the barred gate and the body of the dead man.

Chavez fell in at the rear, watching behind them just in case someone appeared back there, and they hurried up the stone steps and then down the corridor, rushing along until they came to the final door that led across the ground-level room. Martinez held up a hand. He made his way alone to the last door and crouched there. Again he used the radio.

"Six, this is two," came the response. "We have freed three men."

"Roger. Let's get out."

"Roger."

Martinez turned and waved at Chavez. The master sergeant brought the women forward, and Martinez leaned to look out at the empty courtyard of the prison.

Just as he stepped from the room there was a long burst from an AK. Rounds ricocheted off stone and whined away. Martinez dived back under cover but the rounds hadn't been directed at him; the firing was off in one of the other wings of the prison.

"Teams report," said Martinez.

"This is two. We're taking some fire here."

Martinez crawled forward and looked out into the courtyard. He could see nothing, no muzzle flashes, no men running, no sign that anyone was alive.

Over the radio he said, "Three, can you support two?"

No reply. "Four, can you support two?"

A garbled response but Martinez couldn't make it out. "Four, you're broken and garbled."

All he heard was, "Roger."

They had found no one in the prison and both men had worried about that. They wondered if they hadn't broken into a large trap that would spring on them at any moment. Ortega had worried that there had been a breakdown in the security and that the Saudis or the revolutionaries had known they were coming. Gibson hadn't worried at all.

They worked their way through the upper levels and found nothing; they worked their way through lower levels, opened a dozen cells, and found no one imprisoned.

"I think we've been had," said Ortega.

Gibson nodded. "Let's just get the hell out of here."

They whirled and rushed back up the stairs, but the situation changed. There were lights behind them and voices. Ortega leaped to the rear, his back against the stone wall, his weapon ready.

Leaning close, Gibson said, "Now what?"

"Wait."

But the enemy soldiers, or the jailers, were coming closer. Ortega glanced to the rear: the corridor, though dark, was straight with a barred door across the far end. They had nowhere to hide.

Ortega went to one knee. Gibson jumped across the corridor and slipped closer to one of the steel doors. He kept his eyes on the entrance to the corridor.

Two men came down the stone steps. One of them carried an AK and the other had his slung over his shoulder; one was carrying a flashlight but had the beam focused on the floor at their feet.

Ortega snapped off the safety of his weapon, glanced at Gibson, and then aimed at the jailers. He didn't say a word, he just fired on full auto. The weapon stuttered, the bolt slamming back and forth. The rounds snapped out, striking the wall, ricocheting.

Gibson leaned out and fired a quick burst. The muzzle flash lit the corridor like a strobe light. The enemy soldiers stood out in naked relief as the bullets struck them. One staggered back, sitting hard on the steps and then slipping to the side, sliding down into his own blood. The other was thrown against the wall, bounced off, and struck the floor. Neither knew what hit them.

"Go," said Ortegta.

Gibson ran forward, stopped, and crouched, feeling for the throat of the closest man. Satisfied that he was dead, he checked the second and then climbed the stairs. He dropped to one knee and checked the corridor.

Ortega rushed forward, stepped over the bodies, and said, "Get going."

Together, they ran up the corridor, stopped, and listened. Still no sound in the prison; no alert had been sounded. The jailers hadn't discovered them yet.

They made their way back to the surface but stopped short of the door. Ortega was searching the darkened courtyard, wondering where the jailers were, when a burst of fire jerked him around. He saw the muzzle flashes as one fired into the doorway opposite him. Ortega raised his rifle and aimed over the top of it. He squeezed the trigger and felt the weapon kick. The muzzle flash wiped out his night vision. The rounds hit the wall behind the enemy soldier. He stopped firing and whirled. Ortega fired again and the man collapsed, tossing up his weapon.

Now the courtyard was swarming with the enemy. A dozen ran from a tall building that might have been a barracks. Lights were coming on. Two, three, and then half a dozen, blazing down into the courtyard.

Ortega slipped back into the shadows. The AKs opened up, the muzzles strobing and the tracers flashing. Rounds slammed into the stone walls and whined off into the night. Ortega fired at three men running across the courtyard. Two went down, tumbling. Neither moved. The third dropped to a knee and shot into the doorway. Ortega heard the rounds snap past his head.

Firing erupted from one of the other doors. No sound, just the muzzle flashes as the other Green Berets used their silenced weapons. The third man fell, tried to sit up, and then collapsed.

One of the floodlights popped, flared, and went out. Ortega turned his weapon on the two he could see and fired into them. The rounds tore at the wall around them and then found the lenses, shattering them. The courtyard was plunged back into darkness.

Now the radio came alive. Martinez was trying to coordinate the men. Gibson listened and then said, "We've got to get going."

Ortega moved closer to the door. Firing had tapered off and none was coming from the courtyard. Someone, somewhere else, was firing. Ortega nodded and pointed at the door opposite them. They had to reach it.

"I'll cover," said Ortega. "You go."

"Right." Gibson crouched in the door like a sprinter getting ready for a race. "Now," he said, and leaped up, running.

Ortega moved into the doorway, searching the walls and the windows for the enemy. He caught a glimpse of movement near a window and fired at it. Something fell.

Gibson reached the other side and dived through the door.

As he disappeared a dozen weapons opened fire, chewing up the door, the wooden frame, and the stone wall.

Ortega stepped out, saw the muzzle flashes, and fired into them. One man shrieked, the sound like tires on dry concrete. As he jumped back rounds smacked the door near his head.

Over the radio he heard, "Come on."

"On three," he said. "One. Two. Three." He sprinted from hiding, dodged right and left, stopped suddenly, and then ran straight to the door. The enemy shot at him, the bullets kicking up dirt around him. He dived through and rolled away. For a moment he lay panting on the floor.

Outside, the firing increased, more weapons brought to bear. Gibson returned some of the fire and then glanced over his shoulder. "You hit?"

Ortega struggled to sit up. Sweat stung his eyes. "No. I'm fine."

Gibson slammed the door, found the locking bar, and said, "Let's get out of here."

Ortega got to his feet and ran across the room. He hit the wall and hesitated, reached out, and pulled open the door. Nothing outside, but that's what they had seen at the other end.

Over the radio Martinez said, "Rally on me. Rally on me."

Firing was still tapering off around them. Ortega whipped open the door and saw that the courtyard was empty except for the bodies. No evidence that the enemy was close.

"Go," he said.

Gibson ran, and no one fired at him. Ortega followed a moment later and dived through the door behind Gibson.

Martinez knelt in the shadows at the side of the door and watched the courtyard. He'd seen Gibson and Ortega spring toward him and dive for cover. He'd heard shooting and had fired a couple of times, but not much was happening.

Chavez had moved the women out of the line of fire. Neither were combatants and he didn't want them hit by a stray round. He wanted to get them out clean.

"We're going to have to move," said Chavez, crouching in the dark near him. "We give them time and they'll get reinforcements."

Martinez nodded. He used the tiny radio. "All units, fall back to here. Rally on me. Acknowledge."

One by one they did. While he stayed at the door Ortega moved toward one of the windows and ripped the shutters from it so that he could see out.

"On the right," he called.

Martinez moved around and stared into the darkness. A dozen shapes were moving slowly forward, sticking to the shadows. They wore robes and kaffiyehs and carried AKs, the shape of the weapon as distinctive as the sound.

"Use your grenades," said Martinez, pulling the pin on one and dropping it. Leaning out the door, he tossed it underhanded at the oncoming enemy. "Fire in the hole," he called as he ducked back.

A moment later there was an explosion. Dirt, stone, and shrapnel rained against the walls. Someone screamed in terror and abruptly ceased.

There was a wild burst of firing, sounding like the enemy trying to cover his retreat. Martinez stretched out on his belly and sneaked a peek. Nothing moved in the courtyard.

"Chavez," he said. "Let's get going. Take the point."

"Yes, sir."

The sergeant moved to the door and peeked around the corner. Keeping his back against the wall, he stepped out, slipped along the wall, his head swiveling as he looked for the enemy, listening for sounds of their return. When he reached the final door, he opened it quickly. He dived through, rolled, and saw no one. The enemy was not coordinated, hadn't tried to block their escape.

Using the radio, he said, "We're clear."

"On the way," said Martinez.

A moment later Ortega passed the door and stopped, guarding the area. Seconds later both women came through, followed by Gibson and then the captain. He hissed something at Ortega, who joined them in the room.

Martinez was on the radio again. "All teams, report to me."

"Six, this is five."

"Go," said Martinez.

"We're on the opposite side of the courtyard. Coming at you."

"Roger," said Martinez. "We'll cover."

He moved around so that he could look out the door. Two shapes sprinted from a doorway across the courtyard. When they were halfway, there was a single burst of AK fire. Green tracers bounced off the stone. Banse and Munyo dodged right and left in a strange leaping gait. Martinez leaned out the door and fired up at the single rifleman.

Banse and then Munyo rushed by him. They dived into the room, out of the line of fire. Banse rolled over, sat up, and started laughing. "Damn, that was scary."

The radio crackled again. "Six, this is three. Coming at you with the male crew."

"Roger."

"Six, this is two. We're on our way, too."

"Come on in. Let's snap it up."

"Roger."

There was a burst of fire. Martinez saw a muzzle flash but heard no sound. That was one of the silenced weapons. Over the radio he heard, "Six, we're on the move."

"Provide cover," said Martinez as he leaned out.

This time no one fired at the men as they ran across the courtyard. Martinez worried about that, afraid that the enemy had pulled back and would attack them as they tried to get out of the prison. If the marines had arrived, they should be able to escape. If.

Two men worked their way along the wall and suddenly jumped into the room. A moment later Alvarez and the crewman ran across the courtyard. The single AK opened fire. Both Martinez and Jones shot up at the rifleman. There was a long burst, the muzzle flash slowly climbing as if the enemy had been hit.

An instant later Jones was running across the open courtyard. As soon as he joined them Martinez said, "Chavez, take us the hell out of here."

"Yes, sir."

RIYADH, SAUDI ARABIA

Ramey came down from the control tower and stood in the debris-littered hallway. There was an odor of cordite and blood in the air, and he tried to ignore it, concentrating instead on the civilian standing in front of him. The only light was from a lantern set on the floor, a glaring, white light that washed out the colors around it.

As soon as he approached the civilian he asked, "Who the hell are you?"

"Morris Reisman. I'm a reporter."

"Oh fuck," said Ramey. "That's all we need, a fucking reporter."

"What's going on here?" Reisman asked.

Ramey looked at the two marines. "You should have shot him when you had the chance."

"Yes, sir," said one of them.

"Major," said Reisman.

"That's captain," said Ramey.

"Captain. I'm on your side here, I don't want to make trouble."

Wild Bill turned and looked behind him. "Where's Sergeant Jenkins?"

"He's down the corridor, sir."

"One of you find him." Ramey turned his attention to Reisman. "Okay. I'm going to let Sergeant Jenkins brief you. I don't think there's anything that you can do. We'll be gone in an hour."

"That's fine," said Reisman.

From upstairs came another voice. "We got some trouble coming, Captain."

Ramey looked at Reisman. "You stay right here." He turned and ran back to the steps, rushed up them, and entered the control tower again. He moved toward the windows.

A corporal pointed. "Looks like someone's coming from that direction."

Ramey saw two armored cars followed by a couple of trucks and jeeps and then another few trucks. "Give me the radio," he said. "Bullyboy Two-Six, this is Six actual."

"This is Bullyboy Two-Six actual. Go."

"Roger. Move your people to the west side of the airfield. We've got reinforcements coming in from that direction. Lightly armored."

"Roger. On the go."

Ramey gave the handset back to the RTO and watched as one platoon appeared on the tarmac below him. They fanned out as they ran across the airfield toward the oncoming enemy. A small group of men broke off and ran to the south. They jumped down into a slight depression and began to set up a machine-gun nest.

The platoon splintered as Bullyboy Two-Six tried to set up a defensive line. Carrying LAW rockets, a single Dragon rocket launcher, and a couple of heavy machine guns, they spread out in a thin skirmish line, taking up positions in the available cover, depressions between the runways, near a small checkerboard painted building, and behind the approach radars and lights.

The captain watched them scatter and then turned his attention to the approaching enemy forces. He could feel the fear climb into his belly. He hadn't expected the enemy to respond this quickly; he'd counted on them holding back and not probing the area until he'd gotten his men out of there.

"Third platoon is spread through the terminal," said a corporal.

Ramey nodded. He knew what the man meant. His force was spread much too thin for a concentrated attack. He had to reorganize them quickly. He snapped his fingers and held a hand out. The RTO snapped the handset into it.

"Bullyboy Three-Six, this is Six actual. Rally your people near the aircraft."

"Roger that. On the move."

Ramey looked at his watch. "Five minutes at the most."

"Yes, sir."

As they neared, the column fragmented, spreading out to hit on line rather than in column. One of the armored cars turned, heading for the first of the machine-gun crews. The rounds from the SAW-249 didn't have the penetrating power of the old Browning M-2 .50-caliber. Ramey didn't think the machine gunners would be able to stop the car.

But the point became moot. Two men ran toward it and stopped fifty yards short. One slipped to a knee and tugged at the object he held. Ramey knew that he was removing the cotter pin and extending the tube of the disposable LAW rocket. Ramey didn't have much faith in the LAW, but it was lightweight, easy to carry, and did have stopping power—if it fired.

The team fired. There was a bright flash as the rocket ignited and a streak as it dived toward the armored car, but the rocket didn't detonate on impact. It hit the sloped armor, bounced, and exploded in a blinding flash of fire ten or twelve feet in the air.

A machine gun on the armored car began to fire. The whole front sparkled as all the gunners opened up. They were tearing up real estate, rounds chewing the ground and tracers bouncing high, tumbling into the night.

The LAW team leaped up and ran back, away from the armored car. One of the machine gunners turned toward them, firing. One marine stumbled and fell. The second caught the burst in the back. He was lifted from his feet and thrown to the ground.

"Shit," said Ramey.

At that instant the armored car exploded. A ball of fire boiled upward, illuminating the ground around it. A single man leaped from it, his clothes ablaze. He ran fifty feet and then fell, rolling over twice. The flames consumed him.

The second car turned toward the bazooka team, firing machine guns at them, the rounds dancing around them. A marine popped up, fired, and dropped back to the ground. The rocket exploded in front of the armored car, the ground mushrooming up around it. One machine gun fell silent, and then the car reversed, backing out.

Firing erupted all along the line. Tracers lashed out. The muzzle flashes told Ramey exactly where his marines were. He watched as a dozen of the enemy fell. A few turned to run. And then the second armored car erupted in flame.

"Yeah," yelled the corporal beside him, "all fucking right."

Ramey noticed a squad of Arabs breaking from the main group, running to the west and then turning. He used the radio. "Bullyboy Two-Six, they're flying to flank you on the west."

"Roger that. I got them."

The Arabs slowed, then stopped. They disappeared for a moment and then reappeared, running directly at the flank of Bullyboy Two-Six's line. Ramey wanted to alert him again but stayed off the radio. An instant later the flank exploded as Two-Six opened fire on the Arabs. They disappeared in the smoke and flame of hand grenades and automatic-weapons fire.

The enemy advance sputtered. The firing became sporadic as the Arabs retreated, leaving their dead and burning vehicles in their wake.

"That takes care of them," said the corporal.

"That was beautiful," said Reisman. "It's good to see a military unit operating with confidence."

"How the hell did you get up here?" Ramey asked.

"Just walked on up." Reisman pointed at the burning armored cars. "Took them right out."

"If you're going to write about this, be sure to say that the fucking LAW rockets bounced off the armored cars. It's about worthless to a combat unit."

"Had the same problem with them in Vietnam. Wouldn't fire, wouldn't detonate, and when they did they wouldn't penetrate the lightest armor."

"Nothing's changed," said Ramey.

"Sir," said the corporal. "I've got movement on the east."

"Shit." Wild Bill turned, used his binoculars. "Second force coming in from there." He snapped the handset to his ear. "Three-Six, you're going to have to deploy to the east. Got somebody coming up from there."

"Roger that. On the move."

"Two-Six, fall back about fifty yards and take up positions there."

"Roger."

"Why'd you do that?" Reisman asked.

"Soviet doctrine," said Ramey. "The favorite weapon of the Soviet is the mortar. I'm gambling that these forces have had Soviet training, and therefore the next thing we can expect is a mortar attack. Those two burning vehicles make perfect aiming points."

Reisman nodded. In Vietnam almost every ground attack was preceded by a massive mortar attack. Level all the buildings and inflict as many casualties as possible before committing the assault troops.

Almost as if to prove that Ramey knew what he was talking about, the mortars began to fall. Dull pops and small explosions erupted on the airfield. Ramey saw his men getting out, moving to the rear, away from their earlier positions. The mortars walked the line, but his men were gone.

With the mortars still falling, the enemy began to advance. This time they were using the terrain for cover, maneuvering around the obstacles. They had no armor support.

"Two-Six'll be able to handle that," said Ramey. He turned toward the other attacking force.

They had spread out and were moving slowly forward. A flare suddenly shot into the air, exploding into a falling cascade of bright green that burned out rapidly. With that, the enemy suddenly began to rush forward, their weapons firing. Three-Six's platoon seemed not to notice, letting the enemy get closer.

"Come on," said Ramey. "Come on."

The enemy kept running forward, firing, firing, firing. Tracers cut through the night. Green tracers and white ones. They hit the ground and bounced, tumbling upward. The muzzle flashes sparkled like thousands of fireflies on a warm evening in June.

Then, suddenly, the marines fired everything they had. Grenades detonated in the enemy lines. Men fell. Men staggered. Men vanished. Machine-gun bullets ripped into them. Rifle fire cut them down. In seconds it was all over. The attack had disintegrated. One man stood dazed for a moment and then toppled to the ground. A second fled toward the rear, his rifle lost in the terrible carnage behind him.

Ramey turned back to the other platoon. The mortars had stopped, and the men rushed forward into the first line of defense, firing at the ground. They hammered at the positions, but the marines were no longer there.

Two-Six fired then. Grenades and machine guns. The sudden burst of fire caught the enemy by surprise. A dozen men fell and the rest turned to flee. They ran from the field, past the burning hulks of the armored cars, past the bodies of their dead, and off the airfield.

"That should hold them for a while," said Ramey. "Now they'll come at us with a company."

"How soon?" Reisman asked.

"An hour, maybe a little more. With luck, we'll be gone by then."

"No, sir," said the corporal. "Here they come now." He pointed out the window.

From the city came a long column led by half a dozen tanks. There were armored personnel carriers, armored cars, and even antiaircraft guns. It was the big push.

"We can't hold the airfield now," said the corporal.

"We have to. Where in the hell are the Green Berets?"

RIYADH, SAUDI ARABIA

They reached the wall of the prison with no trouble. Cline and Davis had searched the immediate area, looking for signs of a trap, places where the guards could position themselves to fire down into the courtyard, and had made sure that the exit was ready to be used. They had also set it up so they could blow a hole in the wall if they needed it.

As they ran up Martinez pointed and said, "Go on through."

Cline dropped into the channel that led under the wall and began crawling away; Davis was right behind him. Martinez waved at the men and they formed a semicircle around the channel, guarding it.

"Get the women through now," said Martinez. He was crouched near the edge of the channel, his CAR-15 in his hands. He was looking up at the walls around them, searching for the enemy.

Marie Frankowski dropped down on her belly, grunted in sudden pain, and ignoring it, crawled into the channel. Elizabeth Shawn was right behind her. When both women had disappeared, Banse followed and then Munyo.

"The men now," said Martinez, and the procedure was repeated until all the flight-crew members were gone.

Espinoza and Ortega slipped out of sight, followed by Gibson and Brown. Before the last four could go, a dozen men burst through the door and ran screaming at them. Martinez didn't have to say a thing. Everyone opened fire at once. The M-16s and CAR-15s ripped at the enemy soldiers. They fell one by one. A couple tried to return fire. A few turned to run but were cut down before they could find cover inside the building.

With the sounds of the gunfire still echoing, Martinez yelled, "Let's go."

Alvarez dived into the channel and scrambled from sight. Chavez followed, then Jones. Just as Martinez dropped into it the door burst open again and more Arabs poured out. Martinez dropped his CAR-15 to the concrete of the channel and jerked out his hand grenades. He pulled the pin and threw, getting into a rhythm. The grenades detonated. Dirt and sand mushroomed and rained back. Small clouds of dust and smoke drifted. Martinez used his last three grenades, all of them CS. They popped, the flame at the bottom spreading the gas in thick, gray clouds.

That slowed them. Martinez picked up his weapon and dived forward, scrambling along the gritty channel on his elbows and knees. As soon as he was clear he jumped up and then out of the channel. Pointing back, he said, "Destroy it."

Munyo took two hand grenades, pulled the pins, and threw them into the channel. "Fire in the hole!"

The men and women scattered, diving for cover. One grenade exploded and then the second. Dirt and dust boiled up out of the channel. Martinez glanced at it, unsure if it had been destroyed. He wasn't sure that he cared. The smoke and dust would keep the enemy out of it for a moment.

"Go!" he yelled, and Banse, Alvarez, and Munyo took

off across the open ground, heading for the wall and the marines hidden there.

Firing rippled from the walls. A dozen small weapons began to fire. Rounds smashed into the ground, kicking up small geysers of sand. Tracers rained down and then bounced away.

Martinez stepped away from the wall and aimed at the top of it. He fired on full auto, his rounds kicking up small clouds of dust. An instant later the marines began to shoot. Automatic weapons, machine guns, and grenade launchers began to hammer the enemy positions. Return fire slowed and then stopped.

"Go!" Martinez ordered. "Go!"

The remainder of the people were up and running. One of the flight crew stumbled and fell, but Espinoza grabbed him, hauling him to his feet. Together the two men ran forward, Martinez bringing up the rear. He looked at his destination, his head down, running as hard as he could. He neared the wall and dived over the top of it, landing on a shoulder and rolling.

He spun around and crawled back to the wall, poking his CAR-15 over it. He could see the bullets hitting the prison, but no one was inside shooting back. He ducked back, moving along the wall, searching for the marine officer.

When Martinez found him, he said, "We're ready to get out of here."

The marine nodded. He used his radio and said, "Third squad, let's go."

Some of the marines along the wall peeled off, running back and then turning to the right.

"You get all our people out?" asked the marine.

"All that we could find."

A hummer roared up and slid to a stop. Martinez said, "Get the women."

Both Frankowski and Shawn climbed into the lead vehicle. The men, Hansen, Williams, and Crawford, were pushed into the second, and then both vehicles took off, racing back to the airfield.

One of the marines ran up. "There're tanks coming up to the west."

"Shit."

"You got anything to stop tanks?" Martinez asked.

"Got some LAWs and a Dragon."

"Let's go get them," said Martinez.

The marine officer nodded. "First squad, break off now."

Martinez waved at them and yelled, "Follow me."

The men stopped firing and a few of them reloaded their weapons. Martinez ran along the wall, ducking down so that he wouldn't be a target. The men strung out behind him, keeping low. At the end of the wall he heard the noise from the diesel engines and the clanking of the tracks on the concrete of the street.

"Over there," said the marine.

Martinez nodded. The problem with armor in the city was that it couldn't maneuver easily; if the lead tank was destroyed, those behind it couldn't spread out to go around it. They had to back up and find an alternative route. Tanks were designed to work in open terrain, to move quickly, overrunning lightly fortified positions.

Martinez spotted a man with a LAW rocket. Grabbing him, he shouted, "Come with me."

They ran around the side of a building and then, staying close to the wall, headed toward the sound of the tanks. As they approached a second corner Martinez held up a hand, then slipped forward slowly. Before he reached the corner, the tank clanked into the intersection. Martinez dived for the ground.

"Hit it," he called.

The marine slipped to a knee, opened up the LAW, and aimed at the side of the tank. Martinez knew that most of them had heavy armor on the front but light armor on the sides and rear, the assumption being that the enemy would be in front of them.

He lowered his head and closed his eyes. The rocket whooshed over his head; there was an explosion and he felt the heat wash over him. Looking up, he saw that the tank had been holed and that flames were shooting up through the hatch. Some of the small-arms ammo was cooking off with quiet poppings.

Martinez grinned. The tank blocked the street, black

smoke pouring from the rear. He rolled to his side. "Head back."

"Yes, sir." The marine threw away the empty cardboard tube and turned to run.

Martinez followed, listening to the sounds behind him. He heard some firing: single shots from small arms and then a detonation from one of the tanks. A moment later he heard a second explosion that sounded like another LAW rocket.

When they reached the wall, the marines had all pulled back. The hummers were lined up, ready to go. No firing was coming from the prison. It was dark.

Martinez found the marine officer. "We're ready to pull back to the airfield," the marine said.

Martinez used the radio. "Fall back, fall back."

The rest of the force straggled in. Two men were dragging a third. As they approached, Alvarez said, "Banse got hit."

"Bad?"

"Dead."

"Shit."

"The column is turning toward us," said one of the marines. "We'd better get out of here."

The marines scrambled into the hummers. One by one, they turned, heading back to the airfield. Martinez stood near the edge of the wall, watching the last of his men and the marines get into the hummers. He glanced along the wall and saw two bodies lying by it. Marines suddenly appeared, grabbed them, and dragged them back to vehicles.

"We're loaded," yelled the marine officer. "Everyone accounted for."

"Go!" Martinez yelled, climbing into the rear of the last one.

They turned sharply and began to bounce across the open ground, ignoring the streets. Martinez bounced off the seat and reached up, trying to hold himself in position. He glanced to the right and saw the last of the buildings slip behind them.

Ramey watched the battle in the city from his post in the control tower. He was about to deploy his men to receive the attack when the lead tank exploded in a rolling ball of flame. Dense black smoke curled up into the night sky, slowly blending into it.

A moment later another of the tanks blew up. There was some firing from the enemy column, tracers and muzzle flashes marking the positions of the enemy soldiers. Very little fire in return. The marines were pulling back.

"Hummers coming in," said the corporal.

Ramey turned and saw the first of the hummers burst through the fence around the airport. He put the handset against his ear and said, "Blue Bonnet Six, this is Bullyboy Six."

"Go ahead."

"We are ready for the choppers."

"Roger that. Inbound your location. Say status of the airfield."

"Currently cold. Might be some triple-A on the perimeter but we haven't seen it."

"Roger that. You'll see us in about one zero mikes."

"Roger."

Ramey studied the column. It hadn't moved since the tanks had been hit. The Arabs had scrambled away from it, fleeing to the rear, some of them throwing away their weapons. Armored cars still burned on the airfield; some of the structures were on fire and others had already burned to the ground. The fence had been holed in a dozen of places. Bodies were scattered throughout.

"Okay," said Ramey. "Let's get out of here."

Reisman moved forward and raised his camera. He shot a number of pictures, concentrating on the burning vehicles, and then turned to photograph the town.

"They'll never turn out," said the corporal.

Without lowering the camera, Reisman said, "Sure they will. I've got that new low-light film. Incredible stuff. Almost allows you to shoot by starlight."

"Come on," said Ramey. "We're moving out."

Reisman lowered the camera and took a final look around. "Okay. I'm right behind you."

The men in the tower ran down the steps. Ramey had thought about destroying the equipment there but realized it would do no good. It would cripple the airport, but not the ability of the enemy to attack them. He left it alone.

He came out of the tower, the men falling in behind him as he ran for the other end of the room. They ran through the splintered door and down to the main level of the terminal.

"Let's go, boys," Ramey yelled. "We're getting out now."

They reached the doors and spread out, Ramey pushing them open. The desert heat slipped in. He ignored it and stepped out. Nothing moved and the only points of light were the burning vehicles and buildings. Most of the fires had burned down.

Ramey ran along the side of the building and then stopped. He glanced to the right, at what had been a machine-gun nest, and saw bodies close to it, the enemy soldiers cut down by the machine gunner, but the nest had been abandoned, moved to the perimeter to help in the defense there.

The RTO approached him. "Captain. The choppers."

Ramey took the handset. "This is Bullyboy Six actual."

"This is Blue Bonnet Six. We're zero-two out."

"Roger."

"Do you have strobes?"

"Blue Bonnet Six, be advised that we are not prepared for extraction. We'll need another five to ten minutes."

"Roger that. We'll make an orbit, but be advised the longer we're up here the more likely it is that the bad guys will spot us."

"Roger. We'll hurry." Ramey glared at the RTO. "Give me the company freq."

"Yes, sir."

"Three-Six, this is Six actual."

"Go."

"Withdraw from your positions and head toward Two-Six."

"Roger that."

"Two-Six, how's it look at your end."

"The perimeter here is secure. I've got no movement anywhere around me."

"Roger. We'll be moving toward you for extraction. Get your people deployed for that."

"Roger."

Ramey gave the handset back to the RTO. The men from the terminal were straggling out and deploying along a makeshift skirmish line. He spotted one of the NCOs. "Sergeant, get the men moving toward Two-Six's position."

"Yes, sir."

Ramey wiped the sweat from his face and then glanced at his watch. The ruby numbers were barely visible. He was surprised that only an hour had passed since the landing. It seemed much longer.

A squad sprinted from cover near the terminal building. They fanned out, running toward the perimeter. Third platoon was retreating, too. All that was missing were the Green Berets and the hummers.

As he thought this, the first of the vehicles roared around the end of the terminal building. It slowed for a moment and then, seeing the marines moving out, took off in the same direction.

That was the last of Wild Bill's problems. He waved a hand and yelled, "Let's go."

The marines at the terminal all took off running. Ramey kept his eyes on the perimeter but still saw no sign of movement. He reached Two-Six's position and then snapped his fingers. The RTO snapped the handset into his palm.

"Blue Bonnet Six, this is Bullyboy Six. We are in position for pickup."

"Roger that. Inbound your location. Can you give us strobes?"

"Roger. Be advised that we're on the south side of the field. There are two burning vehicles close to us."

"Roger. I have them in sight." Then, after a moment's hesitation: "Be advised that there is a column coming at you from the west."

"Is it close?"

"Shouldn't reach you for fifteen minutes."

"You'd better hurry, Blue Bonnet."

"Roger, we're on the way."

• • •

From the trailing hummer, Martinez saw the helicopters in the west. The sky was just beginning to pale, some of the stars fading as the band of light expanded toward the zenith. He leaned forward and touched the driver. "You'd better hurry."

"They won't leave us," said the marine.

Martinez didn't say a thing; he knew the man was right. American soldiers and marines did not leave one another behind. Interservice rivalry died on the battlefield. Americans took care of other Americans.

"Just step on it."

The hummer crashed through the fence and raced along the terminal. When the driver cleared the end of it, he turned again, crossing the tarmac, past the C-141 in which Frankowski and the others had landed, the wreckage of other planes, and the bodies of the enemy killed in the assault on the airport.

Now he could hear the roar of the chopper's turbines and the pop of their rotors. These weren't the small Apache assault ships, but giant HH-66s, the replacements for the older and slower HH-53s. These new ships carried two pilots and half a dozen enlisted crew, some of them manning the miniguns mounted in the doors. Anyone firing at them would get a wall of lead in return.

As they shot across the runways toward the perimeter the choppers touched down in swirling clouds of dust and sand. Their landing lights flashed and went out, the nav lights blinking dimly.

"Come on," said Martinez. He wanted to get there. He wanted to get the hell out of Saudi Arabia and onto the deck of the carrier waiting for them.

The hummer accelerated and then suddenly slowed. The driver stood on the brake and the wheels locked. They slid forward and then stopped abruptly. As they did so the doors flew open and the men piled out.

Martinez watched them run for the last helicopter in the line. He turned, scanning the airfield for anyone who might have been left behind. He saw the hummers sitting abandoned, the burning armored cars, the smoking remains of the various buildings and equipment. Standing at the far end of the PZ was the marine captain. Martinez raised a hand in salute. The marine returned it, and both men ran for the closest chopper.

Just as he climbed on board the helicopter rose to a hover. It hung there for an instant, the dust and sand sucked up with the rotor wash creating a dust storm that seemed impenetrable. The nose dropped slightly and the aircraft began to move. An instant later they broke out of the dust storm and Martinez saw the first of the enemy vehicles rolling out onto the airfield.

"Just in time," yelled one of the marines.

Martinez nodded as a line of emerald tracers flashed past them.

The minigun opened fire with a sound like a slow-moving buzz saw that slowly picked up speed. In an instant it looked as if a red ray was being fired, every fourth round a tracer that reached out and danced around the lead vehicles of the enemy column. Some of the tracers bounced upward, but the other slugs slammed into the column. The lead vehicle stopped and the second one burst into flames.

And then they were out of range. The minigun stopped and the gunner turned, grinning and holding a thumb up in the air. "Damn, I've always wanted to do that."

Martinez watched as the burning vehicles on the airfield slipped to the rear and then disappeared until the only sign of the battle was the jet-black smoke against the light gray of the morning sky.

Suddenly, he relaxed. They had pulled it off. They had gotten in, and out with the prisoners. He felt very good.

EGLIN AIR FORCE BASE, FLORIDA

Even though the messages wouldn't come through for hours, Gleason, Bloch, and Brizzola were parked in one corner of the message center waiting for the word. They sat at a desk, away from the others who were working, not talking to each other. Just waiting for the word to come down.

Gleason's aide had been sent out to find Cokes and then sandwiches and then coffee. He'd brought in the evening papers, stopping so that one of the guards could search the newspaper to make sure he was sneaking nothing in. He then stood to one side and waited patiently, wishing that he could head on home. They'd been there from the moment the aircraft had landed in Israel. It had been an all-night watch and he was getting tired.

Gleason, Bloch, and Brizzola weren't getting tired; they were getting nervous, even though they knew that there would be no radio communications once the assault force was on the ground, unless something had gone wrong.

They had learned that the aircraft with the Green Berets had taken off from Israel when the computerized message had been handed to them. They knew the moment the Green Berets had bailed out and they knew that the C-141 had landed in Riyadh, leaving the marines on the ground there. They knew that both aircraft had gotten away without anyone shooting at them. But that was all they knew for the moment.

Brizzola had taken to pacing between the rows of desks and computers and old-fashioned teletypes. He had stared over the shoulders of some of the clerks, who quickly blanked their screens in case Brizzola was not cleared to see what had been printed there, even if he was allowed free access to the message center. He looked for the young woman he'd seen there before, but she was gone, either on her day off or because her shift was over. Had she been around, it wouldn't have been quite so boring.

Returning to where the general sat, his eyes closed, Brizzola looked at him, an old man who seemed young to be a marine general. It all boiled down to perspective. When he was a kid in the marines, the senior officers all seemed so old. Maybe sixty or seventy. Now they seemed too young, as if the average age of the generals was shrinking. Brizzola knew that wasn't right. It was all perspective.

He sat on the corner of the desk, his left foot bouncing. Gleason opened an eye and said, "You have to learn to relax. That's the only thing you can do now."

Brizzola nodded and wanted to ask a half-dozen questions, but already knew the answers. He had to sit back, like the coach of a football team, and let the men do their jobs. He knew they were well trained and well equipped. It was out of his hands. They would either succeed or they'd fail, and there was nothing he could do about it.

"An hour?" said Bloch.

Gleason looked at his watch and then shrugged. "Maybe a little more or a little less. Depends on the breaks."

Bloch got up and walked around the desk. He looked

as if he'd thought of something and then decided against it. He picked up a packet of messages and thumbed through them, looking for something, anything.

"Relax," said Gleason. "You'll live longer."

A clerk, a marine lance corporal, appeared in front of them. "I have a message that might interest you."

Bloch reached out for it and then realized that the general should have it first. Without glancing at it, he handed it over to Gleason.

"That was the most amazing display of self-control I've seen in a long time," said Gleason, grinning. He scanned the message and then handed it to Bloch without a word.

"Embassy says something is going on at the airport."

"Which we already knew," said Gleason. "I wish they hadn't put that out. Codes can be broken."

"Enemy knows it already," said Brizzola.

"But the Russians don't," said Gleason. "With the way things have been going lately, I'd prefer that they didn't know until our people were out cleanly."

"They won't do anything," said Brizzola. "They don't want a confrontation with us."

"Exactly," said the general. He closed his eyes again.

Brizzola tried to force himself to relax, but his mind was working too fast. He was going over the plans, the intel reports, the mission, again and again. He could think of things they might have overlooked. He could see things that they hadn't thought about.

The clerk appeared again and handed over another message. This time Bloch scanned it because the general had not opened his eyes.

"They've requested the choppers," he said, his voice rising in excitement.

Gleason opened his eyes but didn't sit up any straighter. "Word on casualties?"

"No, General. Just that they've requested the choppers. I don't know if they got our people or not."

Gleason nodded. "We'll just have to be patient."

Brizzola stood up and walked toward the front of the message center. It was cold and bright and noisy in the cavernous room. A hundred people worked a hundred dif-

ferent computers or radios or teletypes. Printers clattered.
Line printers sounded like angry bees caught in a bottle.
The shredders destroyed the classified documents that no
one wanted or needed. Brizzola wished it would all stop
for a moment, just to give him a rest. He wondered how
the people who worked there put up with it day after day.

A clerk opened a drawer on his desk and Brizzola saw
a copy of *Penthouse*. He wished he could confiscate the
magazine but knew he had to ignore it. It would have
taken his mind off the waiting. He had returned to the
general's desk and was wondering what to do next when
the clerk was back for the third time.

Gleason opened his eyes, took the message, and sat
up. "That's it, gentlemen. They're out. Casualties are light
and they've got our people."

"Yeah!" Brizzola yelled.

Bloch looked solemn, took Gleason's hand, and shook
it. "Congratulations, General."

"I did nothing," said Gleason, smiling broadly. He
looked at his aide. "Why don't you go home for the day?"

"If you're sure you won't need me again today, General."

"Go," said Gleason. He then turned his attention to
Bloch and Brizzola. "Let's get back to the office and clean
up the messes there. By that time it should be late enough
to get a drink somewhere."

John Frankowski lay in bed, the TV on but the sound
inaudible, staring up at the ceiling, watching it brighten
as the sun came up. He had heard no news about Marie
for a long time. There had been diplomatic communiqués,
and telegrams, and regular updates, but none of them told
him a thing. Marie was being held by a revolutionary
council that didn't want to arrange a prisoner trade. They
didn't even want to acknowledge they had taken any prisoners. The last he had heard, she was alive, but had been
sentenced to death.

He thought of that and turned away from the glowing
TV screen to stare at the window, the drawn blinds failing
to keep the light out. The sun sat on the horizon, a glowing ball of orange that looked as if it would never move.

The doorbell startled him. Visitors didn't show up with the sun if it was good news. They waited until a decent hour to bring it. Frankowski got up, knowing what it would be. He pulled the blinds to the side and looked out to see the staff car parked on the street. His heart skipped a beat and he wondered if he was going to pass out.

He'd heard the stories from his mother. How she'd lived on a street where two or three women had husbands in Vietnam, and how they dreaded the army staff cars. Every time one of the cars had turned onto the street, each woman prayed that it would stop at one of the other houses.

Frankowski had never thought that he'd be in that position. He was the man. The air-force staff car coming with the bad news should not be coming to him. He heard the doorbell ring again and the sound of knocking. He shouted, "All right!" but the noise didn't stop.

He pulled his robe from the closet and put it on quickly. He hurried to open the front door. Not wanting to see the men outside, he turned away and headed back toward the living room.

"John," said one of the officers. "I have news."

"I know," said Frankowski, moving to sit down.

"How? It on the TV already?"

"I just know." He sat down, staring at the floor.

"They got her out," said the second man. "She's on a carrier in the Persian Gulf."

"What?" Frankowski's head snapped up. "What'd you say?"

"Marie's fine. They got her out of prison this morning and she's on one of our carriers in the Persian Gulf. They'll be flying her out of there in a couple of hours."

"Oh, Jesus Christ," said Frankowski. "I thought you were going to tell me that she was dead. I thought that was why you came by so early."

"She's fine."

Frankowski sank back in the couch. The relief flooded over him. He wanted to giggle or drink or just stand up and shout. A hundred, a thousand ideas washed through his mind, each screaming for attention.

"You okay?"

"I'm fine," said Frankowski. "I'm perfect."

"We just got word, and I didn't think you'd mind if we woke you up."

"I wasn't asleep anyway." He stood up, unable to sit still. He walked around the room, touching things as if to reassure himself that this wasn't a dream. He looked at his friends. "When will she be back."

"She'll be flown to the hospital in Wiesbaden, Germany, for a physical and examination. Then she'll be allowed to fly on home."

"I always wondered about that. What if the person— what if she wants to come straight home?"

The one officer shrugged. "I think she'll need the time to decompress. Get used to the idea that she's free again."

"I want to see her."

"Oh Christ, John, we've got the flight arranged for you already. You'll be there when she arrives."

Frankowski moved to the door and then stopped. "What should I take?"

"Uniforms. Civilian clothes. And something for Marie. She lost everything she had with her. Anything that she'll be comfortable wearing."

Without a word Frankowski walked back to the bedroom and spotted the bear sitting on the chair where Marie had left it. A small golden bear wearing an old red stocking cap and a shirt that said "M and M." She called the bear Pieces because it represented pieces of chocolate. The bear would have to go to Germany. Marie always left Pieces behind in case something happened. She didn't want to lose the bear. She'd been right about the last trip.

Frankowski pulled down a suitcase and then stepped back to sit on the bed. He didn't know whether to laugh or cry. His emotions bubbled in him and he told himself that men didn't cry, especially fighter pilots. But he was so damned glad that Marie was safe, he just didn't know how to react.

Finally he took a deep breath and started to pack. There was nothing else for him to do.

"The good news," said Wheeler, "is that we're not going to deploy. For the moment."

Sandi Paulding, sitting in the conference room with half a dozen other staff officers, breathed a sigh of relief.

"Or rather," said Wheeler, "we're not going to deploy to the Middle East as you might have suspected, given the world situation and what happened five years ago."

"Thank God for that," said one of the officers.

Paulding wasn't ready to thank God or anyone else for the moment. She was wishing she could just go back to the university and forget about playing soldier, though she was making more money than she would be at the university.

"Plans are under way for us to move toward the Big Bend area of Texas and spread out along a line there to inhibit the invasion of refugees from South and Central America."

"Christ! This is an armor unit. Not a bunch of border cops," snapped a man.

"The orders have been cut." Wheeler was quiet for a moment, suddenly understanding why he hadn't delegated the briefing to a subordinate. No one was happy about being called to active duty and then sent to one of the worst sections of Texas to play border patrol.

"For how long?" Paulding asked.

"Until the current crisis has been resolved."

She looked at Wheeler and thought about that. She knew there was some turmoil in the Soviet Union, what was left of it. She knew the Vietnamese were again growling at the Chinese, who were shooting their own people as fast as they could. In the Middle East the Arabs were shooting at everyone including their own people and the Iraqis were still fighting with the Iranians and everyone else, but were limited by their inability to take the fight to anyone but each other.

Wheeler took a deep breath. "I don't know. The president is worried about the situation in the Middle East. The Saudis have made progress in reestablishing their government, but the fighting continues."

"I'm not interested in a lot of esoteric maneuvering," said Paulding. "I want to know how long."

"That information has not been supplied."

Paulding shook her head. The world seemed to be going to hell in a hand basket and now she was going to watch it from somewhere in the Big Bend area. Not what she'd had in mind when she was attending the monthly reserve meetings.

"We'll get a complete briefing later," said Wheeler. "Right now all I can tell you is that we'll be on active duty for a year. Toward the end of that time, Washington will take another look and decide whether to keep us on or release us."

"This another benefit of the peace dividend?" asked a man.

"I'm not sure what you mean," said Wheeler.

"He means," said Paulding, "that the peace dividend required the reduction of the military forces. Money was saved and the army shrank. Now, with the world situation changing, the solution is to call up the reserves."

Wheeler shrugged. "What can I tell you? We've been called to active duty, but I don't understand the bitching. Each of you knew that it was possible when you signed up. You were all willing to take the benefits of the reserves, the extra pay, the free travel, training, and everything else. Well, now it's time to pay the piper."

"Shit!" said one of the officers.

Wheeler had to grin. "Okay, so I agree. But we're stuck with this until the situation stabilizes."

Paulding rocked back in the chair and ran a hand through her hair. "I hope it stabilizes soon."

"I wouldn't count on it," said Wheeler. "You can hope, but I wouldn't be surprised to see us serve the whole year."

"Great."

EGLIN AIR FORCE BASE, FLORIDA

Martinez felt better after the long flight. The C-141 was specially equipped so that he and his men were able to sleep most of the way. Both male and female load-masters, masquerading as flight attendants, had offered good food, cold drinks, or had left the men alone to sleep. The team took advantage of that.

They landed in Florida and were taken to their quarters to clean up. Their equipment and weapons were surren-dered to the marines, who loaded them into a truck to be taken to the Rapid Deployment Force compound. Marti-nez was told that his only function was to get the men to the compound in an hour to meet with General Gleason.

Martinez was picked up by a staff car, a green Ford that had air-conditioning that did little to cool the interior. He had been waiting outside in the stifling Florida heat, which was more oppressive than the desert of Saudi Ara-bia, his sweat staining the clean BDUs he had donned.

The uniform had a jungle camouflage, unlike the desert ones he'd worn during the raid. A fresh-starched uniform, which had wilted in the heat, one that gave no clue about where he'd been.

When they reached the Rapid Deployment Force compound, Martinez was surprised by the change. The once nearly deserted area was alive with soldiers and marines. Thousands of them in combat gear and wearing BDUs. They carried their weapons with them and wore the new Kevlar helmets.

The car stopped at the gate to the fenced compound. In the past, the guard hut had not been manned. Now an armed MP stood there and the gate was closed. The driver held out an ID card and the guard examined it. He asked about Martinez, checked his roster, and then opened the gate.

"What the hell is going on here?" Martinez asked as they passed through the gate.

"In the last two days a thousand marines and five hundred soldiers have been assigned to the RDF. Security has been increased."

"I can see that."

Armed guards stood beside the doors at the headquarters building, too. Both men stood at attention, looking more ceremonial than anything else. Martinez opened the door of the car and got out. "Thanks for the lift."

"Yes, sir."

He walked up the steps and was surprised as both guards saluted him. He returned it and entered the building. The last time it had been dimly lit with only a few of the offices being used. Now it was brightly lit, with the clatter of computer printers, ringing phones, and men and women hurrying around, many of them carrying stacks of paper. All were dressed in jungle BDUs. Martinez didn't like that. He'd hoped that he'd be out of the jungle environment for a while.

A sergeant ran up, a young man who looked like a teenager, but the stripes on his sleeve suggested that he'd been around for a while. "Captain Martinez?"

"Yes."

"Please follow me, sir."

They headed upstairs, down a hallway that was as brightly lit and as busy as the one below it. Martinez glanced into an office packed with people. One man was screaming at another, who only shook his head. Things had certainly changed.

The sergeant opened a door and said, "The briefing will be held here, sir."

Martinez entered and was surprised to find Gleason, Bloch, and Brizzola already there. Most of his team sat in the chairs surrounding the conference table. Cups of coffee sat in front of them.

Gleason gestured and said, "We'll begin now."

Martinez took a vacant seat. "What in the hell happened here?"

Gleason grinned. "Your little expedition into Saudi Arabia, put together with a makeshift force and sent out in a matter of hours, seems to have impressed the powers that be. Since you got in and out, accomplished your mission, and the casualties were extrememly light, we've been completely revitalized."

"Jesus."

"Full strength in a matter of hours," said Gleason. "Everything I want, I get. Hell, I could requisition a private fighter or a private helicopter and get it. Probably both."

Martinez shook his head.

"It's the way things work," said Gleason. "Congress doesn't see the immediate need, or you fuck up somehow, and your funding is gone. Then you're needed and you pull off a spectacular mission and they hand you the keys to Fort Knox."

"I'm impressed," said Martinez.

Gleason grinned. "I'm authorized to offer you a direct commission into the marine corps as a major." When he saw Martinez hesitate, he amended, "Or a lieutenant colonel."

"No, sir," said Martinez. "Thanks, but no thanks."

Gleason nodded. "I'd have been disappointed if you'd said anything else. Now let me hear about that mission. Everything."

"Yes, sir." Martinez looked at one of the coffee cups,

wished someone had offered him one, and then forgot about it. "As you know . . ."

An hour later he finished. The other team members had covered their roles, explaining exactly what they had done once they got into the prison. Gleason and his staff took notes the whole time.

When they were done, Gleason looked at Martinez. "Offer of a direct commission to lieutenant colonel still stands."

"No, sir."

"Then I'd like your team assigned here for the next few weeks anyway. You could help us get ready to deploy."

"Into Central America?"

"What makes you ask that?" Gleason asked.

"The battle dress. All camouflaged for the jungle."

Gleason grinned again. "Hadn't thought of that. It's the uniform that most of the troops arrived with. Tropical. Effective camouflage in more ways than one. But no, we're going into Saudi Arabia."

"When?" asked Martinez, knowing that he shouldn't have.

"Three weeks max." Gleason glanced at his two operations officers and then continued, "Saudis have now pretty well crushed the revolt. Our little operation helped them. They now control most of their country again. We're going in to be stationed at a small outpost near the sea. A little more American presence in the area just in case a few people think they can move in."

"And you want us to go in with you?" Martinez asked.

"That's what I'd like."

Martinez thought about it and then shook his head. "I'm sorry, General, but we've trained to operate in Latin America. We're out of our depth in the Middle East. The mission worked because it was a standard go in and get out. Direct action."

"Can't change your mind?"

"No, sir."

Gleason stood up and held out a hand. "Then thanks for you help. I still wish you were a marine."

Martinez grinned broadly. "And I still wish you were Special Forces."

John Frankowski, wearing a civilian suit, stood in the operations building at Wiesbaden, Germany. He could see the airfield easily and watched as the gray and silver C-141 landed and then taxied. As it maneuvered on the field a cheer went up from the waiting people, the families of the people on the plane, the captives freed during the raid by American forces.

Frankowski couldn't cheer. He was worried about his wife. She, and Elizabeth Shawn, were the only women to have been held captive, and he was afraid of what might have been done to them. Afraid that the Arabs had taken liberties with them.

The cheering, a sudden burst of noise, surprised and then annoyed him. He wished they would just shut up and leave him alone with this thoughts.

The plane came closer and then stopped on the tarmac right outside. A pickup truck with a ramp was driven out and parked under one of the doors.

In the operations building, the crowd pushed forward and then someone opened a door. The people surged toward the opening. They spilled out onto the patch of grass, pressing toward the short wire fence that separated the tarmac from the operations building.

Frankowski stayed where he was, watching as the first of the people appeared in the hatch of the C-141. Two crew members exited and then turned, as if waiting for the others.

Frankowski recognized Richard Hansen. He stopped and waved to the crowd. He was grinning broadly and didn't look too bad. Maybe he'd lost some weight, but that was all. Behind him appeared another man. They stayed there, listening to the cheering from the crowd.

"Come on," said Frankowski. Now he felt trapped. He didn't want to leave, afraid that he wouldn't see Marie as she exited the plane.

Another shape appeared as the two men got out of the way, but that wasn't Marie either. Frankowski knew she'd be the last off. She always was. Even under these circumstances.

And finally, there she was, standing in the hatch, a hand to shade her eyes as she searched the crowd for him. He could see the disappointment as she failed to spot him. She dropped her hand.

When she did, Frankowski ran to the door and pushed his way out. He shouldered the crowd out of his way and shouted, "Marie! Right here! Marie!"

He reached the front and felt the fence against his legs. He stepped over it onto the tarmac and ran at her. She had spotted him and turned, running.

They met, hugged and kissed, suddenly oblivious of the crowd around them. Photographers took pictures and the TV news was there with videotape running, pushing at each other to get a picture of the faces.

She broke the kiss and said, "I didn't think you were coming. That you were here."

"Waited inside."

"Why?"

He couldn't explain it, so he ignored the question, pulling her close again. He whispered in her ear, "I brought Pieces."

"Pieces?"

"Your bear."

She began to laugh. She pulled him close and hung on. "I know it's over now," she said. "If you hadn't brought the bear, I'd worry. But it's all over."

"How are you?"

"Fine. Hurt my ribs, but the doctors on the carrier took care of that. I'm a little sore, but fine. I want something to eat and drink and then I want to get away from everyone for a while. Just you and me. And Pieces."

"I think the doctors want to talk to you. Examine you."

She looked at the cameras and pulled away from him. Holding his hand, she tugged him toward the operations building. The reporters wouldn't be allowed in there.

As they walked she said, "Doctors on the ship examined me and found nothing really wrong. No need for this.''

Frankowski wondered about rape. He wanted to know if she had been touched by her captors but couldn't think of a way to ask the question. Then, suddenly, he decided that it didn't matter to him. It wasn't like she'd gone in search of an affair. If she had been raped, it would be the same as if the captors had beaten her. It would be an act of violence against her. He'd still want to kill them, but his feelings for her would not be any different.

He moved closer to her, letting his hip bump into hers. She was looking at the cheering crowds, waving at them. In corridor in front of them, air-force people tried to get the crowd to move back. They ran the gauntlet quickly and found themselves in one of the VIP waiting rooms.

As the noise from the crowd faded and the last of the reporters was chased away, Frankowski turned to his wife. "How are you doing?"

"I'm fine. It was a little rough and the food was terrible, but it wasn't that bad. I had faith.''

John turned and looked her in the eyes. In her beautiful eyes. He grinned. "You going back to flying?''

"Sure," she said. "Why not?''

He pulled her close. "Can't think of a single reason.''

Reisman walked into the city room and listened as his fellow journalists burst into applause. One by one they stood up, clapping. Someone shouted, "That was one hell of a story.''

Reisman clasped his hands over his head like a boxer who'd just won the championship. "You have to live right," he announced.

There was more cheering as two men and two women came forward carrying the cake. Sparklers glowing red and green were set on it rather than candles. They brought it closer and set it on a desk.

"The Pulitzer Prize," read Reisman. "Aren't we being a little premature?''

"For the only reporter to cover the rescue in Riyadh

at the airport. I don't think so.'' Carmichael held out a cake knife.

Reisman took the knife but didn't move. ''The sparklers?''

''Let them burn,'' said Carmichael.

One of the women stepped forward and began removing them. ''You men are such sissies.''

Once the sparklers were gone, Reisman moved in and began cutting the cake. Someone came forward with paper plates and cups of punch. As each person was served he or she drifted away to eat in peace.

When Reisman finished cutting the cake, Carmichael said, ''Come with me.''

Reisman turned and spotted Webster. She'd been hanging back, at the rear of the crowd. She had a cup of punch but no cake. He winked at her. She'd been waiting for him at the airport the night before and they had gone to her apartment rather than his. It had seemed to be the thing to do.

She'd prepared for his arrival, had disappeared for a moment, and then returned wearing a white teddy complete with garters and white stockings. She was carrying a bottle of champagne and two glasses.

Reisman was impressed. There wasn't an ounce of fat on her. She looked good in white. He'd wanted to ask her a dozen different things, but the questions evaporated as she leaned over to pour the champagne.

''How you been?'' she asked.

Reisman sipped the champagne and then reached out to grab her, slipping a hand inside the teddy. ''I'm fine. You?''

She kissed him and then said, ''Fine. Bed?''

''Sure.''

Now she was standing at the edge of the crowd, watching as Carmichael dragged him into his office. Carmichael closed the door and took a seat behind his desk. He waved at one of the other chairs. Reisman dropped into it.

''I'm trying to think about your next assignment.''

''That shouldn't be difficult.''

Carmichael shook his heads and picked up a pencil, rolling it between the palms of his hands. ''You've kind of screwed yourself. I know that you were working a China angle here, but I think that's gone."

"So what am I going to do?" Reisman asked.

"Well, your adventure into Saudi Arabia has caught the notice of the powers that be. They want me to give you a freer hand. Go where you think the action is."

Reisman sipped his punch. "I've been where the action is."

"There are heightened tensions in a number of areas," said Carmichael. "Maybe something will strike your fancy."

"Such as?"

"There's talk of American assistance, military assistance, into Central America. The Argentines are making noises about the Falklands again."

Reisman thought about Martinez and his merry band of Green Berets. They had come from that area, but they seemed to think the major problems were drug-related. The Cubans moving drugs to undermine the United States.

"I don't think so."

"Got some unrest in Uruguay. Might be Communist-inspired," said Carmichael.

"And might not. In fact, it might not even matter."

"True. Also heard something about a revolt in Tibet. They don't like the Chinese."

"So who does?" Reisman asked.

"None of that appeals to you?"

"Hell, Ralph, I just got back. I haven't even unpacked yet and now you want me to go shooting off into another area of the world."

"Lots of things happening out there," said Carmichael. "We've got to cover them. The people have a right to know."

Reisman couldn't help laughing. "The people, huh?"

"Well, somebody's got the right to know." He grinned. "Maybe it's just me who has the right to know."

"Let me think this over for a couple of days. Catch my breath." Grinning, he added, "I did turn in one hell of a story, though."

Carmichael nodded and opened a desk drawer. He pulled out a cigar and stuck it in his mouth but didn't bother to light it. "Well, then, welcome back. Let me know what you want to do next. Where you want to go next. The world is percolating. Beginning to boil."

Reisman nodded and said, "And it's a good thing, too. Otherwise we wouldn't have anything to do."

About the Author

Capt. Kevin D. Randle, USAFR, has had a long military career in two branches of the armed forces. He flew helicopters for the army during the Vietnam War, serving with the 116th and 187th Assault Helicopter Companies at Cu Chi in 1968-69. While in Vietnam, he was decorated with the Silver Star, the Distinguished Flying Cross, the Army Commendation Medal for Valor, and forty-one Air Medals. Upon his return to the U.S., he graduated from the University of Iowa, and went on to serve twelve years as an intelligence officer in the Air Force. He is the author of numerous articles and books, and contributed significantly to the VIETNAM: GROUND ZERO series by Eric Helm, and WINGS OVER NAM by Cat Branigan. He currently lives with his wife, Debbie, in Cedar Rapids, Iowa.

Global War

BY CAPT. KEVIN D. RANDLE, USAF

The twilight of the twentieth century. The Cold War is long dead, the war in the Gulf has been won. Yet a series of geopolitical changes destabilizes a dozen major governments around the world, and armies on seven continents are thrown into a new age of high-tech warfare from which there is no escape. Amid the mounting chaos, US Army Capt. Frank Martinez and his crack team of specialists are called upon to bring American military know-how to hot spots in the far corners of the globe.

BORDER WINDS

Flashpoint: Nicaragua. Castro's successor, desperately searching for allies in Latin America, foments a Sandinista coup in Nicaragua—stunning both Moscow and Washington.

Flashpoint: Texas. Tensions are high along the border, as American intelligence catches wind of a Mexican plot to invade the U.S., and a dangerous paramilitary survivalist group mobilizes resistance.

Flashpoint: Uruguay. Reports of a Castroite rebellion send US and Soviet warships on a course straight to the South Atlantic.

Look for GLOBAL WAR *Book 2 in 1992 wherever Bantam Falcon books are sold. Turn the page for an exciting preview . . .*

THE JUNGLES OUTSIDE MANAGUA, NICARAGUA

There was one last chance to pull it off and if it failed, Jesus Castillo, along with his men in the jungle and those who supported him in Managua, would forfeit their lives. He slipped back, away from the edge of the jungle, hiding himself in the deep shadows. Even with the sun high in the morning sky, the jungle was a dim and damp protective.

"We are ready," said Julio Llanca.

Castillo lifted a hand and wiped the sweat from his face. He pulled the soft, camouflaged hat from his head and ran a hand through his soaked hair. He rubbed his hand on the front of his fatigue shirt leaving a ragged stain.

"Another few minutes, we must wait for the signal."

"Certainly, sir."

Castillo watched Llanca move off, crouching near a sergeant and then disappearing into the thick foliage. He checked his weapon, an old AK-47 that had been given to him twenty years earlier when the Sandinistas had been courting the Soviets, receiving military aid from them.

It was a reliable weapon. Parts of the stock had been worn thin during the years and there were scars on the receiver group where shrapnel had hit. But the weapon was sound and as reliable today as it had been in the past. Not a spot of rust on it.

"Colonel," said a voice behind him. "They're beginning the move now."

"Thank you, Sergeant." Castillo thumbed the selector switch on his AK to the single shot and then back to safe. He was never sure if it was better to move through the jungle with the weapon ready to fire or not. A wrong step, a vine or branch and the rifle would discharge. But in the beginning of a firefight, in case of an ambush, it was better to shoot back. A fraction of a second could mean the difference between life and death.

Again he moved to the very edge of the jungle. The trees, bushes, vines, ferns, and flowers stopped abruptly, as if they had been hacked away with a giant knife. The ground dropped away gently, leading down to a camp occupied by government soldiers. Normally they stayed behind their barbed wire fences, but in the last three weeks, as rumors of coups had ripped through the capital, the members of the elite Managua Freedom Brigade had quietly moved to the camp. They were waiting to see if they'd be needed to put down a revolt.

For the last two weeks, Castillo and his men had waited in the jungle, watching. They had kept moving, patrolling, searching the enemy position, but the commanders in the camp had decided it was best not to move. Let the people think the soldiers were content to sit back.

"First radio message is in," said a man standing close to Castillo. "They're going to move."

Castillo looked at his watch though it told him nothing. The attack signal would be broadcast. It was not timed. He nodded but kept his eyes on the enemy camp.

There was movement behind the wire. A soldier, his rifle shouldered, marching inside the perimeter. It was for show and nothing more. A real guard would not be so easy to watch. He would be hidden where he would be able to fire at the approaching enemy. The soldier with the rifle was an ornament and nothing more.

The radio operator, an earphone of the headset pressed against his ear, reached down and twisted a knob. He sat back, glanced at Castillo and nodded. "We are ordered to move."

Castillo knew what that meant. Other soldiers, in other areas, but in Managua, and the cities surrounding it, would begin the attack. Everyone moving at once so that no one could alert the government stooges.

The single guard had moved off so that he was walking away from them. It would be ten or twelve minutes before his path brought him around so that he would see the Castillo and his soldiers attacking.

Without a word, Castillo rose to his feet. He glanced right and left, watching as the line of soldiers stood with him, each wearing camouflaged fatigues and carrying the weapons supplied by the Russians, and later by the Cubans. Waving a hand, Castillo left the cover of the jungle and stepped out into the sunlight.

He hesitated an instant, and then began to run down the hill, toward the camp. His eyes swept the fenceline and the structures behind it, including the guard towers, though they were unmanned.

There was no indication for the base that anyone saw them coming. Castillo knew that he had the advantage of complete surprise. There had been no hotilies for months and the government soldiers had slipped into apathy. They were unprepared for any type of military action. Before they could react, the fight should be over.

In less than a minute, Castillo was crouched at the base of the chainlink fence. Sweat was dripping down his face and side. His breathing was rapid, but the short run down hill hadn't taxed him.

Two men with bolt cutters were snipping at the fence near the posts. They would take out a section of it twenty feet wide. The rest of the assault team had fanned out in a semicircle, protecting the rear. The second wave was at the edge of the jungle, waiting for the fence to fall.

As it did, the single guard appeared again. He stopped, looked at the assembled armed men, and tried to pull his rifle off his soldier. Castillo fired once from the hip. The bullet slammed into the guard's chest, driving him back. He dropped his rifle, fell, and rolled. Blood spurted from the hole in his chest, first a fountain, then a bubbling and finally nothing.

The men rushed through the hole, spreading out, filtering through the camp. Castillo and a squad ran toward the headquarters building. It was close to the front gate with three flagpoles in front of it. A howitzer, probably for display rather than combat sat pointing at the road leading to the camp.

Castillo reached it as two men came out the door. Both were dressed in pressed uniforms, one with a pistol holstered at his side and the other holding a rifle. A single shot on a military reservation was not an uncommon occurance.

But the man with the rifle saw the armed soldiers running at him and recognized none of them. He swung his rifle around but before he could fire, a burst hit him, stitching him from the throat to the groin. He was pushed back, to the wall, and fell to the ground, his blood splattering the grass.

Castillo fired at the other man. The round hit his shoulder and spun him. As he slipped to a knee, he tried to drawn his weapon, but a dozen shots were fired at him. A window behind his head exploded, and bits of wood from the building flew. He tried to dive for cover and was hit a second, then a third time.

They ran to the steps, jumped up them, and then Castillo stood aside as one of his men kicked in the door. They burst through. Two men inside scrambled for an exit, but were cut down. Another stood up slowly, his hands raised above his head. Castillo didn't care. He killed the man with a shot to the heart.

"Upstairs," yelled Castillo. He pointed to the rear of the office.

Two men broke from the main group and ran up the stair. There was a shout and then a burst of fire. Something hit the floor.

Castillo snapped his fingers and pointed at the main door. A man spun to guard it. Before Castillo could point to the rear, a couple of the soldiers ran through the office, kicked open another door, and took up positions at the rear.

"Let's clear the building," ordered Castillo.

The rest of the soldiers began searching for anyone hiding. They dragged one man from a closet and pushed him to the floor in front of Castillo. Without hesitation, Castillo shot him, putting the barrel of his rifle against the man's head. When he pulled the trigger, the man flipped to his back. Blood poured from the wound, grey-green brain splattered the floor as the man drummed his hands and feet on the wood.

Another group of soldiers appeared, pushing a lone woman. She was dressed in a short skirt, blouse and sandals. She fell to her knees in front of Castillo and refused to look up at him.

A man ran into the room and stopped in front of Castillo. He began to lift his hand in salute and then remembered that soldiers didn't salute in the field. "We have taken the main barracks. The soldiers had surrendered."

"Good."

"We hold the armory as well. The weapons are locked in there. We don't have the key."

Castillo waved a hand. "It doesn't matter now. We'll open it later."

"Yes, sir."

"Where is Major Fontes?"

"He is with the men who stormed the motor pool."

"Casualties?"

"No, sir. They surrendered without a fight. They had no weapons."

Castillo couldn't help grinning. That was what happened with bureaucrats and bean counters began to run military operations. Rifles and pistols were dangerous so they were locked up to prevent accidents. Then, when the soldiers needed their weapons, they were locked away where they were of no use.

Castillo turned and walked to the window. There were shards of glass lying on the floor, sparkling in the afternoon sun. Clouds were building to the west but that wouldn't matter now. His soldiers had shelter.

He noticed that three of his men were standing near the gate. They had moved a machine gun, it looked to be a 12.7 mm anti-aircraft weapon of Soviet design. The men were manning it, using it to stop any vehicles approaching.

He turned and looked at the man who had joined them. "We hold the camp?"

"Yes, sir."

Castillo nodded. There had been little firing and it had stopped five minutes earlier. He glanced at the radio operator who had stayed close during the assault. "You may radio the code for success."

"Yes, sir."

"Do we have guards out in the whole camp?"

"Yes, sir. Guards on the captured soldiers, the motor pool and the arms lockers."

"We get the radio room in time?"

"I don't think they managed to get off a distress signal. We knocked down the antenna farm before anything could be broadcast."

Nodding, Castillo kicked his way into the commander's office. The chair had been knocked over and one pane of glass had been broken but there was no other damage. He righted the chair, pushed it behind the desk and sat down. He reached out, rubbing his hand across the desk, almost as if caressing it. There was a sharp pain in his hand and he jerked it back. A sliver of glass was embedded in his flesh, a drop of blood around it.

He pulled the glass from his finger and sucked the blood off. The door opened then and Castillo looked up. The soldier standing in front of him wore a dirty uniform with one sleeve ripped.

"Looks like you ran into it," said Castillo.

"Yes, sir, but we were able to overcome them easily. Major Cruz wants to know what to do with the prisoners."

Castillo took a deep breath. "All right. I think we'll shoot the senior officers, captains and above, the senior NCOs and hold the others." Standing, he said, "Let's go find Major Cruz and take care of it."

"Yes, sir."

Castillo walked toward the door. It had been easy to take the camp. The question was, could they hold it. That was always the question.

THE SPECIAL FORCES ISOLATION AREA
PANAMA

Army Special Forces captain, Francisco Martinez, sat in the air conditioned briefing room, listening to Jose Espinoza, one of the communications NCOs give a lecture on first aid and snake bite during the briefback. That was the thing about the briefback, the FOB commander and this team asked everyone every question they could think of. The commo man might have to answer medical questions, the demolitions man might have to describe how to field strip the light weapons and the medic might have to explain the techniques of dropping a bridge.

Martinez was a small man, only five nine, with a slender build but he was surprisingly strong. He was wiry and hard. He had short cropped black hair, brown eyes and an olive skin that was sun darkened so that he looked as if he had been born in Panama or one of the surrounding countries. He spoke fluent Spanish, though those in the know could tell it was Texas Spanish, heavily accented with the inflections of the region.

He glanced to the right where Colonel Cameron Boyce sat. The Special Forces officer was listening intently to what Espinoza was saying. Cameron was an old man to be in the Special Forces, now pushing fifty. But Cameron had three tours in Vietnam, had run quiet operations into Latin America to eliminate guerrilla bands and drug lords, had survived the beginning of Desert Storm when Special Forces teams had dropped into Iraq before even the air war had been launched, and was as knowledgeable about SF operations and Latin America as anyone in Panama, the CIA or the Pentagon.

Boyce leaned over and whispered something to Major Kirby Lombard. Lombard nodded and said, "Sergeant Gibson, what are the check in times for net control?"

Gibson, who had been sitting to one side, looking as if he was uninterested, stood up and answered, providing a comprehensive list of times and frequencies.

Martinez looked at his watch and realized they'd been at it for nearly four hours. They had been over everything from the moment of insertion to the reasons for extraction, locations for extraction, emergency procedures, and limitations as dictated by the Department of State. Every aspect of the operation had been considered, analyzed, studied, and then intergrated into the overall plan.

Boyce sat up in his chair and looked at the assembled officers and men. Speaking to his team, he asked, "Are there any additional questions or comments?"

Lombard said, "You have made arrangements for resupply?"

Martinez took the question. "Yes, sir. There are four sites close to our base where aerial resupply would be possible with little or no exposure of the flight crews to hostile fire." Grinning, he added, "Not to mention easy access into a couple of local villages where we could resupply if necessary."

"Okay," said Lombard. "I'm happy."

Boyce looked at the rest of his staff waiting, but none of them said a thing. Standing, Boyce walked to the map that was held against the easel by a couple of large, silver clips.

He studied the map, the acetate overlay showing the projected drop zones and the best location for the forward operating base.

"Captain Martinez?" Boyce stood with his back to the assemble soldiers.

"Yes, sir."

Turning, Boyce said, "It's a good plan. A solid plan that protects the secrecy and limits the involvement, or the suspected involvement of the United States if something goes wrong. I think you're a go."

Martinez was standing. A thrill passed through him. It was as if he'd just passed his orals for a Ph.D., won the most coveted part in a television show, been told that his lottery ticket matched the winning numbers, or had won the Super Bowl. He wanted to leap and shout but knew that Army officers did not leap and shout. Shaking, he stuck a hand out and said, "Thank you, Colonel."

"Air assets are available from this moment on. Coordinate with Colonel Curt Jacobs, the Air Force operations officer."

"Yes, sir."

Boyce stood for a moment, studying the younger officer. Finally he said, "I wish I was going with you. This . . ." he waved a hand, "being cooped up to push papers for the bureacrats is not soldiering. It's . . ."

"Yes, sir," said Martinez. "I understand."

"When I was younger, a newly minted second lieutenant, I was standing in the club talking to a full bull. Man was about to retire and pick up his star. I was enving his position. He had the power. He had the money. I was a slave to the orders of everyone." Boyce grinned. "Including the senior NCOs, but he had it all. And he looked at me over his beer and said, 'I'd trade places with you in a minute.' "

Boyce scratched the side of his face. His fingernails made a light sound. "Of course I didn't believe him. He was at the top of his career. At the top of the hill and I was in a valley looking to climb out. Now I understand what he was saying. He couldn't get into the action. For a soldier, that's what it's all about. Rank and power don't matter. It's getting into the field and getting the job done."

"I wouldn't want to be locked up in an office all day," said Martinez, "but the paperwork is important. He realized that the words sounded strange to his own ears.

"To a point," said Boyce. "In the final analysis, it isn't the paperwork or the plan but what happens in the field."

"Yes, sir."

"Good luck to you and your men. It's a good plan. A very good one."

"Thank you, Colonel."

Then, pointing to Sergeant Arturo Chavez, Boyce said, "Have him trim that mustache."

Martinez nodded. It wasn't the first time that his operations NCO had gotten into trouble over his pistolero mustache. Chavez, like most of the team, was a small, dark man with black hair and brown eyes. He was a stockier, more heavily muscled man, who had been in the Army for over fifteen years. The only regulation that he willfully and consistently violated was the one concerning his mustache. He thought that it made him look so much like a bandit that no one would suspect that he was a soldier.

Without another word, Boyce opened the door and stepped into the hallway that lead to the outside. His staff followed him, leaving Martinez and his team in the briefing room. As soon as they shut the door, Espinoza let out a whoop.

Martinez fell back, into a chair, grinning. He looked first at Chavez, and then at his deputy, First Lieutenant Estaban Alverez. "I don't know why I'm so happy about this," he said. "It just means that we're about to go live in the jungle for the next several weeks."

"That's what it's all about," said Chavez. He couldn't stop grinning.

"What we train to do," added Alverez.

"We should be able to hit the field by six in the morning. Boyce said the aviation assets were in place for us."

"Time for a steak dinner," said Chavez. "Equipment, gear, and weapons are all ready to go."

"Okay," said Martinez. "Let's get ready to move."

Chavez turned and said, "Gentlemen, the celebration is now over. We've a little more work to do."

"Someone going to buy beer?" asked Leroy Jones, one of the medics.

"Nope," said Chavez.

"Shit."

Martinez laughed. "I'll buy the beer once we get back."

"Yeah!" said Jones. "I can live with that."

Several hours later, Martinez, along with his team, were sitting in the darkened fuselage of a C-130, orbiting over the Pacific Ocean, waiting to head inbound to the IP and then the DZ. They were using a C-130 rather than one of the newer C-17s. The newer aircraft would have been more comfortable, but the C-130 was in the inventories of nearly every Latin American country. In the dark, with the unit insignia painted in small, flat black letters and numbers, no one would be able to tell who owned the aircraft. It could be anyone.

Martinez sat in the red webbing that was strung along the fuselage for the troops. Lined up in the center of the aircraft and tied down with thick, gray cargo straps, were cylinders that held the spare equipment, batteries for the radios, extra rations and ammunitions, including some heavy weapons in case they needed to defend their camp.

Martinez studied the men that sat in the aircraft with him. His team exec, Alverez, was also Hispanic. He had been born in California but raised in New Mexico, taking some training at the New Mexico Military Institute in Roswell. Like Martinez, he was a young man with black hair and olive skin. He could speak Spanish like a native of Mexico or Spain, depending on assignment, Italian like a resident of Rome, and strangely, Chinese like a man from Hong Kong.

Next to him was Chavez, the team sergeant. Chavez knew everything there was to know about the military, military tactics, and military life. If there was a question to be asked, Chavez was the man to ask because he would answer it. While the rest of the team sat in the darkened C-130 waiting to jump into the night, Chavez was using his flashlight to study his map. Chavez wanted to make sure that everything was wired before they hit the ground.

Gibson, the intelligence NCO, the man with the specific knowledge of the locals, the terrain, and the military forces they would be facing was sitting opposite him. Gibson was one of the three caucasians on the team. There had been four, but Banse had been killed as they had exfiltrated during the Saudi Arabian rescue.

Next to him was Leroy Jones, the only black. He had been selected because of his diminutive size and his ability to speak Spanish made him appear to be a native of Panama. Although he was the senior medical specialist, he was also an expert with explosives and light weapons.

The rest of the team, lost in the darkness of the aircraft,

were Hispanic. The team had been assembled for missions into Latin America. They had operated almost extensively in Latin America except for a brief run into the Middle East because there had been no one else.

It was a good team, thought Martinez. Well trained, used to working with one another and disciplined. Each man knew that he could rely on the others. If one man was in trouble, the others would come to his assistance. No one would be left flapping in the breeze.

Martinez took a deep breath and closed his eyes. For a moment he could visualize the beginning to the mission. The men lined up to exit the troop door on the left side of the aircraft. One man and then an equipment pod. One by one, they'd jump, into the night, using the glow of the stars and the charcoal line of the horizon to guide themselves.

And then he forced his mind away from that. He'd spent five days in isolation, living and breathing the planning of the mission until the briefback. Suddenly the mission was alive. They were on the aircraft, heading into the DZ. Now it was time to let go of it for a moment. Martinez was afraid that he would be over prepared, over rehearsed so that the first unexpected complication would set him off. Now it was time to relax.

It seemed that only a minute had passed. Martinez wasn't aware that he had been asleep. But he felt a hand on his shoulder and opened his eyes to see Chavez grinning at him. The master sergeant had smeared grease paint on his face in a nightmarish pattern designed to mimic the lights and darks of the jungle.

"We're within thirty minutes, Captain." Chavez had to shout over the roar of the four turboprops.

Martinez blinked and tried to focus on his wristwatch. Rubbed his eyes with the heels of his hands. "Everyone ready to go?"

"Ready as we'll ever be," shouted Chavez. He retreated, dropping onto the troopseat.

The loadmaster, an Air Force NCO dressed in a gray, nomex flightsuit, unhooked the cargo straps and wrapped them up, storing them so that they wouldn't be in the way.

Martinez had watched it done a dozen times but it always sent chills through him. It marked the rear beginning of the mission. The last of the waiting was over and it was time to prepare to leap into space.

Michael Brown and Raul Munyo were already checking each others equipment. Robert Cline and Juan Ortega were doing the same thing. Martin Davis was crouched on the deck, examining the seals on the equipment pods a final time.

Martinez stood up and moved to the rear, toward the troop door. He stepped close and looked out the porthole. The silvery landscape that had marked the ocean was gone. They were now flying over land. Jungle. There were no artificial lights, no cities, no sign of life. They could be flying over the jungle as it had been a thousand years earlier. Or a million.

He turned and Alverez was standing behind him. Without a word they began to check each other making sure that all straps were pulled tight, all snaps fastened, all equipment tied or taped down.

"Ready?" yelled Martinez.

"Never ready. Don't like jumping out of perfectly good airplanes."

"This is a C-130."

"Good point."

The jumpmaster moved forward and yelled at Martinez, "We're about ten minutes out now."

Martinez nodded and turned facing his team. "Ten minutes to drop," he shouted over the roar of the engines. "Everyone up and check your equipment."

Once again they ran through the ritual, each man making sure that his equipment was properly strapped and buckled and that the quick-releases on his parachute were secure. Then he checked the gear of the man in front of him, finally turning to complete the check on the man behind him. Chavez, who would be first, and Martinez, who would be last, checked each others. As they all finished, each man handed the other's static line to him and the men placed the nylon webbing between his teeth to signal completion and that they were ready to jump.

Chavez turned and studied the men behind him. Finally, he ordered, "Hook up." Each of the men snapped the metal hook over the metal cable and then yanked on them to show that they were properly fastened and that the cover was properly secured.

The jumpmaster moved forward, grabbed the latch for the troop door, twisted it, pulled in and then pushed up, out of the way. The rush of the slipstream and the roar of the engines filled the interior of the aircraft. Cold air filled the cargo compartment.

"Two minutes," he said, holding up two fingers for the team to see. A tiny red light came on near the hatch.

Chavez glanced back, over his shoulder, and yelled, "Move to the door."

As the men shuffled forward, the equipment pods in front of them, the jumpmaster leaned forward slightly, staring into the darkness in front of the aircraft. The unbroken jungle stretched below him.

The light at the side of the door began to blink and the jumpmaster dragged the equipment pods forward, ready to shove them out.

The red flashing light suddenly changed to a bright, steady green. Shoving the bundles out, the jumpmaster looked up at Chavez and yelled, "Go. GO!"

Chavez moved forward and jumped. Martinez, at the end of the line shuffled forward as the men, one after another, leaped into the night. At the door himself, he brought his feet together on the edge, tucked his chin in, and then put his hands on the framework on either side of the door.

An instant later, Martinez was falling.